FRAGILE LOVE

"I want us to get back together," Russell said. "I miss you, Kirby."

"I miss you, too." Her voice broke as if she was fighting to hold back her feelings. "It seems as if you've been gone forever, Russell."

"I know. It feels that way to me, too. It's especially tough after dinner. I miss hearing the boys running up and down the stairs or playing one of their video games. It's very quiet here."

"Is it only the boys you miss?"

"No," Russell whispered. "You know better than that."

"No, I don't."

"I've never stopped loving you, Kirby. I don't think that I ever will . . ."

* * *

Praise for Lynda Trent and BEST FRIENDS:
With BEST FRIENDS, Lynda Trent serves up a generous slice of contemporary life—reminiscent of Danielle Steel.
—Joan Hohl, bestselling author of *Compromises*

Lynda Trent is a talented author who always touches her audience with emotionally poignant stories.
—*Romantic Times*

LYNDA TRENT

FAMILY SECRETS

ZEBRA BOOKS
KENSINGTON PUBLISHING CORP.

For Joey Mason and Linda Ballard.
Thanks

ZEBRA BOOKS are published by

Kensington Publishing Corp.
850 Third Avenue
New York, NY 10022

First Printing: February, 1996
10 9 8 7 6 5 4 3 2 1

Printed in the United States of America

Chapter One

"So you see," Kirby Garrett said as she strolled from one end of the jury box to the other. She bent her head forward as if she were reasoning with the jury and thinking aloud, her sleek dark hair falling forward, framing her face. "James Eldrich couldn't possibly have committed this crime. His wife's testimony clearly shows that he was home at the time, having dinner with his family. And bear in mind that the clerk who initially identified him from a lineup told this court during cross-examination that his eyesight is poor and he had taken out his contact lenses shortly before the robbery because they were irritating his eyes. You saw yourselves by way of demonstration in this court that without his contact lenses the clerk is so nearsighted that he could not distinguish between the three identically clothed subjects I presented before him."

She gave the jurors a confident smile and leaned on the rail that separated them. She took her time, letting her gray eyes meet theirs as if she were merely summing up the conclusion that was universal and obvious. "Therefore, I ask you to find Mr. Eldrich innocent of robbing the Quick-Mart." She straightened and went back to the defendant's table and sat down next to her client.

"What do you think they'll vote?" Eldrich whispered.

"I assume they'll believe your wife's testimony and find you innocent." She kept a neutral but confident expression on her face. Her thoughts, however, had taken a different turn. Something inside had been nagging at her throughout the trial, something that made her doubt her client's innocence.

Once the prosecution's final arguments were completed and the judge had issued his charge to the jury, the twelve men and women who were to decide her client's fate filed out of the courtroom for their deliberations. Kirby relaxed her tensed muscles but no one in the courtroom could possibly have known it. She was on stage, and until her business there was finished, she would maintain the demeanor that physically matched her exceptional ability as a trial lawyer.

Her father had taught her well, and as one of the most respected defense attorneys in the Southwest, he had set an excellent example for her to follow. No one, except for her father, could have done a better job of defending Eldrich. Now there was nothing more she could do but wait for the jury's verdict. If they found Eldrich innocent, her job was over. If they found him guilty, she would file an appeal. From this point on, it was standard procedure. At the instructions of the bailiff, all those present in the courtroom rose as the judge retired to his chambers to await the jury's decision. Kirby settled back into her chair to wait.

She turned when someone touched her shoulder, then she smiled at Hershal Glassman, the elderly man who headed her law firm. He grinned back. "You did a fine job," he said in a low voice. "I believed you."

"Thanks. I just hope the jury did."

"When you get back to the office, I have a case I'd like for you to review. I left the file on your desk. I'm going to be out of town and you may have to handle it for me."

"Certainly. I'll read it today." Kirby knew Glassman was grooming her to take his place when he eventually retired. The firm of Walker and Glassman had been started by Glassman and her father when they were beginning practice in Houston forty years ago. Her father was now an appellate court judge and therefore no longer a part of the firm, but his distinguished name was still on the shingle. Kirby looked forward to the day when her own would be there as well.

Thirty minutes later the door to the jury deliberation room opened and the jury returned to the courtroom. When the judge returned, Kirby swept her eyes over the jury. She had seen so many jury panels in her years of practice, she could almost tell how each individual felt about the verdict they had reached. Although their decision was unanimous, the body language of two of them indicated that they had at first disagreed with the others, then had had their minds changed. Eldrich stirred nervously beside her.

"The defendant James Eldrich will rise and face the jury," the judge commanded.

Kirby stood with her client, glad he hadn't appeared this nervous earlier in the trial.

"Has the jury reached a verdict?"

"We have, Your Honor," the foreman replied as he handed a slip of paper to the court clerk.

When the judge had read the verdict and it was taken back to the foreman, the judge said, "How do you find the defendant?"

"Your Honor, we find James Eldrich to be not guilty."

Kirby smiled at the jury, then at Eldrich. He was grinning as if he had known all along that he would be found innocent. Kirby shook his hand. "Congratulations, Mr. Eldrich."

He pumped her hand enthusiastically. "You sure did a fine job of getting me off. Thank you."

Kirby saw relief in his eyes, perhaps more than an innocent man would have felt. But it no longer mattered. The case was over.

She gathered up her notes and put everything into her briefcase. Eldrich strode across the room to where his wife and her mother stood waiting for him. His walk was cocksure and springy. He was no longer making an effort to appeal to the jury's sensibilities as Kirby had instructed him. For a second or two she stared down at the familiar, worn table before her, then zipped her briefcase and left.

As she made her way through the crowd in the hall outside the courtroom, she smiled and nodded as various people congratulated her on winning the case. Eldrich had a charismatic personality and the people watching the trial had hoped, for

the most part, that he was innocent. Winning hadn't surprised
her; she won almost all her cases.

As she left the air-conditioned courthouse, the oppressive
July heat assaulted her with a vengeance. Although she had
lived here in Houston all her life and was acclimated to the
Texas Gulf Coast climate, the combination of blistering heat
and high humidity could not be ignored. By August the heat
would be even more unbearable. When she was younger, she
had wondered how people had survived the summers before
the advent of refrigerated air-conditioning; now she wasn't so
sure that it hadn't been easier on them because they had not
had to deal with the drastic contrast of going from comfortable,
cool buildings into the sauna outdoors.

As usual, she walked as quickly as she could the several
blocks to the lot where she parked her car, not only to reach
the haven of air-conditioned comfort she would find there as
soon as possible, but because the courthouse wasn't in the most
desirable part of town. From habit she took care as she hurried
along to avoid the growing population of street people and
panhandling drunks who had hardly sobered from the previous
night's cheap booze. Long before she reached her car, her
blouse was plastered to her back by perspiration that would
not have evaporated even if she hadn't been wearing a suit.

For safety's sake, she glanced around before unlocking the
car, then slipped off the jacket to her suit before getting in. As
soon as she was behind the wheel, she automatically locked
the doors. The car was as hot as an oven but the air-conditioning
soon blasted her with cooling relief. There had been many other
days like this when living in a cooler climate had seemed
appealing, but overall she didn't want to live anywhere else.
She had lived in Houston all thirty-six years of her life, dis-
counting the ones while she was away at college, and not only
did she love the city itself, but all her family still lived there.
And family was important to her.

The Walker and Glassman law offices were in one of the
high-rise buildings a dozen or so blocks from the courthouse,
the ground floor of which was occupied by a prestigious bank.

Kirby punched the elevator "up" button and returned greetings from several of the bank employees who were on their way home. A moment later, the double doors slid open noiselessly and she stepped in. The familiar smells and sounds were like home to her. She had visited her father here on many occasions before she had come to work in his firm and the building held many fond memories for her.

The elevator deposited her on the twenty-second floor. As she stepped off, she ran her fingers through her smoothly cropped black hair as if she could shake free the remaining heat of the streets. It felt good to be here.

Kirby smiled a greeting at the secretary she shared with Glassman and her brother-in-law, Derrick McKinsey. Miss Allerman handed her the messages that had accumulated since Kirby had gone to court.

She shuffled through them as she went into her office. Josh had called and so had Cody, then Josh again. She sighed. That meant she was needed to solve another of her sons' disputes. Josh had just turned twelve, and she had hoped that by now he would have outgrown his need to torment his younger brother. Having been raised herself with only one sibling, and that a sister, she hadn't known what to expect from boys. And her husband Russell hadn't been much help having grown up as an only child. Slipping into her role as mother and dispute arbitrator, she dialed her home number.

"Hello?"

"Josh, are you and Cody fighting again?"

"He started it, Mom. I was trying to watch TV and he kept turning the stereo up as loud as it would go." Kirby rubbed her brow tiredly. It was a wonder the neighbors hadn't called as well. "Put him on."

"Hi, Mom," her youngest said brightly.

"What's going on, Cody?"

"I was trying to do my homework and Josh keeps turning the TV on. You said we were supposed to do our homework as soon as we came in from school since we're going to Grandad's house for dinner." His voice was a bit too innocent to be believed.

"No TV, no stereo. You go up to your room to do your homework."

Cody made a few grumbling noises but he finally agreed.

"Let me talk to Josh again." As Cody handed the phone to his brother, she heard him say in an undertone, "Boy, are you in trouble!"

"Mom, whatever he said, it's not true," Josh said defensively.

"I'm telling you exactly what I told Cody. No TV, no stereo until after you finish your homework. Go to your room to do it and Cody won't bother you." It took more argument to convince Josh, but she finally got an agreement out of him. She looked up to see Derrick standing in her doorway. "I have to go now. Remember, we're having dinner at Grandad's tonight. 'Bye." She hung up and looked at Derrick.

"I hear you won the case," he said, his face split in a wide, superficial smile.

"Yes. I did." She had never cared much for Derrick and wondered what her sister saw in him. He had medium brown hair, hazel eyes, and wasn't bad looking, though he was far from handsome in Kirby's opinion. He reminded her of a beach boy who was approaching middle age ungracefully. His smile was supposed to show he was pleased with her victory; she knew he wasn't.

"Are you going over to Addison's tonight?"

"Of course." She was positive Derrick had heard her say as much to her sons. Her intuition had cautioned her not to trust him from their first meeting when Mallory brought him home to meet the family. "Will you and Mallory be there?"

"Wouldn't miss it. Tara is looking forward to it. You know how she adores her grandmother."

Kirby nodded. It occurred to her that no one ever referred to her parents' house as belonging to them both or to her mother. It had always been Addison's house, Grandad's house, Dad's house. She wondered if her mother had ever noticed that and if it bothered her. But she couldn't imagine her mother being bothered about much of anything. "How is Tara doing in school?"

"She made the honor roll again. I guess she took after me and not her mother." Derrick laughed to suggest that the put-down was merely a joke. The sound of his laughter irritated Kirby almost as much as the slight to her sister.

Stiffly, she said, "Mallory's grades were nothing to be ashamed of."

"Maybe not, but nobody ever accused her of being an egghead. Right? You know I'm right. But of course we wouldn't change her," he added as if it were an afterthought.

"No, I wouldn't." Kirby had always been protective of Mallory. It wasn't just that Mallory was two years younger, but because she was the sort of woman whom people instinctively protected. She and Mallory were as different as two sisters could be. Tara was growing up to be a duplicate of Mallory, so much so that Kirby often found herself amazed and pleased by the similarities. "Is there something you wanted, Derrick? I have a case to review."

"If it's Harris versus Sampson, I'm taking that one."

"No, you're mistaken. Hershal came by the courtroom a little while ago and asked me to read the file. He said he's going to be out of town and wanted me to handle it for him. It's right here on my desk where he said he had put it. See?" she said, jabbing her finger at the thick manila file folder on her desk.

"He changed his mind, then, because he also asked me to do it." Derrick seemed to enjoy her growing aggravation. "It makes sense, when you think about it. I'm the logical one to handle that case."

"I don't see why you think that. I'm as capable as you are of proving Simpson was negligent. The dog that mauled the Harris boy was identified as a pit bull. And if I'm not mistaken, Hershal mentioned last week that Simpson was arrested several months ago for his participation in illegal dog fights. Simpson lives only a block away from where the Harris boy was attacked and he's got a pit bull kennel in his backyard."

"Yes, but it's going to be gory, with the pictures and all. I told Hershal that I'd be better suited to argue the case and he agreed."

Kirby felt her anger growing. "I've seen the pictures that will be submitted as evidence and I neither fainted nor became ill. I'm taking that case if Hershal is still out of town."

"No," Derrick said with his maddening smile. "You aren't."
He winked and left her doorway.

Kirby restrained her desire to throw something at him or
follow him to pursue the argument. Derrick was impossible to
deal with. She would wait and ask Hershal who was to handle
the Harris case.

She slumped back into the leather chair behind her desk and
tried to relax. Someday she would be the head of this firm and
Derrick's underhanded tricks would be a thing of the past. She
would see to that. Hershal had mentioned that he would be
likely to retire before long, and at the age of seventy, he deserved
a rest. Even though he was several years older than her father,
he looked much older and had never had as much stamina as
Addison. She knew Derrick had every expectation of taking
Hershal's place, and although she didn't want to hasten Hershal's retirement, she was looking forward to the day when
Derrick learned that he would be working for her instead of
the reverse. It would be difficult not to gloat.

She closed her door and for the next forty-five minutes
gleaned all she could from the Harris file. Feeling confident
that she could convince Hershal to let her handle the case—if
he actually had been swayed by Derrick—she locked the file
in her filing cabinet and decided it was time to go home. Kirby
loved her job as an attorney, but she loved her home life better.
She and Russell had bought a house in Southampton, an older
and exclusive subdivision of Houston, and going home was
always a balm to her soul. Even when the boys had been
squabbling.

In fact, all her family lived in Southampton. Her parents still
lived in the house where she had been raised on Rice Boulevard,
a stone's throw from Rice University. Mallory and Derrick were
on Bolsover, a block away. She and Russell were on the next
block, Dunstan. All the houses were settled into peaceful gentil-
ity, and ancient live oak trees out front made leafy tunnels of
the streets. While it wasn't as prestigious a subdivision as River
Oaks, Kirby loved it there. It was the sort of place where
neighbors knew each other and it wasn't far from her downtown
office.

Traffic was comparatively light and she soon turned into her drive. An oak tree much larger than the ones that lined the street shaded her drive and most of her yard. This tree was one reason she and Russell had chosen this particular house. It was magnificent, with sweeping limbs the boys had climbed on even as small children.

Kirby unlocked the kitchen door and noted that Ellen, the woman who cleaned her house, had already gone for the day. The house was as spotlessly clean as always. Even with two active boys and Russell to contend with, Ellen worked miracles.

"I'm home," she called from the bottom of the stairs. She heard muffled greetings that meant the boys were at least pretending to do their homework in their respective rooms. She picked up the mail from the hall tree and started leafing through it. She glanced at her watch. Russell should be home at any moment.

She went up to say hello to her sons. Ordinarily she would have swapped her working clothes for more comfortable jeans, but they were expected at her parents' house and Addison preferred a more formal dinner.

Josh's room was nearest the stairs and she stuck her head in the door. "Studying hard?"

"Oh, hi, Mom. I thought I heard you come in."

She went to him and put her hand on his shoulder. Now that he was growing taller, he reminded her strongly of Russell. He had the same brown, wavy hair and green eyes. Even his voice, when it slid into the lower register, was similar to his father's. Of the two, Josh was more inclined toward sports. "How is it coming along?"

"Just fine. I'm almost finished."

"Good. You know how upset Grandad gets when we're late." She kissed the top of his head, reflecting that he would soon be too old to want her to do that.

Cody's room was farther down the hall. When she knocked on his door and pushed it open, he was lying on his bed, studying a model of a space shuttle he had recently completed. "Did you finish your homework?" she asked, even though she already knew the answer. Cody took as naturally to school as Josh did to sports.

"Sure, Mom. It wasn't all that hard. What do you think of this shuttle?"

"You did a wonderful job. I can picture you riding in one someday." She smiled at him. Cody had wanted to be an astronaut for as long as he had known they existed.

He grinned. His hair was also brown, but like Kirby, he had gray eyes framed with black eyelashes. He showed signs of becoming more classically handsome when he was grown than did Josh. His face was also more openly friendly. Cody liked everyone and got along well with everyone but his brother.

"I want you to behave at Grandad's this time. No picking on Tara."

"I'll try not to." He grinned at her as if the possibility of him leaving his cousin in peace was a small one.

"She's not used to having brothers around to torment her."

"Well, she ought to be used to us by now."

This was true, Kirby reflected. Tara was only two years younger than Cody and had lived within a block of them all her life. "Things bother Tara more than they do you and Josh. She doesn't like being teased."

"She's in the third grade," Cody said with the superiority of the fifth grade. "She needs to grow up. Kids at school will tease her if she doesn't stop fussing about every little thing."

Kirby nodded. "I know. But Mallory was the same way." Tara was a lovable little girl, but she had the same helpless air about her as did Mallory. Kirby suspected that Cody and Josh were more protective of Tara at school than they were at family gatherings.

She heard sounds from downstairs. "Get ready to go to Grandad's," she told Cody on her way out of the room.

She met Russell on the stairs and gave him a light kiss. "Put your tie back on. We're going to Dad's tonight. Remember?"

Russell groaned and leaned against the rail. "Is that tonight? I'm bushed. Can't we skip one family dinner?"

"Not when Mom will have already cooked it. You know how she likes to fix just the right amount."

"I know. There are times when I'd like to have seconds." He glumly put the tie back around his neck. "I'll bet she's never had leftovers in her entire life."

"Not that I can remember," Kirby said with a smile. "But that has its advantages." She still thought he was the sexiest man she had ever known. Russell was tall and had the lean body of a natural athlete. His hair was the exact shade of brown as their sons' but his green eyes were flecked with gold, whereas Josh's were a mix of green and brown. She found herself wanting to hug him, but moved away instead. Sometimes his sexiness was a bit overwhelming to her.

"I suppose Derrick will also be there."

"As sure as rain. He mentioned it to me today." Kirby knew Russell disliked Derrick as much as she did, perhaps even more. "How was school?"

"Today was a bear! Every student I have forgot his homework, did the wrong assignment, lost it, you name it. I think they get together and plan how to drive me crazy." Russell taught political science at the University of Houston. Addison was forever telling him it made more sense for him to transfer to Rice so he could walk to work, but Russell refused—possibly because it was Addison's idea. "I got them, though. I assigned enough homework to keep them busy all weekend." He chortled as if he took particular pleasure in tormenting his students.

Kirby laughed. "You're as bad as your sons." She helped him straighten his tie. "There. You look wonderful."

He smiled and came up on the step behind her. "How wonderful?"

Kirby moved away. "There you go, fishing for compliments again. I have to see that the dog has water. Ellen forgets to check and it's so hot outside." She passed him and hurried downstairs. There was no sound behind her as if he were watching her. Kirby didn't look back.

She was greeted in the backyard by Abby. The puppy was half-grown and was already larger than the man at the pound had assured Kirby she would grow to be. Addison had discouraged getting a dog from the pound as he preferred to have only purebred dogs himself, but Kirby liked the idea of saving a puppy and this was the one the boys had chosen. Abby wasn't the brightest of dogs, but she was one of the most lovable.

As usual, Abby had overturned her water dish. Kirby began

filling it as the puppy pranced around, stumbling over her own feet.

Russell hadn't followed her out to the yard and Kirby was glad. She knew he must be wondering what was wrong with her lately. Kirby wondered, too.

She had never been overly fond of making love. Not that Russell wasn't good at it, but it just didn't appeal to her. She loved him, but was content to show it by doing things for him and by being with him in the evenings with the boys. Lately she had found herself becoming uncomfortable if he so much as kissed her. It wasn't something she could explain to Russell so she simply avoided intimacy as often as possible.

She turned off the water and bent to pat Abby. The puppy licked her hand and bounced up and down gleefully. She raced across the yard, turned a tight circle and ran back. Kirby stroked the puppy's soft fur and rubbed her ears. "If you grow to fill out all that skin, you'll be large enough to ride."

Abby took that as a compliment, as she did any sound made by her humans, and ran in more tight circles, her pink tongue hanging out the side of her mouth.

"Ready?" Russell called from the back door. "I know you want to be on time and it's already six o'clock."

"I'm coming." Her mother put dinner on the table at six-thirty every night and everyone was expected to be there on time. She disentangled herself from Abby and went into the house. "She has more energy than a hurricane!"

"I'll play ball with her tomorrow," Josh said as he waggled his fingers at the dog. "I'm teaching her to fetch."

"Good luck," Russell said good-naturedly.

Kirby smiled at him. He hadn't been enthusiastic about getting a dog, much less one the size of a horse, but he had already fallen in love with Abby. Not for the first time she reflected how lucky she had been to fall in love with and marry Russell. He was nothing at all like her father.

Kirby frowned slightly as she picked her purse up off the table by the door. Why would she think such a thing? She had idolized her father all her life. In her opinion, Addison could do no wrong. When Russell had a difference of opinion with Addison, Kirby almost always took her father's side. She had always been proud of the fact that she looked most like him, while Mallory resembled their mother. Kirby and her father both had eyes that were "Walker gray," as Addison termed it—a silver eye color that was a genetic trademark of his family. Why would she have even a fleeting thought of being glad Russell was nothing like Addison? She firmly put the thought out of her head.

Because of the heat and because Houstonians weren't fond of walking when it wasn't necessary, they drove to the Walker house on Rice. Derrick's car was already in the drive and Tara was in the front yard. When she saw them, she waved as if she hadn't seen the boys in school only hours before.

"She can be so geeky," Josh grumbled as he frowned at his cousin. "Quit waving, Cody! You're a geek, too."

"So what? You're a jock." Cody said it as if that were the greatest insult he could say in front of his parents.

"All right, boys," Russell said. "Don't start. And don't pick on Tara this time."

Josh made a growling noise of acknowledgment.

They parked on the street and walked across the clipped lawn. Kirby smiled at her niece. "Hello, Tara. Have you been here long?"

"Not too long. Mom is coming in her own car." Tara gazed up adoringly at Kirby. Her long, curly brown hair was tousled and her chocolate eyes were framed by surprisingly long eyelashes. "Hi, Cody. How's Abby?"

Kirby left the children comparing ideas on what tricks Abby might be capable of learning someday and crossed the yard beside Russell. She knew him so well, she could sense his growing tension as they neared the house. For some reason she could never understand, Russell truly disliked Addison. She could well understand why he detested Derrick.

"Well, hello there, Kirby," Derrick said as they entered the house. The glass of bourbon in his hand was half-empty. The liquor cabinet was always his first stop.

"Hello, Derrick," she said automatically. "Is Mallory going to be much later? You know Mom likes us to be on time. Why didn't you come together?"

"She wasn't ready as usual so Tara and I came on ahead."

Derrick shook hands with Russell without speaking to him.
"Can I get anyone a drink?"

"No," Russell said.

"Perhaps some Chablis," Kirby answered. She went into the
den and greeted her father with a smile. "Hello, Dad."

"Hello, Kirby, Russell. I guess the boys are outside?"

"They're talking to Tara. Does Mom need help in the
kitchen?"

"Probably." Addison gave her his most endearing smile.
Russell had once said Addison's smile and physical appearance
could get him any political position he wanted and Kirby agreed.
With his thick, silver hair—which matched his "Walker gray"
eyes—and regal bearing, he looked like the sort of father one
would expect to see on a traditional greeting card.

Kirby left the men and went into the kitchen. Although Jane
Walker had a woman in to do her heavier housework, she
preferred doing her own cooking. She had been careful to teach
her daughters all she knew, but Mallory was the only one who
followed her example. Kirby had never cared for cooking and
would rely on TV dinners if it wasn't for Ellen. "Hi, Mom."

"Hello, Kirby. I didn't hear you drive up. Will you put
ice in the glasses for me?" Jane moved about the kitchen,
orchestrating the family meal. "I hope you're all hungry. I
seem to have fixed enough to feed an army." As always, Jane
looked as if she were a bit flustered by life, her brown eyes
glancing with concern from one steaming pot to another. She
loved to cook but the organization of getting it all on the table
at once was difficult for her.

Kirby hid her smile. Since she was accustomed to cooking
only for Addison, Jane's estimation of what constituted a large
meal was skewed. She knew when they returned home, Russell
would head for the pie Ellen had left on the counter top to
cool. Although he was slender, Russell preferred to eat much
more than Jane had ever prepared at a meal.

"Was Tara out there?" Jane asked as she spooned mashed
potatoes into a serving bowl, the rim of which was decorated
with a delicate rose pattern. "I couldn't get her to come in the
house." The heat of the kitchen was softening her hair spray,
and one of her permed locks had fallen toward her face. Her

hair, once a lovely shade of brown, was liberally flecked with silver now, and Kirby knew Addison was pressuring Jane to dye it.

"I guess she was watching for the boys. They're planning ways to train Abby."

"I just can't believe you actually got such a large dog. She will eat you out of house and home by the time she's grown." Jane shook her graying head. "I always liked small dogs myself. I guess I never will get over losing Tinkerbell."

"I know you loved him." Kirby had always thought Tinkerbell was an odd name for a rat terrier that hated small girls and had bitten Kirby on many occasions. She had never had any affection for the animal at all and had had to feign sorrow for her mother's sake when the dog finally died of old age. She took the ice from the freezer and started filling the crystal glasses.

"Mallory will be late. I just know she will, and dinner will be stone cold." Jane looked out the window to see if Mallory's car was in the drive. "I don't know what to do with that girl."

"She's never too late," Kirby said placatingly. "You know how she is."

"Do you think I should take all these rolls in? It seems like an awful lot just for the family."

"I would if I were you. The boys are ravenous these days."

"It's because they're growing taller. The Walkers are always tall."

"So is Russell," Kirby reminded her. "I think I hear a car." She picked up the tea pitcher to fill the glasses.

Jane looked back out the window and sighed with relief. "It's Mallory, thank goodness. She's coming in the side door."

Mallory rushed into the kitchen as Kirby was returning from putting the glasses of iced tea on the table. "Am I late? Say I'm not late, Mom. Hi, Kirby. I saw the kids out front. Aren't they growing fast?" She put a quick kiss on Jane's cheek and dropped her purse onto a kitchen chair. "I'm glad I'm not late." She shook her head, and her long dark hair fluffed around her face in luxurious waves. Like their mother, her eyes were dark and expressive.

"Well, you almost were. What am I going to do with you?"

Jane pretended to scold. "Go get the children and tell them to wash up."

Kirby and Jane finished putting the food on the table and Jane gave the settings one last check before calling the men in to eat. Jane took great pride in presenting an elegant table and it didn't matter to her if only the family was present to enjoy it.

They found their usual seats and Addison started carving the roast. "It looks good enough to eat," he said with his usual joke. He had made the same comment all Kirby's life. When she was young, she had thought it was some sort of blessing over the food.

"Kirby won her case today," Derrick said with as much pride as if he were responsible for her success. "She did a good job. I think Eldrich was guilty as sin, myself."

"I believed him," Kirby said rather tartly. "Pass the peas, Josh."

"Good for you," Addison said. "Derrick was just telling me he's been asked to take the Harris case when Hershal is out of town."

Kirby glared at her brother-in-law, who smiled back. "I'm not so sure that's what Hershal had in mind. I intend to ask him tomorrow." She handed the peas to Russell.

"Grandma, we're going to teach Abby to sit up and fetch and all kinds of things," Tara said to Jane. "I'm going to help them teach her." At eight, Tara looked like a small replica of Mallory. In time, Kirby thought, she would be uncommonly beautiful.

"Train her," Addison corrected. "You teach people and you train dogs. Eat some carrots, Tara, they're good for your eyes. You want your eyes to be pretty when you grow up."

Tara slid lower in her seat and didn't answer, but she let Mallory put a couple of carrot slices on her plate.

"Is the roast all right?" Jane asked anxiously as Addison took the first bite. "I hope it's not too tough. Is it tough, Addison?"

"No, it's fine."

Russell tasted it. "It's great, Mrs. Walker." Unlike Derrick,

Russell had never fallen into the habit of addressing Kirby's parents by their first names.

Jane smiled at him as if he were one of her own children. "Pass the rolls to Cody, Mallory. He didn't get any bread. Now don't get too full, children, I made a pie."

Cody and Josh grinned at each other.

"They love your pies, Mom," Kirby verified. "We all do."

"Well, I've always loved to cook, you know."

"Jane would have made a farmer a good wife," Addison said off-handedly.

Jane's forehead crumpled as if she weren't too sure if that was a compliment or not. She seldom knew exactly what Addison meant when he made a comment like that. "I have more tea if anyone wants any," she said to cover her confusion.

"I can't stay long," Mallory said as she passed the carrots to Derrick. "I told a friend I'd meet her at the mall in an hour."

"Can I go?" Tara asked.

"Not tonight, honey. It's a school night and I may be out past your bedtime."

Tara stared glumly at her plate. "Do I have to eat all my carrots? I hate carrots."

Mallory gave her a reproving look. "Tara made an A on her homework. Tell them about it, honey."

"It was easy. I just had to look up some words and make up a story to use them in."

Jane nodded approvingly. "The Walkers have always been bright in school. If you keep on the way you're going, Tara, you may be valedictorian of your class. Wouldn't that be nice?"

"She's too young to know what that means," Addison said. He winked at Tara.

Tara turned her head and pretended to be studying the embroidery design on the tablecloth.

"Well, anyway," Jane said, "everybody eat up and we'll have some peach pie."

Kirby glanced at Mallory as she ate. Something was going on with her sister but Kirby wasn't sure what it was. Mallory frequently met a "friend" at the mall or for a movie or for dinner, but she never mentioned the friend by name. Kirby didn't know of any woman that Mallory was particularly close to. Was it possible that Mallory was having an affair? Kirby certainly couldn't blame her if she was. Derrick was enough to drive anyone to see other men.

The meal went on as usual, the conversation ebbing and flowing as it had on countless other occasions, Addison occasionally correcting Jane's comments and Derrick doing the same to Mallory. Kirby had never noticed that they shared this irritating trait. She reminded herself that in her father's case, he meant no harm, while Derrick's words had barbs in them. Beneath the cover of the tablecloth, she rested her hand companionably on Russell's thigh. He covered her hand with his.

Kirby had loved Russell for as long as she had known him. It was as close to love at first sight as she had ever come. She wondered if he knew that. Kirby had always found it difficult to express such things, even in the throes of first love. It was even more difficult for her to demonstrate her love physically. She had never been fond of touching.

She never lost sight of how lucky she had been to find Russell. He wasn't at all what her father had wanted for her. Addison had wanted lawyer sons-in-law to go into the family law firm. Mallory had conformed; Kirby had not. When Kirby insisted on marrying Russell instead of one of the men favored by her father, she had come dangerously close to rebellion. She glanced down the table at her father. Looking back on it, she was amazed she had been able to pull it off.

Her heart went out to Russell. Would he ever know how much she loved him? Surely he must. Russell understood how difficult it was for her to express such sentiments. But as she ate, Kirby idly wondered why she was like that.

Chapter Two

"Go get it, Abby. Go get it, girl!" Abby bobbed up and down around Josh's feet growling at his shoes while she totally disregarded the ball he had thrown. "Mom, this dog isn't ever going to learn anything," Josh complained as he bent over to pet the puppy.

"Give her time," Kirby said. She straightened from weeding her flower garden and watched as Cody trotted after the ball. She hid her smile. Abby was proving hard to train, but the boys were teaching each other to fetch.

"Let me try. She minds me better," Cody said. He showed Abby the ball and she slobbered on it excitedly. "Go get it, Abby!" The dog ran three yards, stopped, watched the ball bounce against the fence, and ran back to Cody.

"She's young yet," Russell said.

Kirby shaded her eyes against the glare of the sun to look up at him. "I didn't hear you come out."

"There's a telephone call for you."

"Good. I wanted an excuse to stop doing this." She stood and dusted her hands on her shorts. "If I didn't like flowers so much, I'd never touch the flower beds. It's so hot this year."

"I never saw a summer in Houston that wasn't hot." Russell grinned at her and put his arm around her shoulder companionably as they walked toward the house.

Kirby walked a half step faster so that Russell's arm fell away from her. "Who's on the phone?"

"It's Derrick."

Concern replaced her smile. "Why would he be calling me on a Saturday?"

"I didn't ask."

A sense of urgency quickened her pace. As she breezed into the kitchen, the cooler, drier air was a welcoming relief, though momentary, as her thoughts snapped back to the question at hand. She picked up the receiver. "Hello?"

"Kirby, this is Derrick." He always started off his calls to her like that, as if he wasn't sure she would recognize his voice even after this many years. "I'm afraid I have some bad news."

Her stomach knotted. "It's not Dad, is it?"

"No, thank God. It's Hershal Glassman."

"Hershal? What's wrong? Is he sick?" She sank onto the nearest chair.

Derrick paused. "He's dead."

For a moment Kirby couldn't make sense of what he was saying. She had the sickening feeling that this was some sort of terrible joke on Derrick's part. "Dead? That's not possible. I saw him yesterday at the office and he was perfectly well."

"It was his heart. Addison just called me. They've taken him to Parkland Funeral Home."

"I can't believe it." Russell's presence behind her startled her and she turned and met his eyes. Covering the phone, she said, "Hershal has died. Derrick says it was his heart." To Derrick she said, "He told me his doctor put him on a restricted diet, and I knew he was taking a prescription medicine as well as nitroglycerine. But I never knew it was this serious."

"Heart problems are always serious." Derrick's patronizing tone irritated her.

"Dad called you?" Why hadn't he also called her?

"I just got off the phone with him. He said I was to call you. I think he and Jane have already gone to the funeral home. I'm going, too, as soon as I change clothes."

"I'll be there as soon as I can." Kirby told herself that Addison had called Derrick and not her in order to save time. Hershal had no children or living kin to help his wife during a crisis like this. Naturally Addison would need to be there for her. She hung up and looked at Russell. "Hershal is dead," she repeated. She still found it hard to believe. Despite the medications he was taking, he had seemed healthy.

"Do you want me to go with you?"

She shook her head. "No, you stay here with the boys. I'll get dressed." She hurried up the stairs to her bedroom, where she shucked off her clothes and rummaged through her closet. Numbness from the shock was settling in and she couldn't decide what to wear. Nothing too bright in color, she decided. Mrs. Glassman was of the old school and might be offended. On the other hand, black seemed to be too much. She pulled a navy dress off the hanger.

As she dressed, Kirby's thoughts focused on work and which cases Hershal's death would impact. She might have to work nights in the coming week or so to sort through his case load. She had often teased Hershal about being the most disorganized man she had ever known. His office was like a magpie's nest. Tears stung her eyes. She was going to miss Hershal a great deal.

She put on enough makeup to look presentable and grabbed her navy leather purse. A quick glance in the mirror told her she looked better than she felt. The numbness that had at first blocked her feelings was giving way to a mounting sense of loss, and she felt too close to tears. Kirby blinked them back. She hated to cry and almost never did. Not even now at the loss of a man who had been almost a second father to her.

Russell was waiting for her in the kitchen. He put his hands on her shoulders and looked into her eyes. "Are you sure you're okay to drive?"

"Of course I am. He's at Parkland. It's not even that far." She managed a smile. "I don't know when I'll be home. It depends on whether Mrs. Glassman needs me or not."

"I understand. I'll hold down the fort here. Call me if you need me."

Kirby nodded and fished in her purse for her keys as she went out the door. Only when she reached the car did she realize that she had left without kissing Russell, even though he had obviously expected her to. She told herself that he would understand. She didn't feel up to inspecting her motives for not remembering something so automatic in their parting.

Parkland Funeral Home was only a short drive down Holcombe Boulevard. From the street it looked like a colonial mansion. Only the discreet sign on the small, carefully manicured front lawn designated it as a place of business. Addison's and Russell's cars were parked out front. Kirby pulled into the nearest space and hurried through the heat to the building.

Inside there was silence. Even though people were gathering there and moving about, an inherent hush prevailed. The scent of carnations battled with the more basic, cloying sweet smell that permeated all funeral homes. The walls were done in pastel shades of peach and green over a plush, dark green carpeting. The couches and chairs formed several small conversation areas, each of which was guarded by impressively large floral arrangements that looked as if they were permanent decorations. Addison, Jane, and Derrick were seated in one of the conversational groups, leaning toward an elderly, slightly frumpy woman who was softly crying.

Kirby went to them and sat next to Mrs. Glassman. "I'm so sorry," she said sincerely. "I got here as quickly as I could."

Vanessa Glassman reached out and patted Kirby's hand. "You've all been so good to come. I don't know what I would have done without you." Her voice broke and fresh tears coursed down her cheeks. Her pale eyes were red from crying.

Kirby had many questions but didn't know how to ask any of them. She had rarely dealt with the death of someone she knew so well.

"He had gone out to get the paper," Mrs. Glassman said as if she had been over this many times already. "I wondered what was taking him so long so I looked out and there he was, lying on the sidewalk, all curled up." Her eyes implored Kirby's as if she wanted someone to explain to her how something like this could have happened. "He was already dead. I called the ambulance right away, but Hershal was already gone."

Kirby pressed the elderly woman's hand in a gesture of reassurance. "He was a good man. We're all going to miss him."

"Is there anyone else that needs to be telephoned?" Jane asked. "I'd be glad to do it for you."

Mrs. Glassman shook her gray head. "There's nobody. Nobody at all. You know, when we were younger, we thought about having children, but it was never the right time. You know?" She looked at Addison for confirmation.

He nodded. "I know. Time goes by so quickly."

Mrs. Glassman drew in a wavering breath. "So quickly. I'm all alone, I guess."

"No, you have us," Jane said hurriedly. "And there must be others. Some friend or cousin."

"Well, I do have a cousin in Freeport. Her name is Mavis Jordan. I haven't seen her for years and years, but we were very close as girls."

"There now," Jane said comfortingly. "You're not alone. In Freeport, you say? Why don't I go and call her?"

Mrs. Glassman nodded. "Her husband is named Al. I guess it's listed that way."

Jane left to find a phone she could use.

"Would you like to stay at our house tonight so you won't be alone?" Kirby offered. She had no guest room, but she knew Josh and Cody wouldn't mind sharing a room for a few days.

"No, I'd rather be at my own place, thank you anyway." Mrs. Glassman sighed and more tears gathered. "I just don't think I'll ever be able to go out and bring in the paper again without crying. He was just *lying* there."

Addison patted her other hand. "I'll help you until you're back on your feet and I'm sure Derrick will, too. At Walker and Glassman we're family." He gave her his most confident smile.

"I just can't think what else needs to be done," Mrs. Glassman said in a listless voice. "I know there are other things I should see to, but I can't think right now."

"Jane will know what to do." Addison rose. "I'll go see when viewing will begin."

Jane returned. "I found your cousin and she says that she and Al will be here as soon as they can. You won't be alone tonight. If they're late arriving, you can stay with us."

"You've all been so kind."

Kirby watched as her father consulted with one of the funeral directors across the room, then he looked at his watch and nodded.

"We weren't at the hospital any time at all," Mrs. Glassman was saying. "Hershal was already gone. I told them to bring him here. I guess that's what he would have wanted. We never talked about it."

Jane gave her a hug. "Of course you didn't. I'm sure this is exactly what Hershal would have wanted."

With interest, Kirby watched her mother saying all the right things and helping Mrs. Glassman with all the details she was too upset to deal with alone. Clearly, her mother was in her element at a time like this, quite the opposite of most other times when she seemed to be confused and too shy to speak at all. To Kirby's surprise, it occurred to her that she didn't know her mother very well. It was so easy to let her fade into the background by comparison to Addison's charisma. Even Mallory eclipsed her.

Addison rejoined them. "You'll be able to see him at seven o'clock tonight. Until then, I think it would be best if you go home and lie down."

"I couldn't possibly do that," Mrs. Glassman objected. "I have to stay here. What if Laura and Al arrive and can't find me?"

"I gave Laura your address and phone number and ours as well," Jane said. "She'll probably go to your place first."

"Yes," Mrs. Glassman said reluctantly. "I suppose you're right."

"I'll be with you. I won't leave you there alone," Jane assured her. To the others, she said, "Derrick, if you'll give Addison a ride, I'll take Vanessa home in our car." Jane often turned up her words at the end of a sentence as if she were asking a question.

"Certainly," Derrick said. His voice was too loud for the solemn room. "I'm parked out front, Addison."

"I'll be back at seven o'clock," Kirby said. She leaned over and gave Mrs. Glassman a hug. The woman smelled of lavender, powder, and soap. "Is there anything I can do for you in the meantime?"

"No, Kirby. You've done more than enough just coming down here on your day off." Mrs. Glassman seemed in a daze, as if her mind refused to be aware of her widowhood. "I'll see you all this evening." Jane took her arm and they walked slowly to the door. The funeral director, looking as bereaved as any of the mourners, held the door open for them, then returned to his post.

Kirby was glad to escape the frozen serenity of the funeral home. As she sat in her car waiting for her air conditioner to cool it and breathing deeply of the hot air, she realized there was something about funerals that terrified her, something that she had never thought to question until now. It was as if she had been holding her breath, forgetting to breathe. With her next breath, she was aware that the scent of carnations still clung to her and she wanted nothing more than to wash it away.

The funeral for Hershal Glassman drew a larger crowd than Kirby had expected. Although the Glassmans had no family to speak of, Hershal had made many friends—and from the looks of it, they had all come to pay their last respects. Mrs. Glassman's cousin, Mavis, had proven to be of little help, but that didn't matter. Jane had taken charge, while calling no attention to herself, and had everything running smoothly. Because Mrs. Glassman had only Mavis and Al to sit with her in the family pews during the service, she asked Addison's family to join them.

All during the service, Kirby fought the urge to run from the room. The cloying scent of carnations hung in the air, and the preacher seemed to take forever delivering the eulogy. Kirby was glad when the final song was sung and everyone had filed by to see Hershal one last time. She had walked by the casket because it was expected of her, but she had avoided looking inside. In her opinion it was barbaric to view the deceased. She put her hand in Russell's to force herself not to run away. His warm hand tightened on hers, and for the moment, she felt protected.

The cemetery was peaceful and beautifully landscaped with large trees shading the graves. The procession followed the hearse along the winding road around the older section to the canopy that had been erected over the grave site. Serving as pall bearers, Addison and Derrick, together with four other men Kirby presumed to be from the Glassmans' church, removed Hershal's coffin from the hearse and set it on its stand over the open grave.

Kirby walked by Russell's side to the folding chairs, waited until the widow and her cousins were seated, then sat next to him on the second row. As the preacher spoke, Kirby stared at the spray of white carnations on the bed of greenery that covered the casket, finding it hard to believe Hershal was inside.

For everyone concerned, the graveside service was mercifully short. Kirby paid her last respects to Mrs. Glassman, shook Mavis's and Al's hands, and was glad to escape to the car.

"I hate funerals," she confided to Russell as they waited for Addison and Jane to join them in the car.

"So do I. I'd much rather be cremated."

She looked at him in surprise. "You would? You've never mentioned that before."

He shrugged. "Are you okay? I could feel you trembling during the last prayer."

"I'm fine. It's just the smell of carnations. I can barely tolerate it."

He seemed puzzled. "I didn't smell anything. I thought the flowers florists used these days didn't have an aroma."

"These did!" She watched Jane hug Mrs. Glassman one last time, then her parents began making their way to the car. Kirby waved at her sons, who were standing by Tara and Mallory and would be riding home with the McKinseys. "The boys are growing so fast. Look at them. They're almost as tall as Mallory."

"They're going to be good-looking men." Russell sounded as if he hadn't noticed them lately either. "When did they get to be so tall?"

Jane opened the back door and slid in. Addison got in on the other side. "Are you going to the Glassman house?" Jane asked Kirby as she fastened her seat belt.

"I hadn't planned on it."

"We have too much to do," Addison said as if that settled the discussion. "She won't miss us."

Jane closed her lips and gazed out the window at the expanse of tombstones.

"Did you want to go, Mom?" Kirby asked, hoping she didn't.

"No. That's all right. Your father's right." She sounded as if she would have accepted his decree, even if she had chosen differently.

As they drove home, Kirby said, "I guess this means that I'll step into the place of senior partner. It would have been better, I think, if I already had become a full partner, but I suppose no one will find it too confusing." When Addison didn't answer, she glanced back at him. "Right?"

"I don't think this is the time nor place to be discussing business," Addison said firmly.

Kirby felt the sting of his correction as if she were a troublesome child. Addison was the only person in the world who made her feel this way. For the rest of the ride she was silent.

Kirby arrived at the office early the following morning so she would have plenty of time to start sorting through Hershal's belongings and papers before Mrs. Glassman arrived to get his personal effects. She was surprised to see Derrick was already at work and especially to find him seated in the office that had been Hershal Glassman's.

"You're here early," she commented as she approached the desk, expecting Derrick to vacate Hershal's chair so she could sit down and get to work. Yet not only did Derrick show no sign of moving, but the glint in his eye signaled he was up to his old tricks again. He would provoke her in an attempt to make her angry and get an emotional response from her, thus proving his superiority. He had done this many times before, but only once, the first time, had he been successful. She wasn't sure whether he couldn't tell when his stock strategies weren't working or he wasn't creative enough to come up with something new. Kirby was ready for any barb he might use to rile her. Continuing to smile, she said, "There's no need for you to straighten up things in here. It's my job, really."

"No, I want you to start reviewing the Mangano case. It'll be your first murder trial, but I think you can handle it."

Kirby laughed. "Excuse me? It's not your place to assign me cases. I'm the one in charge now, not you."

"On the contrary. I'm the one Hershal chose to take his place as head of the firm. I've already arranged to have my name added to the sign in the foyer. That reminds me, I need to tell Miss Allerman to order new stationery as well." He checked his watch as if he were already running short of time.

Kirby felt her temper rising. This wasn't one of his barbs; he was serious. "Look, Derrick, I don't know where you got this idea, but I've been with the firm two years longer than you. Before Dad left to become a judge, he was grooming me to run this place. You know that. Eventually, he wanted me to take his place at the head of the firm, and I know Hershal had the confidence that I could do it. He as much as told me so."

"All I know is that I've read the written instructions Hershal had prepared in case of his demise. And he appointed me." Derrick's ingratiating smile spread quickly. "I feel sure it was with Addison's blessings."

"You know Dad isn't supposed to influence anything in the firm as long as he sits on the appellate court. It would be a conflict of interest."

"Kirby, don't embarrass yourself and Addison by complaining to him about this. After all, as you said, Addison is supposed to have no influence whatsoever regarding the business of this law firm." Derrick turned back to the disarray of paper and briefs covering Hershal's desk. "I'd love to argue with you about this, but I really have more than enough to do. You'll find the Mangano file on your desk."

Maintaining the appearance that she was unruffled by this, she stared at him for a moment, trying to decide what to do. Then she turned and left the room. By the time she reached her office, she was so angry she was trembling. Derrick didn't have sense enough to run this firm! He wasn't half the attorney she was. Hershal had often told her this in private. He hadn't cared for Derrick personally and she'd often seen him reviewing Derrick's work as if he had little confidence in his abilities. Although Hershal had never said so, she felt sure he'd only kept him on because he was Addison's son-in-law. She couldn't believe Hershal would make such a decision. But the only other possibility was that the decision wasn't Hershal's. And that path of reasoning led to Addison.

She shook her head. That wasn't possible. Her father wouldn't go against the rules like that. He could lose his position on the appellate court for doing such a thing. Kirby had complete faith in her father's honesty.

So why was Derrick suddenly the new head of the law firm and she was right where she had been? Had Addison set up this line of succession prior to his becoming a judge? And if he had, why had he given Kirby the impression that he was grooming her for the position? She knew Derrick wouldn't have courage enough to falsify whatever document Hershal had left that designated his successor. He would know she'd be watching out for anything that didn't seem on the level where this was concerned. She wanted to see the document herself but decided it was pointless. Her asking or demanding to see it would only give Derrick more to crow about. The only viable possibility was that she had misread Hershal. Thinking back, she couldn't remember Hershal ever actually telling her he would one day yield control of the firm to her. How could she have been so gullible?

Feeling a deep sense of betrayal, Kirby shook her head to cast off the negative emotion and concentrated on viewing this situation dispassionately. It was one of the valuable coping skills her father had taught her. "You've got to be tough to succeed," he'd said. "Your emotions will get in your way if you let them. If your adversary ever knows you're hurt or disappointed by what he's done, he'll continue to press his advantage. Never let the bastards get the best of you."

Resolute that she had her emotions properly locked away where they wouldn't interfere, she picked up the case file on Julio Mangano and got back to work. She was familiar with an overview of the case. Mangano was accused of murdering his business partner, Luis Chairez. The murder had made headlines since the two had co-owned the chain of Guadalupe Mexican Restaurants so popular with Houstonians. Although Hershal already had done much of the preliminary work, she would have to go over most of it again. Kirby would have been eager to have this case, had the circumstances been different. But at the moment, she had no choice and would have to make the best of it.

On the first page were Hershal's scrawled handwritten notes. Obviously he hadn't expected anyone else to read them and he hadn't taken the time to make them legible to eyes other than his. As she began deciphering them, his words leaped up at her with a visceral punch she hadn't expected.

Kirby reread the entire page of notes carefully to be sure she hadn't misunderstood. Mangano had all but confessed, yet as his attorney, she was expected to prove his innocence, regardless. Had Derrick known this and assigned this case to her because she mistakenly had mentioned to him at one time that the moral issue of defending someone she thought was guilty bothered her? Was he trying to make things so uncomfortable for her that she would leave the firm rather than work for him?

She closed the folder and pushed it away. There was no need to become paranoid over this. Derrick was too lazy to have read Hershal's notes. Of course there was the possibility that Hershal had told him this case would be difficult to win. He had sometimes done that sort of thing.

Kirby bit her lower lip thoughtfully. She wished she could challenge Derrick's assertion that Hershal had wanted him to take over, but Derrick would have some sort of proof. If she was going to work with the man every day without Hershal as a buffer between them, she was going to have to make some effort to get along with him. Accusing him of something like this could give him cause to make her life even more unbearable. He wouldn't fire her because of the risk of displeasing his still powerful and influential father-in-law. But he could and would make her life at work a hell because he knew she would never complain to her father. Even though it hadn't been necessary, Addison Walker had drilled it into her that to be a successful and respected attorney, she would have to fight her own battles and prove her own worth. Despite the crap from Derrick she might have to wade through, she was going to continue establishing her own reputation. She was, after all, her father's daughter.

Again she opened the Mangano file. She always had been able to shut out unpleasant thoughts with concentration on her work—and this was to be no exception.

Julio Mangano and Luis Chairez had become estranged several years before when Chairez had divorced Mangano's sister. Neither had been willing to sell out to the other so the partnership had remained intact, but with each giving orders against the other's wishes. Since the restaurant chain was widespread, they rarely had to be together, so the business hadn't suffered drastically.

According to the DA's charge, on the night of June 19, Chairez and his ex-wife had had a bitter quarrel over child support for their five children. He had reportedly struck the woman and called her several derogatory names. She promptly told her brother, and Mangano had gone looking for Chairez. He supposedly had found him in one of their restaurants that was closed for remodeling, chased him into the storeroom, and shot him. Mangano's assertion was that he and his brother interrupted a burglary in progress and the burglar shot Chairez before running from the scene and vanishing.

Kirby muttered under her breath. From the way Hershal had written about the burglar, it was obvious that he felt this was an addition to the original story. That meant Mangano was a fool as well as a murderer. He hadn't even figured out a possible alibi. The prosecuting attorney would rip the burglar story to shreds.

Derrick stepped into her office and dropped a paper onto the file. "I knew you'd want to read Hershal's succession instructions for yourself, so here they are."

She glanced at the document which had been witnessed and notarized. At the bottom was Hershal's distinctive signature. There was no reason to read it. Kirby let it lie where he had tossed it. She leaned back in her swivel chair and waited in silence. It was another ploy passed on to her by her father that frequently worked for her.

Derrick frowned. "Aren't you even going to read it? I just want you to know I'm not lying about this."

"There's no need for me to read it. Just tell me this. Was it Hershal's idea?"

"Probably. At any rate, it's done. Now we can work together in harmony or . . ." He paused to let her imagination fill in the blank.

"I have no intention of leaving the firm my own father worked so hard to build. Surely you didn't think I would." Her eyes locked onto his, daring him to break the contact.

Derrick looked away. "Of course not. I wasn't suggesting that you should."

"No?"

"I'm considering bringing in several more attorneys over the next couple of months. I've been keeping my eyes open and there are two that appeal to me. I'll talk to them by the end of the week and see if they're interested."

"It would seem this appointment isn't a surprise to you. How long have you known Hershal was going to do this?"

"For several months. I didn't mention it to you because we've never been close and I expected Hershal to be with us for a number of years. There was no reason to upset you."

"I see." She wasn't going to make this easy for him.

"I talked to Addison and he agreed that there was no reason to tell you."

"Dad knew?"

"Of course."

"I don't want to hear any more, Derrick. I don't know why Hershal made this decision, but it appears that he intended for you to be in charge so that's that."

"Addison—"

"Derrick, you and I both know Dad can't have any say in how the firm is run. That would be a violation of ethics. Surely you aren't suggesting my father would do such a thing."

"Certainly not." Derrick drew himself up straighter.

"I have work to do." She bent over the file in a dismissing gesture. For a while he stood in the doorway glaring at her but she ignored him. After a time he went away and she heard him go back into Hershal's office.

Kirby sighed and tossed her pen onto the file. Her father had nothing to do with this. No man was more honest and above-board than Addison Walker. Since she was a small child, Kirby had deified him, and she would never believe he would do anything wrong. Not her father.

That meant Hershal had made the decision on his own. For reasons she would never understand, she had shown him in some way that she wasn't as capable as Derrick, though Kirby couldn't fathom what way that could have been. Derrick was a good lawyer or Addison wouldn't have taken him into the firm, son-in-law or not, but he wasn't likable. She told herself she was letting her personal opinion of him color the issue. That wasn't professional.

Once again she picked up the Mangano file. She put the copy of Hershal's letter in the top drawer of her desk to read later when Derrick wasn't likely to walk in and see her. In the outer office she heard the secretary starting the pot of coffee and sorting the mail. Kirby pressed the button on her intercom. "Miss Allerman? Make an appointment for me to meet with Julio Mangano this afternoon."

"Yes, Mrs. Garrett."

Kirby leaned back again. One way or another, she was going to win this case and prove to Derrick and everyone else that she was twice the lawyer he was.

Chapter Three

Julio Mangano sauntered into the interrogation room of the Harris County Jail, his black eyes scanning Kirby from head to toe as he approached the opposite side of the table. "You must be my new lawyer," he said as he turned his chair around, straddled it, and leaned his forearms on the back of the chair.

"Yes, I must be," Kirby answered in a manner and tone intended to counter his initial belligerence. From his raised eyebrow she could see that she'd gotten his attention. "In case they didn't tell you, my name is Kirby Garrett." She made no move to shake his hand, correctly guessing he wouldn't either, and flipped one of her business cards onto the scarred tabletop in front of him as she laid down her briefcase and took her seat. Without looking at him, Kirby opened her briefcase and took out her case file, a yellow legal pad and a tape recorder. "Do you mind if I record this?"

"Yes, I do. I don't like recorders. Mr. Glassman never recorded nothing."

"All right." She put the recorder back into her briefcase and picked up her pen. "Tell me in your own words what happened on June 19."

"I already told Mr. Glassman and he wrote it down."

"As you know, Mr. Glassman has died. I've read his notes

but I need to hear the story myself if I'm to defend you. Now what happened on the night Luis Chairez was killed?''

"He was married to my sister Marie, you know? They've got five kids. Marie and all of them kids have been living with me since he ran out on them. It's not easy on Marie. She didn't get nothing in the divorce, and she can't get a job good enough to take care of all of them. I don't mind supporting them," he added hastily. "She's my sister, you know? But it ought to be her husband's place."

"I understand."

"Marie went to Luis and told him she was going to take him back to court if he didn't start paying child support. Luis got mad. She said he called her some filthy names and he hit her. Naturally Marie came to me and told me what that rotten sonofabitch did." Mangano glared at her. "His sonofabitch brother was there, too. Fernando. He, too, called my sister names. Marie said when Luis hit her, Fernando laughed and told him he ought to hit her again and teach her not to talk to men that way. Marie told me all of this."

"What did you do?"

"I got real mad, you know? Don't nobody have the right to talk to my sister that way. Nobody! Especially not some bastard who ran off with a *puta* and left his wife and kids all alone! And that goes double for his fucking brother!"

"Try not to get so excited. I want you to remember everything accurately." Kirby watched the vein pulse in Mangano's temple. His obsidian eyes were as sharp as a straight razor and his voice had dropped to a dangerous pitch. "What happened next?"

"I went looking for them. Luis was right where Marie left him in a restaurant we were buying for the chain and remodeling to look Mexican. Fernando had already left."

"Was anybody else there? Any witnesses who can say Chairez was alive when you left?"

"No. Wasn't nobody there at all."

Kirby wrote it down. This was a variance from the burglar story noted by Hershal.

Mangano shifted in his chair and clasped his hands together as if he was restraining himself. "I told him not to ever touch my sister again or I'd kill him *and* his brother."

"Are you positive that's what you said? It won't look good to the jury if you threatened to kill him." She hoped he would take the hint and recant his words.

"I'm telling you what happened. Okay?" He glared at her. Kirby nodded. Mangano continued. "I told him he was a sonofabitch and a lot of other things."

"Were you saying these things in a normal tone of voice or were you shouting?"

"I was in his face and yelling." Mangano showed no remorse.

"Could anyone have heard you?"

"I told you there wasn't nobody else there. How many times I got to tell you?"

"Continue with what happened."

"He pushed me and I shoved him back. Then we got after it, you know? Fighting. I hit him in the face and he started running. I chased him into the back room. It's like a storage room, you know?"

"Is this the room where his body was found?"

"Yeah." Mangano paused a moment as if he was trying to recall something. "There was a burglar in there, hiding. He shot Luis and ran off."

Kirby put down her pen and leaned back to study Mangano. "A burglar? In a storeroom of a restaurant that's closed for remodeling? He must have heard the argument, yet he didn't go out the back door? I assume there must be a back door."

"Sure there is. It wouldn't meet the frigging fire code if there wasn't."

"Why didn't this burglar simply run away? Why did he shoot Chairez?"

"How should I know? He just did."

"And then he ran away." She watched him. The man was the worst liar she had ever seen. No jury would believe him. And because he was the only witness, he would have to take the stand.

"Yeah, right out that back door."

"Where did he go from there?"

"How the hell should I know?"

"Can you describe the man?" Kirby picked up her pen again.

"He was wearing a black ski mask. I didn't see his face."

"A ski mask? In June? In a building he must have thought would be empty? Mr. Mangano, you've got to help me if we're going to prove your innocence."

"Look, I'm telling you what happened. Marie will back me up."

"Marie was there? I thought you said you went alone."

"I was. But I told her all about it when I got back home."

"That makes it hearsay evidence. It's not admissible in court. Did you call the police when Mr. Chairez was shot?"

"Hell, no. He wouldn't have done it for me. Besides, he was dead."

"Are you sure he was dead? Did you check for a pulse or check to see if he was breathing?"

"No. He was dead. I could tell."

"You left the scene of the crime without notifying anyone?" Kirby leaned forward. This wasn't in Hershal's notes. "You left him just lying there?"

"I told you he was dead. What did you expect me to do for the bastard, sing him a hymn?"

Kirby frowned at him. "Do you want to go to prison, Mr. Mangano? Murder carries a possible death penalty. Is that what you want?"

"Hell, no."

"Then help me out. Did you call the police?"

"Sure I did. Whatever."

Kirby had never interviewed anyone so unremorseful over having killed someone. She had assisted Hershal in a number of murder cases, but virtually all of those clients had at least tried to come up with alibis or claim it was a crime of passion. "Did you have a gun with you when you went to see Mr. Chairez that night?"

"Sure. I always carry one in my car."

"But was it on your person when you went into the building?"

"Yeah, I stuck it under my belt and pulled my shirt over it so no one could see it, you know?"

"Why would you take a gun with you into the building?"

"I knew Luis was in there and Luis was a big man. For all

I knew, Fernando was still there, too. I didn't want them to beat me up."

"So it was self-defense," she said with a spark of hope. "Where is the gun now?"

"I lost it."

"You lost it!"

He shrugged. "It happened. What can I do about it now?"

"I don't suppose it was the same caliber gun that killed Mr. Chairez."

"It might have been." His black eyes bored into her. "I don't recall what kind it was. Just a gun. You know?"

"I know." She sighed. "What's your sister's phone number and last name?"

"Her last name? It was the same as that no good bastard's. Chairez. Her phone number is the same as mine. What do you need to talk to Marie about?"

"I need to verify her side of the story. We'll need her as a character reference and to tell the jury you went there in her defense."

"Leave Marie out of this. She's been through enough already."

She glared back at him. "Look, Mr. Mangano. If you don't cooperate with me, you're on your way to the pen. If I tell a jury what you've just told me, you're as good as convicted."

"He hurt my sister!"

"That doesn't give you the right to murder a man!"

"I told you the burglar shot him." He gave her a mirthless grin. "Maybe Fernando was the burglar. Maybe you ought to arrest him, too."

Kirby snapped her note pad shut and thrust it into her brief-case. "Think about all of this and try to remember something that I can use to prove your innocence. I'll be back in touch with you."

"I'm not so sure I want a woman lawyer defending me. Isn't there some man in your office? A man would understand better."

"Yes, we do have a number of men on staff. One of them is named Derrick McKinsey. Are you requesting he handle your case instead of me?" She hoped Mangano would let her off the hook.

Mangano shook his head. "What's the point? I guess you'll be okay."

Kirby went to the door and signaled the guard to let her out. She would be glad to see the last of Mangano for the day.

When she returned to the office, she went into to see Derrick. He was on the phone with Mallory.

"I don't care what Tara says. She's not old enough to decide where she will go or what she will do. You're her mother. You handle it." He listened for a minute. "Mallory, I'm trying to work here. Yes, put her on." He motioned for Kirby to come in and sit down. "Tara, this is Daddy. What's this about you not wanting to go over to Grandad's house? . . . Well, honey, that's not good enough. Your mother has something to do today and you're not old enough to stay home alone . . . I don't want to hear another word about it. Put your mother back on." He waited. "Mallory, that wasn't so difficult. Yeah, right. I've got to go." He hung up.

"Tara doesn't want to go to Dad's house? Since when?"

"She's been pulling this for the last few days. I don't know why. I guess she thinks she's too old to need supervision during the day."

"She's always loved going over there."

"Who knows what a girl is thinking? How did it go with Mangano?"

Kirby shook her head. "The man is as guilty as they come. I don't want to handle this case. He even said he would be more comfortable with a man as his lawyer. He all but told me he killed Chairez! And didn't even sound remorseful! Have you met this character?"

Derrick nodded. "I went over the case with Hershal a couple of times. I figured you'd want it. If you pull it off, you'll make a name for yourself."

"Derrick, if I pull it off, I'll be setting a murderer free! I can't do that."

"You have to. You're a lawyer. It's your job to defend your clients."

"I'm not so sure Mangano wouldn't kill again. I mean, the man has no remorse at all and he's still mad at Luis Chairez's brother! This burglar he mentioned is obviously a fabrication. No jury would ever believe it."

"The burglar was Hershal's idea." Derrick grinned and steepled his fingers. "You should have heard the original version."

"Hershal made up a lie for him?" Kirby was so shocked her mouth dropped open. "He invented the burglar?"

"I was there when he did it. He suggested to Mangano that if someone else had been there and if that someone else had killed Chairez, that would let Mangano off the hook."

"But it's a lie! I can't let my client perjure himself on the stand!"

"Don't put him on the stand. There are ways around it." Derrick gave her a placating smile. "I know this isn't a pretty trial. You'd probably be more interested in some civil case. But here at Walker, Glassman and McKinsey we deal in a harder-edged clientele. It's a decision I made when I took over."

"This is the first I've heard of that. And I can handle criminal cases as well as you can. Probably better."

"Then you can prove yourself with Mangano. And I don't intend to inform you of every decision I make, when I make it. You'll hear about the changes when everyone else does. Don't forget, you're not the head of this outfit. You just work here."

"Don't you become patronizing with me, Derrick! I'm in no mood for your chauvinism."

He threw up his hands in pretended fear. "Don't go PMS on me. I'm just trying to conduct business here."

Kirby stood and strode to the door. "Does that mean you're refusing to take the Mangano case?"

"You got it, baby," he said cheerfully.

She crossed to his desk and leaned over it until her face was inches from his. With a stern expression and businesslike tone, she said, "If you ever call me 'baby' again, I'll sue you for sexual harassment. Got it, Derrick?"

He laughed and said, "Meow."

Kirby left the office before her anger became visible and before she did him physical harm. In the sanctity of her own office, she fumed. With Derrick at the helm, she wasn't sure she could or would continue working there. To leave was a big decision. Her father had built the practice into one of the most prestigious in Houston. Of course neither he nor Hershal were here now. In time the firm's prestige might drop. Kirby knew she was a good attorney and that she could probably keep the firm's reputation as untarnished as it had been when Derrick inherited it, but was that what she wanted?

The button for Derrick's line lit up on her phone, meaning that he was talking to someone. Likely Mallory. If he spent all his time on personal crises, she would be left doing all the work. Kirby was positive she wasn't going to let that happen.

She dropped the Mangano file in the tray marked *McKinsey* and went to the file cabinet to get another of the cases she was currently developing. Derrick could handle Mangano or the man could find another law firm altogether. Kirby couldn't defend him in good conscience, knowing the man was a killer.

She was well into the file of a man accused of armed robbery when her phone rang. She answered and smiled when she recognized her caller. "Dad! I didn't expect to hear from you today."

"I was just wondering if my favorite daughter would like to meet me for lunch tomorrow."

"I'd love to."

"How about Caruso's?"

Kirby paused. "All the way out Westheimer? Will you have time?"

"I've already cleared it with my secretary. I picked Caruso's because I know it's your favorite."

"Okay. Sure. I'd never turn down an invitation to eat there." Kirby pushed her papers into a neater stack. "Is something wrong? We usually don't make such a production out of lunch."

"Well, maybe we should. You and I haven't been spending much time together lately. Whenever I see you, the family is around and we don't really get a chance to talk."

"All right." Kirby told herself she was being foolish to suspect something was wrong despite Addison's assurances. "I'll meet you there at, say, noon?"

"Sounds good to me."

After she hung up, Kirby was still bothered by the niggling

concern that Addison had sounded a bit too cheerful. She shook her head and told herself she was imagining it.

At noon Kirby turned off Westheimer and parked in The Great Caruso's parking lot. She hadn't been to the restaurant in several months and was looking forward to the treat. A glance about told her Addison's car wasn't in the lot.

She entered through the glass revolving door and was greeted by a man with a professional smile. "Two," she said. "Non-smoking, please." She followed him into the dining area.

As she waited, she studied the menu and listened to the waiters sing. That was one of Caruso's drawing cards. The waiters frequently sang solos from operas as they went to and fro between the tables. Some of them were particularly good. The ambiance was also exquisite; the music, soft lighting, abundant greenery, and pristine tablecloths made Caruso's a wonderful place to escape for an hour or so. Russell had never cared for the place, since he didn't like opera. Kirby had heard and enjoyed operas all her life.

Addison joined her moments later and ordered wine for them both. Kirby wouldn't have done that since she still had an afternoon's work ahead and wine, even a single glass, tended to relax her and somewhat slow down her usually quick mind. "I have a client coming in at two-thirty," she said as Addison consulted the menu. "I'll have to keep an eye on the time."

"I canceled all my appointments for the afternoon. I was hoping you had done the same."

"You know how it is when you're making a living," Kirby said with a smile. "Somebody has to mind the store."

"What do you mean by that?"

Before she could answer, the waiter appeared silently, pad in hand. Kirby ordered and took a sip of wine while her father instructed the waiter and sent him away. Avoiding direct eye contact with Addison, she said, "Derrick is being his usually overbearing self. He shoved a case off on me that I'm almost certain to lose. I think he did it just to make me look bad. You know how he is. He wants the easy, high-profile cases for himself. I get stuck with a sure loser."

"You mean the Mangano case?"

Kirby looked up in surprise. "How do you know about Julio Mangano?"

"I read the papers. I try to keep pace, even if I'm a step removed from the law office."

"The papers didn't say we were representing him. Did Derrick talk to you about it?"

Addison rested his forearms on the table with the wineglass between his fingertips. "Derrick did mention it in passing. No details, of course."

"He shouldn't have done that. This is a murder trial and will automatically be appealed, if the prosecution wins. What if it lands in your court?"

"A conviction is not likely. Not with you representing him. You're underestimating yourself."

She shook her head. "I'm not taking that case. I told Derrick he'll have to do that one or tell Mangano to find another attorney."

"That's not what law is all about," Addison said. "I can't believe you would have a man settle for some other firm when you would do the job better."

Kirby leaned closer and lowered her voice. "He's guilty. I'm positive of it. If I represent him and prove his innocence, a killer will be turned loose on the streets. You haven't met him, Dad. He's a dangerous man."

Addison spread his hands in a gesture of reasoning. "You can't know that."

"Yes, I can. If you had talked to him, you'd see what I mean."

"Kirby, a man is innocent until proven guilty. I can't believe you would go against this basic precept. It's what our judicial system is based upon."

"I shouldn't be talking to you about this at all. We could both get in trouble for having this conversation."

"No one can hear us." Addison glanced around the area to verify that no one was listening. "I'm asking you to take the case."

"Why?"

"Because I think you can win it. If you do, it will mean a feather in your cap, professionally speaking."

"Not this case. I won't do it."

"Kirby, every man who is charged with an offense has the right to the best defense possible."

"I know all that. I went to law school. Remember?"

"If you take only the cases that are open and shut and shun the ones that make you stretch, your career will go nowhere. You'll end up defending penny-ante cases that no one cares about. What if I had done that?"

"That's not fair. I'm not taking the easy way out. I just don't want to defend this particular man." She glanced around. "Dad, I don't feel right about discussing this. It's not ethical."

Addison laughed as if she were being charmingly foolish. "I don't mean to make you feel uncomfortable, baby."

Kirby felt a curling distaste beginning in her middle but she couldn't have said why. All her life, Addison had called Mallory and her "baby." He called Tara that as well. It was his favorite term of endearment. "I know you don't. Let's forget it."

"Derrick is very upset over it. I want you to tell him you'll take the case."

She narrowed her eyes thoughtfully. "Did Derrick call you yesterday? Is that why you asked me to meet you for lunch?"

"It's not uncommon for a man to take his daughter to lunch, I don't believe. Derrick did talk to me, but lunch was my idea."

"I think I should go. I can't discuss this case with you." She stood up but Addison caught her wrist and pulled her gently back down.

"Don't go. I won't talk about it anymore. I know you'll do what's right. After all, you are my daughter."

Kirby fell silent as the waiter placed their food before them. Across the room a waiter was singing a strain from *La Traviata*. Addison seemed to be totally engrossed in eating his salad while Kirby listlessly stirred her lettuce around. She was no longer hungry.

If anyone had even suggested that Addison might overstep the bounds of propriety, she would have been offended. Yet here he was discussing a case he should know nothing about! Did Derrick keep him apprised of all the cases or was this an exception? He could claim the discussion was about the best interest of her career, but Kirby still was uncomfortable. Addison shouldn't have become involved at all.

There was no one she could consult about this. Derrick obviously wasn't a person she could trust and Russell was far from impartial when it came to her father. Besides, she never told him anything about Addison that might fuel the dislike between them.

"So what have you decided to do about Mangano?" Addison asked as he started on his ravioli.

"I'll take the case," she said stiffly. All her life she had done what her father expected of her, with the exception of marrying Russell. In this matter there was no other choice. Addison would be angry with her if she balked on this, and it was never wise to do something that would provoke his anger.

"That's a good girl. I knew you'd do the right thing." He smiled beatifically at her.

Kirby tried to eat her food without thinking about what had just happened, but the best she could do was to pretend.

Derrick was watching for her to return from lunch. When she passed by his office, he motioned for her to come in. "How was lunch?"

"Why did you talk to my father about the Mangano case?" Kirby demanded. "You know that's a conflict of interest for him to know about it."

"I didn't go into any detail. Did he say that I had?"

Kirby didn't reply.

"I just don't want to see you throw your career away."

"Don't worry about my career, Derrick."

"All the same, I was glad to hear you're going to take the case and stop making waves."

"How do you know what I've decided?"

Derrick faltered as if he had been caught in a slipup. "You said you had."

"No, I didn't." Kirby remembered that Addison had a car phone. He could have phoned Derrick as soon as they parted at the restaurant. Kirby's eyes narrowed and she stared at Derrick coldly. "Have you talked to Dad since I saw him at lunch?"

"Of course not." Derrick's eyes were a bit too guileless, making Kirby even more suspicious. "But you are taking it, aren't you?"

Kirby signed. "Yes. I suppose I am." Turning her back on Derrick, Kirby went to her own office and closed the door, wanting to be alone to think.

All that made sense was that Addison had told Derrick of her decision. But why would he do that? For that matter, why had he gotten involved at all? Kirby had been a lawyer long enough to know that most lawyers bent or broke the rules from time to time. Until today, she would have said Addison was one of the rare exceptions, one of those who never considered bending the rules at all.

She disliked thinking that her father wasn't perfect. It had seldom happened.

Kirby opened a drawer of her desk and took out a birthday card Addison had sent her two months before. She had meant to take it home but kept forgetting it. For that matter, she didn't know why he had sent it to her at work in the first place. She had received one at the family party for her from both her parents that was signed in Jane's flowery handwriting. At the time she received the card at work, she had thought it was special that her father wanted to give her a card that only the two of them shared.

Suddenly, panic seized her. She was staring at the depiction on the card of a father with a small girl on his lap, both of them smiling lovingly. Terror ripped through her and she started to shake. She heard a child crying and smelled the overwhelming scent of carnations. There was a blur of blue and white. Her ears were ringing and her mouth was uncomfortably dry. She couldn't stop staring at the card, even though it was shaking visibly in her hand.

With a choked cry, she threw the card away from her and covered her face with her hands.

Slowly the terror faded away. Kirby carefully took a shuddering breath and looked around her office. Her skin was slick with perspiration and her breath was coming in short gasps.

What had happened to her?

She forced herself to breathe more normally, though she felt dizzy and disoriented. She hugged herself and her hands felt icy through the silk of her blouse. What on God's earth had happened? She had heard of people having panic attacks but had never experienced one herself, and frankly, she had been skeptical of such things being a reality. Everyone felt uneasy at one time or another, but this had been far more than mere uneasiness.

Cautiously she picked up the card and looked at it again. It was the same card she had seen off and on for two months. When she received it, she had felt singled out, special. Now it was all she could do to look at it. The man seemed so big and frightening, the little girl so terribly vulnerable. Her hands began trembling again.

Kirby dropped the card in the wastebasket and pushed the basket away. Whatever it had triggered, whether it was a bona fide panic attack or not, was still lingering near. She certainly didn't want to repeat the experience.

There was a soft knock on her door. Straightening her jacket and touching her hair to be sure it was in place, she forced her voice to be calm and called out, "Come in."

Miss Allerman opened the door. "Your two-thirty appointment is here. A Mrs. Bateman."

Kirby looked at her watch in dismay. Had half an hour gone by since she'd left Derrick's office? How could that be? "Give me a few minutes, please. I haven't finished reviewing her file."

Miss Allerman nodded and closed the door as she left.

Kirby fought down the urge to cry. She had rarely been so frightened in her life. Not only could she not explain the terror, but half an hour had vanished. She drew in deep breaths to calm herself. Panic wouldn't solve anything. Everyone lost track of time once in a while. It didn't mean anything. As she rose to go to her filing cabinet, she avoided looking at the wastebasket where the card lay on top of other discarded papers.

She pulled out the Bateman file and returned to her desk. She had a job to do. If she was going to fall apart, she would have to do it later, on her own time. The thought made her smile and that automatically relaxed her a bit.

Quickly she scanned her notes. The Bateman case was a simple property dispute. Nothing traumatic about it for anyone but the parties directly involved. She pressed the button to signal Miss Allerman to send Mrs. Bateman in to see her.

The panic attack or whatever it had been was gone now, and in retrospect, Kirby told herself she was remembering it as being worse than it had been.

But she still avoided looking in the wastebasket.

Chapter Four

Kirby finished her summation and sat down. The jury watched her with no more expression than if she were a television set. Behind her she could hear Maria Chairez sniffling. Maria had been crying off and on during the entire trial. Because of Kirby's advice, she had brought her children with her most days, all five of them scrubbed clean and behaving like small adults. Kirby was hoping to portray Mangano as a family man who was protective of his sister and her children.

After the prosecution's final arguments, the judge instructed the jury, then both judge and jury left the courtroom. This particular courtroom had no windows and she was feeling somewhat claustrophobic. Closed spaces had never bothered her before, and Kirby didn't understand why claustrophobia would suddenly start cropping up in her life.

Even though it was early October, already autumn according to the calendar, the weather outside was still steaming hot most days. Kirby knew cooler days had to come soon and no one was more anxious than she. Her blouse was still plastered to her back under her suit jacket even though she had been indoors for several hours. This particular judge apparently preferred warmer rooms and had set the thermostat accordingly.

"How long will it be?" Mangano asked.

"I have no idea. If the jury hasn't decided by about five

o'clock, the judge will probably call a recess until tomorrow morning. Until the jury is through with its deliberations, we'll all just have to wait." She hoped the wait would be a long one. That would mean they were at least considering things in Mangano's favor. She had represented him to the best of her ability, having put her assumption of his guilt out of her mind. After all, she could be wrong.

After about an hour, the judge declared a recess and left the courtroom. Maria Chairez leaned forward and touched Kirby's shoulder. "I want to thank you for what you have done for my brother." Her accent was heavier than Mangano's and she was obviously shy. It had embarrassed her when Kirby had shown the jury the photos of her bruises after her last encounter with her ex-husband. Kirby had disliked doing this in front of Maria's children, but she had to make Chairez appear to be as evil as possible to make a case for Mangano's reason for killing him.

She had convinced Mangano to let her defend him by admitting to the jury that even though Julio fired the shot that killed Chairez, he had done so under the influence of sudden passion—he had feared for Maria's life and was afraid Chairez might kill her the next time he beat her up. Mangano had argued with her at length that a burglar had fired the fatal shot, not him, but Kirby finally won his trust—even though there was a risk, though she deemed it slight, that the jury might find him guilty of voluntary manslaughter.

At four-fifteen, the judge reconvened the court and called for the jury to return. When the judge ordered the defendant to stand, Kirby rose with Mangano and waited in silence for the verdict. Even though Maria was on the bench behind the rail, Kirby could sense Maria's tension. One of the Chairez children began whispering and Maria hushed him quickly.

"Your Honor, we find the defendant not guilty of the murder of Luis Chairez."

Maria sobbed in relief. Kirby could hear the children rustling around behind her. She didn't look at Mangano.

When the judge dismissed the court, she gathered up her papers and shook Mangano's hand. He grinned at her as if he had known all along the jury would decide in his favor. Because he had no remorse for having killed Chairez, he had assumed no one would object.

Now that the case was over, Kirby was glad to be away from Mangano and hoped she would never have to see him again.

Mallory put her arm around Tara's shoulders and smiled proudly at her, then turned back to her daughter's teacher. "I'm so glad Tara is doing well in art. She's always loved to draw."

Tara's teacher, Mrs. Lydick, nodded and moved out of the way of other parents who were studying the papers taped to the wall. "I was so glad you were able to come for Parent-Teacher Night. It means so much to the children. There was some disagreement about us having it so early this year, but I think it's really better for everyone to get to know each other as soon as possible."

"Mom? Melissa Puricelli is over there. Is it okay if I go talk to her?"

"Sure, honey."

Mrs. Lydick waited until Tara had moved away. "May I speak frankly, Mrs. McKinsey?" She looked about her as if trying to determine that they were out of earshot of all the others.

"Of course." Mallory hoped the teacher wasn't going to question Derrick's not being there. He had flatly refused to come because he had courtside seats at a basketball game.

"I've been a bit worried about Tara lately."

Mallory frowned. "In what way? Is she misbehaving?"

"Not really. All children go through spells when they become somewhat of a discipline problem. The two pictures I displayed are ones Tara drew soon after school started. I decided not to put up her more recent ones. Lately her pictures have been, well, disturbing."

"I don't understand."

Mrs. Lydick motioned for Mallory to follow her to her desk so they would be even farther away from the other parents and children. She unlocked her desk and took out three pictures. Even to Mallory's unschooled eyes they were different from the ones on the wall. The colors were darker and the drawings less precise. The adults were drawn huge and threatening and the child in each one, presumably Tara, was tiny, huddling in one corner.

"Tara did these?"

"When she turned in the first one, I assumed she was simply having a bad day. But she's consistently drawing like this now. Has something changed in her life?" Mrs. Lydick seemed uncomfortable. "I don't mean to be prying, but I thought if there was some problem at home, I might be able to help Tara somehow."

"There's no problem at home." Mallory thought carefully. "Nothing has changed at all."

"Sometimes children misinterpret arguments. I've seen drawings crop up like this when a divorce is about to happen, something like that."

Mallory lifted her chin resentfully. Tara's teacher had no business prying into her personal life. "Derrick—my husband—didn't come tonight because he had made other plans. We aren't divorcing. Did Tara tell you that we are? She has no reason to think such a thing. She and her father are quite close."

"No, no. Not at all. I was only using that as an example."

Mallory frowned at the pictures. "They are unsettling, aren't they?"

"This one," Mrs. Lydick said, "was an assignment on families. That's why I thought perhaps . . ." Her voice trailed off discreetly.

"No, Derrick and I rarely argue." This wasn't true, but she wasn't going to admit that in front of a stranger. Besides, they had always argued. Why would it suddenly start bothering Tara? "What were these other assignments?"

"This one is 'What Chore Do You Dislike Most?' and this one is 'My Summer Vacation.'"

Mallory frowned. In both a large man was bending over the tiny child. The last one was in a room with blue furniture and something about it seemed familiar to Mallory. "We didn't take a vacation this year and we don't have blue furniture," she said as much to herself as to Mrs. Lydick.

"Kids seldom are that accurate. The color of the furniture

may only mean a blue crayon was closest to hand. Each table has to share a box of crayons, you see."

Mallory nodded. "I'll tell Derrick about this, but I can't think of a single thing that's changed at home. If anything, Tara is less of a problem than ever. She's staying in her room more or watching TV."

"She's a bit livelier here at school. Of course the year is just starting and it takes the children a while to calm down and get back into routine."

"Tara has been misbehaving? I mean, she's not perfect, goodness knows, but she's so quiet at home lately." Now that she thought about it, Tara had been rather too quiet. When her nephews were eight, they were louder than ever and practically lived in the backyard. Tara preferred to stay in her room or in the den with Mallory and watch TV. "Frankly I was enjoying the peace for a change. Last year she and her cousins were into everything."

Mrs. Lydick smiled. "It may be nothing at all. If there's one thing I've learned about children, it's that they can be unpredictable. Maybe Tara is just going through a phase."

"I'm sure that's it," Mallory said with relief. "She's a good girl."

"My goodness, yes. I wish I had a classroom full of students like Tara. I just thought I should tell you about the difference in her pictures."

"Thank you." Mallory watched Tara with her friend across the room. They were giggling like any other eight-year-olds. There was nothing to worry about. Mrs. Lydick was only being cautious. She decided there was no reason to tell Derrick anything after all.

Five days later, Julio Mangano made headlines again. Fernando Chairez's lifeless body had been found floating in Chocolate Bayou and this time Mangano had been seen running from the scene of the crime.

"I won't defend him," Kirby stated flatly. "You can do it or you can let him find another attorney, but I refuse to defend that man again."

Lynda Trent

Derrick gave her a parental frown. "We can't let our personal objections interfere with our business. You did a superb job before. You can do it again."

"You aren't listening to me. I didn't say I can't, I said I won't. Hasn't it occurred to you that if I hadn't managed to convince a jury to let Mangano out of jail, Fernando Chairez would still be alive? The man had a family. Three small children, according to the paper. Now he's gone forever."

"From your argument in the courtroom, I gather his family may be better off without him." Derrick smiled. "He sounds like a particularly unsavory character."

"You're not his jury, Derrick. I can't believe you could say that. All I had to go on was the word of the man who is now his murderer! For all we know, the Chairez brothers might have been wonderful people. We don't know that Mangano didn't give his sister those bruises himself! I certainly believe he was capable of it."

"Why are you getting so worked up? You don't know these people. Not really."

"Something has been bothering me. You said Hershal gave Mangano the idea of fabricating that burglar nonsense. Why did he do that?"

Derrick shrugged. "Hershal knew Mangano was guilty. We talked about it. He told Mangano to tell everyone a burglar did it because he thought no jury would believe it. Mangano would be found guilty."

"He was setting up his own client? No. Hershal wouldn't do such a thing!"

"Kirby, I don't know why you're so damned determined to see the world through rose-colored glasses, but people aren't all good or all bad."

"I don't think that," she snapped. "You know I don't."

"Hershal was just an ordinary man. He had faults like anybody else."

"He was like a second father to me."

"That doesn't have anything to do with how he made his living. I'd heard him say that sometimes you have to cut your losses and go on. He knew Mangano was guilty. He also knew there would be an automatic appeal so he would have at least one more shot at representing him in court. And frankly, he wanted the money. The Guadalupe Restaurants make a fortune. Mangano could afford it.''

"No," she flatly denied. "I don't believe that of Hershal. He would no more do that than Dad would."

Derrick laughed. "I agree with you there. I imagine that's where he got the idea in the first place."

"Dad hasn't had anything to do with the office since he became a judge. I know he doesn't!"

"Whatever you say. Look, I've got a lot of work to do and I can't sit here talking to you all day. If you need something to do, I can take care of that."

"I'm doing more than my share now," she said stiffly. "Now that you come in late and leave early, I'm working twice as hard as you are."

Derrick gave her another of his irritating smiles. "That's one of the perks of being boss."

Kirby left and shut the door behind her harder than necessary. She hated dealing with Derrick. He always knew just what to say to bring her to the boiling point. And she was just as determined that he not know he was succeeding. If this wasn't the law firm her father had founded, she wouldn't put up with it another minute.

In her office, she looked at the stack of cases she had been given to work. Derrick assigned her all the rough ones, while he kept the plums for himself. He came off looking good and her credibility was shrinking.

Kirby got her purse and went to Miss Allerman's desk. "I'm going to be gone for a while. Will you take any messages for me?"

"Of course, Mrs. Garrett."

She drove downtown to the Harris County District Attorney's Office on Fannin. Leon Zimmerman had been the DA for a number of years and never had been a friend of her father's. In fact, Addison had never said a good word about the man as far as Kirby knew, but she had formed a different opinion of the man from having seen him work in court. She was glad he'd agreed to see her without an appointment when she had called.

"Mrs. Garrett," he said with a nod of greeting. "What can I do for you today?" He motioned for her to take a seat in one of the chairs in front of his desk, showing no sign that he intended to rise and shake hands. Peering over the half-frame spectacles that he wore for reading, he said, "You're Addison Walker's daughter, aren't you?"

"Yes, I am."

Zimmerman nodded. "I've known Addison for many years. I recognize you from the Mangano case."

"I know you and my father don't see eye to eye on most issues, but I hope you won't hold that against me."

"Why should I? I don't agree with a lot of people. That doesn't mean they're my enemies." He removed his glasses and looked directly at her. With what she could only describe as a twinkle in his light blue eyes, he said, "Besides, I'm almost always right, and sooner or later those who disagree with me recognize that."

She found herself smiling. She liked the man. "I'm wondering if you have a position for me here in the DA's office."

Zimmerman's face didn't register surprise, but his eyes narrowed speculatively. For a long moment he didn't answer; he was studying her. Although his weather-seamed face seemed more suited to that of a cowboy than a lawyer, his penetrating eyes were sharply intelligent. "Why?"

"As you said, I was in charge of defending Julio Mangano for the murder of Luis Chairez recently. I didn't want to take that case, but I ended up with it when Hershal Glassman died."

"Yes, I was sorry to hear that Mr. Glassman died. You did a great job defending him, but it seems your client is in a peck of trouble again."

"He's not my client. I've told Derrick McKinsey I won't take the case."

"Oh? I had heard you were." His cropped hair was an even mix of brown and gray and stuck up untidily about his head. Kirby had seldom seen anyone who looked less like an esteemed district attorney.

"It wouldn't surprise me if Derrick has accepted it in my behalf and hasn't told me. He would do such a thing." She clasped her hands in her lap. This was difficult for her. "I have a moral problem with knowing a man is a murderer and being in large part responsible for his release. Especially when he kills again. I might be able to convince a jury that he's innocent this time, too, but if he's killed twice, he could easily do it again."

"That's the court system for you. Everyone is entitled to counsel."

"I want to work here because I believe I would be happier as a prosecuting attorney. I'm a good lawyer, Mr. Zimmerman. A very good one. I want to use my abilities to put criminals behind bars, not to set them free."

"I see."

"If it's a matter of credentials, I can supply you with whatever you want to see."

"That won't be necessary. I'm familiar with a number of your cases. Frankly, I didn't think you had a ghost of a chance of getting Mangano free. I know him from other occasions when that temper of his has gotten him into trouble. So you want to work here. Does your father know about this?"

"I haven't discussed it with him. It's something that's been in the back of my mind for a while now, but I don't ask his opinion on everything."

"He won't be pleased. Addison and I never have hit it off. We've been at odds more times than I can remember, and you'd be leaving the family firm on top of it all."

"Dad will understand." She wondered if that was true. "I'm not happy working there. With Dad no longer involved with the firm and Hershal Glassman gone, it's not the same."

"I understand."

"Do you have an opening?"

"I will have next month."

Kirby waited for him to elaborate. When he didn't, she said, "Does that mean you'll consider hiring me?"

"I'll certainly give it serious thought. I have a number of applicants for the job, naturally. I'm not making any promises."

"I wouldn't expect you to. I'm sure you need time to think about it." She stood to go.

"I'll be in touch with you." He smiled and his face crinkled into pleasant wrinkles.

"Thank you."

Kirby went back to her car and sat there for several seconds, thinking over what she had done. While it was true that she had considered applying at the DA's office for some time, it was out of character for her to do so without so much as mentioning it to Russell or her father. Kirby wasn't given to acting on impulses. Normally she wanted to look at any issue from every possible angle, and both Russell and Addison's opinions were important to her. All the same, she wasn't sorry she had talked to Zimmerman.

But what would her father say?

That night she and Russell sat up long after the boys were in bed. "Is something bothering you?" he asked as he turned off the TV.

"I did something today that I probably shouldn't have done."

"You punched Derrick?" he asked hopefully.

"I wish I had. No, I went to the DA's office to talk to Leon Zimmerman."

"Plea bargain negotiations?"

"No. I asked him for a job." Kirby watched to see if Russell would be upset. "I know it would mean a big cut in my salary, but I don't think I can bear to work with Derrick another day."

"Zimmerman hired you?"

"No, but he said he'll be needing to hire another assistant soon and that he'll consider me. Maybe I'm reading too much into it, but I think he's impressed with my capabilities."

"He should be."

She smiled at him. "So what do you think? I know I should have talked to you, but Derrick pushed me over the top today. It was talk to Zimmerman or have reason to defend myself in court."

"It's a big step. You know your dad won't be pleased."

"No, but I'm sure he'll understand. At least I hope he will." She sighed. "He really will be mad, won't he." It was a statement, not a question; she knew her father too well to think otherwise.

"He'll be livid, I'd say."

"But what else could I do? I can't break off from the company and start my own firm. Dad would certainly see that as hostile to the firm he and Hershal worked so hard to build. The DA's office seemed to be the best choice. And I like the idea of sending criminals to prison, not freeing them simply because I'm good at defense."

"I agree. I know that Mangano thing upset you a great deal."

"Before the trial, he all but told me he was guilty. But since he never *said* he was, I had to defend him anyway. Now he's killed the other Chairez brother! I feel as if it's partially my fault."

"What will you feel when you have to argue to send a man to prison when you think he's really innocent?"

"I don't think that happens much. The state has to be pretty damned sure of a person's guilt before the case is presented to a grand jury. And then the grand jury won't bring an indictment if they don't agree. After all that, if an innocent man gets convicted because of a poor defense, he has the right to appeal. Don't you see the difference?"

"Yes, but I know how altruistic you can be."

"That's not a fault, necessarily." She crossed her arms over her chest.

"Hey, don't get mad at me. I'm on your side. I'm just playing devil's advocate."

Kirby put her face in her hands and rubbed her forehead. She'd thought about all this so many times she was worn out. "I know. I'm sorry."

"I'm glad you applied at the DA's office. I like Zimmerman."

"I didn't know you even knew him."

"I've met him through the college. He's been out to talk to my classes from time to time."

"So you don't think I've lost my mind? What about the cut in pay?"

Russell took her hand in his in a comforting gesture. "That's no big deal. We were saving most of your earnings anyway. So our nest egg will grow slower. We can manage."

She squeezed his hand. "You're a good person, Russell. A lot of husbands would want me to stay with the firm and not make financial waves."

"It's been a long time since we sat and talked like this." He rubbed his thumb over the palm of her hand. "We used to sit up late and talk all the time."

"I remember. Our life is faster paced now. There are the boys and we're both working. By this time of night, I'm usually exhausted."

"Maybe in the DA's office you won't be working late so often and we'll have more time together. I'd like that."

Kirby gave his hand another squeeze before withdrawing hers. "I'd like that, too."

"Would you really?" Russell studied her face as if he didn't believe her.

His doubt put Kirby on the defensive. "Of course I would. I miss getting to see the boys more. They're growing up faster than I would have thought possible. And I almost never have a chance to visit with Mallory these days."

"And me?"

"Of course, you too. Russell, don't do this."

"Do what?"

"Put me on the defensive by suggesting that I'm avoiding you. I hate it when you do that."

He was silent for a moment. "I didn't mean to upset you. It seems as if we can never have a conversation anymore."

"I'm trying. It's just that I'm under a lot of pressure lately."

"This has been going on for well over a year. Maybe longer."

"I have no idea what you're talking about." She got up and busied herself straightening the throw pillows on the couch. She didn't want to look at him because she knew it was true.

"Yes, you do. I know you too well to believe that."

"It's late. Let's go to bed before we have another argument."

"Damn it, Kirby, we have to talk sometime! If we keep on this way, our marriage isn't going to make it!"

In a frosty tone, she said, "That's good to know, Russell. I appreciate your telling me this at a time when I need your support more than ever. It's not like I have anything else to worry about."

"Okay then, prove me wrong. Let's go to bed."

She turned away. "I'll be up soon. There are some things I need to do first."

For a long time, he sat there watching her. Kirby pretended it didn't bother her to feel his accusing glare knifing into her. Then, without another word, Russell left the room.

When she was alone, Kirby sat down and leaned her head back on the couch cushions. What was wrong with her life lately? She loved Russell and she wanted to be married to him. It wasn't her fault, was it, that she didn't have the same sexual urges she had had when they first married? She was thirty-six now and had sons who were almost grown. She was no longer a starry-eyed bride working her way through law school and living on a shoestring. It was only natural that they had been closer then and that her libido had been stronger. They had been starting a life together, a family. He had no right to make her feel guilty like this.

That argument would probably be convincing to everyone but Russell and herself. Something else was wrong and she didn't know what it was. She wanted Russell, but she tended to want him primarily when he wasn't around or when making love wasn't possible. He had suggested that she should see a marriage counselor but Kirby was resistant. Seeing a counselor would be the same thing as admitting that her marriage was failing and she couldn't bear that. She could just imagine what Addison would say if it got back to him that she and Russell were having marital problems. The attorneys in her family sometimes represented others seeking a divorce, but they never sued for one themselves.

She tidied up downstairs until Russell had had time to go to sleep, then she climbed the stairs hoping that sleep would come for her soon, as well.

Chapter Five

Two weeks passed and Kirby decided she had acted prematurely in talking to Zimmerman. Derrick seemed to be going out of his way to keep from upsetting her, and the office settled into a calm it hadn't known since Hershal Glassman died. The sign on the entry doors and the directory in the bank lobby now read, "Walker, Glassman and McKinsey," and since Derrick had hired the two new lawyers, the workload wasn't so unbearable.

Derrick had moved his things into the larger office Glassman had occupied and had offered Kirby his old office. Kirby turned it down. "I know where everything is in my office and I don't want to have to go to the bother of moving. Let Haufman or Jeffers have it."

"If you say so. I was only giving you first choice."

"Thank you, but no."

"Mallory says you two had fun the other night."

Kirby glanced at him. She was trying to file some papers and would rather Derrick leave her alone. She was currently handling a case of spousal abuse and divorce and the paperwork was becoming an avalanche. But like Derrick, she was trying to be less antagonistic so she was cordial. "What night was that?"

"Last Thursday. The night you two went shopping."

"I'm glad she enjoyed it." Kirby realized she had filed one folder under the first name and not the last and had to correct the mistake before she could continue with her work. Derrick was a distraction and she wished he would go away.

"So you were with her?"

She glanced at him. "What's that supposed to mean?"

"Nothing. I just meant I'm glad she had a good time."

"Derrick, I'd love to talk to you, but I have to get this file in order. Mrs. Harper will be here soon for another consultation."

"Okay. I'll be on my way. I want to see if Jim or Kyle needs anything."

Kirby nodded without looking up. Jim Haufman and Kyle Jeffers seemed capable of moving into their offices without Derrick's help, but at least it got him out of her office.

She sorted through the file tabs and put the rest of the papers away in order. Miss Allerman usually did this for her, but with two new men in the office, the secretary was busy helping them get settled in.

Kirby sat at her desk and took the Harper file out of her basket of cases to be reviewed. Then it struck her. She and Mallory hadn't gone shopping on Thursday; it had been Tuesday. Thursday she and Russell had gone to see the middle school football game with the boys. Josh would be old enough to try out for the team next year and he wanted to see every game possible.

Of course, Derrick could have confused the days, but now that she thought about it, he had seemed to be fishing for something—such as determining whether Mallory was really with her sister or if she had gone someplace else.

For a minute Kirby silently debated calling Mallory, then picked up the phone and dialed her number. She stepped around the desk as the phone rang and pushed her door shut. "Mallory? What are you doing?"

Mallory sounded out of breath. "You barely caught me. I had errands to run after I dropped Tara and the boys off at school. I heard the phone ringing and ran in from the drive."

"Is everything going all right with you?"

"Sure. Why do you ask?"

"Derrick was in here a minute ago and he wanted to know if we had fun shopping last Thursday."

Mallory was silent for a beat too long. "I guess he was only making conversation."

"We weren't together Thursday. I saw you on Tuesday."

"Oh, that's right! Well, you know how he is. Derrick can't remember his own birthday unless I remind him."

Kirby frowned. She had always been able to tell when Mallory was lying. "What did you do on Thursday?"

"Not much. I think I may have gone over to Dad's house to pick up a dress Mom has been sewing for Tara."

"So you were with Mom that night?"

"Hey, what's going on? Why the third degree?"

"I didn't mean for it to sound like that. I guess I've been in court too often in the past few days." She thought for a minute. "Mal, you'd tell me if something was going on, wouldn't you?"

"In a heartbeat. I've never been able to keep anything from you," Mallory said a bit too lightly.

"I know. That's why I'm asking."

"If you don't believe me, ask Mom," Mallory said with more of an edge to her tone.

"I'm sorry. I really am."

"That's okay, but if there's nothing else, I have a million things to do."

"Sure. I'll talk to you later." Kirby hung up more suspicious than ever. Although Derrick had never suspected, Kirby knew Mallory had been involved with a man the year before, though that was over now. Now that she thought about it, there had been other instances when Kirby had thought Mallory's excuses were unbelievable, though she had never questioned her.

As kids in school, Mallory had always been the one to flirt and had dated more than Kirby. At one time or another she had dated most of the football team and at least half the baseball team. Mallory had always liked the opposite sex.

Kirby slowly sat back down and opened the file. Mallory was a grown woman and capable of running her own life, but Kirby had always felt very protective of her. If Mallory was heading for trouble, it was Kirby's responsibility to point her sister in a safe direction.

The name of the file left in the basket caught Kirby's attention. It read "Julio Mangano." With growing disbelief she grabbed the file and read it again. Derrick was assigning the case to her despite what she had told him!

Kirby shoved away from her desk and stalked out of her room and down the hall to Derrick's office. She didn't bother knocking. He was talking to Haufman, one of the new lawyers. Kirby tossed the papers on Derrick's desk. "Why the hell was this on my desk?" she demanded.

Haufman stood and eased toward the door. Derrick turned the folder so he could read the name. "I've assigned you to the case. You defended him successfully before. He asked for you again."

"I told you I will not represent this man again!"

Haufman said, "I'll leave you two alone," then he escaped down the hall.

Kirby continued glaring at Derrick. "Well?" she prompted.

"I'm not going to argue with you. I'm the one who has to decide who takes what case and that's all there is to it."

"No, it's not. I would have represented anyone but Julio Mangano, but I refuse to take this one! Give it to Haufman."

"He doesn't have your experience. Neither does Jeffers."

"Then take it yourself!"

"I have my own cases to represent." Derrick was as angry as Kirby by now. He rose from behind his desk and tried to intimidate her with a glowering look.

"Then tell him to go elsewhere!"

"Kirby, don't back me into a corner on this!"

"You're insisting I handle Mangano?"

"Yes!"

Kirby straightened. "I quit."

Derrick blinked. "You what?"

"You heard me. I quit. I'm out of here. Finished. I'm history."

"You can't quit! This is your father's own firm! It's the family business!"

"You can represent the family by yourself. I won't stay here and put up with your dictates. Not when I think you're only doing this to irritate me. It worked. I quit." She found she was actually enjoying this. The expression on Derrick's face was worth two fat paychecks. "I'll clean out my office today, or I can give you two weeks' notice, whichever you prefer."

"Get out of here! Now!" Derrick's face was growing redder by the second and a vein throbbed in his temple. "Get out of my sight!"

She smiled. "See you around. By the way, Mrs. Harper will be here in about an hour. If I were you, I'd spend the time reading her file."

When she got to Miss Allerman's desk, it was evident that the older woman had heard the entire exchange. Fortunately the waiting room was empty. "I need some boxes. The kind computer paper comes in would be perfect."

"Yes, Mrs. Garrett." Miss Allerman rose slowly. "Are you . . . That is, I couldn't help but overhear . . . Are you . . .?"

"Leaving? Yes, I am. I need the boxes to pack the personal belongings that are in my office."

"I'll bring them right in." The woman continued staring at Kirby as if she couldn't believe what was happening.

Kirby gave her a smile and went to her office. Her knees almost buckled as she dropped into her desk chair. The enormity of what she had done was settling in. She had quit her job! And Zimmerman hadn't yet offered her a position and she didn't know if he would. She was out of work! Kirby bit her lower lip as she looked around. This was the office she had moved into the week she passed her bar exam. Her father had helped pick the prints on the wall and had bought the desk to fit her wishes. He wasn't going to be happy about this.

Miss Allerman stepped into the room, carrying two boxes. "These are all I have on hand, Mrs. Garrett. I can get you some more by tomorrow if I ask around at the other offices, I think."

"Two will be plenty." Kirby took the boxes and ushered the woman out so she could shut the door.

Clutching the boxes to her, she was overwhelmed at what she had done. She had no job! What would Russell say? She had no doubt that he would be supportive, but what would he really think? It was so unlike her to make snap decisions of any magnitude. This one would affect the rest of her life and she had made it in the heat of an argument. What was happening to her?

She was suddenly in a hurry to pack up and get out of the building. The walls seemed to be closing in on her.

Kirby went to her desk and started loading all her personal property into the boxes. She owned surprisingly little. It all fit into the two boxes with room to spare. She shouldered her purse, stacked the boxes into a configuration she could handle, and looked around the room for one last time. There was an excellent chance she would never see it again. With emotions roiling in her, Kirby left.

When Russell came home from classes, she was waiting for him at the door. "I've done something rash," she said.

"Oh? That doesn't sound like you. What is it?"

"I quit my job." She watched him to see his real reaction. He stared at her. "You did? Good for you."

"You're not angry?"

"Why should I be? We talked about it, remember?"

"We discussed me going to work for Zimmerman. He hasn't called me about an opening. I simply quit. Just like that."

Russell put down the papers he had brought home to grade and pulled her into his arms. "What happened?"

"Derrick was being himself. He tried to force me to take the Mangano case and it was one straw too many. I couldn't do it. We argued and I quit. I've already cleared out my office."

"You stuck with him longer than I would have."

"But now we have only one paycheck."

"So when you get on with the DA's office, we'll have a pay increase. It won't be so much like a cut then."

She hugged him close and breathed in his familiar scent. "You really understand, don't you?"

"After all these years, you're still underestimating me."

"I haven't told the boys. I wasn't sure how to do it. Dad doesn't know, either. I dread him finding out."

"He has to know sooner or later. I'll bet Derrick called him before you were out of the building."

"No, Dad isn't supposed to know anything about the firm since he's an appellate judge. Derrick would have no reason to tell him."

"Kirby, the world isn't as pure as you'd like to think."

"I don't think it's so pure," she said as she pulled away. "You underestimate me. I'm as discerning as you are."

"I didn't intend to make you angry." The too familiar reserve was back in Russell's voice. "I only meant that no one, especially your father, plays strictly by the rules."

"What's that supposed to mean?"

"Forget it. Do you want to go out tonight and celebrate your freedom?"

"No. I certainly don't feel like celebrating. I feel more like hiding in my room."

"If you regret it that much, call Derrick and ask if you can come back."

"You know I won't do any such thing!"

"Then let's look on the bright side."

Kirby sighed. She didn't know what she had expected of Russell, but this wasn't it. "Nobody celebrates losing a job," she muttered as she pushed open the kitchen's swinging door and went into the dining room. "What if we can't make ends meet?"

"We'll lie about the boys' age and send them to work. I'll quit my job, too, and they can support us for a change."

She glared at him. "Can't you ever be serious?"

"Hey," he said, catching her and making her stop and face him. "I'm sorry. What do you want me to do and say? I'm trying to keep you from feeling down about this. It's really not the end of the world. I bring in a good salary. That's how we've been able to save most of yours. We aren't going to starve over this."

Kirby shook her head. She felt like crying so she didn't look up at him. She hated for anyone to see she was about to cry. "I guess I'm just upset."

He hugged her again. "Come on. Let's tell the boys."

Josh and Cody took the news better than she had expected.

Cody's first question was, "Now you can take us to school once in a while instead of Aunt Mallory always doing it? And you'll be here when we come in? Great!"

"Mallory and I will swap out on driving you to and from school. This doesn't mean I'll be home indefinitely—just until I get another job."

"Don't look too hard," Josh said. "We're in no hurry. It's boring being shut up in here with Ellen and the shrimp until one of you comes home from work." He playfully punched at Cody, who jabbed back.

That night when Kirby and Russell were alone, she said, "I guess I'll get the kitchen painted this week. I've been putting it off until I had time."

"I meant to do it for you, but with that extra class this year, I've been swamped, too."

"I know. I like painting. I don't mind doing it." As she sat in front of her dresser mirror brushing her hair, she studied her reflection for the first time in who knew how long. Couldn't Russell see the worry in her eyes? Despite his reassurances, she was still worried and rather afraid. There was still the matter of breaking the news to Addison.

Russell got into bed and rose up on one elbow to watch her. "I've always liked that gown."

She glanced down. It was a white satin one he had given her two birthdays back. She seldom wore it because the tiny straps and low cut made her feel too naked. Abruptly she stood and turned off the overhead light. Even the softer light from Russell's bedside lamp was still too bright, so she hurriedly slid into bed. "Are you going to turn out the lamp or read?"

"I was thinking we might do something else. I still want to celebrate." He put his arm over her and drew her toward him.

Kirby stiffened, more by reflex than conscious thought.

Russell pretended not to notice, though she was certain he had. He bent over her and tenderly kissed her lips.

Kirby tried to kiss him back and to pretend nothing was wrong. After all, she did love him. When she was away from him, she wanted him to hold her like this. But as always, it was different when it actually happened.

His kiss became more insistent and Kirby tried to match his

growing ardor. His bare skin was warm and smooth beneath her hands. Russell never slept in pajamas and this bothered her more than she could ever tell him. Even in the early days when their loving had been so passionate, Kirby had worn a gown to bed and had promptly put it on again after they had made love. In recent years she hadn't taken it off at all unless Russell insisted.

When his hand cupped her breast, Kirby cried out and pushed him away. She sat up, gasping for air as if she were smothering. She was shaking all over. Russell lay back on his pillow and stared stonily up at the ceiling. This was not a first.

"I'm sorry," she said without looking at him. "I just don't feel like it tonight."

"You never feel like it, do you?" His voice was cold and distant. She could tell from the tenor of his voice that he was hurt rather than angry.

"That's not fair, Russell." She stole a glance at him and saw his pain in the tight lines of his compressed mouth. "I'm sorry," she repeated.

"I don't suppose you want to tell me what was wrong this time?"

Still refusing to look directly at him, she hugged her knees to her chest.

"I noticed the gown you're wearing and I thought . . . well, I guess you know what I thought."

"Russell, please. Don't do this to me. Not tonight."

"What's so different about tonight?"

"I quit my job! I'm upset!"

"Kirby, if it wasn't the job, it would be something else. A headache or one of the boys would be feeling bad or you would have to get up early for some reason. There's never a good time for us to make love anymore."

"Maybe it would be a good idea for me to put the boys into one room and you move out of this room for now." Even to her, her voice sounded small. She didn't really want him to do that. She just didn't want him to touch her.

"No. I'm staying in here and so are you." His words were curt. He rolled over and turned out the lamp.

Kirby drew a deep breath in the concealing darkness. She

was uncomfortable with the dark lately, actually afraid. But at this moment, it felt like a place to hide. Russell didn't know about her new fears. She didn't know how to explain them since she seldom had been afraid of anything. There was no excuse for her to suddenly become fearful of so many things from the dark to closed rooms to the scent of carnations.

"If I thought it was only that you're strung out from quitting your job, I could understand that, but . . . " He was silent for a while. "Kirby, are you seeing someone else?"

"What? Of course not!" She turned in his direction. He was invisible in the darkness but she sensed him there inches away, so close that if he moved his bare leg, he would touch her. Unobtrusively she eased closer to her edge of the bed. "I've never had an affair! What a thing to ask!"

"I didn't think you were, but I had to know." He touched her arm and she jumped. "Will you do me a favor? Let's talk to a counselor. Only a few times. If he or she says there's nothing wrong, I'll assume it's all my fault and I'll never mention it again."

"There's nothing wrong with me. You go see a counselor if you're so set on it," she said tersely.

"Marriage counseling only works if both people go. You know that as well as I do."

"All marriages go through rough times. This is just a phase."

"Okay, then see a counselor for another reason. If you're under so much strain you don't ever want me to touch you, maybe the problem is something other than the marriage."

"So now you're saying I'm crazy? Thanks, Russell."

"I didn't say that!" He drew a calming breath. "I'm not trying to make you angry. I'm trying to find a solution."

Kirby rolled away so her back was toward him. "Good night."

"That's it? The conversation is ended?" He was angry.

Kirby closed her eyes tightly. A ball of fear was knotting in her middle, but she didn't know why. Russell would never hurt her no matter how angry he became. All the same, she felt panic rising. She tried to reassure herself the room wouldn't be so dark if her eyes weren't closed, that there would be moonlight coming in from the windows, that she wasn't alone in the dark with an angry man. But nothing seemed to help.

After a while the bed moved as if Russell had turned his back to her, too, and Kirby began to relax. It was over for tonight. In the darkness, tears stung her eyes and this time she wasn't able to blink them away. No matter what she might say to Russell, she was becoming aware that something was going very wrong within her. And she was afraid of confiding her doubts and fears to anyone, professional or not. If she ignored them, perhaps they would go away.

Before the end of the week Kirby received a call from Leon Zimmerman. He offered her the recently vacated position as an assistant DA and she instantly accepted. As quickly as she could, she changed into business attire and went down to see the office she would occupy and meet the rest of the staff.

Zimmerman greeted her with a smile and a handshake and escorted her directly to her office. The walls needed painting and the metal desk was scuffed and dented in a couple of places. Nothing about the place could be called beautiful, nor could anyone deny that it was a far cry from the palatial offices of Walker, Glassman and McKinsey. "I love it," she said with a smile. It was true. Derrick wasn't lurking down the hall and the Mangano file would never show up on her desk.

"Then you can start on Monday?" Zimmerman was watching her as if he was still trying to figure her out.

"I certainly can. I'm looking forward to it."

"Great. I like enthusiasm. We don't have many hard-and-fast rules here. The main one is that if you get dissatisfied or have a personality problem with someone in the office, you're to talk to me instead of just quitting. I'm a firm believer in communication."

Kirby was a bit taken aback, considering the manner in which she had left her other position, but felt sure his emphasis on that rule was coincidence. "So am I, Mr. Zimmerman. I think you'll find me easy to work with."

"I think I will at that. And my name is Leon. We're all on a first-name basis here. It makes us more of a team."

"That's fine with me. It's Leon from now on."

"Just so I know, what did your papa think about you taking this job?"

"I don't know yet. I'm going to see him this afternoon."

"I'll listen for the explosion."

Kirby smiled but she was afraid he might be right.

"It's good to see you again, Kirby," Addison said as he closed the door to his chambers. The walls were lined with legal reference books, all richly bound in leather, and interspersed among them were Addison's various certificates of graduation and commendation, gilt-framed and prominently displayed. The carpeting was deep-toned and plush, the furnishings expensive and the lighting subdued. A portrait of Addison, Jane, and their two daughters, painted some twenty years earlier, adorned the wall directly behind his desk, and on his desk were framed enlargements of snapshots taken of Kirby and Mallory when they were little girls. The ambiance of serene strength and power was Addison's trademark and ever familiar to Kirby.

"We'll be over for dinner on Sunday, of course, but there's something I want to talk over with you before then."

"I understand," Addison said as he sat behind his massive oak desk and motioned for Kirby to take the leather chair she usually occupied during her visits. "I've talked to Derrick and he's ready to take you back. I told him that you've always had a temper—certainly more of one than Mallory." He laughed. "I guess you got it from your mother's side of the family." It was a standing joke between them. Jane and her family were the epitome of reservation and shyness.

"I must have," Kirby responded by rote with a smile. Then his statement about Derrick sprang to her consciousness and she sobered. "I didn't expect Derrick to talk to you about my leaving the firm. I wanted to tell you myself."

"He just happened to mention it to me when we were talking the other day. I told him you were probably upset about something and when you cooled off you would be willing to pretend it never happened." He gave her a fatherly smile as if he had ironed out the whole issue.

"You really shouldn't have done that, Dad. I'm not going back to work with Derrick."

"Now that's not what I want to hear," Addison said, his smile firmly in place. "We don't need divisiveness in our family, and I'm certainly not getting rid of Derrick. He's married to your sister."

"I know that. What I'm trying to tell you is that I've accepted a job somewhere else."

Addison's smile receded. "You have? Which firm?"

"The District Attorney's office. I'm working for Leon Zimmerman starting on Monday."

Addison fell silent and stoic, except for his eyes. The intensity of his gaze told Kirby he was shuffling thoughts quickly. At length he calmly said, "I see."

"I hope you aren't going to be upset with me. I know you and Hershal started the practice from scratch and that you've built it into a firm that commands respect, but you and Hershal aren't there now and I don't like to work with Derrick. I particularly dislike working *for* Derrick. I don't know what Hershal had in mind when he left Derrick in charge, but it's a disaster up there these days."

Addison made no comment. Kirby wondered again if the decision to make Derrick a full partner had been made entirely by Hershal. She had expected Addison to question her allegation but he was only staring at her.

After a time Addison nodded. "I think you've made a good decision," he said thoughtfully.

"You do?"

"Zimmerman is tough to go against. It can't hurt to have a Walker in his ranks." He smiled as if he were only joking.

"Dad, you shouldn't say things like that. What if someone overheard and thought you meant it?"

"No one can hear us in here. I'm positive of that."

"You still shouldn't say it. Now that I'm working in the DA's office, I'm loyal to them. You still don't have a Walker in the enemy camp. For that matter, the DA can't be *your* enemy any longer. You have to remain impartial."

"I am. You know I am." Addison's rich baritone timbre soothed her. "I thought you'd realize I was only joking."

Kirby let go some of the tension in her muscles. "You're not angry with me for working in Zimmerman's office?"

"I could never stay angry with you. No, I was more upset when I heard you had walked out on Derrick."

"I wouldn't put it quite that way. I can't go into my reasons, but they were good ones." She watched him with mounting skepticism. His response seemed out of character for him. She had been positive he would be angry, if not furious. But then, it had been a long time since Addison had gotten into one of his terrible rages.

"I'm sure they were." He smiled at her again. "Now, I want you and Derrick to put all this behind you. You're both family and will see each other every Sunday at dinner and on other family occasions. I don't want disruption to come of this. You know how that would upset your mother."

"Yes. I intend to be civil to Derrick. I can't like him, but I don't have to show it."

"That's my good girl." He stood to signal the visit was over. "I'm glad you came to tell me the news about Zimmerman, Kirby. I wouldn't want to have heard it from other sources."

"No, I wouldn't do that to you."

He patted her shoulder as he walked her to the door. "I'm looking forward to seeing you on Sunday."

She turned the knob and stepped into his secretary's office. "I'll see you Sunday, Dad. When I get home, I'll call Mom and tell her the news."

"Yes, you do that. She sets great store in knowing what you and Mallory are doing. I believe she's been worried about you lately."

Kirby nodded. Her mother was a natural worrier, even with less provocation than Kirby having walked out of the family law practice. As she went into the hall, she was surprised how relieved she felt. Her father had taken it awfully well.

Chapter Six

Kirby smiled to put the woman seated across from her at ease. Connie Chandler didn't return the smile. Neither did her daughter, Kayla. "What can I do for you, Mrs. Chandler?"

Connie glanced at Kayla, who ducked her head and stared at the floor while she kicked her sneakers against the legs of the chair. "I don't know quite where to start. It's my ex-husband."

"Yes?" Kirby prompted when the woman said no more. "Is it a matter of delinquent child support?"

"No. I wish that's all it was." Connie took Kayla's hand. "Gary took Kayla on a father-daughter campout a couple of weeks ago. It sounded innocent enough to me. Kayla was excited about going. I assumed from what Gary said that several fathers and daughters from his church would be there, too. It turns out it was just the two of them."

Kirby was taking notes. "What happened on the campout?"

"Gary . . . well . . . he raped Kayla."

The girl turned away and looked as if she was trying hard not to cry. She was obviously embarrassed. Connie was even more upset.

"He raped her?" Kirby looked more closely at the girl. "How old are you, Kayla?"

"I'm six." She refused to make eye contact with Kirby and

her face was a pasty white, making her scattering of freckles more pronounced.

Speaking gently to Mrs. Chandler, Kirby said, "Please tell me exactly what happened."

"Gary, my ex-husband, picked her up for visitation the way he usually does after school. I work so she always calls me before she leaves the house to tell me that she's going. Like I said, she was excited about it. We used to camp out, the three of us, before the divorce, but that's been almost a year and she's missed it. Up until now, Kayla has adored her father." Connie put her arm around Kayla, who unobtrusively shrugged it away.

Misery filled Connie's eyes. She was on the verge of tears. "I didn't have any way of knowing what was going on until he brought her back on Sunday. Then he told me it had been just the two of them and not a church function like I had figured. I noticed Kayla was real quiet, she's usually a little chatterbox, but she wasn't saying much of anything. I figured she was just tired."

"Were you upset when you learned it had been just the two of them?"

"No. I had no reason to think he would hurt her. Certainly I never thought he would do something like this!"

"When did Kayla tell you what happened?"

"She told me last Friday when it was visitation time again."

"She didn't tell you for two weeks?"

Connie shook her head. Kayla continued sitting in stony, embarrassed silence. "He had told her not to say anything. He said if she did, he wouldn't love her anymore, that it was supposed to be a secret between the two of them."

"How did she tell you about it?"

"All last week I could tell something was bothering her, but I couldn't get her to tell me anything. The closer Friday came, the more upset she was getting. Finally, Friday morning before going to school she flat out said that she didn't want to see him. She claimed she was sick. I could see she felt all right so I started asking questions. Finally she said he 'hurt' her."

Kirby put down her pen after making the notes and studied Kayla's profile. "Kayla, what did you mean by he 'hurt' you?"

Kayla shrugged and refused to speak.

"Just what I said. He raped her."

"Are you certain, Mrs. Chandler? There are many ways she could have been hurt. Perhaps she meant he struck her."

"He didn't hit me!" Kayla snapped, her face screwed into a frown. "He hurt me another way."

"Can you tell me about it?"

Kayla shook her head and compressed her lips.

"She's embarrassed," Connie said. "You can understand why, I'm sure."

"Of course. Kayla, I'm not trying to make you uncomfortable. I just have to know exactly what happened. If this goes to court, you'll be expected to tell your side of the story. Otherwise he won't be punished for hurting you."

Still looking down, Kayla reluctantly said, "We took the tent and went to a place we used to go camping when Daddy still lived with Mommy and me."

"It's not a real campground," her mother added. "It's a place on some land outside of Livingston, near the lake."

Kirby motioned for Mrs. Chandler to let Kayla tell what happened in her own words. "You took a tent?" Kirby prompted. She hated making the child so uncomfortable, but she had to know the details to determine if a crime had indeed been committed.

Kayla nodded. "I had my sleeping bag and Daddy had his. The first night nothing happened. The next day we fished in the lake and went swimming. But that night, Daddy said for me to sleep with him in his sleeping bag so we wouldn't get too cold."

"And did you?"

"I didn't know I wasn't supposed to. When I was little, I got in bed with Mommy and Daddy," she said defensively.

"I understand. My children have done that, too."

"You have children?" Kayla looked at Kirby for the first time. Her hazel eyes were full of hurt and fright.

"I have two boys. Both a bit older than you are. What happened when you got into the sleeping bag?"

"He lay down, too."

Connie shifted restlessly. "Is it necessary for her to tell this again?"

"I'm afraid so. Then what happened, Kayla?"

"Nothing for a while. I was almost asleep. Then he started touching me." She dropped her eyes again and her voice faded.

"Where did he touch you?"

"Between my legs."

Kirby nodded encouragingly. This was almost as difficult for Kirby to hear as it was for Kayla to relate. "What did you do?"

"I didn't know what to do. I played like I was asleep. He kept doing it and I was getting scared because I know you're not supposed to touch yourself there." She kicked the chair leg harder. "Then he laid on his back and put me across his lap. That's when I saw he wasn't wearing any pants. I got really scared then and told him to stop. But he didn't. He hurt me." As the girl gave the remaining details of what happened, her voice dropped to a whisper, and she looked at neither Kirby nor her mother.

Kirby was silent for a moment as she fought to control her emotions. There was no question in her mind that Kayla was telling the truth. "Mrs. Chandler, did intercourse take place?"

"Of course. That's what she just told you." The woman looked at Kirby as if she were talking nonsense.

"Which doctor examined her?"

"I didn't take her to a doctor."

"Why not?" Kirby was surprised.

"Two weeks had passed. I figured a doctor wouldn't find any evidence after that long."

"The police should have advised you to get her examined immediately to document any physical changes, such as whether her hymen is still intact."

Connie was quiet for a moment. "I didn't call the police. I thought I should talk to you folks first. Should I have called the police?"

"Technically it's not necessary. Our office will report this to them for you, but because they are so understaffed, our office will likely handle the investigation. You will need to take her to the doctor right away."

Kayla gave Kirby a suspicious look. "I hate going to the doctor's office."

"I know, but it's really necessary this time." Kirby smiled, hoping the girl would see her as less threatening. "I know this must be very difficult for you, Kayla. I'm going to do all I can to help you and to make this as easy as possible."

"I want Gary put in prison for what he did to her," Connie said angrily. "I'll do whatever it takes to get the s.o.b. put away. And I'm not letting him see her for visitations anymore, either. Gary says if I don't, I'll be in contempt of court because of the court-ordered visitation. But I don't care. He's not going to have a chance to hurt her again!"

"I agree. This can't be allowed to happen again. You'll need to talk with your attorney about petitioning the court for a change in visitation and perhaps getting a temporary restraining order to keep him away from both of you for the moment. And don't worry about the contempt of court issue. Your attorney can handle that for you, too. Under such circumstances, most judges will rule based on the child's best interest."

"But I don't have an attorney. My divorce attorney has moved and I don't know any others. Can you recommend one who will be really good?"

"I could have before I took this job, but in my position as an assistant to the district attorney I can't make recommendations or do any direct referrals. The best I could do is give you a list to choose from." Kirby wanted nothing more than to do the paperwork for Connie or direct her to a competent attorney, but ethics prohibited her from doing so. "If you'll excuse me, Mrs. Chandler, I need to discuss this with the district attorney. Can you wait a few minutes?"

"Of course."

Kirby went to find Zimmerman. To her relief, he wasn't busy. "I need to talk to you. I've just been talking with a Mrs. Connie Chandler and her daughter, Kayla. It seems that Kayla was raped by her father. He and Mrs. Chandler are divorced and the rape happened while Kayla was with her father during a visitation. Naturally Mrs. Chandler doesn't want Kayla to spend time alone with Mr. Chandler so I advised her to get an attorney to petition the court for temporary orders to restrict the father's contact with the girl for her protection and to preclude the possibility that he would try to intimidate her. The woman wants the girl's father prosecuted and is adamant that she isn't going to allow the girl to be alone with him ever again, and I don't blame her. I told her not to worry about a contempt citation under the circumstances. What is our procedure for reporting this to Child Protective Services?''

''Slow down, Kirby.'' Zimmerman shook his head. ''There is no question that you're anxious to help this woman and her daughter, but we have to be sure we can make a case against the guy. Did she bring a copy of the examining doctor's report?''

''No, Kayla hasn't been to see a doctor yet, but I advised her mother to do so immediately. You see, this happened a couple of weeks ago and the girl didn't tell her mother until last Friday.''

Concern clouded Zimmerman's normally placid features. ''Then we won't have any sperm samples for DNA testing, and after this long, any bruises or other physical evidence is unlikely to show up.''

''But an examination will show that her hymen is no longer intact, thus evidence of penetration.''

''I'm afraid that's not conclusive. A number of things other than a penis can tear a hymen. She could even have done it herself.''

''I hardly think that's possible!'' Kirby snapped, revealing more of the anger she was feeling than she intended. Lowering her voice and tempering her tone, she said, ''You didn't see or hear her when she told me about it. I have no doubt the girl is telling the truth about what happened.''

''I'm not saying it didn't happen. It probably did. What about other witnesses?''

''There weren't any—just the girl and her father.''

''That's too bad.''

''But the girl is surprisingly articulate for her age and I think her testimony would be viewed as credible.''

''What about other occurrences of sexual molestation?''

''This was the first time.''

''What else have you got? Torn clothing? Anything?''

''Nothing, but can't we—''

"Kirby, if we don't have any more evidence than this, we won't stand much chance of getting a conviction. If we press it and lose, we've put that little girl and her mother through hell for nothing. I've seen a lot of incest trials and they're almost as traumatic on the child as the actual rape." Zimmerman sighed. "It makes me sick, too, but these are the facts. It's the father's word against his daughter's, and assuming that the father has no priors and the defense can produce believable character witnesses, we may have insufficient evidence and therefore no case. What do you know about the father?"

"I didn't take time to ask, yet; I was more concerned with the girl's immediate welfare. But Mrs. Chandler and Kayla are still in my office."

"Go back and find out all you can about him. It's probably too much to hope for, but maybe he's got a record of molestation or something else we can use against him."

A tight knot gripped Kirby's stomach. She knew the law as well as Leon Zimmerman did. The state would have to prove beyond a reasonable doubt that Gary Chandler raped his daughter—and the burden of proof was the prosecution's. Of course the man's background and credibility were pivotal, and she was upset with herself for not having asked about that before coming to Leon. It wasn't like her to let her emotions interfere with her work, but the anxiety she felt for this vulnerable, young girl had sidetracked her thoughts. She'd have to watch that in the future so Leon wouldn't think she was less than competent.

It wasn't her faux pas, however, that was causing her stomach to churn—it was the realization that despite the best efforts of the district attorney's office, a rapist might go free due to a lack of evidence and have the chance to repeat his heinous crime.

"Leon, if we aren't able to get this man convicted and put away, we can't prevent him from having unchaperoned visitations with her, can we? Isn't there something this office can do to protect her?"

"That's the worst part. We can't."

"I can't let that happen!"

"You have no choice. Mrs. Chandler can go back to the domestic relations court and try to convince the judge the child is at risk of being incested, but I can't hold out much hope for that."

"Why on earth not?"

"In divorce situations, one spouse will frequently accuse the other of terrible offenses, including incest. The judge will most likely assume Mrs. Chandler is making it up to get back at her ex-husband."

"In my opinion she's not doing that. I believe her."

"She may be telling the truth. I'm only telling you what my own experience has been in cases like this. How old is the girl?"

"She's six."

Zimmerman grunted in disgust. "It's a damned shame. I agree that if it's true, the man ought to be put in the pen where he'll have the opportunity of becoming the sweetheart of the cell block. But it seldom happens that way. Until we know what sort of reputation the man has, all this is mere conjecture. I'd go with you to talk to Mrs. Chandler and the girl, but I'm due in court in fifteen minutes. If you come up with something substantial, let me know and we'll see what we can do."

Connie Chandler looked up expectantly when Kirby returned to her office. Kayla glanced up, too, but ducked her head again. Kirby wanted to sweep the little girl into her arms and reassure her that she was safe and would never again be hurt by her father, but instead she found the switch to her emotions and turned them off. She'd always known how to do that and routinely used the technique to her advantage in the courtroom. The only drawback was that she sometimes had trouble turning her emotions back on and, thus, some people perceived her as too cool, too aloof and decidedly dispassionate. For the most part, it wasn't a problem—except with Russell. Picking up her yellow legal pad and pen, she methodically resumed her questioning. "I need some background on Mr. Chandler. What sort of work does he do and does he have any trouble keeping a job?"

"He's been with the same accounting firm for twelve years, and has been given commendations for his work. He became a CPA as soon as he graduated from college."

That won't help, Kirby thought to herself. "Does he have any close friends?"

"A few, I suppose. He plays golf with his boss and two other guys pretty often and afterward they have a few beers there at the clubhouse bar."

"Does he drink to excess? Ever get drunk?"

"No."

"Other than traffic tickets, has he ever been arrested?"

Connie gave a mirthless laugh. "Gary? Not him. He's never been in any sort of trouble. He certainly doesn't have a criminal record. Why, he's even a deacon in our church and coaches a Little League team. To look at him, you'd think he was Mr. Clean himself. But I know better."

"What do you mean?"

"He used to buy porn. He didn't know that I knew, because he kept it hidden, but I did. One day I found one of those dirty magazines in the drawer where he kept his socks. I started looking around and found a whole box full in the top of our closet. I sure never thought he was into it that much." Connie glanced at Kayla as if she wished she wasn't having to talk in front of her.

"Kayla," Kirby said as she reached in the lap drawer of her desk where she kept change. "Why don't you go out to the waiting room and ask Mrs. Parsons to buy you a soft drink? There's a vending machine down toward the elevator."

The girl took the money and left.

"Thank you. I hate to talk about things like this in front of her. Gary is a bastard, but since the divorce she's been so defensive of him. All that has changed now, but I still hate to discuss matters like pornography in front of her. She's still so young."

"I understand. Tell me what sort of magazines they were."

"You know, like the ones the convenience stores keep under the counter. Mostly, though, they were the kind I think you'd have to go to one of those adult bookstores to buy. It was awful. It made me sick. I mean, adults can pose for dirty pictures if they want to, but I don't want them in my house. What if Kayla found them instead of me?"

Kirby nodded thoughtfully. Knowing he was into pornography could be very useful. "Is it possible that he took pictures of Kayla?"

Connie's eyes widened. "That never occurred to me!"

"It's not likely he did since she didn't tell you when she was revealing the rape. If we could prove he did something like this, we could nail him on child pornography charges."

"What do you mean? Don't we have enough to put him in prison already? He raped Kayla!"

"I believe you, but the DA said we don't have enough evidence to get a rape conviction. If she had been taken directly to a doctor while he could still get sperm samples or if there were bruises that could be documented, that would be a different story."

"But I didn't know about it in time!"

"I know. I understand. I'm only telling you the reality of the situation. If there's no way of winning the case, we don't want to put Kayla through having to testify in court. Right now she still has her privacy. Only you and a handful of people know about it. That will change if we put her on the stand and accuse a man who apparently has a spotless reputation."

"I thought children testified out of court and it was video-taped."

"Sometimes it's done that way with the extremely young ones. Kayla is six, however, and the judge might insist that she give her testimony on the stand in court."

"I hadn't thought of that." Connie looked as if she was about to cry. "But what about the dirty magazines? Won't they prove he's not all he pretends to be."

"That may help strengthen our case, but we'd have to prove that his interest in porn was directly connected to the rape and we'd have to establish that he was the one who bought it. That it was his magazine. There's controversy over whether reading porn increases the probability of sexual crimes. In other words, there are a lot of men who read *Playboy* who aren't rapists. The jury could even question if he was the one who bought it."

"Well, I certainly didn't buy it and put it in that box in the closet! That pervert sonofabitch I was married to bought it! I knew he bought those magazines from time to time, but I never dreamed it meant he was capable of raping his own daughter. If you people can't help me, I don't know what I'm going to do."

"We aren't going to give up just yet. Go home and search everywhere for anything he may have left behind. Get Kayla to a doctor for an examination and get her into counseling. A therapist will know how to ask questions that may be admissible in court. Above all, don't try to plant any ideas in Kayla's head. Even if they turn out to be true, the judge will have to throw it out as inadmissible if Kayla says you prompted her. Do you see what I mean?"

Connie nodded. Her eyes filled with tears. "You're telling me we don't have an open-and-shut case like I thought we did. That it doesn't matter what happened to my daughter."

Kirby met her eyes squarely. "It matters to me, Mrs. Chandler. I'm not writing this off by any means. We need to do some investigation before we can go ahead with it. We don't want to risk taking him to court and having him found innocent when a bit more work can give us better evidence." She added, "I believe you. I don't think either of you are making this up."

"All right. I'll see if Gary left any of that garbage behind. If I find something, should I call you?"

"Yes. And get Kayla into counseling. Even if we never prove her father raped her, she will need professional help to heal from this."

After Connie was gone, Kirby buried her face in her hands. She was shaken and starting to tremble; her nerves had been steady as long as Connie was there, but now the emotions all of this had evoked were besieging her. The mental picture of Kayla's description of the rape by her father was horrifying. Kirby felt nauseous just thinking about it, yet she found it difficult to put it out of her mind.

Sheer determination got Kirby through the rest of the day but the Chandlers' visit still haunted her. At last she escaped to the sanctuary of her home.

"You haven't said more than a handful of words since I came home," Russell commented as he eased himself into his favorite chair in their comfortable den, preparing to watch the evening news. "Has something upset you?"

Kirby looked up from the book she was pretending to read. "A woman and her six-year-old daughter were in today accusing the child's father of incest. Six years old! And from the way the little girl told the story, I believe her."

"No wonder you're upset," Russell commiserated. "People like that should be buried under the jail."

"Yeah, should be. But in this case, there's not enough evidence to sentence him to a slap on the wrist, much less send him to prison. That's what's bothering me."

"That's really rough!"

"This is the first incest case I've ever been involved with. Leon says we don't have a leg to stand on. And I guess he's right. That's what burns me so. If the man did this once, he will almost certainly do it again. He may have been molesting children for years and no one told on him before now! Russell, it's just not right!" Kirby's eyes, blazing with anger, were fixed on Russell.

"Hey, take it easy. I'm on your side. You're right."

"I'm sorry, Russell. I didn't mean to jump down your throat. I'm just upset."

"It's understandable. Is there anything I can do?"

She drew a calming breath and managed a smile. "Not unless you follow him around and catch him molesting a child." The words made her feel sick. "I doubt this is the first time Chandler has done something like this." She wondered why she felt so certain of that.

"He's a real winner, isn't he?"

"His visitation rights will likely be suspended while Child Protective Services conducts their investigation, but if we can't prove he's molesting his daughter, he'll have unchaperoned access again." She looked back at the book in her lap. "I'm going to go up and read. Maybe that will get my mind off this."

"I'll be up later." Russell watched her leave the room, then turned back to the TV. The image of one of the news anchors flickered before him but he was not paying attention. He had never seen Kirby so upset over a case, not even murder. At one time, she would have wanted to be with him when she was strung out over something so he could comfort her and lend his support. Now she preferred to work things out alone. Virtually everything.

Their marriage was falling apart little by little and there didn't seem to be a damned thing he could do about it.

Mallory swayed to the music blaring from the jukebox by the dance floor. On the bar in front of her was an empty glass with a salt-encrusted rim.

"Hey there, pretty lady," a man said as he slid onto the stool beside her. "I've been noticing you from across the room. Are you here by yourself?"

"Not anymore." She smiled as she took inventory of him. Good looking, though not handsome. Well dressed in a suit and tie, but looking a bit rumpled as if he had come to the bar straight from work. "I'm Mallory."

"No last name?"

"No last name." She let her eyes sweep over him knowing he was watching her. "How about you? Do you have two names?"

"No, my name is just plain Bob. Who would have guessed that in a city the size of Houston, the only two people with one word names would meet?"

"Well, Just Plain Bob, I think we should celebrate the coincidence." She signaled the bartender to bring her another margarita.

Bob was still staring at her. "You don't look like a woman who'd be alone very often. Married?"

"Does it matter?"

"Not to me. Just curious."

She sipped the drink, then leisurely licked the salt from her full lips. Judging by the sparkle in Bob's eyes, the seductive move wasn't wasted. "I like this place."

"This is my first time here."

"Let's dance. I love to dance." Her first drink on an empty stomach had mellowed her and, as always, had put her in an amorous mood. After she had downed her second, she could pretend Derrick had never existed.

Bob led her to the center of the dance floor and drew her

close. Mallory didn't object. He was tall and had dark hair, as did most of the men she chose. Other than the fact that tall, dark men were dangerously exciting to her, she had no idea why she was drawn only to men fitting that description. Derrick was merely of average height and his hair was an uninteresting medium brown. What a shame it was that her daddy had not known her preference before choosing a husband for her. She might have had a chance at a happy marriage.

Mallory ground her hips against Bob's, and from the response she felt, she knew he was pleased with her. Her soul merged with the sensuous rhythm of the music and she closed her eyes. Derrick thought she was at a church fund raiser so she had several hours of freedom. She couldn't keep from laughing at how easily he was deceived.

"Is something funny?" Bob asked, leaning back so he could see her face, apparently ready to join in the laughter.

"I was just thinking about someone I know."

"Should I be jealous?" He wasn't deft at flirting but he was trying.

"No, he's as dull as dishwater."

"I haven't heard that expression in years."

"No? It fits him perfectly. He's as sharp as oatmeal." She laughed at her own wit.

Laughter came back to her from someone at one of the tables surrounding the dance floor but she couldn't see who it was through the dense cigarette smoke that clung in the air like the Houston fog on a wintery night after a cold, drizzling rain. She would have to remember to tell Derrick that some of the others at the meeting were chain smokers since neither she nor Derrick smoked and she knew from experience that her clothes would reek. She would be sober by the time she got home and knew it wasn't likely he would get close enough to smell the margaritas. She looked up through her eyelashes at Bob. Picking up men was the most exciting thing she had ever done. She was good at it.

"Why don't we go somewhere less public?" he suggested.

Mallory pretended to consider his suggestion before answering, as if she hadn't expected it. "Well . . . okay. Where did you have in mind?"

"My apartment is less public."

"Sounds good to me. I'll follow you in my car."

Bob paid both their bar bills while Mallory downed a hefty swallow of her margarita, finishing off the drink without wasting a drop. Although she would have preferred sipping the drink, she had to make good use of her time away from the house.

She got into her car and followed Bob onto Westheimer. Although rush hour was long since past, the thoroughfare was still congested with traffic. But Mallory didn't care; she loved the excitement and bustle of the city. Besides, a small town would provide her with fewer choices on nights like this. One of the few good traits about Derrick was that he was determined never to move out of town.

Bob turned into the parking lot of an expensive apartment complex. Mallory wasn't surprised; she was good at judging her conquests and picking the right fishing holes. The Schooner wasn't a place to go for those without money.

As he guided her into the inner courtyard, he put his arm around her shoulders and Mallory hummed the tune they had been dancing to, matching her steps to his. Some of her friends from church lived in these apartments. The chance of being seen in a place she shouldn't be by someone she knew was almost as exciting as picking up a man. But not quite. Nothing was that exciting. She put her arm around his waist.

"You're friendly. I like that."

She smiled up at him. "So do I."

As they waited for the elevator, Mallory gazed across the pool at the opposite set of buildings where her friends lived. Their lights were all on; most likely they were home. If they looked out now, they would see her. Mischief danced in Mallory's eyes as she watched to see if she would be caught this time. She had never been caught before. Not a single time.

The elevator took them to the fourth floor and Bob unlocked the second door on the right, turned on the lights, and waited for her to enter his apartment first. "I like your place," she observed. "There's lots of greenery. I love plants." She went to a small tree on the opposite side of the living room and touched the leaves gently. "I've never been able to make anything grow."

"Neither can I. I just replace them as they die." He came to her and put his arms around her. "I don't have any margarita mix but I have bourbon."

"That's fine with me. Straight up." She followed him to the built-in bar and took a glass of amber liquid as he poured one for himself. "Isn't this a beautiful night?" She crossed to the patio doors and drew the curtains back so she could look across the pool again. No one ever saw her. Maybe she had become invisible. She giggled. "Did you know alcohol makes me invisible? It's true, you know."

"You must not have had enough then because I can still see you. You're beautiful."

She turned and smiled at him over the rim of her glass. "Am I?" She loved to flirt, to lead men down the path of her choosing. It was so easy when a person knew how. "How beautiful am I?"

He came to her and pulled the drapes back into place. "You don't really want to talk, do you? I was hoping we might do something more interesting."

"I love to do interesting things." She smiled provocatively up at him.

As he led her to the bedroom, Mallory drank a third of her bourbon. She would have to pretend an orgasm. She always did. But before that happened, she would have a man's complete attention and he would hold her and touch her and maybe even talk to her in a soft voice. All that was worth having sex with him. She kicked off her shoes and fell into his bed.

Kirby moved restlessly in her sleep. The nightmare was back again.

She drifted down a long hall that seemed vaguely familiar but distorted somehow. She passed closed doors that stretched on forever. The walls were pale blue, and she was aware of the faint scent of carnations. The ceiling seemed impossibly far above her and carpeting muffled the sounds of her footsteps.

She knew she was searching for something but had no idea what.

At the far end of the hall, she opened the door and entered a blue room. In the middle of the room was a bed and on the bed lay a man. As she watched, he got off the bed as if moving in slow motion. He signaled for her to come to him and her panic began to rise. She shook her head and started to back into the hall.

The man was coming toward her, moving quickly now. She couldn't see his face. She never could in this nightmare. But she knew he was bent on hurting her. She felt herself trying to scream but no sound came from her mouth. As he closed the distance between them, she turned and started to run, flailing her arms to ward him off. Still no scream and she felt as if she were choking on the absence of sound.

This time the familiar nightmare took a slightly different turn. Before she could reach the end of the hall, he caught her. His hand closed on her arm and she struggled and tried to cry out, but he only laughed and started dragging her back down the hall toward the room where she had found him.

Kirby awoke with a scream and found herself sitting up in bed. Russell was shaking her arm and saying, "Wake up, Kirby. You're having a nightmare. Wake up."

She jerked away from him and wrapped her arms about her body. "I'm awake! I'm awake!" All the same, she glanced around the room to be certain the man hadn't somehow followed her out of her dream.

"Are you okay? I've been trying to wake you for almost a minute." Russell looked worried. "You were fighting me but wouldn't wake up."

"It was the nightmare," she said needlessly. "The one I have sometimes."

"The same one? With the man chasing you?"

"Yes, but this time he caught me."

"Maybe you dreamed that because I was shaking your arm."

"I don't know." She didn't want to discuss it. She wanted to be alone with her fears. No one could hurt her if she was alone. "I don't know!" She left the bed and reached for her robe. "I don't want to go back to sleep. I need to move around a bit. Do you want anything from the kitchen?"

"Not at this hour of the night." Russell switched on the lamp. "Kirby, you need to do something about these nightmares of yours."

"Everyone has nightmares. Even you."

"Yes, but not the same one over and over and not several nights a week. This has been going on for years and lately they've occurred more often."

"I have a high-pressure job. That's all it is."

"You don't believe that, do you? It doesn't make any sense. Not when it's the same nightmare every time."

"I don't want to talk about it. It's still too real to me." She pulled the robe about her and belted it.

"Come back to bed. I want to talk to you."

She sat on the foot of the bed and looked at him in silence.

"I want you to see a therapist."

"No. We've had this discussion before. Almost as many times as I've had the nightmare."

"Damn it, Kirby, I could be right, you know. There's nothing wrong about seeing a therapist. If anything, it's a status symbol."

"Not to me."

"Do it for me. Just a few times. Maybe you'll find a way to get rid of the nightmares."

Kirby's nerves were still on edge. "Russell, stop nagging at me! I don't want to see any therapist and I'm damn tired of you hassling me about it!"

Russell glared at her. "I wasn't aware that it was a hassle for me to care about your well-being."

She jumped to her feet. "Don't go sanctimonious on me! I hate that! Just leave me alone!" In the absolute silence that followed, she realized she had been shouting.

He got out of bed and grabbed up his pillow. "Fine. If that's the way you want it! I'll be in the den if you want me." He yanked the coverlet off the end of the bed and stalked from the room.

Kirby sat back down on the bed. What had gone wrong between them? She wanted to go after him and bring him back to bed, but the nightmare was still too near for her to think rationally. There would be time for clear thinking in the morning.

She lay back down. She didn't want to go downstairs now that Russell was down there. He might interpret the action as a desire to prolong the fight. She only wanted to be left alone so she could get her thoughts under control again.

Kirby slipped back into bed and closed her eyes, trying to fall back asleep. But no matter how hard she tried to relax, she remained awake. She didn't sleep for the rest of the night, but that wasn't unusual for her.

Chapter Seven

"I want to assign an investigator to watch Gary Chandler for the next few days. I've got a feeling we could get something on him if we tried."

Zimmerman put down his chipped coffee cup. "Gary Chandler? Oh, yeah. Kayla Chandler's father. Child Protective Services is on that. Have they come up with anything?"

"No, they haven't. I just talked to Shelby Yost. She hasn't had time to conduct even her initial interview. We've got to do something. We can't just sit here and do nothing."

"Kirby, if you take every case personally, you'll soon be old and gray. You've got to change what you can and forget the rest. It's the only way to stay sane in this business."

"I can't do that. Not when a six-year-old child has been raped. Will you assign a man to watch Chandler?"

"No, I can't. I've already told you we don't have enough evidence to work up a case. Besides, all my staff investigators are up to their armpits with other work and my budget is too tight to hire an outside PI. I told Gunderman all that we knew on this and he agreed that it would be a waste of police department manpower to put one of his overworked CID investigators on this. For all we know, no law has been broken. I'm telling you, I've heard stories from ex-spouses that would curl your hair and that didn't have a grain of truth."

"I believed Mrs. Chandler and it was obvious that Kayla wasn't lying. A six-year-old wouldn't know enough about sex to make up the things she told me."

"Kids lie," Zimmerman said bluntly. "I've got kids and they do it all the time. I'll bet yours do, too."

"This was different. How could she make up sexual details that were so believable unless she had firsthand knowledge?"

"Maybe she watches a lot of TV."

Kirby scowled at him.

"Look, I'm not trying to make out that the kid's a liar. But any half-ass lawyer could poke holes in that story without even trying."

"So what do we do? Let him rape her again? I can't sit back and allow that to happen."

Zimmerman stared at her in concern. "Do you get this worked up over all your cases?"

"No, of course not. But if you had heard her—"

"I know. I've heard the same story a dozen times. I also know that most of the men accused of this get off without so much as a slap on the wrist. If they are tried and convicted and given lengthy sentences, they aren't in long because of jail overcrowding and early releases. You know all that."

"Don't you see how *wrong* that is?" Kirby asked in a controlled tone that belied the burst of anger she was trying to suppress.

"Hey, don't hang the messenger. I'm only telling you how it is."

"Any man who would rape his young daughter should be dealt with harshly! He certainly should be behind bars so he can't do it again!"

"What if he's falsely accused? You told me yourself that he's well thought of and even coaches a Little League team. The man's a bleeding deacon, for Chrissake! You'd never win a case like that. Not unless you'd caught him in the act and the DNA confirmed it was him without a shadow of a doubt. I'm telling you, forget it."

Kirby picked up her own coffee cup. "I have work to do."

Zimmerman caught her arm as she tried to leave the coffee

room. "Wait a minute. I'm not the enemy. Don't be mad at me. I'm on your side."

"Then tell me who you'd get if you had money in the budget."

He thought for a minute. "If I were to hire a PI to follow Chandler, I'd get Bill Davies."

"Bill Davies?"

"He's a retired cop. Worked for me for a while, and he still does some surveillance. In my opinion, he's the best there is. But it doesn't matter because we're already stretching our budget so tight that Lincoln's beginning to squeal. Even if we had the money, this Chandler thing is a lost cause."

Kirby nodded. "I understand but I don't agree."

She went to her office and looked up Davies' number. When he answered, she said, "I'm Kirby Garrett with the Harris County DA's office. What do you charge for local surveillance?" His reply was reasonable. "I'd like to hire you to watch a man by the name of Gary Chandler."

"What's he supposed to be doing? Drugs?"

"No, I have reason to believe he may be a child molester."

"All right. Tell Zimmerman I'm back."

"Actually, I'm hiring you myself. Does that change things?"

"Only if your checks bounce. Are you sure you can afford me on a county worker's pay?"

If the man was trying to be funny, Kirby felt he needed work on his delivery. If not, their relationship was destined to be short. She decided he was inept at levity and hoped it wouldn't affect his investigative ability. "Don't worry about the checks. I'm an heiress and only work for the county for fun."

"Hey, that's not bad. I really like working with people with a sense of humor. You got a picture of the guy?"

"I can get one. Can you come by my office tomorrow afternoon?"

"How's four o'clock?"

"Perfect." Kirby hung up and smiled. Zimmerman had confidence in the man; everything was going to be all right. Without hesitation, she dialed Connie Chandler.

*   *   *

"Tara, turn me loose," Mallory said with growing impatience. "I'm only going shopping, not to the moon. You stay here with Grandma and be a good girl."

Jane leaned over her granddaughter. "I thought we might bake some cookies. I know you like to help me in the kitchen."

Tara looked up at her grandmother. She knew she was fighting a losing battle. Reluctantly she released her mother's hand.

Jane took Tara's other hand and straightened up. "Don't worry, Mallory. She will be fine once you're gone."

Tara noticed her mother was looking at her with that sort of confused expression she sometimes had. Like when she couldn't decide which blouse to buy or when she was getting ready to cook and stared into the pantry as if the choices of things to cook were too difficult. "It's not like her to be so clinging," her mother said to her grandmother.

Jane patted Tara's hand. "She's just going through a stage. Aren't you, Tara?"

Tara shrugged and looked at the floor. She didn't like being asked questions she didn't understand and it was too embarrassing to admit she didn't know what an adult meant sometimes.

Before leaving, her mother kissed the top of her head and Tara noticed she was wearing her favorite gardenia-scented perfume. "'Bye, honey. I'll be back as soon as I can."

Tara didn't answer. She was accustomed to Mallory being gone for hours if she was gone at all. She couldn't understand how anyone could enjoy shopping as much as her mother did. She had decided it took her mother a long time to shop because she took forever making up her mind. Tara disliked going to the mall. She supposed that was why she was usually left in the care of her grandparents.

Jane started toward the kitchen and Tara followed close behind. Her grandparents' house was as familiar to her as her own. There was a quietness here that seemed to defy motion. She could close her eyes and know where she was by the smells of the potpourri her grandmother kept all around the house and the smell of food baking. It seemed that every time she was over, her grandmother was baking something.

She climbed onto the stool by the refrigerator and watched her grandmother start thumbing through a cookbook filled with nothing but cookie recipes. Tara could already feel her mouth start to water. Nobody could make cookies like her grandmother.

"Let's see. Which cookie is your favorite?" Jane said as she leafed through the pages.

"Chocolate chip," Tara said promptly. She smiled because she knew her grandmother already knew this but asked it every time.

"Chocolate chip. Of course." Jane found the recipe and propped the open book against the coffee canister. "Would you help me measure the flour?"

Tara pulled the stool closer and opened the flour canister. Even before she'd learned to read, she had known the larger one held flour and the next smaller was the sugar. She had been helping her grandmother make cookies since she had been old enough to toddle into the kitchen. She peered into the canister. "It's almost empty."

"It is? Dear, dear. I forgot to refill it. I'll just go out to the freezer and get another bag."

Tara hopped off the stool and followed, right on her heels.

"Are you coming with me? It's rainy out. You stay in the house. I'm only going across to the garage."

"I don't mind rain," Tara said hastily. "I like to walk in it."

"Well, come on then. But don't dawdle or you'll have wet clothes. I don't have dry ones for you to change into today."

"I'll hurry." Tara beat her grandmother across the drive to the garage. She waited under the overhang until Jane opened the side room door.

Jane had always kept the freezer out here, even though it would have been handier in the kitchen. Unlike her mother's, this freezer was the long kind that opened from the top. When she was younger, her cousin Josh had convinced her it was a coffin that was wired to stay cool inside. She had been afraid of it for months. His brother Cody had finally admitted that

Josh was lying, and once again she was able to get near it without being afraid.

It was kept in a storeroom on one side of the garage with its own separate door. The hedge clippers, empty gasoline cans, gardening paraphernalia, and lawn chairs were kept here as well. At one time Tara had viewed it as a place of adventures. Now she never came here alone.

Jane lifted the lid and a rush of cold cloud billowed out. She lifted out a bag of flour and handed it to Tara. "Is it too cold for you to carry?"

"No, Grandma. I can carry it." She peered into the box as always to see the orderly stacks of frozen vegetables and meats. The cold air smelled good.

"Let me close it up," Jane said. "All the cold is getting out."

As Tara stepped back to give her grandmother room, she heard a car pull up in the driveway and stop, then the sound of a car door opening and shutting. Quickly she moved closer to Jane, getting in her grandmother's way and almost causing her to fall.

"For goodness' sake, Tara, I nearly stepped on you, child. Come on. Let's go back inside where it's warmer. It's starting to rain, and from the feel of it out here, I believe that cold front the weatherman promised us is passing by right now."

Tara moved out of the way again, but she stayed close by her grandmother. As they left the side room, she saw her grandfather's maroon car parked in the drive. He had already gotten out and crossed to the house in the rain. The kitchen door was closing behind him. Tara reached out and touched her grandmother's skirt for reassurance. Thunder boomed in the distance and the rain suddenly increased in intensity.

Jane hurried her across the drive as the gusty wind drove the rain sideways across the yard. "I'm half drowned!" Jane declared as she pushed Tara into the house ahead of her. "Move over, Tara, before I wash away."

Addison smiled as he turned and saw Tara in the doorway. "Why hello, baby. I didn't know you were coming over today."

"Mallory went shopping. Tara and I are baking cookies."

Tara hugged the bag of flour to her chest as she solemnly gazed up at her grandfather.

"Has the cat got your tongue?" he asked playfully.

"No. Hi, Grandad."

"That's better. Would you like to come in the den and watch TV with me?"

"No, thanks."

"Why don't you go ahead?" Jane encouraged. "I'll call you when the cookies come out of the oven."

"I want to help you."

"I guess I'm not needed," Addison said with a long-suffering look at Tara.

"Bring the flour over here," Jane said. "I'll fill the canister and we can get started."

Addison left the room and Tara relaxed a bit. At least now she knew where he was.

"Your grandad wanted to visit with you," Jane said as she poured the cold flour into the canister. "You haven't been over as much lately and he misses you."

"I guess I'm growing up too fast." This was the excuse her mother always gave her father when Tara did something out of the ordinary.

Jane chuckled. "I guess you are for a fact. Before you know it, you won't want to make cookies with me anymore, will you?"

Tara smiled at her. "I'll always want to do that." She put the tip of her finger in the flour. "I like to touch it when it's right out of the freezer. Why do you keep it there, Grandma?"

"It keeps bugs out of it. You know, weevils."

Tara nodded. "Why don't you keep the sugar in there, too?"

"It makes sugar turn into a rock. It's too damp, I guess."

Tara thought about that and tried to get a mental picture of a rock made out of sugar.

Jane went to the door that led into the laundry room and Tara jumped off the stool and followed her.

"Have you become part of my shadow?" Jane asked with a laugh. "I'm just getting an apron out of the dryer."

"I wanted to watch."

"It's not all that interesting." Jane opened the dryer and

pulled the clothes into a laundry basket. "There it is. Do you need one, too?"

Tara nodded and Jane tied a checkered apron around her waist.

"There now. You look like a proper cook."

They went back into the kitchen as Jane tied her own apron. Tara climbed on the stool and leaned her elbows on the counter top.

"Why don't you go tell Grandad that we're making chocolate chip cookies and visit with him a while? He was saying just the other day that he wished you'd come over more often."

As a surge of fright gripped Tara and her eyes grew round, she struggled to hide her fear from her grandmother. "I've just been busy," she mumbled, her head tucked down. "You have homework in the third grade."

"I guess that's right. You really are growing up fast. Homework. Goodness gracious, it seems like you should still be a toddler."

She thought for a minute. "Grandma, if something was bothering me, could I talk to you about it?"

"Of course you could. You can tell Grandad and me anything. Is something wrong?"

"No. I guess not." She stuck her finger back in the flour. It was already warming to room temperature.

"Get your finger out of there."

Tara wiped her floury finger on her jeans, leaving a white streak on the denim.

Jane brushed it away. "Get the chocolate chips out of the pantry for me. Do you remember where they are?"

"Sure." She slid off the stool and crossed the kitchen. By standing on tiptoe she could reach the tin Jane used to store baking chocolate. She took off the lid, got a package of chips, and put the tin away.

As she turned around, Addison stepped into the kitchen and stopped between her and her grandmother. He looked straight at her for a moment, then said, "Come with me for a minute, Tara. There's something I want to show you."

"I'm helping Grandma."

"It won't take long and you can come right back."

"Run along," Jane said. "I'll wait until you're back to put in the chocolate chips."

Tara swallowed nervously. There was no escape. Still clutching the bag of chocolate, she followed Addison across the kitchen to the doorway that led to the den.

Tara stopped in the doorway and watched him cross to his favorite chair, sit down, then pat his pants pocket. "Guess what I've got in here."

"I don't know." She didn't go any closer.

"Come see."

Tara felt as if her heart were in her throat. Slowly she went to him. Addison straightened out his leg so she could reach into his pocket. Tara closed her eyes and wished she were a thousand miles away. Her fingers searched and found a candy bar. With relief she pulled it out. "Candy?" she asked.

"I know you like that kind." His eyes were too alert and he had that odd smile on his face.

Tara stepped back as she unwrapped the candy.

"Why are you so shy around me lately?" Addison asked. "You're my favorite granddaughter."

"I'm your only granddaughter," she corrected.

"You'd be my favorite if I had a dozen others. Why don't you come sit in my lap and let's watch TV together."

"I'm too big to sit in laps."

"Since when? You sat in my lap last summer. You weren't too big then."

Tara frowned. "I don't like sitting in your lap anymore."

Addison's face crumpled into a frown. "You don't? Why, even big girls sit in their grandads' laps. There's nothing wrong with it."

She shrugged and looked down at the carpet. What would he do if she turned and ran back to the kitchen?

"Your mommy sat in my lap when she was your age. So did Aunt Kirby. They didn't think they were too old."

"I don't know." She had no idea how to answer him. On one hand, she didn't want to be rude and up until recently she had adored him. Maybe she was wrong not to like sitting in his lap and all that went with it.

"At least come give me a kiss. That's small payment for candy, I should think."

Tara sidled closer and aimed a kiss at Addison's cheek. At the last moment, he turned and she kissed his mouth instead. He laughed as she jumped back. Tara fled from the room.

By the time she reached the kitchen, her heart was pounding and she felt as if she were going to cry. She could still smell him and feel the sensation of his lips touching hers. Tara wiped her mouth on her shirt sleeve as hard as she could. She wished she could tell her daddy and that he would make her grandad stop doing these things.

"What's that in your hand? Is your grandad giving you candy before dinner again?" Jane smiled indulgently. "Put it on the counter until later."

"I don't want it." She hated this kind of candy now. It reminded her of her grandfather. She shoved it along the counter and it collided with the sugar bowl. She hated having to search his pockets for treats. Sometimes she touched his private parts by accident and that embarrassed her, though he seemed to like it.

"I was about to come and get you and the chips. It's time to mix them in."

Tara climbed back on the stool and surrendered the bag. It was rather squashed from being gripped tightly against her body but the chips looked fine as her grandmother poured them into the bowl.

As she stirred, Jane said, "I talked to Cody earlier today. He said he got a hundred on his English test."

"Cody is real smart."

"So are you. And so is Josh if he would only apply himself."

"I had a test in math. I failed it. I'm not smart at all."

Jane was instantly sympathetic. "That's not true, Tara. You're just as smart as Cody. I imagine you didn't study hard enough for the test. You have to study, you know."

"I know. I don't like school anymore." She tapped her shoe against the rungs on the stool. "I don't have hardly any friends."

"Now I know that's not true. What about Melissa Puricelli? She's come over here with you several times and the two of you were giggling every time I looked your way."

"I like Melissa okay." Tara didn't feel happy enough to have a friend. Not even Melissa. She was pretty certain that if Melissa knew about the things her grandfather did when he was alone with her, she wouldn't want to be friends at all. Tara wouldn't dare tell her or anyone.

"I'm going to make an apple pie for Sunday dinner. Maybe Melissa would like to come over with you."

"Maybe." She couldn't ask Melissa to come over. What if something happened in front of her, or worse, what if her grandfather touched Melissa? "I think she's going to be busy on Sunday."

Jane gave her a questioning glance but didn't ask questions. "Stir the chips carefully or they'll go everywhere." She handed the spoon to Tara.

She carefully stirred the mixture, fishing out only a few chips to eat as usual, while her grandmother checked the oven temperature.

"Do you want to go watch TV while we wait for them to cook? I imagine cartoons are on by now."

"I'd rather stay in here with you."

"I'm always glad to have your company." Jane sat at the table and began peeling carrots for dinner. Tara sat beside her and put her head on Jane's shoulder. As if she had not seen this done many times before, she watched the orange slivers of carrot peel fall onto the paper towel and listened as the peeled carrots dropped with a plunk into the bowl of iced water beside the towel. She would rather be watching cartoons but she wasn't about to leave the safety of the kitchen and go in the den with Addison.

"I've been following your man Chandler for a week now," Bill Davies reported to Kirby. "That guy doesn't do anything out of the ordinary. His lunch hour he goes to St. Anthony's Elementary School but he never speaks to anyone. He just sits in his car, watching the kids play."

Kirby nodded. "That's exactly what I thought he might be doing. Does he do this every day?"

"So far. Should I keep on following him?"

"What about his evenings?"

"As I said, nothing out of the ordinary. Every day after work he goes straight home, okay? Except for Tuesday. That night he went to the park near his place and coached a kids' baseball team. You know, the season's over for the kids, but I guess the boys are still getting together one day a week. You know how kids don't ever want to stop doing something that's fun."

"He didn't do anything suspicious there?"

Davies shook his head. "Of course, they were all boys. No girls. I guess he's not interested in boys."

"That's good news." Kirby took out her checkbook and wrote him a check. "This will cover the coming week. If you see him do anything other than his routine, let me know."

"Sure." Davies handed her a folder. "These are the snapshots I took of him at the playground the only day he got out of his car. Pretty good pictures, if you ask me. Like you can see, he just stood there and watched them play. Does his daughter go to St. Anthony's?"

"No, she's in public school." Kirby opened the folder. Davies had enlarged the photos so any details would show. As he had said, Chandler wasn't doing anything suspicious. "Does he have any idea you're following him?"

"No way. I'm careful. Like Zimmerman once told me, I'm the best."

She smiled at him. "You're doing good work. I'll talk to you in a week if not before."

Davies grinned and touched his forehead in a mock salute. "Next week."

Kirby spread the photos out on her desk and leaned over them. Maybe there was something she had missed in her first glance at them. It didn't seem innocent to her that Chandler would spend his lunch hour watching elementary school children at recess, especially when his own daughter wasn't at that school. Was it possible that he was also an exhibitionist?

She studied the photos in detail. Chandler wasn't an unattractive man. With his dark suit and conservative tie and his hair well groomed, he looked like any young corporate executive. As Connie had said, to a casual observer, he appeared to be spotlessly clean of any misconduct.

She concentrated on the children. Did any of them seem to stand out from the rest? She was surprised to see a girl who looked a great deal like Kayla in the foreground of most of the pictures. Was she the reason Chandler had left his car that day? She was playing near the fence and in several shots she was looking at him as if she was curious. Had Chandler said something to her? Surely not, since at least one teacher would have been watching them closely.

In the last picture Chandler was going back to his car. He had his right hand in his pants pocket and was reaching for the door handle with the other. Something about the expression on his face made her catch her breath. He wasn't anyone she knew. He didn't even resemble any of her acquaintances. But there was something about his stance that was tugging at her memory.

Suddenly Kirby was eight years old again. There was an acrid taste in her mouth that reminded her too much of baking soda and she felt as if she were choking. Her eyes were clenched shut and she was fighting for air. She felt fabric beneath her hands. The kind of fabric in men's suits. She thought she was going to die.

As quickly as the flashback occurred, it was over. Kirby was gripping the top of her desk and gasping for air. Her heart was pounding and she jerked her head around to be certain she was alone. For a terrible moment she thought she was going to throw up.

She dropped into her chair and clasped her trembling hands in her lap. Still desperately vulnerable, she wrapped her arms around her body. The awful taste was still in her mouth and the texture of that coarse fabric still on her hands. She wanted to run from the room but was too terrified to move.

What had happened? Nothing like this had ever happened to her before. For those few seconds she had been in a different place and a child again. What was happening to her?

As her eyes filled with tears, she reached for a tissue. This was ridiculous! Had it been another panic attack? This was entirely different from the other time.

The memory of the taste was fading, and she couldn't relate it to anything familiar other than a tube of baking soda toothpaste she had once tried. She had thrown it away after one use and never bought it again. But this certainly wasn't toothpaste she was tasting.

Was she going crazy? Kirby had never known anyone who'd had a nervous breakdown, and she wasn't positive what one was, really. Did it start like this? She couldn't recall being this frightened in her entire life.

Unexpectedly, the door to her office opened and she jumped. Mrs. Parsons gave her a curious look. "I'm sorry. I guess I should have knocked but I didn't want to bother you. I just need to file these for you."

"Yes. Thank you." A fine sweat was slicking her face. Kirby blotted it with the tissue.

"Are you not feeling well?"

"No. I'm fine. I just had a moment of dizziness. That's all." She couldn't possibly describe what had just happened. She didn't understand it herself.

As Mrs. Parsons went to the file cabinet to finish what she had come to do, Kirby began gathering up the photos of Gary Chandler. She pretended nothing was wrong. Eventually she felt more like herself and logically deduced that what she had experienced was another panic attack, this one indeed as frightening as their reputation. It couldn't have been anything else.

Chapter Eight

Jane smiled and lifted the teacup to her lips. Her party was going smoothly but that was no surprise. Jane would be the first to say that she might not be as quick-witted as Addison or Kirby, but she had a true talent for creating successful parties.

The chairwoman of the Harris County Republican Women was a woman named Freddie Rae Powers. Jane had known her for many years though she didn't consider herself to be Freddie Rae's friend. Jane had always been so absorbed in making a home for Addison and being a mother to their children, she had very few close friends at all.

"As usual, your party is a success," Freddie said as she helped herself to another of the tiny cucumber sandwiches Jane had spent the morning preparing. "I always say, if you want to go to a grand party, you must go to the Walkers."

"Thank you. I do love to give them."

"I hear Addison has his sights set much higher these days."

"Yes, he does, but he's such a capable man." Jane had no idea what Freddie Rae was talking about. Addison didn't confide anything in her. He never had. "He and Kirby seem to have all the brains in the family. Mallory, I'm afraid, takes after me." She smiled at her daughter across the room. Mallory was listening intently to a gesturing woman in a pink flowered hat.

Freddie Rae followed Jane's gaze. "Oh, dear. Trudy Harrison

has her trapped over there. I'm sure she's recounting every detail of her gallbladder surgery again. And those hats! No one wears hats like Trudy!''

"Well, Mallory hasn't heard about the operation," Jane said doubtfully. "I'm sure it's instructive to her."

Freddie Rae laughed. "Dear Jane. How you do put things. What a sense of humor you have!"

Jane thanked her but she had no idea what she had said that had caused Freddie Rae to make the comment. "More punch?"

"No, no. I'm practically stuffed as it is." She reached for a celery stick filled with cheese. "Really now. What do you think about Addison's interest in the Supreme Court?"

Jane had many years of practice hiding her surprise. "I'm sure he will do a magnificent job. He does so well at everything." So that was it, she thought. Addison was aspiring to be on the Texas Supreme Court. She wondered if that would mean having to move to Austin. Jane had lived in Houston all her life and didn't want to leave her children and grandchildren.

"So supportive! But that's really our job, isn't it? I don't care what all those liberal women say. It's a wife's job to support her husband in everything he tries to do."

Jane nodded absently. She was wondering why Addison hadn't told her about such an important matter, but then he never talked with her about politics because it all was so confusing to her.

"Raymond Stansfield will be in town next month. I can't tell you how excited I am to meet him. I've followed his career for years, but I've never met him in person."

"He's quite nice, really. Addison has known him for quite a while. I don't know him as well, of course, but I like his wife."

"I'm sure I will, too. Virginia Stansfield will make a lovely First Lady."

"Yes, she will. Assuming he's elected, that is."

Freddie Rae laughed again. "You're such a card, Jane!"

Jane smiled uncertainly. "You'll get to meet them at the party next month. Addison has asked me to host it."

"Surely you won't have it here," Freddie Rae said as if that was quite out of the question.

"Oh, no. It will be much too large for my house. No, Addison has reserved a board room at the Warwick."

Just then Mallory came to her mother's side. "It's a wonderful party, Mom. Dad will be so pleased."

"I was just telling your mother the same thing," Freddie Rae gushed. "By the way, Mallory, is your husband considering joining the political circuit?"

"Not that I know of. Derrick is perfectly happy where he is. He's head of the law firm, you know."

"Yes, so I heard. He's such a capable young man. He reminds me of your father in so many ways."

"Does he? I had never noticed any similarity at all."

"Oh, but there are some, of course. Any psychologist will tell you that it's quite common for daughters to marry men like their fathers. Sons do the opposite. They marry women like their mothers. It's a known fact."

"I had no idea." Mallory seemed fascinated by this information. "I suppose there is some resemblance, even though Dad is taller than Derrick and his hair was darker before it turned gray. They're both lawyers and in the same firm. Or they were until Dad became a judge, that is. Mom, do you think Derrick is like Dad?"

"I had never thought to notice, but I suppose they could be alike in some ways."

Mallory considered this another moment or two, then looked at her watch. "Mom, don't be disappointed, but I have to run. I have another appointment."

"You have to leave so soon?"

"I'm sorry. I made the appointment without realizing your party was set for today." She looked genuinely contrite.

Jane gave her a brief hug. "Run along then. I'm glad you came."

"So am I. I always love your parties." She threw a smile at Freddie Rae. "Goodbye. It was so good to see you again."

"Such a good girl," Freddie Rae said as Mallory left. "She's a real credit to you, Jane. Where's Kirby today?"

"She's at work. She's with the district attorney's office, you know."

"Yes, I heard. Was Addison upset over her leaving the family firm?"

"No, not at all." Jane had been a bit surprised at this herself. She had fully expected him to go into one of his rages. Instead, he had taken it in stride and had made no scene at all.

"Maybe someday Kirby will go into politics, too."

"Perhaps." Jane thought this was highly unlikely, but she wanted to leave the possibility open in case she was wrong. It wouldn't be wise for Freddie Rae to remember later that Jane had said Kirby wasn't interested in politics if it turned out that she was. "Have another rum ball?" She passed the plate to Freddie, who took several.

Mallory was glad to escape the party. Her mother did a wonderful job of putting them together, but Mallory was tired of hearing about operations and politics. She found it hard to remember who was running for what position, and with the election year coming up, there were more names and causes than ever to keep straight. She was glad Derrick had no political aspirations.

A glance at her watch told her she would have to hurry. She was to meet Bob at his apartment in ten minutes and traffic made it impossible to get anywhere in that length of time.

She eventually reached Bob's apartment and parked in one of the visitor spaces. It was curious that she still didn't know his last name, but then he didn't know hers either. In a way that made it more exciting.

She rushed into the elevator and pushed the button for the fourth floor. Bob wasn't the only man she was seeing, but he was one of the few she had seen more than once. Mallory liked diversity and she didn't want to be with any one man long enough for him to get the idea she would leave Derrick for him. Her affairs were purely for pleasure, not a search for a permanent change in her life.

Bob opened the door almost before she stopped knocking. "You're late."

"I'm sorry. I had another appointment today."

"Not another man, I hope."

Mallory laughed. "My mother had a party and I was expected to be there."

"I can accept that." He put his arms around her and pressed his pelvis against hers. "I've been looking forward to this all day." The bulge in his pants attested to the truth in that statement and that pleased her.

"So have I." It was true. The guilt wouldn't come until later, along with the dull ache of incompletion. Sometimes it bothered Mallory that she never had an orgasm with a man but she told herself that a lot of other women probably didn't either and she could always take care of that herself. Still, it would be nice to find some man who could take away this craving for sex for at least a few minutes. Perhaps today would be the day.

"I had trouble getting off work this afternoon."

"I'm worth it," she said with confidence.

"You certainly are." As he nuzzled her neck, Mallory let her head roll back with pleasure. "You already want me. I can tell."

"You're right again." She turned him in the direction of his bedroom. "I'm glad no one lives with you. That would be so inconvenient."

"Actually I was thinking of asking you to move in."

"Move in?" Mallory stopped and looked up at him. She took the opportunity to start unbuttoning her blouse. "I can't move in here."

"You could leave your husband."

Mallory thought quickly. She had forgotten that Bob knew she was married. "No, I can't do that."

"Come on, baby. At least consider it."

The endearment struck home and she smiled provocatively. "I'll think about it. Call me that again. I like it."

"What? Baby?"

She made a purring sound and rubbed against his chest. "I don't know what it is, but that word always turns me on. It makes me think of danger."

Bob laughed. "You're a strange one."

"I'm a woman of mystery."

"I don't even know your real name."

Mallory smiled and shrugged. She had told him her name

was Mallory. Did that mean his wasn't really Bob? Somehow that was exciting, too. She caught the waistband of his pants and led him into the bedroom.

Bob hastily took off his clothes and lay in the bed. Mallory began to strip, but ever so slowly, letting him watch her with his hungry eyes. She had his full attention and loved it. Especially knowing she was completely in charge. That was one thing all her affairs had in common—she was the one who controlled them. If a man became too demanding or possessive, she simply stopped seeing him.

Without taking her eyes from him, she dropped her skirt and stepped out of it. Her blouse soon joined it, leaving her clad in nothing but a sheer, pink teddy and matching garter belt. It had excited her at the party to know she was dressed so provocatively under her conservative clothing. She could tell by the look in Bob's eyes that her seductive costuming was having the desired effect, and a quick glance at his lower torso told her he was more than ready for her.

He sat on the side of the bed and pulled her to him. With a groan, he buried his face between her breasts. Mallory murmured as he kissed her nipples through the filmy fabric. She loved to be touched, to be held. One of the things she liked best about Bob was that he talked to her as they made love.

"You're so beautiful," he said, sliding the slender strap off her shoulder. "I can't believe the way you're made." He drew the strap farther down, exposing her breast. "God, look at that!" He covered the nipple with his mouth and sucked it eagerly.

Mallory wished foreplay could go on forever; she really liked that better than intercourse. Unfortunately, her lovers didn't share that opinion.

"I want you. Come to bed."

"Not yet," she said with a sexy smile. "I want to tease you first." She pushed the other strap off her shoulder and the teddy slid lower, caught on her breast for a heartbeat, then fell to her waist. Bob covered her breasts with his hands, then Mallory backed away until she was just out of reach. With a sensuous shift of her hips, the teddy drifted to the floor. Only her garter belt and hose remained.

"Come closer," he said in a hoarse voice.

"Maybe. If you're good."

"I'll be good. Come on, baby. Let me touch you."

The words lit fires of erotic passion in her. She moved just within fingertip range and Bob obliged by stroking her nipples with a feathery touch that made the buds rise to turgid, throbbing points. Mallory was growing more excited by the moment and moved closer. One hand remained on her breast, the other slipped between her thighs.

"You're ready for me. Come on. Lie down."

"Yes," she said, licking her lips. "Tell me what you want me to do." Her pulse quickened with the danger of giving up some of her control. But it was only a little.

"Lie down. Here."

Mallory did as he said and lay on her back in the middle of the bed. Her breath was coming quickly. This could be the day she would finally be satisfied!

"Spread your legs. Wider." Bob was getting into this. She could tell by the way his eyes had darkened and the way his body was responding without her ever having touched him. "You heard me, baby. Spread them wider."

Mallory parted her legs as wide as she could. Bob knelt between them. This was progressing faster than she usually allowed but it felt right; it held the hint of possible fulfillment. Maybe going too slow had been the reason she never had reached a climax during intercourse.

As Bob entered her, he groaned with obvious pleasure. Mallory put her arms around him. Waves of desire already were building in her. Today would be the day! She knew it would be!

He started moving inside her, stoking her passion. Mallory moaned as her body responded. She held her thoughts firmly on Bob and what he was doing to her. If only she could keep her mind in control! This could be it!

Soon he increased the pace and she knew this meant he was nearing his completion. Mallory's eyes fell on the print of a famous painting he had hanging on the wall. At once her attention was broken—only for a moment, but that was enough. As he ground out his passion, hers faded. It was gone. As near as she had come, she had lost it. Mallory was so disappointed she wanted to cry. Instead she responded with what Bob expected to hear. "Yes!" she shouted. "Yes, yes!" She pushed her hips against his and wrapped her legs about him. After holding the position for several seconds, she relaxed. It was over. Again.

"Damn, but you're good!" Bob rolled off her and held her to his side. "I've never known any woman who was so hot!" He sounded smugly pleased as if he assumed no other man had ever pleased her as well as he did.

Mallory smiled at him and put her arm across his chest. This was a good part of lovemaking, even if it always came at a time when she was again sexually frustrated. At least he was holding her and talking to her in a gentle voice.

She only half-listened to him, though. What he was saying wasn't important. All that mattered was that he was holding her and that she still had his complete attention. Next time. Next time she would climax for sure. She remembered to keep smiling and to kiss his shoulder from time to time to keep him talking to her.

Kirby closed her eyes and sighed. She was again working late at the office, wading through case after case involving sexual crimes against children. At first the facts had sickened her. Now she was so tired and had read so many, the emotional impact was gone.

She heard a sound and looked up to see a large man standing in her doorway. Her first impulse was to run, then she recognized Zimmerman.

"What are you doing up here so late?"

"I'm looking for some obscure precedent that will help me find a way to prosecute the Chandler case."

Zimmerman looked puzzled. "Chandler case?" Understanding hit him. "Not that again. I thought you let that drop weeks ago."

"It's still bothering me. I don't know why. Maybe it's because I'm so positive Chandler did it."

"Pardon my bluntness, but there's no way in hell that you

could know that for a fact. You're becoming obsessive about this. I figured the Lemke case would keep you busy all week.''

''Leon, a little girl was raped! Someone needs to be obsessive about it! I can't ignore it.'' Kirby frowned up at him. ''I'll work on the Lemke case during regular work hours.''

He crossed the room and sat at the table opposite her. ''Look at you. You're buried in a pile of law books and it's nearly midnight.''

''Midnight! Is it that late?'' She looked at her watch and groaned. ''I had no idea I'd been here so long.''

''Come on. You've worked enough for one day. You have other cases that need your attention tomorrow. Cases we have a chance of winning. Besides, your husband must be worried sick by now.''

''No, Russell will have been asleep for an hour or so. He's used to me coming in late.''

''You do this regularly?''

''I do lately. You're getting your money's worth in me.''

''Not if you work yourself to death. Come on. The library is closing for tonight.''

Kirby shuffled her notes into a stack and put them in her briefcase. She knew he was right, but she hated to stop the search. Somewhere in all this, there had to be some case she could use as a precedent to put Gary Chandler in prison where he belonged.

Zimmerman turned out the light as she left the room and they walked down the hall together, turning off lights as they went. Kirby smiled at him. ''I have to admit, I dread leaving when I work late. I hate to turn out the lights and know that I'm the only one in the building. It's really creepy here after everyone else is gone.''

''Yeah? I've always thought of it as peaceful.''

Kirby glanced behind them at the dark hall. ''Lately I've been having strange fears. I suppose they're panic attacks. I don't know what else to call them.'' As soon as the words were out of her mouth, she wished she hadn't been so honest. Zimmerman might lose confidence in her and that wouldn't do. She tried to pass it off with a laugh, and in a joking manner said, ''I've even become afraid of the dark.''

"You'll outgrow it, kid." He winked at her. "Go on to the elevator and I'll turn off this last one."

Kirby didn't argue. She usually ran for the elevator as soon as this light was out. The dark always closed in on her and she imagined hands reaching out to grab her. Instead, she nodded to him as if she were accepting a common courtesy and walked ahead with a confident stride. When the elevator doors opened, she stepped into its brightly lit interior and held the door for him.

As they left the elevator on the first floor, Kirby glanced in both directions out of habit. At the end of the hall on her left were several members of the cleaning staff polishing the floors. As they passed by them on their way to the parking garage entrance, one of them was singing bits of a song as he worked. Another laughed at something a third said. Although the cleaning crew was honest and familiar to her, Kirby found it difficult to walk near them on the nights she was here alone. She was grateful for Leon's presence, even though she had no reason to fear the crew. She hoped she wasn't becoming paranoid on top of having panic attacks.

Even though the parking garage was well lit and she told him there was no need, Zimmerman insisted on walking her to her car. He waited for her to get in, then shut her car door and Kirby automatically locked it. She was secretly glad he had walked her over. At night her imagination filled the cavernous garage with dangers.

"You drive carefully," he called through the rolled-up window.

She smiled and nodded as she started her car, this time making direct eye contact. Kirby had always had a knack for reading people's faces and accurately assessing whether there was truth or deception behind their words and actions. Now she was relatively sure that Zimmerman had seen through her attempts to cover her fears and insecurities and was concerned about her. But to her relief, his concern seemed to be for her personal welfare and not her professional competence. He might prove to be as fatherly as Hershal Glassman had been, and nothing would please her more.

Although the drive home was relatively quick and uneventful,

Kirby always found the absence of traffic more unnerving than the fracas during rush hour. And for the last month or two, it had been even more unsettling. It was not until she was in the house and had locked the door behind her that she felt even marginally secure.

Russell had left lights on for her in the kitchen and the living room and one on the stairs. He had always been thoughtful that way. Kirby sometimes wondered what she would do without him.

After checking all the outside doors to be certain the house was locked, she went up to their bedroom. As she undressed, Russell stirred and sleepily called her name.

"It's just me. Go back to sleep."

He rose up enough to look at the clock. "It's after midnight?"

"I had a lot of work to do." She hoped he would go back to sleep. She didn't want to argue tonight.

"The boys asked if you still live here. I told them I wasn't sure."

"I'll come home earlier tomorrow. I promise."

Russell propped himself up on his elbow. "If I didn't know you so well, I'd be certain you're having an affair."

"Yes, I am. With a library of law books. You can't imagine how exciting it is." She took a gown from her drawer and went into the bathroom to change.

"You could change in here," he called to her. "You used to do that."

Kirby sighed and stared at her reflection in the mirror. "Go back to sleep, Russell. I have to take off my makeup and comb out my hair. I'll be to bed soon."

She heard no reply and knew he was lying back down. She undressed and pulled on her gown. Even when she was alone, she didn't like to be naked longer than was necessary. It made her feel too vulnerable. By the time she washed away her makeup and brushed the hair spray out of her hair, Russell was asleep.

She got into bed without waking him and checked the alarm. Morning would come too early.

Sleep came quickly and, with it, the nightmare. She was in the long hallway. The flowery smell was cloying sweet and she had the sensation of blue all about her. As always, she went to the door at the end of the hall and opened it, even though she dreaded what she would find there. The man was on the bed. This time he was calling to her and his pants were unzipped. His hands were busy playing with himself.

Panic hit her and she ran. No matter how hard she tried, she couldn't outrun him. Her feet seemed to be sinking in mud rather than the carpet, whereas he was able to move with lightning speed. As always, he caught her and pulled her back to the room, ignoring her screams and protests.

Kirby bolted upright, gasping for air. As always in this nightmare, she awoke choking and unable to get enough air into her lungs. The physical sensations were as disturbing as the dream. Some nights she was afraid she wouldn't be able to get enough air in and would pass out.

To her relief, Russell didn't wake up this time. She lay back down but didn't close her eyes. The nightmare was still too real. Hugging the covers to her, she stayed awake as long as she could before exhaustion won out.

Mallory lay in bed waiting for Derrick to finish his nightly ritual of flossing, brushing his teeth, and examining his hairline to see if it had receded further since the night before. All day she had been thinking about Bob. She had come so close to climaxing the day before that she was encouraged to think it could happen someday. Derrick was the handiest person to experiment with.

"Are you ever coming to bed?" she called.

"In a minute. Did you get my navy suit from the cleaners?"

"I forgot. I'll do it tomorrow."

"I don't ask you to do much. Write yourself a note."

"I'll remember." She hoped he wasn't going to start another fight. She needed him to be nice to her tonight.

Derrick came into the bedroom. As always, he was wearing pajamas, top and bottom.

"Do you always have to dress to come to bed?" she asked. "I couldn't begin to sleep in all that."

"It's turned cold. You know how I hate to be cold." He hurried into bed.

"I can warm you up." She slid closer and matched her length to his. "See how warm I am?"

"Mallory, do we have to do this again? If you worked as hard as I do all day, you'd look forward to going to bed for rest and not sex." He made no move to embrace her.

Mallory wasn't going to give up that easily. She kissed the tender part of his neck and he flinched. Moving up his throat, she licked the inner curve of his ear.

"Stop that!" He rolled away. "I told you I'm tired."

"Drunk is more like it." She lay back and frowned up at the ceiling.

"You're a fine one to point a finger. How many did you have tonight?"

"Why should I keep count when I know you'll do it for me?" The mood was spoiled. He wouldn't touch her now. She glanced at the clock. Would she be able to slip out to the Schooner this late? Derrick was sure to go to sleep quickly.

"Maybe I'd feel more like having sex if you weren't always coming on to me," Derrick grumbled. "A man doesn't like to feel pressured about something like sex."

"If I left it up to you, I'd probably still be a virgin." She ran her hands over her body beneath the thin gown she wore. She couldn't understand why he didn't want her. It wasn't as if she had let herself go since their marriage. She dieted almost constantly. Kirby said she was getting too thin, though Mallory thought she could still stand to lose a few pounds. "Why don't you like to make love with me?" she asked.

"God!" Derrick ground out. "I'm trying to go to sleep, for Christ sake! I have a busy day tomorrow. If you're going to feel sorry for yourself or get on a crying jag, do it in another room."

Mallory glared at him through the darkness and got out of bed. "Anything is better than lying here next to you!" she retorted. She yanked her robe out of her closet and left the bedroom.

She hated living with Derrick. If it wasn't for the stigma in her family of a divorce, she would have left him years before.

No Walker had ever divorced and she was afraid to tell Addison that she wanted one. He would never understand. Addison had introduced her to Derrick and had encouraged her to marry him. Derrick was as much a part of the family as she was, maybe more.

Mallory went into the den and poured herself another Scotch. She knew she was drinking too much. So was Derrick. Was he doing it for the same reason she was? It was the only way to numb herself out enough to stay married to him.

She sat on the couch and curled her legs under her but didn't turn on the TV. She preferred the silent darkness. There was already enough alcohol in her system that she couldn't feel the drink, but the taste was soothing. Mallory liked the taste of alcohol. That was one reason she drank so much. Derrick might say she was addicted, but she was positive she could stop drinking anytime she felt like it. She just didn't want to.

On the end table beside her was a clay figurine Tara had made in art class. She had said it was a clown but it didn't look much like one. Mallory picked it up and smiled. Tara wasn't particularly good at art, though she tried. Mallory had never been good at it either. She hadn't been good at much of anything. Kirby had inherited all the brains and talent. Her parents had said so often. In a way this had been liberating. Mallory had never had to study as hard as Kirby and hadn't been expected to bring home high grades. Sometimes she wondered if she would have made better grades if more had been expected of her.

Mallory was worried about Tara. Something was bothering her but Mallory had no idea what it was. She had had another conference with Mrs. Lydick, but Tara's teacher had no clue either. None of the other children was bullying Tara, and Melissa Puricelli was still her best friend, but something about Tara was different.

Sadly, it occurred to Mallory that she was no more cut out for motherhood than she was for marriage. It wasn't her fault that she had an unusually high sex drive, but maybe it was her fault that Tara was unhappy. At least Derrick had that much going for him—he was a good father.

She wished she hadn't thought of Derrick again. He could

help her if he wanted to. There had to be some way he could satisfy her sexually. When they made love, he held off for a while, but when he was ready, he came. Once that happened, she was on her own. He said it was her own fault for not being more responsive.

More responsive? If she responded any stronger, she would explode! Mallory leaned her head back against the couch cushions. Maybe she just expected more from sex than it could deliver. Maybe all women felt like this and just didn't talk about it. Sure, it was different in novels, but those were fiction. Not one of her friends had ever told her what it felt like during lovemaking. She didn't know anyone well enough to ask, not even Kirby.

If all women felt this frustrated, however, why didn't they talk about sex all the time? It was never far from her mind.

She wondered if she could ask Kirby about it. Kirby was certain to be honest about what she was feeling. She could be bluntly honest. Mallory told herself she would find a way to work the question into a conversation in the near future. It wouldn't be easy. As much as Mallory enjoyed having sex, she thoroughly disliked talking about it.

Chapter Nine

"Is this blouse all right?" Mallory asked, critically turning left and right in front of her mirror.

"It's pretty." Kirby glanced at her wristwatch. "We're going to be late again if you don't hurry. Mom likes for people to show up on time."

"I know." Mallory frowned at her reflection and started unbuttoning the blouse. "Maybe the blue one I bought at Macy's."

"Mal, I've already had time to take Tara over to stay with Russell and the boys. You've changed clothes three times! Just wear anything. We aren't going to see anyone but Mom."

"I like to look nice when I go out. Besides, I may do some shopping before I come back home. Tara needs new shoes."

"If you're not ready in five minutes, I'm leaving without you."

Mallory pulled on the blue blouse and buttoned it as she stepped into a different pair of shoes. "You needn't be so compulsive about being on time. It's not like we have an appointment with Mom."

"No, but she asked us to be there by two. It's five 'til now. It takes that long to drive the three blocks down Rice. You know what it's like on a Saturday during football season."

"Okay, okay. I'm ready. Well, almost. You go ahead to the car and I'll catch up in a second."

Two minutes later, Mallory joined Kirby, who hurriedly backed her car out of Mallory's driveway. "I may as well go down an extra block and turn at the light. At least that way traffic has to let us in."

"I'll be glad when football season is over."

"This is the last game. Russell says Rice isn't going to make the playoffs this year. That's why there's so much traffic."

"I hate sports." Mallory pulled down the visor and looked in the lighted mirror. "I should have freshened my makeup."

"You haven't been up that long, if I know you."

"Thank goodness Tara isn't an early morning person. Derrick was already gone to the links before either of us woke up."

"Is everything all right between you and Derrick?"

Mallory was silent for several seconds. "Sure. Why?"

"I'm worried about you. You have so much frantic energy but you don't seem to get much of anything done."

"Thanks, sis."

Kirby threw her a smile. "Come on. Tell big sister what's going on."

Mallory sank back against the seat and shoved the visor out of the way. "I had hoped it wasn't that obvious. Derrick and I are having lots of arguments. That's all."

"It may not be obvious to anyone but me. It's just that I know you so well. Is there anything I can do?"

"No. It may not even be his fault." She stared moodily out the window.

"Russell and I have been arguing quite a bit, too." Kirby wasn't sure how to discuss what was bothering her most with anyone, even Mallory. "He says I should get into therapy."

"Therapy? You? You're the most balanced person I know."

"I think so, too. It's just that I've been having so many nightmares lately."

"How can you and Russell argue about nightmares? What kind of nightmares are they?"

"It's the same one, over and over. I guess I shouldn't be burdening you with this. Russell and I will work it out." She sounded more positive than she felt. For the past week she and

Russell had barely spoken at all and she was miserable over the distance between them. As much as Kirby detested clinging women, she was terrified of losing Russell.

"I can't imagine you two having problems. I would have said you're the perfect couple."

"There's no such thing." Kirby stopped at the red light. Even though the game wasn't for hours yet, cars were already packing into the parking lot at Rice Stadium. "Would you look at this traffic?"

"Derrick says it's a grudge match. I didn't even ask who they're playing. You don't want to tell me about the nightmare?"

Kirby tensed. Why had she mentioned the nightmare? She didn't want to talk about it at all. Especially the details. If she minimized its significance, maybe Mallory would drop the subject. In a lighter tone, she said, "It's just the usual. I'm being chased down a long hall. I guess everyone has had that dream."

"I haven't. I never remember my dreams at all."

Kirby was unexpectedly curious. "Then how do you know you haven't dreamed it?"

"Don't turn into a lawyer with me." Mallory glanced at her. "This nightmare must be troubling you a great deal if Russell wants you to go into therapy because of it."

"You know how Russell worries. He thinks therapy can cure anything." Kirby couldn't talk anymore about the nightmare. Even the memory of it was deeply disturbing. She had to change the subject without being too obvious; otherwise, Mallory would continue to press her for the details. After a pause, she said, "Besides, it's not just the dream. Lately we haven't been very . . . intimate."

"You're not having sex?" Mallory exclaimed. "I would leave Derrick in a New York minute!"

"Marriage is more than two bodies rubbing against each other," Kirby said in exasperation. "Russell's engine never seems to idle lately, if you know what I mean."

"Really? Russell?" Mallory grinned and looked interested. "I wouldn't have thought it of him. He's always struck me as the intellectual sort."

"He is, but that doesn't mean he doesn't want to make love." The light turned green and she pulled out onto Rice Boulevard. "I still love him. That's not it. But I work so late that I'm tired when I get home. I seem to be tired most of the time. Maybe it's just that I'm getting older and I'm not as interested in sex as I used to be."

"Damn! I hope I never get that old." Mallory laughed as if she didn't think that was even remotely possible. "But Derrick probably prays for it. It's a shame you and I are too moral for mate swapping. It sounds as if that could solve both our problems."

"Can't you ever be serious?" Kirby frowned at the slow-moving traffic ahead. "I should have known you'd try to turn this into a comedy."

"Hey, I didn't mean anything by it. I didn't realize it was so important to you."

"Well, it is." Kirby hit the brakes quickly to avoid rear-ending the car in front of her. The traffic had stopped behind the line of cars trying to turn into the stadium. She looked at her watch. "We're late."

"Okay, so you can stop worrying. If we're already late, there's no reason to worry about it any longer."

"I don't think you could possibly be my sister. You must have been swapped for the real Mallory at birth."

"Or maybe you were. No, you're too much like Dad. And I look like Mom. I guess we're sisters after all. Darn! We'll just have to make the best of it."

Kirby leaned her left elbow on the armrest and tried not to be so tense over the traffic jam. "Looks like we aren't going much of anywhere for a while. Tell me about the problems you're having with Derrick."

"It's nothing. Not really."

"I don't believe you. Why is it you can ask me details about my private life and won't share your own? That's really irritating."

"That's not true. At least not completely true. It's just that it's easier for you to talk about personal things. That's all."

"Easier? I wish it were true. But there's no point in arguing.

Listen Mallory, we're sisters and we need to be there for each other. I know something is bothering you and I want to help.''

"Then let me do it my way, okay?"

"I'm listening."

Mallory drew a deep breath. "Kirby, when you and Russell make love," Mallory began slowly, "do you . . . you know?"

"I don't understand. Do I what?"

"Never mind. I can't talk to you about this."

"To be perfectly honest, I've never really liked making love."

"Never?"Mallory asked, leaning closer.

Kirby hadn't intended to be so blunt. The admission that she didn't enjoy lovemaking had slipped out. But from the tone of voice and inflection of Mallory's response, she could tell that it had been important for Mallory to know this. Probing carefully, she said, "No, I don't. Do you?"

"I like being held and talked to. It's just that I can't seem to climax." She laughed as if it were of no importance.

"Not ever?" Kirby couldn't conceal her surprise. Lately she had begun having the same problem. She had thought she was the only one who didn't have climaxes easily and repeatedly.

Mallory looked out the window. "Well, I don't mean that, of course. Just forget I mentioned it. Isn't that Mom in the yard?"

Kirby peered halfway down the block. "Yes, that's her. She's probably come out because we're late. Can you believe this? We can see the house and can't drive there. We should have walked. It would have been quicker than this."

"Don't tell her I said Derrick and I are having trouble. Okay?"

"I never repeat anything you say to me in confidence. Don't you tell her about me either."

"Deal."

"Maybe we should both get into therapy. We might qualify for a group rate." She smiled at her sister.

"We would probably drive some counselor bananas."

Knowing that their conversation would end in moments, Kirby impulsively said, "There is something I've been wanting to ask you. You don't have to answer if you don't want to. Are you having an affair?"

"Me?" Mallory looked too amazed. She didn't meet Kirby's eyes. "Of course not. What a question! Why, are you?"

"Absolutely not. I was just wondering. Late one night last week as I was on my way home, I thought I saw you coming out of an apartment building."

"You're seeing things, sis." Mallory looked out the window again.

The tension had increased between them with her question, which meant that Mallory must be lying. She had never been able to make Kirby believe she was telling the truth when she wasn't. Kirby didn't pursue it. It was none of her business.

The traffic crept forward and at last they were able to turn into the Walker drive. "Finally!" Kirby turned off the car and opened the door. "Hi, Mom."

Jane looked up. "You're late. I thought I saw you trapped in traffic down the street." She was snipping the dead blooms off her chrysanthemums. "I don't know if these will bloom again this year or not. They didn't do well this season. It's been so wet."

"You always have a beautiful yard, Mom," Mallory said. "I wish I could find an interest in gardening. I don't ever seem to have the time."

"You just have to take the time. It will be easier as Tara gets older. After all, the outside of your house makes an impression on everyone who drives past." She patted Mallory's shoulder. "Come in the house, both of you. We have a lot to do if we're to make the party a rousing success."

"You're the one who has a talent for planning parties," Kirby said. "I don't know why you need us for this."

"I've planned it, but I need help in assembling the place cards. I want a little autumn arrangement at each plate and my fingers aren't as nimble as they once were."

"So that's it," Kirby said with a laugh. "You only want us for our glue guns."

"Why, no, dear. That's not it at all." Jane wasn't quick at humor.

"I know, Mom. I was just teasing."

Kirby followed her mother and sister into the house. It was so familiar to her, she was certain she could walk through it blindfolded. Jane hadn't rearranged the furniture for as long as Kirby could remember. When she bought new couches or chairs, she always placed them right where the old ones had been. Because she had decorated the entire house in her signature colors of Wedgwood blue and white, the old and the new blended perfectly and without any noticeable ripples of change.

Jane had set up two card tables in the den and had arranged neat piles of an assortment of dried flowers and ribbons on them. "Mallory, you print the place cards. There's the calligraphy pen and ink. Here's a list of names. When you finish, give the card to Kirby and she will hot glue the flowers. I'll show you the picture I'm copying. Then give the card to me and I'll attach the ribbon. All right?"

"Okay." Kirby sat at the table and studied the pictures of various designs of place cards her mother had clipped out of one of her craft magazines.

Jane pointed to the most elaborate one. "This is the one we're doing."

"You would pick the most difficult," Kirby said wryly.

Mallory laughed. "She always does. Don't you remember the favors we made for my twelfth birthday party? We worked on them for days!"

"I don't remember that." Kirby cocked her head to one side as she tried to bring up the memory. "I don't recall that at all."

"You must, dear. We worked ourselves silly over it." Jane laughed at the memory. "I did overreach that time."

"Kirby, you're just not thinking hard enough. You sang and I played the piano. You were fourteen and said your social life would be ruined if you had to sing in public. Don't you remember?"

"No, I don't," Kirby said rather abruptly. "I'm sorry. I don't remember anything that happened when I was fourteen."

"You must. That was the year you had that huge crush on Brandon Cates."

"I don't even remember anyone named Brandon Cates." She picked up some of the dried flowers. She wanted to change the subject. It bothered her that she couldn't remember any of this. She felt ridiculously close to tears.

"I can't believe this." Mallory exclaimed." You've always had the best memory of anyone I ever knew. You can read something twice and have it memorized! Why don't you remember that party?" Mallory looked genuinely confused.

"I don't remember anything between the ages of about eight and sixteen."

"That's just not possible," Mallory said bluntly. "That's practically half your life!"

"Now don't tease her, Mallory. I'm sure she's exaggerating." Jane picked up a red flower, a blue one, and a tiny spray of white prickly flowers. "Put them together like this and hot glue them to the right corner. I want red, white, and blue on each card. If the red flowers seem skimpy like this one, add another to it. I just couldn't find decent red flowers. I hope these will do. Your father is counting so on this party. Raymond Stansfield is the guest of honor. This is to kick off his presidential campaign in Houston so it's very important that everything go well."

"The red flowers are pretty. Don't worry. Everything will be fine," Kirby reassured her. "Your parties always are successful. I don't know why you worry so."

"They're successful because I make them be. That takes a lot of concentration." Jane showed her exactly how to glue the flowers in place. "I'll start making bows." She measured three strands of ribbon in red, white, and blue.

Mallory still looked worried. "Kirby, are you serious about not remembering eight years of your life?"

"It's not a big deal. Start lettering the cards or we'll never get finished."

"It is a big deal. Don't you remember going to grade school and starting high school?"

"I know I went to St. Clair just like you did." Kirby avoided Mallory's eyes.

"I do wish you girls were sending your children to St. Clair. It has such a wonderful curriculum. Addison was adamant that you go there."

"I know it's a good school, but the boys like public school. Josh wants to play every sport."

"Sports are taught at St. Clair. Both you girls were cheerleaders."

"I know, but it's not quite the same. Russell went to public school and he was determined the boys should, too."

"Tara wouldn't dream of attending any school the boys didn't go to," Mallory added. "You know how close the three of them are."

"All the same, St. Clair is wonderful and I've never regretted sending you two there."

"Remember the Great Dane we had?" Mallory asked.

"We never had a Great Dane," Kirby said.

"Yes, we did." Jane smiled in remembrance. "We got him the summer before I bought Tinkerbell. He was a lovely animal, even if he was as clumsy as they come. You named him a funny name. What was it? Pie something or other?"

"Pyewacket," Mallory said, watching Kirby. "We named him after the cat in *Bell, Book and Candle.*"

"Of course. Pyewacket." Jane cut another section of ribbons and tied them in a tricolored bow. "I could never remember what his name was, so I just called him Pie."

"What happened to him?" Kirby said. She couldn't remember the dog at all but she was determined not to let Mallory or Jane see that this frightened her. How could she possibly have forgotten a Great Dane named Pyewacket?

"He was run over. In the street out front of the house. You cried for days." By this point, Mallory was staring at her.

"I suppose that's why I forgot. I must have been traumatized by him getting killed." Kirby refused to meet Mallory's eyes.

"I'm sure that's it," Jane said. "He was so attached to you. More than to Mallory, really."

"Kirby, it worries me that you've lost those memories," Mallory said, nervously chewing her lower lip. "Maybe you should go in for a checkup. Mom, does Alzheimer's run in our family?"

"No, not at all. I had a cousin named Rachel Ann who became a bit odd, but she was always peculiar and she didn't have Alzheimer's."

"I wish I hadn't told you. I don't want to go to a doctor. This memory has always been missing. It's not something that has happened recently."

"How do you know, if you don't remember it?" Mallory countered.

"I had a physical only two months ago."

"I'm sure she's fine, dear. No one has complete recall. Why, you probably don't remember every detail of your life either. Do you, Mallory?"

"But Mom . . ."

Jane turned to Kirby. "Would you go back to the guest room and get the extra glue sticks I bought? I can see we're going to need them."

"Sure, Mom." Kirby was glad to escape. It would give her mother time to get Mallory's mind on another subject. She could kick herself for admitting the memory loss. It was a secret she had kept for years. Even Russell didn't know. Because she had no explanation for it, she had never told anyone. She found it frightening and tried never to dwell on it. Normally, she was pretty good at ignoring it.

Unlike most of the houses in the neighborhood, the Walker house was a rambling ranch style instead of being two-storied. The guest room was at the end of the hall that ran the length of the house. Showcased along the wall were many of the watercolors Jane had painted in her earlier years. Kirby had seen them so often they were invisible to her.

She opened the door to the guest room and gasped as another flashback seized her.

Somewhere music was playing and the song was "April in Paris." That song always made her feel slightly nauseous, but now the sensation was multiplied many times over. She felt overwhelmed by panic and dread. It was as if someone's hands were on her, reaching up under her dress and pushing down into her panties. A child was sobbing, though faint and seemingly far away.

As suddenly as it had happened, the moment was over.

Kirby grabbed the door frame to steady herself. The room was empty and smelled musty, like any room that had been closed off and seldom used. It was also silent—no music, no man, no crying child.

Feeling as though her trembling knees might buckle, she sat on the chest at the foot of the bed in which her mother stored quilts and unused bedspreads. Her hands were shaking as well, and a cold sweat covered her face and body. She was panting as if she had been running and feared she would hyperventilate and faint.

Kirby leaned forward and buried her face in her hands. What was wrong with her? Was she going insane? Tears were hovering just behind her eyelids and she had to struggle not to cry. She had told herself that the other flashbacks were flukes and that she would never experience anything like that again. That they were panic attacks at the most.

That didn't explain the things she saw, felt, heard, and tasted. No panic attack she had ever heard described made the victim feel as if they were in the middle of a nightmare and in different surroundings.

"Are you having trouble finding the glue sticks?" Mallory called out as she came down the hall looking for Kirby. "Mom says they're in the closet on the shelf where she keeps all her crafts." When she entered the guest bedroom and saw Kirby, she rushed to her side. "Are you all right?"

"I'm fine," Kirby lied.

Mallory turned as if to call Jane, but Kirby grabbed her arm. "Don't call Mom! I don't want to worry her."

"What's wrong with you? You look as if you're about to pass out. Do you need to lie down on the bed?"

"No!" Kirby rubbed the dull ache in her forehead. "Why did you come looking for me?"

"We thought you must have gotten lost. You've had more than enough time to get the glue and come back."

Kirby felt the panic rising. She thought she had been in the room only a couple of seconds at the most. On unsteady legs she went to the closet and found the glue sticks in plain sight along with Jane's other crafts and odds and ends.

"You're going to the doctor and that's all there is to it," Mallory said flatly. "Look in the mirror."

Kirby gazed at her reflection. It was easy to see why Mallory was worried. She was not only pale, but her eyes seemed haunted and she was visibly quivering. "All right. I'll go to the doctor. But don't tell Mom. Promise?"

"I won't say a word to her if you really do go for a checkup. And tell him about your memory loss, too."

"That might be better suited to a different kind of doctor," Kirby said in an effort to lighten the moment.

"I'm not joking, Kirby."

Kirby looked into the mirror again, but this time the reflection of a Jenny Lind bed covered with a polished cotton bedspread caught her attention. She turned to see it better. The spread was a floral design in blue, pale green, and white. Beside the bed was an antique end table with a bowl of Jane's favorite potpourri, a blend of carnations and roses. "Mal, did anyone ever sleep in this room when we were little?"

"In here? No, this was always the guest room." Mallory looked around. "When we had company they slept here, but no one lived in here. Mom never used it at all until a few years ago when she became interested in crafts. Even now, she only stores things in the closet. Why do you ask?"

"I don't know. I was only wondering." The urge to run out of the room was strong and it took all her willpower to walk calmly with Mallory into the hall and shut the door behind them. It seemed to take forever for the two of them to get back into the den.

"There you are," Jane said with relief. "I was about to come looking for both of you."

"I just had trouble finding the glue sticks," Kirby said lamely.

"You did? But I always put everything in its place. Has someone been into my closet?"

"No, Mom. Kirby was just looking in the wrong place," Mallory said quickly. "The glue was right where it should have been."

Kirby sat down and started gluing the dried flowers to the stack of place cards Mallory had printed in her absence, pretending nothing unusual had happened and trying not to think about the room down the hall.

* * *

Jane passed the bowl of sweet potatoes to Addison and waited to speak until he had served himself. "The girls were over today. We finished most of the place cards for the party. They're on the card table there in the corner."

"Good." He reached for a dinner roll.

"Would you pass the potatoes back, please?"

Addison nudged the bowl a little closer to her.

"I think the cards turned out quite nicely." Jane hoped he'd at least look at them. It was too much to expect him to compliment her. He took notice of nothing but his food. "How was your day, dear?"

"Same as always." He sighed as if he would rather be anywhere other than within conversational distance with her.

"Mine was busy."

"You already said that."

Jane ate in silence, a silence marred only by the faint click of sterling silver against fine china. If she didn't make conversation, Addison would eat every meal without saying a word, then retreat behind his newspaper until time for whatever television show he wanted to watch. He didn't even talk to her as they were preparing for bed and hadn't for years. Jane had the burden of carrying on any communication between them.

"I hope I haven't left any names off the guest list."

Addison fixed his accusing steel gray eyes on her. Jane looked down at her plate. "You aren't sure?" he asked.

"Of course I am. I'm sure I couldn't have missed anyone," she added quickly. "I went over the list several times. Every one is there."

"Good. Don't screw up."

"I won't," she said in a contrite voice. "I never do. Not when it's something as important as this."

He grunted and continued eating.

"Mallory and Kirby are so much help. I would never have had time to do all the place cards myself. Not and do such a nice job. Would you like to see them after dinner?"

"Not really. I've seen place cards before."

"But this is such an important dinner, I thought—"

"Jane, do we have to go on and on about something as trivial as place cards? I've had a hard week. The court dockets are overflowing, and I'm going to have my hands full next week as well. I don't want to talk about place cards."

"All right, Addison." Jane felt wounded. He never wanted to talk about anything that interested her. But then he never had. She knew not to upset him. Despite the public image he portrayed, Addison had a vicious temper. She and their daughters had always tried to avoid his rages. When she had once told her father about the rages, he had told her not to upset her husband. It was good advice and Jane tried to follow it, but she wasn't always sure what would provoke him.

The meal continued in unbroken silence. She found herself trying not to touch her fork to the plate in order to keep the quietness unbroken. The effort made her nervous. She longed to ask him how he had spent his Saturday, but Addison certainly wouldn't be pleased if she did. He maintained that, after working hard all week, what he chose to do on the weekends was his own business.

Jane wondered if he was having an affair. She was reasonably sure he had been involved with someone when the girls were small. He had shown all the signs. She had never found any proof that it was true, but she knew something had been going on with Addison during those years. Since then, he had behaved quite normally. So he probably wasn't seeing anyone. Maybe.

At times Jane was almost envious of women as young as her daughters. If they wanted a divorce, none of their peers would be shocked or think negatively toward them. It was more or less accepted these days among the younger generation. Not at all as it had been when Jane was their ages. Her parents would have disowned her and never spoken to her again.

There were times she still thought how nice it would be to have her house all to herself.

Jane glanced at Addison. Fortunately he never tried to guess what she was thinking. He seemed to take it for granted that she didn't think at all. It was to be expected, she supposed, since he was so much smarter than she was, but all the same, it would have been nice if he had ever asked what she was thinking. At least it would have been if he'd asked at a time when she wasn't thinking how pleasant it would be to be divorced from him.

Addison wasn't a bad husband. She often told herself that. He never had blatant affairs. He drank too much, but he never became staggering drunk. While he never went to church, he didn't object if she did. Her mother had pointed out all this to Jane the one time she had gone to her for advice after she and Addison had had an argument. Her mother had been certain of the fact that Jane was lucky to have a man like Addison. But there were times she wished she wasn't so lucky.

And he hadn't struck her in quite a while.

Addison finished his meal and laid his napkin on the table. Jane knew from long years of living with him that this meant the meal was over. She put her own napkin on the table beside her plate. Without a word, he stood and started in the direction of the den. As Jane cleared the table, she finished eating dinner. It was easier to do it this way than to explain why it took her longer to eat a meal than it did him.

The kitchen was the one room in the house that was most her own. Addison had never cooked a meal in his life, as far as she knew, and he almost never came in there. Jane washed the dishes by hand, taking her time. She had a dishwasher, but she seldom used it except on Sunday evenings when the whole clan was over for dinner. With only Addison and herself in the house, it was easier to wash the dishes than to load the dishwasher and unload it again when it was finished. She actually liked the feel of clean, wet china.

By the time her kitchen was spotless, Addison was engrossed in a movie. Retrieving the book she had been reading, Jane went upstairs, once again to be alone.

What were marriages supposed to be like these days? Jane knew from her magazine articles that with young couples, each partner was expected to share the chores and contribute to the income. But what about older couples?

At least these years weren't as turbulent as the earlier ones. Addison had mellowed to some extent. He had been very strict with the girls and her. That was how Jane always thought of it—strict. When the girls were growing up, Addison had frequently beaten them mercilessly. Jane had learned the hard way that they got hurt worse if she tried to go to their aid. Usually, Jane had ended up beaten as well.

She sat on the edge of the bed and stared at the wall. How many times had she sat in this very spot and hugged one daughter, trying to still her sobs, as the other screamed for Addison to stop hitting her? As always, the memory made her nauseous and guilty.

But what could she have done? Her parents would have told her to be obedient and return to her husband if Jane had taken the girls and left him. No one she knew went to marriage counseling back then, or therapy. Besides, Addison was the one who needed help, not her. Jane had never struck anyone in her life.

At times she forgot what her early marriage had been like. Remembering helped put things back into perspective. Addison was no longer an emotional time bomb that might explode without warning. Or at least not as often. Both girls had survived the beatings with no noticeable damage. They had husbands and children of their own now. Kirby was even a successful lawyer.

Jane thought for a minute about the difference it might have made if she had been able to get a job back then. A job that could have supported her and her children.

But that had been out of the question. Addison had always said Jane wasn't smart enough to work. Her father had told her no women in her family had ever held jobs and that it wasn't right for her to consider looking for one. Somehow it had seemed unfeminine.

Jane sighed and looked around the expensively furnished room. Her life would have been very different without Addison. Her daughters might not have married nearly so well without his counseling and suggestions.

It was foolish of her to have regrets after all these years. Foolish and rather ungrateful.

Putting the memories of her past behind her, Jane lay back on the pillows and started to read.

Chapter Ten

"I don't think I should be going to this party," Russell said for the third time.

"You didn't go to the dinner. Dad will think it's odd if you don't go to the house either."

"Kirby, I didn't go to the Republican Fund Raiser because I'm Democrat. It would have been stranger if I had gone."

"Dad understands that. But this is different." She looked in the mirror to inspect her makeup. She was still dressed in the black sequined dress she had worn to the fund raiser. Her high heels were uncomfortable and she wished she could change, but none of her other shoes would match the dress. "He's only asking a few people over. Just the men at Derrick's office, the mayor, the party members responsible for putting together the fund raiser, and the Stansfields."

"Sounds like the sort of party I try really hard to avoid. Is my collar straight in the back?"

Kirby straightened his collar and helped him on with his suit coat. "I particularly want you to meet Raymond Stansfield. He could be the next President of the United States."

"So could several other people."

"Russell, don't be like that. How could I possibly explain to Dad that you didn't want to come?"

"He already knows I'm as staunch a Democrat as he is a Republican. Are you sure he expects me at all?"

"Of course he does. All the family will be there. Except the children, of course." She stepped back to look at him. "You look great!"

Russell grimaced. "Kirby, it's nine o'clock at night. I really don't want to dress up and go anywhere."

"You're already dressed now. I'll go tell the boys we're leaving."

Soon they were in the car and heading to the Walker house. Kirby broke the silence by saying, "You won't feel it's necessary to announce that you're a Democrat, will you?"

"Do I ever embarrass you?" His voice was tense. He really didn't want to go.

"No. I just wanted to remind you."

"I'm not a fool, Kirby. I know who the guests are and how to behave."

"I didn't mean it like that. Look, if you're going to snap at me all evening, go back home and I'll go by myself."

"No, you insisted and I'm already dressed and in the car. I'm going with you."

Kirby stared out the window. "What's happened to us? I miss the way we used to be."

"You mean before you decided your job is the most important thing in your life and that you don't want me to touch you? I miss that, too."

"Sarcasm never solves anything."

"Thank you for correcting me yet again."

Kirby finished the ride in silence, glad to reach her parents' house and be able to relax, smile, and escape Russell. These days she found him easier to love when he wasn't around. She found her mother in the kitchen putting lady fingers and cream cheese sandwiches on a tray. "The dinner was beautiful! Everything went so well."

"I thought so, too. Your father said the roast beef was a bit on the dry side. Did it seem dry to you?"

"Not at all. And if it did, that was the cook's fault, not yours."

"I love parties at the Warwick," Jane said as she inspected the tray one last time. "Everything always runs so smoothly."

"Do you want me to carry that out for you? You don't want to spend every minute in the kitchen."

"This is the last tray." Jane handed it to Kirby. "Put it by the fruit bowl."

Kirby carried the tray to the dining table, which was laden with finger foods and two kinds of punch. Even though they had just eaten, several of the guests were gathered around the table. Addison motioned for her to join him. She instantly recognized the man and woman beside him.

"Kirby, this is Raymond and Virginia Stansfield," Addison said. "Ray, this is my eldest daughter, Kirby Garrett. She's an assistant district attorney these days."

Raymond shook Kirby's hand, then Virginia did the same. Kirby found she was almost shy in their presence. "I've heard so much about you from Dad, I feel I almost know you."

"We've been friends a long time." Raymond grinned at Addison. "We go back a long way."

"Are you here alone?" Addison asked.

"No, Russell is over there talking to Freddie Rae Powers and her husband."

Addison's smile slipped a notch as he located Russell. "Take care, Raymond. We've been invaded by Democrats."

"Oh?"

Kirby felt uneasy. Maybe Russell hadn't been invited after all.

Addison's smile was back in place. "Actually, only one and we have him surrounded."

"I'm surprised you have a Democrat in your family," Virginia said. "It must make for interesting visits."

"Russell rarely talks politics," Kirby said quickly.

"In-laws," Addison said with a laugh. "What can you do with them?"

Kirby was upset she had been placed in the position of having to defend Russell when they had just had another argument.

She regretted having brought him at all. Sometimes it was difficult to know what her father expected of her.

Virginia glanced at Russell. "Your husband is very hand-some. Do you have children?"

"Thank you. We have two boys, ages twelve and ten. We left them at home glued to the TV."

"I remember when our children were that age. They grow up so fast." Virginia sounded genuinely regretful that her son and daughter, both active in politics, were no longer small. "I enjoyed being a mother. Of course grandchildren are wonderful, but they aren't quite the same."

"I have a few years before my boys reach that age. I'm enjoying having them at home." She found she really liked Virginia. If they'd lived in the same town and if Kirby hadn't been so in awe of them, she and Virginia might have become friends, despite the fact that Virginia was Jane's contemporary.

"You're with the district attorney's office? I would have thought you would be in your father's law firm."

"I was for a long time. I decided it was time for a change," she said smoothly.

"Is your sister a lawyer, too?" she asked with a nod toward the opposite side of the room.

Kirby glanced in the direction Virginia had indicated and found Mallory accepting a drink from one of the male guests. By the brightness of Mallory's smile, Kirby guessed this wasn't her first drink of the evening. "No, Mallory never showed much interest in law. Her husband is head of the family's firm, however."

"So I was told."

Addison left Raymond talking to Trudy Harrison and made his way across the room to Russell. "May I talk to you for a moment?"

"Of course." Russell excused himself from the Powerses and followed Addison out the door that led to the rear patio.

"I was a bit surprised to see you here tonight."

"So am I." Russell didn't like Addison, and when they were alone, he made no pretense about it. "Kirby insisted that I come."

"I'm hoping you remember how important this gathering is. Raymond Stansfield may well be our next President."

"I'm aware he's running."

"I don't want anyone connected to my family saying or doing anything to upset him."

Russell stared at him. "Let me get this straight. You brought me out here to tell me not to do anything to embarrass you?"

"I wouldn't have put it so bluntly, but yes. I've worked hard to get where I am and nobody is going to screw it up for me."

"I'll keep that in mind." He was no longer able to speak congenially.

"That includes not drinking too much." He looked pointedly at the wineglass in Russell's hand.

Russell tossed the wine into the pool and handed the empty glass to Addison, his eyes daring the man to go any farther with this line of conversation. "I assume you'll also give the same instructions to Derrick? He's already had too much to drink and could use some of your advice. I don't need it or want it."

A vein pulsed in Addison's temple. Otherwise he seemed in perfect control. "I've never liked you, Russell."

"I've never liked you either, Mr. Walker. And you don't intimidate me."

Addison turned on his heels and went back inside. Although the night was chilly, Russell stayed on the patio. He considered going home and having Kirby call when she wanted him to pick her up, but Addison would view that as a victory for his side.

Russell walked to the edge of the lighted pool and looked in. Apparently Addison had been waiting until after the party to have it closed off for the winter and the water was clear and blue. He heard the patio door open behind him and hoped it wasn't Addison returning.

"It's pretty, isn't it? Even if it does look so cold."

He turned to see Mallory. She handed him one of the two glasses she had in her hands. "Thanks."

"I saw you out here all alone and thought I'd come talk to you." She strolled along the edge of the pool and Russell walked with her. "I hate these parties."

"So do I." Of all the Walker family, Russell was fondest of Mallory. "Your father just told me to mind my manners." She smiled and he saw a faint resemblance to Kirby.

"That always makes me want to do something really scandalous. Does it you?"

"Yes."

"You know, you and I are a lot alike." She gazed through the glass door. "It's a shame Derrick and I have so little in common these days. Look at him in there. You'd think it was his party."

Russell watched Derrick exchange a laugh with one of the prettier women in the room. He was obviously flirting, though Russell couldn't hear a word he was saying. "I've never thought you two were a perfect match."

"Well, I guess I'm stuck with him."

He turned to her. "There is such a thing as a divorce if you're that unhappy."

"Not in this family there isn't. Can you imagine what Dad would say if I told him I wanted to divorce Derrick? He would go into orbit!"

"If you're miserable living with him, you should do it anyway." He looked at Kirby, who was still talking animatedly to Virginia Stansfield. "Life is too short to spend it in unhappiness."

"Kirby loves you."

Russell chuckled, but with little mirth. "Right. Especially lately."

"She said you two have been having some problems."

"Who doesn't?" Russell couldn't imagine Kirby confiding in anyone, not even Mallory.

"You can work it out." Her words slurred slightly and she took another sip of wine. "I've always thought you two were a perfect match. Will you get me another glass of wine?"

"I will in a little while. I think you'd better let that one settle first."

Mallory put her fingertips to her lips. "I'm not acting drunk, am I? Tell me I don't look drunk."

"You don't." It was a small lie. "I just don't want Addison and Derrick to get angry with you."

She went to the diving board and sat down. "I don't want that, either." She patted the board beside her and he joined her. "I like you, Russell. You're just like a brother to me."

"I like you, too, Mal. Do you want me to get you a cup of coffee?"

"No, I'll be all right after I breathe some more of this fresh air." She took a deep breath. "I'm glad it's finally turning cool."

"Is there any way I can help you with Derrick?"

"No. We just don't like each other." She stared at the patio door. "Look at them in there. It's like we're watching them on TV with the sound turned low. They all seem to go together. Do you know what I mean?"

"Yes, I do."

"And we don't match them. You and me, I mean. Why is that?"

He shrugged. "Maybe they don't go with us. It could be the other way around. 'To thy ownself be true' and all that. You and I are a majority of one."

"I like that. Did you make that up?"

"No, Henry David Thoreau beat me to it."

"I remember studying about him in school. God, I haven't thought about school in years!" Her face grew sad. "Do you think I'm getting old, Russell? I think I'm getting old."

"I'm getting you some coffee. Stay here until I get back, and don't walk too close to the edge."

Mallory watched him go. It was such a shame, she thought, that Derrick wasn't like Russell. Kirby had always been the lucky one. She was intelligent and successful and had a husband who wasn't like Derrick. Lately Mallory had begun to think Kirby was their father's favorite, even though Mallory was positive she had been the favorite when they were children.

Mallory felt the tears coming and didn't try to stop them. She had always cried easily, and if it smeared her makeup, it didn't matter. Not when she was the least favorite of everyone and had to stay married to that bastard Derrick. She wallowed in self-pity until Russell returned with two cups of coffee.

"Thank you," she said as she took one. It was warm in her hands and she suddenly realized she was cold.

"You've been crying."

Mallory sniffed. "Only a little."

Russell took a clean handkerchief from his pocket. "Here. Your mascara is running."

Mallory dabbed at her eyes. "Is that better?"

"Here. Let me."

She turned up her face obediently. If only Derrick ever treated her so gently, if he showed her half the respect Russell did, she would love him forever. "I wish you had a brother I could run away with."

He laughed. "I wish you had a sister."

She giggled. "Silly! You're married to my sister already!"

"That's right," he said as if that fact had slipped his mind. "I feel better now. You always make me laugh."

"I wish Kirby laughed as easily. She used to, you know. We used to laugh all the time." He sipped his coffee. "Careful. It's really hot."

"You and Kirby are going to work it out. I can tell these things. I've got crystal balls." She giggled again.

"Drink your coffee," he said with a grin, feeling a little bit better.

Inside the house, Kirby was enjoying her conversation with Virginia. It was easy to see why this woman was being called "the darling of the press." She had an openness about her that cut through the tedium of obligatory small talk in a group brought together by a goal instead of friendship.

". . . and my daughter said, 'If that was your dog, you wouldn't want to put a ribbon on him either.'"

Kirby laughed. "That sounds like something my Cody would say." She felt a touch on her shoulder and turned to see Derrick. "Hello. Mrs. Stansfield was just telling me the funniest story."

"Call me Virginia, please."

Derrick forced a smile at Virginia, obviously not interested in hearing a funny story. "Kirby, I need to talk to you."

"Sure." He had been drinking heavily; his eyes were bloodshot and glassy. She was about to suggest they go into the kitchen when he interrupted her.

"What is your husband doing with my wife out by the pool?"

he demanded in a voice loud enough to be heard by everyone in the room.

"How should I know? I assume they're having a conversation." Kirby felt her cheeks getting hot and knew a blush was rising. Derrick was inferring that Russell couldn't be trusted with Mallory.

Virginia excused herself tactfully.

"That was really cute, Derrick," Kirby snapped. "What do you suppose Virginia thought about you saying such a thing?"

"Probably not as much as everyone thinks about Russell and Mallory carrying on like they are." His speech wasn't slurred but Derrick could drink an enormous amount and show little outward signs of inebriation. "They've been out there for nearly an hour!"

"So what? She's my sister and he's her brother-in-law."

"You're not that blind, are you? Mallory flirts with any male over twelve. I've watched her." He was only a few steps away from causing an angry scene.

"I'll go talk to them," Kirby said to placate him. She caught her mother's eye and motioned with her head. If anyone could get Derrick to sober up, it was Jane.

Jane stepped up to Derrick's side and immediately assessed the situation. "Will you come with me to the kitchen? There's something I need your help with."

Derrick glared at Kirby but he left with his mother-in-law.

Kirby made her way through the crowded room to the patio door and looked out. Russell and Mallory were out there, as Derrick had said, but they were only sitting on the diving board and talking. Both were drinking coffee so she knew Mallory must have had too much to drink, too. As she watched, Russell smiled at Mallory and said something that made her laugh. Jealousy sparked in Kirby. She had always been jealous of Mallory's popularity with men.

Even when they were girls, Mallory had been an accomplished flirt. She seemed to have been born knowing how to talk to men and keep their undivided attention. If Kirby hadn't loved her and been so protective of her, they might not still be so close.

Protective? Kirby turned the word over in her mind. What

had **Mallory** needed protection from? It struck her as an odd thing to think.

She went out to them and said, "Russell, I think it's time for us to go."

"Sit down, Kirby. Russell was telling me about the boys trying to train their puppy. I wish I could have seen it."

"I'm sure you will next time." Kirby noticed they were sitting closer than was necessary. Had she been foolish to be so trusting of Russell? "Let's leave, Russell."

"All right." He actually looked reluctant. This didn't help dispel Kirby's jealousy. "I'll see you in a few days, Mal."

" 'Bye." Mallory waved at him and wandered back toward the house.

Once Mallory was far enough away not to hear her, Kirby asked, "What were you two doing out here?"

"Talking," he said as if that was obvious. "What else would we be doing?"

"You were practically sitting in her lap. Derrick is pretty upset. He told me to come out here and get you away from his wife."

"For God's sake! She's my sister!"

"Your sister-in-law," Kirby corrected coldly. "I'm leaving. Are you coming with me?"

He gave her a long glare, then started for the gate.

Kirby frowned after him. She couldn't leave without telling her parents and the Stansfields goodbye. Lately Russell made everything so difficult for her.

She said her goodbyes as quickly as possible, not at all sure that Russell wouldn't drive away and leave her there. They only lived a couple of blocks away but it wasn't safe to walk alone after dark. Especially not dressed as she was, wearing high heels that were so difficult to walk in that running would be impossible.

Russell was waiting for her in the car, but he didn't speak when she got in. His rapid acceleration leaving the house jerked her head back. "Cute. I'm impressed," she said sarcastically.

"I don't know what's wrong with you lately, but you're turning into a Class A bitch."

"I am not! You were the one making a scene with my sister."

"Are you saying you actually think I was flirting with Mallory? Tell me the truth now!"

"How should I know what to think? For all I know, you may be flirting with every female student on campus. I have no idea if you can be trusted at all."

"I can't believe you're saying these things." Russell's voice was strained with anger.

"I can't help but wonder what Derrick saw you two doing that upset him so much. He almost caused an unpleasant scene."

"Derrick was drunk. He's always drunk."

"So was Mallory."

"Nothing happened between us that you or anyone else couldn't have heard. We were just talking. It was your idea for me to go to that damned party in the first place. And by the way, I was neither invited nor welcomed. Your father made that abundantly clear."

"That's nonsense." She stared stonily ahead.

"You think I'm lying? Call him and ask for yourself."

"I won't do any such thing."

"Maybe you could ask Derrick. You seem to take his word over mine. Maybe I should ask what you were doing talking to him."

"You're making a fool of yourself."

"I'm not the one that applies to. You were pretty foolish dragging me away from the party like that. Mallory must know that you suspected something."

Kirby knew this was true and she was embarrassed, though she certainly wasn't going to let Russell know. She knew she had overreacted but was in too far to back out. She retreated into cold silence.

"So now you aren't talking to me?" He pulled into their drive, turned off the engine, and glared at her through the darkness.

Kirby got out of the car and fished in her purse for her house keys as she walked. He got there first and opened the door. She brushed past him and went upstairs.

Russell had always hated getting the silent treatment and she knew it hurt him more than any argument could. She clamped her lips shut and refused to say a single word.

"Don't do this to me, Kirby," he warned. "Talk to me. Let's work this out."

She turned away from him and drew back the covers on her side of the bed.

"Shit!" he muttered. He grabbed up his pillow and the comforter from the foot of the bed and stalked out.

She could hear him downstairs, moving angrily about. After a while she heard him turn the TV on and knew he wouldn't be back upstairs until he was positive she was asleep. Most likely he would stay down there all night.

Kirby kicked off her high heels and struggled with her dress zipper until she freed herself from the dress. Of all the nights for him to start an argument. Tonight had been so important to her father and she hoped Russell hadn't ruined it. She refused to think that he could have been as innocent as he claimed. As often as he wanted to have sex, maybe she had hit a nerve in accusing him of flirting with Mallory and his students. Kirby was thoroughly miserable as she took off her makeup and got ready for bed.

"I've got just what you wanted," Bill Davies said as he tossed a folder of photos on her desk. "We caught him!"

She opened the folder to a series of photographs of Gary Chandler talking to a pretty little girl through the school yard fence, then luring her out the gate and into his car. The last photo showed the girl back out on the sidewalk, a dazed and frightened expression on her face. In the background was Chandler's car driving away. Davies' camera had caught it all.

"When she started to cry, I went up to her. She told me Chandler hurt her. Said he took pictures, too. I took her to her teacher. The principal called her mother and the police. Later we all went downtown and a couple of Gunderman's detectives took statements from all of us. The license plate number I gave them tagged Chandler and the description matched. The mother signed a complaint on the spot."

Kirby smiled and ruffled through the photos again. "Great work! Do you know if the little girl is willing to testify?"

He nodded. "So will her teacher. The teacher was so upset

she wanted to tear Chandler limb from limb. I got all the paperwork in this folder here. Names, addresses, etcetera.''

"Did they know you had Chandler under surveillance?"

"The CID guys know what I do for a living. But the others don't. And I didn't tell them anything about that. All they know is that I saw the girl get out of Chandler's car crying and went to see if she needed help. I figured I'd leave it up to you as to what you wanted to make public and what was to be between us.''

"You did an excellent job. Thank you. It will probably be better if we don't mention the surveillance before the trial. I don't want the defense or our liberal press or anyone trying to twist it into some sort of entrapment scheme. And the less time we give them, the better.''

Davies grinned and she noticed for the first time that he had a chip missing out of one of his front teeth. ''I'm glad to help get slime balls like Chandler off the street. I'll make a good witness in court, too, since I'm a retired cop. I'm looking forward to it.''

Kirby nodded. ''We both are.'' As soon as he left, she dialed Connie Chandler's work number.

Gary Chandler was arrested and charged with indecency with a child, a second-degree felony. His facade of being a well-mannered, mild-tempered good citizen vanished when he was locked in jail and had significant trouble posting bail. Kirby enjoyed his discomfort. Despite his protests that he was innocent and claims that his ex-wife had set him up out of spite, the grand jury indicted him two weeks later.

On the heels of his indictment for molesting the Brooks girl, Connie Chandler officially filed charges against him for raping his own daughter. Because of his standing in the community, Chandler's story was in all the Houston papers. The evening news interviewed two members of his church and a colleague at work. They all expressed doubts that he was even capable of doing something so terrible. But Connie Chandler and Evelyn Brooks were interviewed by a local radio talk show host and they were equally convincing of his guilt. Kirby was certain she could put him in prison for what he'd done to the Brooks girl and it could be for as much as twenty years.

"I know you want to handle this case," Zimmerman said to Kirby.

"Yes, I do. I want to see to it that this sonofabitch gets all that's coming to him!"

Zimmerman's brow furrowed. "One thing worries me. I'm afraid you've become too personally involved with this. What happened to your talent as a lawyer to distance yourself from cases you're working on? You have to remember that you weren't the little girl who was raped by her father."

Kirby shot him a quick look. "Of course I know it didn't happen to me! My father would never do such a thing!" She paced the width of his office and back again. "I can't believe you'd even suggest such a thing about my father!"

Zimmerman was watching her in surprise. "I didn't accuse Addison Walker of doing anything. Why are you getting so worked up?"

Kirby stopped and clasped her hands together. He was right. "I'm not worked up. I just know Dad wouldn't do such a thing."

"I'm sure you're right. I wasn't accusing him," he repeated. "I was cautioning you to remain objective. Maybe I should assign the Chandler case to someone else. I could take it myself. You have the Erickson murder coming up. Your hands are already full."

"No! No, it's important for me to see this all the way through."

"There's one other matter. If Bill Davies was there to take pictures of the Brooks girl being lured into Chandler's car, the defense will ask why he didn't put a stop to what he assumed was going on."

Kirby frowned as she thought. "He didn't know anything was happening that needed to have been stopped until later. He was hired to maintain surveillance. And that's what he did." Kirby had been so intent on getting evidence on Chandler that she hadn't instructed Davies to prevent Chandler from hurting another young girl. In retrospect, she wondered why it would have been necessary for her to have done so. Surely Davies had assumed Chandler wouldn't hurt the girl sitting in his car out front of the school. Although it would only have been circumstantial evidence for him to have lured the girl into his car and then release her unharmed, it would have helped prove his inclination toward being in private with little girls. She felt terrible that the Brooks girl had been molested, but now Chandler could be stopped and put behind bars.

"I know that. I'm only playing devil's advocate. It might damage our case."

"No, it won't. Chandler molested that girl and Davies not stopping him doesn't make it any less a crime."

"Unless the defense lawyer can turn this around as entrapment. Chandler has money. He'll hire the best, I'm sure."

"I've thought of that. I'm not worried." Kirby lifted her chin defiantly. "He committed a crime and he'll be punished for it."

Zimmerman leaned back in his chair. "I remember back when I first started this job, I had your confidence and optimism. It was an uncomfortable time and I'm glad I outgrew it."

Kirby smiled coolly. "I hope I never do."

He chuckled. "We'll see. We'll see."

Chapter Eleven

"You're working late again?" Mallory asked in frustration. "You've worked late every night this week."

"That's the way it is for those of us who have jobs."

"Cute, Derrick. You're the one who has always said that you don't want me to work."

"And you sure don't argue about it, do you? You like being kept."

Mallory glared at him. "If I were being kept, I'd have someone here to sleep with."

"Damn! Is sex all you ever think about?" he demanded as he slammed his briefcase shut. "You've got a one-track mind!"

"It probably seems that way because you never think of sex at all. You're no better than a goddamned eunuch!"

"Thank you, Mallory. I hope our daughter didn't hear that."

"If she did, she wouldn't know what the word meant. Besides, she's watching TV in her room." Mallory watched him put on his coat. "I had thought we might get the Christmas tree out of the attic and decorate it."

"I'll get it down tomorrow evening." He picked up the briefcase.

"You said that four days ago. Christmas will be past before we get any decorations up!"

"Then *you* crawl around up there and find everything yourself. You've turned into such a goddamned nag!"

"If I have, it's your fault. You never show me any consideration, Derrick!"

"I wonder why." He walked out of the house without saying goodbye. The door slammed behind him.

Mallory's eyes filled with tears and she pressed her fingers against her temples. The headache was building. She always got a headache when she fought with Derrick.

She went to the bathroom and took two aspirin. When she looked back at the doorway, Tara was standing there.

"Are we going to decorate the tree tonight?"

"I wish we were, honey, but Daddy has to work late after all. He promised we'll do it tomorrow. If he doesn't get the tree down when he comes home from work, I'll go up and get it myself."

"Okay."

Mallory hugged her daughter. She hated for Tara to be disappointed about anything. "I love you, honey."

Tara smiled and threw her arms around her mother's neck. "I love you, too, Mommy."

Even though she was too big to carry, Mallory lifted Tara and took her into her bedroom. "What's on TV?"

"It's a really neat show about Rudolph the Red-Nosed Reindeer. Not the cartoon one but a different one."

"Okay if I watch it with you?"

"Sure." Tara scooted over in the bed and Mallory sat next to her and leaned back against the headboard.

Although Mallory was watching the TV, her thoughts were elsewhere. Her body was aching for sexual release and she couldn't get the thought of making love out of her mind. At times it was as if her world revolved around the men she picked up at the Schooner or other places.

She considered calling Bob despite her decision not to see him again, but after a moment she decided against it. The last time she had been with Bob, he had asked her to move in with him and the red flag had gone up. She made it a rule not to see any man too often or too long so they wouldn't read more into the relationship than she intended. Mallory had as much permanence in her life as she could stand now. Because she never gave any of the men her last name or phone number, Bob wouldn't know where to find her.

Besides, she was leery of any man who would ask a woman he hardly knew to move in with him. Other than sex, they shared nothing at all.

"Look at this part, Mom!"

She turned her attention back to the show and laughed with Tara when Rudolph put his nose into a can and got it stuck on his head. "Have you seen this before?"

"No, Cody told me about it. He said it was on last week, too."

Mallory watched until the show was over. "That was a good one. Next time we'll tape it. It's bedtime for you, short stuff."

"Already?"

"I've let you stay up late as it is. Tomorrow is a school day. Remember?"

"I remember." Tara pushed her feet under the cover. "Will you tuck me in like you did when I was little?"

Mallory smiled and stroked Tara's dark hair back from her forehead. "Of course I will." She turned off the light and television and sat back down on the bed. "Go to sleep now. Angels and fairies will watch over you and bring you sweet dreams."

"Sing me the song about the little girl going to bed."

Mallory began to sing Brahms Lullaby in a soft voice. It had been Tara's favorite lullaby all her life. Knowing there wouldn't be many more times before Tara decided she was too old to hear lullabies put a lump in Mallory's throat.

Tara closed her eyes, a smile on her face. She pretended to be asleep by the time the song was finished. Mallory pretended to believe she was sleeping and made a show of tiptoeing out of the room.

Restlessly she ambled down the hall to her bedroom and sat on the edge of her bed. Tara was down for the night and she was alone as usual. For several minutes she stared at the telephone on her bedside table as the battle raged in her head. Unable to defeat the desire that begged to be satisfied but never was, she picked up the phone and dialed the number of the woman who babysat for Tara. "I know it's late, but could you come over tonight? I have somewhere I need to go. Tara is already asleep and Derrick is still at work." She held her breath waiting for an answer, then exhaled a sigh of relief. "Thank you, Mrs. Cotton. I don't know what I'd do without you." Within half an hour she was walking into the dimly lit interior of the Schooner.

Mallory threw a practiced glance around the room. Because it was late and a week night, the clientele was different. She had been reasonably sure Bob wouldn't be here because of the hour. She sat at a table near the dance floor where she would be easily seen and ordered a margarita.

In a few minutes, she caught the eye of a man seated at the bar. He was tall and darkly good looking, though not handsome. She gave him a hint of a smile and made eye contact a bit longer than a glance. He immediately took the bait and came to her table.

"Mind if I sit with you? The place is quiet tonight."

"Have a seat. You come here often?" She knew he didn't because this was almost her second home and she'd never seen this man before.

"Yes, I do. I haven't seen you in here. My name is Randy."

Mallory smiled sexily. "Are you? Randy?"

"All the time."

"My name is Desiree. Like *desire*, but with an extra *e.*" Sometimes Mallory made up a name, especially if she was pretty sure she would never want to see the man again. It made the game more exciting.

"It fits you." He lifted his glass of bourbon but continued to watch her over the rim. "You're one sexy woman."

She leaned forward and lowered her eyelashes. "And you're one sexy man." She knew the rules of this game very well. When it came to flirting, Mallory was a master.

"Do you live alone?" he asked.

"No, I have a roommate. How about you?"

"I have a house not far from here."

"You live all alone in a house?"

"It's allowed in my neighborhood," he said with a grin.

"I'd like to see it."

He paid for their drinks and they left together.

Mallory insisted on driving her car behind his. Once she had run into a problem when her date passed out and couldn't drive her back to her car. Since that night she provided for her own escape.

She followed him to a house in Bellaire and parked behind him in the drive. It was a small brick house and even in the dark she could see that the trim needed painting. She heard a dog bark in the backyard as if it had been roused from sleep by their arrival.

Randy let her into the house, and as was her habit, she quickly surveyed her surroundings. A lot could be learned about a person this way. "This doesn't look like a bachelor's place." She picked up a ruffled throw pillow in a floral design from the couch. There were feminine touches to the furnishings and decorating that a wife or at least a live-in girlfriend might make. "Randy, I don't think you quite told me the truth."

"She's visiting her folks in Mississippi all this week. Does it matter?"

Mallory tossed the pillow back onto the couch. "Not to me." She went to him and put her arms around his neck. "I have an idea. Let's act out my favorite fantasy."

"Okay. What is it?" He ran his hands over her as if he was eager to get started.

"In this fantasy, I'm a little girl. You teach me how to make love."

"Kinky!" he said in admiration. "Rosemary's never gotten into sexual fantasies."

Mallory smiled and on tiptoes gave him a quick kiss. "I'll sit on the couch and you find me here."

"Great!" Randy licked the lipstick she'd left on his lips as he backed away, watching her with growing excitement. "Sit down. I'll be right back."

Mallory went to the couch and sat on it cross-legged as a child would. She pulled her long hair over each shoulder and braided it into two long pigtails. This was her favorite fantasy. It never failed to bring her to the brink of satisfaction. She would never have dreamed of asking Derrick to do it. This fantasy made her too vulnerable.

Randy came around the corner and reacted as if he were

surprised to discover her there. "Hello, Desiree. Were you a good girl today?"

Mallory nodded and looked up at him with a sweet, innocent smile on her face. "Yes, Daddy."

He sat beside her and put his hand on her bare knee. "I have a new game I'd like to teach you."

"Is it a fun game?" she asked. Her heart was racing as Randy drew his hand up under her skirt.

"It sure is. Would you like to play with me?"

"If you want me to, Daddy." She nodded earnestly.

Randy's fingertips grazed the crotch of her panties. Mallory pretended to pull away shyly.

"No, in this game, you sit very still while I make you feel good."

"Okay." She spread her legs wider apart. "Like this?"

"Exactly like this." He touched her with more confidence. "What a good girl you are!"

Mallory lay her head back against the couch and enjoyed his touch. One reason she loved this fantasy was because it relieved her of all responsibility. All she had to do was behave as she was told.

Randy unzipped his trousers and Mallory pretended to be surprised to see he was made differently from her. She touched him in a way she knew would excite him. Since this was her fantasy and she didn't know if he shared her tastes, it was important for him to get a great deal of enjoyment from her actions.

When he finally told her to stand up and slip off her panties, she did as she was told and lay back on the couch, her legs spread. Randy didn't bother to remove her dress. He dropped his pants to the floor and came into her. Mallory closed her eyes and forced herself to stay in the fantasy, not to let her mind perceive reality until she reached a climax.

Randy dropped all pretense of the fantasy and started making vigorous love to her. Mallory almost lost her concentration on pretending that this was her first time. And that was important. She ignored him and let herself feel only the sensations of him inside her. It was so close to the illusive key that she sought, she found herself drawing nearer and nearer.

Suddenly she cried out as much in surprise as in satisfaction. She had reached a climax! It had actually happened! Mallory was so relieved she felt tears sting her eyes. She held desperately to the welcome release, not wanting to miss a second of it. Randy groaned and thrust into her one last time.

He held her close and Mallory hugged him as if she would never let him go. Her breathing gradually slowed and her heartbeat matched that pace, finally returning to normal. She had climaxed! She wanted to thank him and to ask him to do it again, but she was afraid of ruining the experience with a failure.

When he pushed away from her and sat up, she pulled on her panties and stood to go.

"Where are you going?"

"It's late. I'm going home."

"My wife is out of town. You can sleep here."

"My roommate would worry. I have to go home."

"At least tell me your last name and your phone number. Whenever Rosemary is gone, we can get together."

Mallory went to the door and looked back at him. "My name is Desiree Duncan. I'm in the phone book. 'Bye." She stepped out into the night.

Gary Chandler's trial for the sexual molestation of Glenda Brooks started the first week in January and Kirby found it dominating her interest to the exclusion of everything else. She had other cases in various stages of preparation before going to court and she tried to keep her mind on them, but everything paled by comparison to her effort to prove Chandler's guilt.

Chandler had chosen Milton Boone to represent him, a man whose reputation as a successful criminal trial attorney was well known in Houston. It was also known that Boone wasn't above fighting dirty. Winning was everything with him. If Kirby had been less determined, he might have intimidated her.

As she had anticipated, Boone petitioned the court to dismiss the case due to entrapment. The judge, however, ruled that although it was unusual for a prosecuting attorney to hire a private investigator with his own money to help collect evidence, no evidence was presented that the private investigator had by his actions done anything that could be construed as entrapment.

The testimony necessary for the judge to rule on the defense request took most of the afternoon, so the judge recessed the trial until the next morning at nine.

Kirby, along with Evelyn Brooks and her daughter Glenda, remained standing until the judge was gone from the courtroom. "We won that one," she said to Mrs. Brooks with relief. "Boone knew there was no entrapment involved, but tried to get the case thrown out anyway. I expected as much. The man has no ethics."

Connie Chandler, who had been watching the proceedings, waited until Evelyn Brooks and her daughter left before approaching Kirby. "I'm sorry that the little Brooks girl is going to have to testify, but selfishly, I'm glad it isn't Kayla. She's so withdrawn these days. I can barely get her to talk even at home. She just sits in front of the TV or in her room. She doesn't do anything, just sits there."

"Have you started her in therapy yet?"

"No, not yet. When all this started, Gary stopped sending the child support checks and I can't afford counseling on my salary. You told me not to contact him so I can't call and demand that he send the money he owes us." She glared across the room to where her former husband was talking to his lawyer. "Why should he? He's already been arrested."

"I'll mention this to his attorney. He can't use this as an excuse to stop paying court-ordered child support. His lawyer probably doesn't know he's doing it. Boone will want him to appear to be as upright and as honest as possible and being a deadbeat husband doesn't fit that image."

"I hope you're right. We've had a big drop in our standard of living since the divorce. And Gary is still living in that big house and bringing in his salary just as if nothing has happened!" Connie was rightfully angry and bitter because of the injustice.

"I don't expect he will be living there much longer. Huntsville prison is bigger but it's certainly not as comfortable."

Connie smiled for the first time. "I'm so glad we found you.

I was awfully afraid to talk to anyone about what happened to Kayla. I didn't want people to point at her and make cruel remarks. She's been through enough already. If it hadn't been for you, he might have continued hurting innocent little girls for who knows how long."

"You know that even if we get a conviction, and I expect we will, we still won't be able to prosecute him for assaulting Kayla because nothing about this case could be introduced as evidence. Nevertheless, during the punishment phase of this trial, I intend to mention that you filed a complaint alleging that he raped his daughter. The judge may have the statement stricken from the trial record and instruct the jurors to disregard it, but the jury will have heard it and it may help them decide on the maximum prison term of twenty years. Even if we'd been able to get him convicted for what he did to Kayla, the maximum sentence wouldn't have been any longer."

"Incidentally," Connie said, "I looked around for more evidence like you told me, and sure enough, I found some magazines in the storage space behind the garage." She looked embarrassed. "More porn."

"As I said before, it's not necessarily illegal. If it could be sold in a store, it's not condemning enough."

"Well," Connie said doubtfully, "I'm not sure this came from a store. Not a regular one, I mean. The paper was real cheap, and it didn't have one of those slick, professional covers."

"Oh?"

Connie seemed reluctant to talk about it. "The pictures were all of children."

Kirby did a double-take. "Children? Are you talking kiddie porn here?"

"I guess that's what it's called."

"You still have it, don't you? You didn't throw it away?"

"I know better than that. Is this what we needed to cement the case against Gary?"

"It sure won't hurt." Kirby's mind was racing. Gary Chandler being into kiddie porn might be enough to get a conviction against him, especially if the porn was a local product. There had been some speculation at the office about such a ring

operating in Houston, but no one had proof. "Bring me the **magazines**, Mrs. Chandler. I'll see what I can do."

"I really appreciate you going out of your way to help me **and** Kayla. I'm not sure everyone would believe me."

"I believe you."

"Thanks again for what you're doing," Connie said with a **tear** forming in her eye. "I'd better run. I may be able to get **home** before the baby-sitter goes into another hour. If it's more **than** five minutes or so, she charges me for the entire hour."

"Tell Kayla hello for me."

After Connie had left, Kirby returned to her office and called **home.** "Russell, I'm going to be late. There's a casserole in **the** refrigerator. All you have to do is put it in the microwave **for** ten minutes."

Russell sounded irritated. "I'm learning to cook really well **these** days. Do you ever intend to eat with us again?"

"Don't start in on me. I've had a really rough day."

"So have I."

Kirby sighed. "We can talk about it when I come home. Let **me** get to work so I can leave here at a decent hour. Okay?"

"Sure. Why not." He hung up.

She held the receiver for a few seconds, then hung up. He **wasn't** going to be reasonable. Why hurry home to another **argument?**

She opened the folder in front of her and started reviewing **its** contents.

Several hours later, she drove home, dreading the argument **that** was certain to be waiting for her. This time, she decided, **she** would try a different approach.

"Russell? I'm home," she called as she went in through the **kitchen** door.

"You're early. It's not midnight yet."

"Are the boys in bed?"

"Of course. This is a school night. I don't let them stay up **until** all hours like you do."

Kirby refused to be goaded. "I've missed you." She saw **surprise** register on his face. She stepped nearer and put her **arms** around him.

After a hesitation, Russell embraced her. "I've missed you,

too." His voice sounded wary, as if he was wondering what she was up to. "Coming home to Ellen isn't the same. I think she's starting to wonder if you still live here."

"Could we just go to bed?"

"You never go to sleep this early."

"I'm not sleepy." She smiled up at him.

Slowly he grinned. "Bed it is."

Hand in hand they went through the house, checking locks and turning out the lights as they had when they were newly-weds. Kirby discovered she really had missed being with him. When they weren't fighting, she could tell how much she loved him.

Arm in arm they climbed the stairs, and when they were in their room, Russell kissed her. Kirby returned the kiss and held him close. "I really have missed this," she whispered to him. "At times I don't know what gets into me. I get all caught up in the things I have to do and it's as if I forget who we are. Who I am. Does that make sense?"

"Yes. You're a workaholic."

"I try not to be."

"Let's not talk about that now." He kissed her again.

Kirby began unbuttoning Russell's shirt and kissing his skin as she exposed it. He reciprocated in kind. "I like the way you smell," she said as she rubbed the tip of her nose over his chest. "You smell like soap and sunshine."

"I love you, Kirby. I can't tell you how much I want you."

She loosened her skirt and stepped out of it. "Come to bed. I want you to hold me and make me forget there's a world outside this room."

"I can do that." Russell finished undressing and left his clothes mingled with hers on the bedroom floor.

Kirby pulled back the bed covers, and as they crawled into the bed and snuggled against each other, she tried to remember how long it had been since they had held each other naked in the night. Usually she was wearing a nightgown. Russell began making love to her, touching her in all the places she liked best and moving at the slow pace that had always excited her in the past.

Kirby felt her desire growing. She wanted to make love with

him. When it was good like this between them, she wondered why she didn't want to make love all the time. Russell was a superb lover and he made her body sing.

When she was at a fever pitch from wanting him, Russell entered her and they moved together at a tempo that drove her gradually and steadily to greater ecstasy.

Suddenly she panicked. It wasn't Russell that was making love to her; it was a man who hurt her rather than pleased her. Kirby shoved against him. She felt as if she were suffocating under his weight. She couldn't breathe! It was as if he was smothering her! Raping her! She cried out in fright and fought to free herself.

Russell rolled away.

Kirby scooted opposite him and sat up on her side of the bed, her arms wrapped around her body, trembling in terror. What had happened? How could she possibly have a memory of something like that? Nothing even remotely resembling that had ever happened to her! If she had been raped, she would certainly have remembered it!

"What happened this time?" Russell asked from his side of the bed, his voice tight and barely controlled. He made no move to touch her.

"I don't know." She wanted to reach out to him and try to explain what had happened, but she didn't understand it herself. She wasn't even certain she could find the words to tell him what she had seen in her mind. "I don't know," she repeated miserably.

Russell got up and went into his closet. When he came back out, he was wearing his robe. He reached for his pillow.

"Aren't you coming back to bed?"

"No. I'm not wanted or needed here." He stared at her through the semidarkness. "I don't know what's wrong with you, Kirby, but this isn't working."

"I tried! I really did!"

"I don't want my wife to have to go to such effort to let me touch her. Can't you see what that would do to anyone? What if I had to force myself to let you touch me? It would hurt you, too."

"I wasn't forcing myself. I wasn't! It's just that something happened." She gazed up at him, willing him to understand. "Please don't sleep downstairs, Russell."

He stood there in silence for several long minutes. "I'm thinking of moving out."

"You want to leave me?" Kirby's mouth dropped open. It had never occurred to her that he would do that.

"I'm talking about a trial separation. Not a divorce. I need to be alone. I need to think."

"What can you think about somewhere else that you can't think about here?" Panic was spiraling upward within her. She didn't want to lose Russell! "Don't leave me!"

"I think it's for the best."

"But where will you go?"

"There's an apartment complex over on Old Spanish Trail that's got a vacancy and is close to the university. I'll go there."

"You've been looking for apartments?" Her world was slipping askew and she had to struggle to make sense of what he was saying. "You're moving to an apartment?"

"I'm not filing for a divorce," he repeated in that same dull voice that frightened her because of its lack of warmth. "I just need to make some decisions. You do, too."

"Have you told the boys? How can I explain this to them?"

"I imagine they more or less expect it. Josh asked me several days ago if we were about to split up."

"You never told me that!"

"When have I seen you?"

Kirby was stunned. She couldn't believe any of this was happening. "Don't go, Russell."

He looked as if he was considering staying, but shook his head. "I think I have to. We can't go on like we've been. It's not good for the boys or for us. They deserve a better life. If I'm not here, you'll be home more often and they need that. Especially Josh. He really misses you."

Kirby stared at him, her mind spinning wildly. She would have said that was more true of Cody than Josh. With a sinking feeling she realized she hadn't talked to either of her sons much lately. She had been so caught up in her work, she hadn't realized that. "I'll change. Stay here and give me a chance to prove to you that it will be different."

"I'm not doing this to punish you. I'm not sure I want to be here anymore. I don't want you to have to force yourself to be with me or to show me more attention. Don't you see? If it isn't what you want yourself, I don't want it from you."

"When are you leaving?"

"Tomorrow. I'll call my substitute and have him take my classes. I don't want to move my things out while the boys are here. I won't leave tomorrow afternoon without telling them goodbye. Where will you be tomorrow?"

"I have to be in court." She saw the wry expression on his face. "Damn it! It's true! I can't take off tomorrow with no more warning than this. I'm to be in the judge's chambers at nine o'clock!"

"I'll be gone when you get off work. I suggest you come straight home. The boys will need you, not Ellen." He turned and walked out of the room.

Kirby stared after him. She found it difficult to believe the conversation they'd just finished had taken place at all, and that Russell actually meant to leave her. He even had a place already picked out to go to!

She doubled up her fist and struck her pillow. Tears burned her eyes and she couldn't stem them. She muffled her sobs in her pillow. The last thing she wanted was for Russell to think he had to come back upstairs and comfort her. On the other hand, there was nothing she wanted more.

She continued to sob, but Russell didn't come.

Chapter Twelve

For the first time in years, Kirby left work early. She had been upset all day over Russell's threat to leave. By the time the judge recessed the proceedings for the day, she had managed to convince herself that Russell had been speaking in anger the night before and that he didn't really intend to go. They were in love. People who were in love didn't leave each other.

When she pulled into her driveway, she noticed his car was not there. Her stomach muscles tightened as if in preparation to be kicked and she felt sick all over. Still, she denied that he might move out. He was late at work. He had stopped by the grocery store. There were many reasons why his car wasn't in the drive.

The moment she stepped into the house, her denial was destroyed.

"You made him leave, didn't you!" Josh shouted when he saw her. "It's all your fault!"

She saw Ellen slide unobtrusively into the other room to distance herself from the unpleasant scene. Kirby wished she could avoid it, too.

She put down her briefcase. Josh was glaring at her as if he wanted to throw something at her. Cody was curled in a chair, his eyes wide and frightened. "Where is your father?"

"He's gone. He said you knew all about it." Josh came

nearer and she saw he was fighting back his tears. "He said he was moving out and that you would explain when you came home."

Kirby looked from one boy to the other. "He didn't tell you why he was leaving or where he was going?"

"He said you two decided it would be best to live apart for a while. A trial separation. What the hell does that mean, Mom!"

She didn't correct his language. She felt like using stronger words herself. "So he did tell you why he was moving out." She tried to keep her voice calm. She tried to put her arm around Josh's shoulder but he pulled away. "We thought it would be for the best."

"Why! Why would that be for our best?" Josh shouted.

"Josh, stop yelling!" She struggled to regain her poise. "You aren't the center of the universe. He didn't leave you boys, he left me."

Josh gave Cody an I-told-you-so look. Cody lowered his eyes and stared at the arm of the chair as he picked at the design. "What did you do to him, Mom?"

"I didn't do anything." Kirby was finding it hard not to be as angry as her son. "This isn't easy on me either."

"Yeah. Right." Josh paced to the window and back. "Where did Dad go?"

"He said he's found an apartment over on OST. Close to the university."

"Call him up and tell him to come back."

"Josh, it's not that easy." She went to Cody and put her arm around him as she sat on the arm of his chair. He made a halfhearted effort to shrug it off but failed and didn't try again. "I didn't know he had found an apartment until last night. I didn't even know he was looking for one."

"You're not going to blame this on Dad!" Josh stormed. "You're not going to turn us against him!"

"I'm not trying to. I'm only trying to explain to you what happened. We've been arguing a lot lately. I know you boys have noticed it."

"Everybody argues," Cody muttered.

"I know. But we weren't making up between arguments anymore. Your dad and I still love each other, but he felt it would be best if we spend some time apart." She wondered how she was managing to sound so calm when her heart was breaking. She loved Russell, but she wasn't at all sure now if it was reciprocated. "Sometimes married couples need space between them for a while."

"When will the divorce be final?" Josh demanded.

"We aren't asking for a divorce. This is only a separation."

"How do you know for sure?" Cody asked. "You said you didn't know he was looking for an apartment. Maybe he's getting a divorce, too."

"Shut up, Cody!" Josh shouted.

Kirby rumpled her youngest son's hair. He had always been the most logical of the two. "I have to believe him." To Josh she said, "I'm upset, too."

"You sure sound it!" His sarcasm was evident.

"Josh, that's enough! I know you're hurting, but so am I and so is Cody. You're only making it worse."

"Not me! I'm not the one who chased Dad away!"

"Neither did I!" What composure she'd had was slipping away.

"I guess now you and Dad will start dating other people like Brice's parents did!"

"The Mathisons were getting a divorce. I'm not going to date anyone." It tore into her that she didn't know if Russell would or not. If they were separated, he might not feel bound to keep his wedding vows. "Your dad isn't seeing anyone either," she added, hoping it was true.

"How do you know?" Cody asked. His gray eyes were troubled and filled with hurt as he looked up at her.

"Let's just take one day at a time. Okay?"

Cody jumped from the chair and ran from the room. She heard him clattering up the stairs and racing down the hall to his room. The slamming of his door resounded through the house.

"See what you've done?" Josh demanded. "I hope you're satisfied!"

"Stop it, Josh! I'm still your mother and I won't allow you to talk to me like this. If you want to be mad at someone, be mad at your father. He's the one who moved out, not me!"

Josh stared at her with hatred distorting his features, then turned and ran in the same direction Cody had taken.

Kirby heard his door slam even harder than Cody's. She sat where Cody had been and buried her face in her hands. Russell had left. He had actually gone. The tears came and she almost choked on her sobs. Sorrow, hurt, and anger shook her body. The phone rang, startling her, but she didn't want to answer it. Ellen would get it on the kitchen extension. Then she thought it might be Russell and ran, catching it on the third ring. "Hello?"

"Kirby? Is that you?" Mallory asked.

"God, Mal. Can you come over?"

"Sure. What's wrong? You're scaring me."

"Russell has left me." Kirby's voice broke and a sob escaped her. "Please come, Mal."

"I'm on my way."

Ellen came to the door and paused there self-consciously. "I'm through for the day, Mrs. Garrett. I'll be leaving now."

Kirby wrote her a check and asked her to leave the kitchen door unlocked for Mallory. She headed for the den and leaned back on the sofa cushions, suddenly exhausted and too upset to care about safety. She wished she, too, could escape this nightmare by simply leaving the house. In a few minutes she heard Mallory call out for her from the kitchen. "I'm in here."

Mallory rushed into the den and knelt beside Kirby's chair. "What happened? I had no idea things were this serious between you."

"Join the club. Neither did I."

"You mean he didn't give you any warning? He just left?"

"Last night he wanted to make love. I tried. I really did! But something went wrong." She rubbed her forehead. Everything seemed so unreal. "He got mad. No, that's not really true. He became very, very quiet. He said he had found an apartment over on Old Spanish Trail and that he was moving out. Just like that."

"He actually found an apartment and rented it without telling you? That's really rotten!"

It hadn't occurred to Kirby that Russell would have had to rent the apartment in advance for him to be able to move into it on such short notice. "I guess he did. I don't know, Mal. I can't seem to think straight."

"How are the boys taking it?"

"Cody is hurt and Josh is furious. Russell left before I got home and they had plenty of time to work themselves up."

"I'll go up and talk to them."

"Thanks. Right now they consider me the enemy."

"Shit," Mallory muttered as she headed for the stairs.

Kirby remained where she was. Would it be possible to just sit here forever and not have to take any actions or make any decisions? She wondered if Russell had been seeing someone behind her back. Maybe he hadn't moved into an empty apartment at all. The tears returned.

After a long time, Mallory came back downstairs. "I talked to both of them. Josh is really mad but I told him it's not all your fault. That it takes two people to argue."

"I'm going to have problems with him. I can see it coming. You didn't hear how he was talking to me."

"He didn't pull any punches with me either. I think he probably repeated it all to me upstairs. Cody seems lost. He had been crying." She reached out and touched Kirby's knee. "I don't remember the last time I saw you cry."

"I don't either."

"Is there any way I can get in touch with Russell? Maybe I can talk to him and get him to come back to you."

"Thanks, but I don't know exactly where he is. There are apartment complexes all along OST."

"I know." Mallory bit her lip in concern. "I'm not going to leave you alone. How about if Tara and I come over for a few days? Maybe by then Russell will come to his senses and decide to move back."

"I don't know if he'll ever come back. He didn't move out on a whim. He'd already arranged for a place to go." She looked at Mallory. "What if he's moved in with a woman?"

"Russell wouldn't do that," Mallory said quickly. "Not Russell."

"Why not? He's a man." Kirby heard the bitterness in her voice as if it were coming from someone else. "You know what men are like."

"You're just hurt." Mallory started for the phone. "I'm going to call Mom. She can watch Tara this afternoon and give things time to settle down here."

"I don't want Mom to know."

"Kirby, Mom has to know you and Russell are separated. She has to be told!"

"She'll tell Dad. You know she will."

"I know, but it's not something you can keep from him."

"He's going to be so upset!" Kirby chewed her finger as she had when she was a child. "I don't want Dad to know."

"Okay. It can wait until tomorrow. Maybe it'll resolve itself by then and they'll never have to know. Tara will be all right by herself for a while. I'll call and tell her to come over here if she gets lonely."

Kirby nodded, too miserable even to think. She was glad to have Mallory around and taking care of things.

By the middle of February Gary Chandler's trial was drawing to an end. Kirby wasn't sure how she was staying sane. Russell hadn't come home and Josh hadn't forgiven her. Prosecuting Chandler and ensuring that he was put in prison for what he'd done to Glenda Brooks had become an obsession with her. Between her anger at Russell and her anger at Chandler, she had no trouble keeping her adrenaline flowing to combat her mounting fatigue. Her closing argument reiterating the proof of Chandler's guilt, beyond the shadow of a doubt, couldn't have been more compelling if she, herself, had been the victim of Chandler's villainy.

After only two hours' deliberation, the jury found him guilty as charged. His attorney immediately filed an appeal but Kirby was confident the verdict would stand. They had won.

Evelyn Brooks and Connie Chandler both hugged her and cried with relief on her shoulder. Kirby embraced them in return, embarrassed that she felt near tears herself. Now that a guilty verdict had been rendered, the exhaustion Kirby had held at bay came crashing in. This trial had taken more out of her than any defense work she'd ever done.

Back at the office, Zimmerman gave Kirby a long look as he congratulated her on the conviction. "Are you all right?"

"No, I'm not. I wish I could go to sleep and not wake up for a month."

"I suggest you do that. Take some time off."

"I can't take time off. I've only worked here a few months."

"I'll authorize the advancement of some sick leave."

"I have a case load, Leon. I have other people depending on me."

"Have you heard from Russell?"

"Sure. He calls the boys and comes to see them. He's taken them to his apartment for the weekend a couple of times."

"But he's not talking about coming home?"

Kirby shook her head. She was so tired she didn't even hurt anymore. "He's civil to me when I answer his phone calls, but he picks the boys up before I come home and drops them off out front. I've seen very little of him."

"Do you know where he lives?"

"Cody told me." She remembered how angry Josh had been over Cody revealing even this much about Russell to her. Since his dad had been gone, Josh seldom had been civil to her.

"So is he filing for a divorce?"

"Apparently not. I assume I'll be the last to know. Unless he tells Cody, I may not get the word until the papers are served. Josh isn't passing along any information." At least she knew Russell wasn't living with another woman. Both the boys would have mentioned that.

"That's rough." Zimmerman poured himself another of the many cups of coffee he drank every day. "I'm putting you on sick leave as of tomorrow. Take at least a week off." He paused. "It wouldn't hurt you to go out. Have some fun."

She shook her head. "All I want to do is sleep."

For the next three days, Kirby stayed in bed while her boys were in school. Sleep, however, eluded her. She couldn't sleep in the bed she had shared with Russell all those years knowing he wouldn't be there with her that night. On those rare occasions day or night when she did drift into sleep, she was plagued by nightmares.

Her mother came over daily and brought food even when

Kirby told her not to bother. Her father's disapproval over her separation from Russell was obvious by his absence.

"Dad isn't going to forgive me, is he?" she asked her mother.

Jane avoided her eyes. "Of course he will. Russell's leaving just surprised him. That's all."

"He never liked Russell. I'm surprised he's not elated."

"Addison is against divorce. You know that." Jane added, "He doesn't actually dislike Russell. Not really."

"Yes, he does. He's never made that a secret." Kirby pushed the Chinese chicken salad her mother had prepared around on her plate. She was wrapped in her terry cloth robe and hadn't bothered to put on makeup all day.

"It's just that this has come at an inconvenient time. That's all." Jane tasted her tea and added a spoonful of sugar.

"What do you mean?"

"Addison says with the election coming soon, he doesn't want any negative publicity right now."

"That's right. I'd forgotten that he'll have to run for election to keep the judgeship he was appointed to. I wouldn't think my relationship with Russell would have any effect on that. I mean, he is the incumbent."

"Actually, I think it's some sort of appointment he has his sights set on. He hasn't told me his plans, but I know it's important from the way he's acting."

"Mom, have you ever considered asking him? I mean, it's your life, too, you know."

"He will tell me when he wants me to know. Eat your food. You're going to be sick for sure at this rate."

"I think I already am. I have a doctor's appointment for this afternoon."

"Do you want me to watch the boys?"

Kirby smiled faintly. "They can look after themselves. They seem to think they're grown these days." She looked curiously at her mother. "I still don't understand why my separation from Russell would have any effect on Dad getting some appointment. It's not like he's running for President."

"No, of course it's not that. My goodness, he's working so hard to have Raymond Stansfield elected! My guess is that he has his eye on the Texas Supreme Court."

"That would be great! But that's an elected position, too, not an appointment. Unless, of course, there were a vacancy to be filled between elections, which there isn't, unless I'm mistaken. Wait a minute. If he was elected, then that would mean you'd be moving to Austin. Wouldn't it?"

Jane nodded and concern flickered across her face. "Yes, I believe it would mean that."

"Do you want to move? All your friends and organizations are here. Not to mention Mallory and me."

"I know." Jane sighed and rested her chin on the back of her hand. "I've worried about it a lot lately. Your father is a success at everything he does, so I have to believe that if he wants to be on the Texas Supreme Court, that's what he'll do. It's selfish of me not to want that for him, but the truth is, I don't want to move." She looked guilty for having admitted it. "I like it here."

"Mom, are you sure he said he wanted to run for the Texas Supreme Court?"

"Well, no, he actually didn't say that, I just assumed that is what he was referring to."

"It's my guess you misunderstood him. As far as I know, he plans to run for election to the Appellate Court judgeship he was appointed to. And if I'm wrong, and if you don't want to move and leave everything behind, you'd better talk to him about it."

Jane laughed. "I couldn't do that. Addison has our best interest in mind. He understands these things so much better than I ever could."

"Mom, that's feudal."

"Maybe, but it's how our marriage works. I was brought up to believe that a wife should listen to her husband and let him make the decisions. Most people move around these days. I should count myself lucky to have been able to stay in one place for so long. Why, you girls grew up in that house. We've lived there since early in our marriage."

"All the more reason why you should stay there if that's what you want. You and Dad should talk this over." Kirby couldn't imagine not discussing something of such great importance. But then, she reflected wryly, she obviously wasn't such an expert at keeping a marriage together.

"Perhaps I will talk to him." Jane didn't sound convincing.

"Speaking of talking about things, I haven't mentioned this to you before, but I'm having a lot of trouble with Josh," Kirby confessed. "He's become so rebellious. You know his grades have never been outstanding, but now I can't even get him to do his homework. He seems to think he doesn't have to do anything I say."

"Have you talked to Russell about this?"

"No. I don't want him to think I can't handle my own son. Besides, Russell hasn't exactly stayed with me through thick and thin, now has he? I was hoping you might have a suggestion of something I could do to bring Josh around. He's probably just feeling insecure or something—though that's certainly not evident in the way he acts. He actually tries to boss me around and outright refuses to do his chores or to call if he's going to be late coming home from Brice's house."

"I just don't know, dear. He's at such an impressionable age."

"I expected some rebellion from him when he became a teenager, but twelve is a bit early." She ran her fingers through her tousled hair. "God! What if it's worse then?"

"Maybe Addison can have a talk with him."

"I'd appreciate that. Will you ask him?"

"Of course. Finish eating now. You're just playing around with your food like you did when you were little. You need to keep your strength up."

Kirby glanced at the clock. "It's later than I thought. I'll put it in the refrigerator and eat it later. I really will," she said when she saw the doubt on her mother's face. "I'll have to hurry if I'm to get to the doctor on time."

"I'll straighten up in here. You go get ready. I can let myself out. And call when you get back home and tell me what he said."

Kirby dressed and left a note for the boys telling them where she had gone. She reached the doctor's office with two minutes to spare, the rush having depleted all her energy.

After all the hurry, she still had to wait half an hour. When

Dr. Nichols examined her he said, "You seem to be in good health. You're just a bit run-down, that's all. I don't see any reason to be concerned. If your blood work shows a problem, my nurse will call you."

"What about my insomnia? How long can I go without sleep? Since Russell moved out, I've done little more than doze. Every sound wakes me up."

"That's fairly common. You've been through a big emotional change."

"When I do sleep, I have terrible nightmares. Really frightening ones."

Dr. Nichols looked thoughtful. "Surely you're having ordinary dreams as well."

"Not that I can remember. Like I said, I'm not sleeping that much. It's getting to the point where I'm almost afraid to try to sleep."

"Well, that's a problem. Are you crying a lot and having appetite changes?"

"I'm not hungry at all. I've lost several pounds since he left."

"You're suffering from depression." He wrote out a prescription. "Try these tablets. Take one in the morning and two at night and let's see how you do. Also, I recommend that you see Dr. Lauren Jacobs."

"Another doctor? Is she some sort of specialist?"

"She's a psychiatrist. I'm sending you to her because she can prescribe other medication if this doesn't work for you. Depression medications are odd in that some work for one person and not for the next. I've known Dr. Jacobs for several years and I know she's helped a number of my patients with their depression."

"I'm only depressed because Russell moved out. It'll go away in a few days."

"How long did you say he's been gone?"

"About a month."

"Would you say you're coping better now or worse?"

Kirby frowned. "I don't want to see a psychiatrist. There's nothing wrong with my mind."

"Yes, there is. You're depressed. Seeing Dr. Jacobs is no different than coming in to me if you have the flu."

Dr. Nichols wrote the psychiatrist's name on a piece of paper and handed it to Kirby. "You think about it, but I strongly recommend that you talk to her or to someone like her. Depression isn't anything to play around with."

"You're the doctor." Kirby closed the paper in her hand. She had no intention of following his advice.

That afternoon Kirby was surprised to see Tara at her side door. "Hi, honey. Your mom isn't over here if you're looking for her. The boys are down the street but I'm sure you can find them."

"Maybe after a while. Can I talk to you?" Tara seemed nervous.

"Of course. I was just getting ready to make dinner." She hadn't cooked a real meal in almost a week. Today she was trying to convince herself that she could function even if she was too depressed to think.

Tara came into the kitchen and pulled out a chair from the table while Kirby went back to her recipe book. She had never made this casserole before and it was proving to be more difficult than she had expected.

Tara didn't say anything.

Kirby glanced around at her. "What's going on? Did Josh do something to upset you?"

"I haven't seen Josh in days. He doesn't like me anymore."

Kirby went to her and hugged her. "That's not it, honey. He's just upset these days. It's not that he doesn't like you."

"I don't care if he does or not. I like Cody better anyway."

Kirby smiled and went back to the recipe. Tara and Cody had always been as close as brother and sister.

"If something was bothering me, could I tell you and trust you not to tell anyone?"

"Certainly. I always keep your secrets."

"What if it was something really, really bad. At least I think it may be."

"All the more reason to tell me." Kirby reached for her thyme and rosemary.

"But maybe it's not anything at all and I'm just being stupid."

"You've never been stupid. Did someone say you are?"

"No."

"What's bothering you?"

Tara picked up the salt and pepper shakers and shuffled them back and forth between her hands. "What if Grandad told me not to talk about it?"

"That makes it a little different. This problem is something Grandad knows about?"

Tara nodded solemnly.

"Then maybe you should talk to him about it. Especially if he told you not to tell anyone."

Tara put her chin down on the table. Listlessly she pushed the shakers around. After a long time, she said, "I think I'm doing something bad."

"Then you should stop." Kirby glanced at her. "Is this what Grandad knows about?"

"Yes."

"Then he probably said not to tell anyone so your mom and dad won't be upset with you. Is that it?"

"I guess."

"Then you probably ought to do as he says." She read the list of spices and started sorting through her spice drawer for the cardamon. "I'll bet I don't have any cardamon. I can't think of a single reason I would have bought any. I should have read this recipe all the way through before I started it." She dug deeper among the boxes and bottles of spices. "I wonder if ginger could be substituted for it?" When Tara didn't answer, she looked around and found she was alone in the kitchen.

"Tara?" she called, going to the door that led to the dining room. "Are you still here?" There was no answer so Kirby shrugged. Tara had come in and out of their house ever since she was old enough to walk over alone. Probably she had gone down the street to play with the boys.

Returning to the kitchen, Kirby resumed her search for the cardamon.

She paused as she took out the bottle of ginger to substitute for the cardamon. Tara was upset and that was unusual. Normally Tara was full of smiles and giggles. Now that Kirby thought about it, however, she hadn't seen Tara laugh out loud in weeks. "They grow up too fast," Kirby muttered to herself. Surely if something was really worrying Tara, she would have stayed until it was resolved.

Tara wasn't playing with the boys. She was walking home the long way around the block. She was deeply worried but no grown-up seemed to want to hear about it. She didn't know what to do.

The day before when her mother had told her to go to her grandparents' house after school, her grandmother hadn't been home. Tara hadn't realized this until she was already in the house and alone with Addison. There had been no escape.

He had been friendly toward her as he always was, but he had insisted that she play hide-and-seek with him. At eight years of age, Tara felt she was too old to enjoy hide-and-seek with her grandfather, but Addison insisted. She had covered her eyes and he had gone to hide.

She had wandered through the house, looking under beds and in closets, and wondering how she could go outside without hurting his feelings or making him mad. He had been difficult to find. It wasn't until she looked into the guest room that she located him.

At first she hadn't understood what he was doing. He was lying on the bed in plain sight and his hands were covering his lap. She went closer to the bed and he moved his hands and she found herself staring at his penis. At first she had been stunned. She knew boys had them. Cody had shown her his when she was three years old. It stood to reason that grown-up men would have them, too. But Addison's was much larger than Cody's had been and it stood at an angle from his body.

"Want to touch it?" he had asked.

Tara had turned and run from the room, down the hall and out of the house. She had hidden behind the azalea bush until she saw her grandmother drive up and park.

Addison greeted Jane as if nothing out of the ordinary had happened. He was standing in the kitchen with his pants zipped and looking just as he always did. Tara wondered if she had acted stupid in running away. He gave her a grin and a wink when her grandmother wasn't looking but she didn't know what he meant by that. If Cody or Josh had done the same, it would have indicated they shared a secret. Later, when her grandmother had gone into the bathroom, Addison had whispered to Tara that she wasn't to tell anyone about the game they had played together.

That was how Tara knew she had done something wrong. If she had accidentally seen him in the bathroom or something like that, it would be a mistake and forgivable. But she had gone looking for him and that made her an accomplice.

Tara sat on the curb in front of her house, watching the cars go by. This new game of Grandad's was worse than the one where she fished around in his pants pockets for candy. He had even offered to let her touch him! He must think she was a really naughty girl. That was why she was afraid to tell her parents. Even Aunt Kirby had said that if he told her not to tell, she shouldn't. But what was she supposed to do?

She had no way at all of making sure it would never happen again.

Chapter Thirteen

The soft ticking of the grandfather clock punctuated the silence. Jane sipped her honeyed hot tea and placed the cup back in its saucer. "Mallory, I know something is bothering you. What is it?"

"Nothing, Mom." She curled one leg under her as she had when she was a child.

"I know you too well. Are you worried about Tara?"

"Tara? Why would I be worried about her?"

Jane was puzzled. "She's not acting like herself lately. Every time she comes over, she follows me from room to room as if she's afraid of getting lost. She hardly ever smiles anymore."

"She does at home. Her grades haven't been so good lately, but neither were mine. She's a long way from failing third grade, so I haven't given it much thought."

"You haven't seen any changes in her behavior at home?"

Mallory thought for a minute. "She mostly stays in her room."

"That's not natural for an eight-year-old."

"It is for an eight-year-old who has her own TV. I told Derrick she was too young for a TV in her room, but you know how he is when he gets something in his head. He bought it anyway."

"She almost never watches TV over here."

"Maybe she sees enough of it at home. Tara is fine."

"Then what's bothering you?"

Mallory picked up a throw pillow and began worrying its fringe. "Derrick and I are having some problems. Nothing serious. Just . . . problems." She frowned at the pillow. "All married couples have difficulties from time to time."

"That's true. It's just that with Kirby and Russell separated, I was worried. Your father is still upset over Russell moving out."

"I know. He's told me every time I've seen him since it happened. I think everyone should just leave Kirby alone and let them work it out for themselves."

"There's never been a divorce in the Walker family." Jane grew thoughtful. There had been several in her own family, but for some reason they weren't counted. When she had married Addison, she had become, blood and bones, a Walker.

"I know, Mom. I've worried about it, too. The thing is, I really like Russell. I'm not so sure it's his fault."

"Mallory! What a thing to say. Kirby is your only sister."

"I know. But Russell is a nice person. It's not like he hits her or has a girlfriend."

"Not that we know about, at least." Jane was trying to dislike Russell out of loyalty to Addison's point of view.

"I'm positive he's not seeing anyone."

"How would you know that?"

"You can just tell. Men who are on the prowl have a certain look about them."

Jane thought that over. She had never seen any man who seemed to be "on the prowl," as Mallory put it. "What sort of look?"

"I don't know how to describe it. You can just tell. Russell doesn't have it."

"Then why did he desert his family?"

Mallory laughed. "He didn't desert them, Mom. He only moved to another place. Josh and Cody have told me they talk to him every day. He calls them as soon as he comes in from his last class."

"I don't know why Kirby allowed him to move out in the first place." This was an implied question which Addison repeated frequently. Jane had no answer and she wondered if Mallory would.

"What else could she do? Russell is an adult. He can leave if he wants to."

"I just hope you and Derrick don't split up. I don't think your father could stand it."

Mallory frowned. "I don't see how it would affect Dad so much if we did. He doesn't have to live with Derrick. I do."

Jane turned sharply, with as much of a scowl as she could muster. "Then you're considering it?"

"No. Not really." Mallory sighed and looked away. "When he works late so often and barely speaks to me when he's home, I wonder why I put up with him."

"You do it because he's your husband." Jane couldn't keep the shock from her voice.

"This is the twentieth century. Husbands are no longer deified."

"You sound so bitter. I hate to see you like that."

"I'm sorry. I'm trying not to be. It's just that my marriage isn't like yours. I'm not happy with Derrick."

Jane was surprised. Did her children see her marriage to their father as happy? "Addison has his moments, too. He works late as often as Derrick, and if he gets this new position he wants, I have no idea what hours he will be expected to put in."

"New position? What new position?"

"He's got lofty goals, you know. I believe he's hoping to get a place on the Texas Supreme Court. I know he's awfully excited about it."

"You see? Dad talks to you. I don't know if Derrick is excited about anything or not."

At times her daughters confused her. Kirby complained that Jane didn't know what Addison's aspirations were because he didn't confide in her, and Mallory said they communicated better than she and Derrick. What was she to believe? Jane had never been good at discernment. As usual when she wasn't sure what to say or do, she fell back on what Addison would do in the situation. "You and Derrick have a good marriage. It's up to a wife to make it work. Be interesting when he comes home. Pay attention to how his day went. Fix yourself up when it's time for him to come home after a hard day at the office.''

"I could open the door clad only in Saran Wrap and he wouldn't notice."

Jane felt herself blushing. ''Mallory! Of all the things to say!''

"I'm sorry. I only mean that Derrick isn't interested in me anymore. Sexually, I mean.''

Jane hadn't intended to be involved in such an intimate conversation. ''I really don't think you should be telling me this.''

Mallory dipped her head in respectful contrition, an automatic response to even the mildest chastisement from either parent. ''Sorry.''

"Perhaps if you went to a marriage counselor. I understand it's all quite confidential.''

"Can you imagine Derrick agreeing to do that? If he went, he would only say there's nothing wrong with him and that it's all my fault. And it's not!''

"I didn't say it was your fault." Jane had often wanted to see a marriage counselor herself but Addison absolutely forbade it. During one of her rare, rebellious moments, Jane had considered going anyway, but then decided not to risk it. She did little enough that was right in Addison's eyes as it was.

Mallory leaned her head back against the couch and stared up at the ceiling. ''Life used to be so much simpler.''

"Yes, it was, dear." Jane was relieved to have the conversation turn to a more pleasant topic. ''I remember when you girls were still living at home. Those were the happiest days of my life.''

Mallory didn't answer, but sadness clouded her face.

Jane took that to mean that Mallory agreed with her. ''Of course, you have that for yourself now. I mean, Tara is still small and you can be with her every day. You still have your best years in front of you.''

"I suppose you're right." She didn't sound at all convinced.

"I just wish I could somehow do it all for you girls. Live, I mean. I think the talent for living is lost these days. It was so much easier when I was young. The wife stayed home and the husband worked. You had two children and a fenced yard and life went smoothly."

"Except for the two children, I have all that now. Derrick would never let me get a job."

"I know. He's really quite good to you. I think maybe you just don't see it." Jane smiled to soften her words. She disliked finding fault or even suggesting it. "At least we all live close to each other. I feel so sorry for my friends whose children have moved away. They only see them perhaps twice a year. You and Kirby and I can visit anytime we choose." Her voice trailed away. If Addison got that job he wanted on the Texas Supreme Court, she would have to move to Austin. She decided not to think about that.

The grandfather clock chimed the hour with its mellow tones. Mallory sat up. "I should leave. I have some things I want to do before Tara comes home from school."

Jane stood and took both teacups. "I'm so glad you came by. I wish you did this more often."

"I intend to, but time has a way of slipping away from me." Mallory followed Jane to the kitchen and opened the swinging door for her. "Do you want me to wash the cups for you?"

"No, no. It gives me something to do."

Mallory laughed and hugged her. "As if you needed more to do! I wish my days were as productive as yours."

Jane smiled as she took the cups to the sink. What did Mallory think she did all day? She had a woman in to clean the house so she didn't do more than straighten up occasionally. She cooked, but that didn't take all day. "Perhaps if you had another child." She loved her grandchildren and Mallory had been happier when Tara was a baby.

"I don't think that would be a good idea." Mallory looked as if the idea amused her.

"Maybe not. The world is so uncertain these days." Jane had often heard Addison say this and everyone seemed to agree with him. Personally, she thought the world had been much more unstable during the times of the cold war when Russia was still a fearsome giant. But no one ever said that.

Mallory glanced at her wristwatch. "Got to run, Mom. Thanks for having me over."

"Goodbye. Drive carefully."

After leaving her mother, Mallory headed directly to the nearest shopping center. Her mother tried to be helpful, but she didn't understand what it was like to live with a man like Derrick. She had almost laughed when her mother suggested she have another child. Derrick would know for certain it wasn't his. After Tara's birth, he had gotten a vasectomy. Mallory hadn't known of his intention until the surgery was over.

She could still remember how she felt when he gave her the news. It had been worse than a blow from his fist. All her life Mallory had wanted children, a houseful if possible. She knew Derrick preferred small families, but she had figured she could get around that. Now it was impossible.

Derrick loved Tara more than he had thought possible. Mallory knew that was true. And Tara adored him in return. Mallory secretly hoped Derrick now regretted his hasty decision. It had guaranteed he would never have the grandson Addison had expected them to produce.

Had Addison wanted sons of his own and not daughters? He had often said so in anger. Mallory wondered if that was why he had been so harsh with them when they were small.

Mallory was convinced that she would never have treated her children as Addison had, even if she'd had a dozen, and all of them girls! Her eyes filled with tears and she blinked them away. She had a rule not to dwell on memories of her childhood. With practiced ease, she put the thoughts on a blackboard in her mind and erased them.

After parking her car, Mallory walked into the mall. Although she strolled by stores gazing in the windows, she wasn't shopping for anything they were selling.

She sat alone in the fast-food area and sipped a soft drink, her dark eyes roaming the other customers. At last she found one who interested her. He was younger than she usually wanted, but he was alone and he had the randy look that most young men seemed to have. She caught his eye and smiled. He glanced around, decided she meant it for him, and smiled in return.

Mallory felt excitement rising. His hair was long and he was wearing a T-shirt emblazoned with a football team logo. His movements were gangly, as if he wasn't yet accustomed to his height, but that didn't bother her. What did was that at his age, he might not have a place of his own. She consulted her watch. It would mean breaking all her rules, but she could take him to her place. Tara wouldn't be home for over an hour and Derrick never came home in the middle of the day.

The young man sidled over to her as if he still wasn't positive she had smiled at him. "Hi," he said awkwardly.

"Hello. My name is Susan. What's yours?"

"Jason Fielding. I never saw you around here before."

Mallory held her smile in place. Why did men always think that was an interesting gambit to open a conversation? "I've been here. You must not have been looking."

"I sure wish I had." His eyes were growing more certain. "Is it okay if I sit with you?"

She wondered exactly how old he was. Now that he was closer, he appeared to be younger than she had thought at first. "I have a better idea."

She took him to her house. Once he had understood what she was offering, he had become more talkative. He had even tried to flirt.

Once reaching her house, Mallory unlocked the side door and let him in. As she locked it behind them, she said, "How old are you, Jason?"

"Twenty-five," he stammered, obviously lying.

"That's nice. So am I." She concealed her amusement as she preceded him through the house.

"Hey, this is a really neat place!"

"Thank you." She glanced around, trying to see it from his perspective. Her house was nice. Just empty of pleasant emotions.

Upstairs she left her bedroom door open. If anyone came in, she wanted to know. Mallory pulled down the covers on the bed and started undressing. Jason stared at her for a split second, then started shucking off his own clothes. Mallory found she was actually enjoying this. He was so eager and so grateful.

In bed he made up for his lack of expertise with stamina and enthusiasm. Although Mallory never came close to being satisfied, she did enjoy the feel of his strong young arms around her and the firmness of his skin. He was as wiry as a coiled spring and about as patient. He came twice before he rolled over and stared up at the ceiling in gratitude.

"Wow! That was great!"

"It was for me, too." It wasn't a complete lie. She really had enjoyed the exchange and her personal demons were slaked for the moment. She only wished it had fully satisfied her. She heard a noise from downstairs and was instantly alert.

"What was that?" he whispered. "Was that a door closing?"

"Hush!" She listened intently. Someone was moving about downstairs. She swung her legs over the side of the bed and reached for her clothes. "Get dressed!"

Jason needed no encouraging. He already had his faded jeans in hand and was trying to shove both legs into the same hole.

Mallory strained to hear the sounds from below over the furtive noise they were making. It was too early for Tara, so it had to be Derrick. "I think it's my husband."

"You're married?" he gasped.

"Here." She stuffed his underwear in the pocket of his jeans. "Follow me." She took him to the upstairs deck Derrick had installed a few years back as a sunning porch. "You can go down these steps. Just be careful and don't let him see you."

Jason looked as if he was scared half to death. "You never told me you had a husband!" he snapped.

"Be quiet or you'll get to meet him personally!" She shoved him in the direction of the steps. Her adrenaline was pumping double time. This was exciting! She had never come so close to getting caught before.

Once assured that Jason was moving down the steps, she raced back to the bedroom and tossed the covers over the bed, then hurried down to intercept Derrick. "What are you doing home so early?"

He glanced at her as if he had forgotten she might be home. "I forgot some papers I need. Have you seen the portfolio I brought home last night?"

"No, I haven't." She had. It was in the bedroom.

"I think I must have left it by the bed. I was reading them last night and I don't remember moving them this morning." He brushed past her and started up the stairs.

Mallory could feel her heart pounding. Would Derrick know

she had just been in their bed with a man? What if Jason had left something behind?

She hurried up the stairs after him.

Derrick went straight to his bedside table and picked up the portfolio. He frowned at the unmade bed. "Why haven't you straightened up in here yet? The place is a mess."

Mallory sat on the bed and leaned back provocatively. "Have time for a quickie?"

Derrick frowned to show his disapproval and hurried from the room.

Mallory laid back on the rumpled bed and smiled up at the ceiling. Maybe she would do this more often.

Zimmerman finished going over the case workload with his staff of assistants and said, "Any questions?"

Kirby consulted the assignment sheet again. "Just the Cleo Jimpson case?"

"Yeah. Just the one. You busted your butt putting Chandler away." Zimmerman glanced at his own notes. "I'm giving you a breather for a while."

"I don't mind taking more cases. I like to work."

Several of the other attorneys around the conference table frowned at her as if they thought she was buttering up the boss. Zimmerman noticed but didn't react. "I know you do, but if you continue burning your candle at both ends, you'll soon hit burnout and be useless to me. I'm just trying to help you pace yourself."

"Whatever you say." She glanced down at her notes. "Jimpson looks air tight. It won't take much effort. By the way, the Mangano appeal is coming up soon. I'd heard they had requested oral argument and thought you would want me to get prepared to handle that."

"If the court grants oral arguments, which I doubt, I'm having Whittaker work it for us. Since you've represented Mangano as a defendant before, I think it's best for you to steer clear so there won't be any question of conflict of interest."

Kirby nodded though he knew she disagreed. She had told him earlier during one of their private conversations that she had felt partly responsible for Mangano being free when he committed the murder for which he'd been convicted and wanted nothing more than to see to it that his conviction would stand. He wished, for her sake, that he could let her handle the appeal for the prosecution.

"I guess that's it." The other attorneys gathered up their papers and headed for their own offices. Zimmerman watched Kirby stall until the others were gone. "Is there something else?"

"When the Chandler appeal comes up, I want to handle it."

"We'll see." He was good at lying; he had been a successful lawyer for years. As yet, Chandler's attorney hadn't requested oral argument, and if and when he did, Zimmerman was going to handle it himself. He had seen what the case had done to Kirby and he wasn't sure her nerves could take going through it again so soon. She was exactly what he wanted to find in a promising young lawyer. She preferred work to breathing and would pursue a matter until she ran it into the ground. He didn't want to lose her to overwork. "How are things at home?"

"As good as can be expected. Russell still isn't saying when he's coming home. Josh is still furious at me and thinks it's all my fault. Cody's adjusting."

"Separations are hard on kids."

"They're hard on everyone." She put her papers into her briefcase and shut it. "How are things with you?"

"Can't complain. Janet's trying to fatten me up." He patted his thick waist. "Becky and Tom are coming for visitation this weekend. That always puts the house in an uproar. I love it." Zimmerman had always loved kids. Janet was considerably younger than he was and he had been glad to start a second family with her. So far they had two sons, Dylan and Parker. She had told Zimmerman she wanted more.

"The boys are going to Russell's apartment for the weekend. It's going to be quiet at my house. Too quiet."

"You're welcome to come over and help us corral our brood." He grinned at her.

"Thanks, but I'm going to paint the kitchen while the boys are gone."

"Sounds like fun. You can do mine when you finish yours."

Kirby laughed. "I get to choose the color?"

"On second thought, it's fine the way it is. As hard as you've been working, I'm not sure I want to give you a chance to get even with me."

"I love working here." She smiled at him. "I really do. It's entirely different from having to put up with Derrick. I didn't realize what a royal pain in the ass he was until I got away from him."

"Sounds like my first wife."

Kirby was laughing as she left.

Zimmerman watched her go and wished he knew some way to make her happy. He was fond of her. She was already like a daughter to him. In some ways she reminded him of his Becky. He couldn't understand any man wanting to leave her. He shook his head. There was no understanding some people.

From her office phone, Kirby called her house to be sure the boys were in from school. "Cody? I just wanted to check in with you."

"I'm home."

"Put Josh on, please." She had told him to take out the trash before school and he had left without doing it. She was positive he had disobeyed on purpose.

"He's not here."

"Where is he?"

"I don't know. He got in a car with some friends."

Kirby frowned. Lately Josh had started running with a different crowd. Most of them were older and had their own cars. "When he comes in, will you tell him to call me?"

"Sure, Mom."

She hung up and tapped her fingers on her desk with mounting impatience. Josh was becoming more and more of a problem. These days he seldom did anything she asked of him. Spring break was just around the corner and she wasn't sure she wanted him at home with nothing to do. She dialed Russell's number.

His answering machine came on. She had known he wouldn't be home from classes this early. Lately she had found it easier to talk to his answering machine. "Call me when you come home? I need to discuss Josh." She paused. "And I think we need to talk about us." She hung up quickly.

She had put off saying that to him. What would she say if he said he saw no reason to talk about putting their marriage back together? Kirby missed him more than she would have thought possible, and worse, she now could see how his leaving was mostly her fault. That wasn't easy to admit. She wasn't sure she could admit it to Russell at all.

The now familiar rush of panic swept over her as she thought about how much she dreaded having to confront her children's father.

Kirby frowned. That was an odd way for her to label Russell. She had always thought of him first as her husband, not as the boys' father. And since when did she dread confrontations? She made her living by confronting people.

At least this wave of panic hadn't come accompanied by pictures in living color, sounds and smells. That was a relief.

She couldn't understand the scenes that sometimes filled her head. They were like memories, but they weren't memories of anything from her childhood. Not even close. It didn't take a leap of genius to know the pictures dealt with a small girl being sexually abused.

As nausea rose within her, Kirby hurriedly reminded herself that she had never been molested. She didn't even have friends who had been hurt in that way. The pictures in her head couldn't be memories.

They couldn't be!

But there was a familiarity about them that frightened her. She had the terrible feeling that if she just thought about it, she would know what the pictures meant.

Kirby shook her head. There was no one in her family who could have molested her. She had no uncles, no older brothers. There were a few male cousins, but none who had stayed with them for longer than a weekend, and always in the company of their parents. No men in her family had access to her. Therefore the pictures were something else—not memories.

There was one person who might know, however. Mallory had grown up in the same house, experienced the same things, known the same people. Did Mallory have these horrible pictures in her mind, too? Kirby knew she couldn't ask. If the answer was no, she would have revealed too much. Something about the pictures made Kirby reluctant, almost unable, to tell anyone about them.

Again she wondered what it felt like when a person was having a nervous breakdown. Did it start with unexplainable pictures of a child being molested? And bouts of panic so acute that a person felt compelled to run and hide? And smells that should have been pleasant but that were part of the panic itself? Kirby wished there was someone she could ask these things before they drove her insane. Literally.

Chapter Fourteen

"How have you been?" Kirby asked.

"Fine. And you?" Russell seemed as ill at ease as she felt.

"I'm doing all right. The boys miss you."

"I talk to them every day."

"I miss you, too." She clasped her hands in her lap, feeling like a fool. This was Russell, not some stranger. For fourteen years she had slept in the same bed with him, cooked his meals, and had borne their two sons. It was ridiculous for her to be so nervous around him.

"I miss you, Kirby." His voice gentled and he looked away as if he hadn't intended to reveal the tenderness.

"I'd like for you to come back."

He shook his head. "Nothing has changed. We weren't happy together. You know we weren't."

"I can change that. If I have a nightmare, I won't wake you. I'll try harder this time." She heard the desperation creeping into her voice and hated herself for it. She had told herself she wouldn't beg.

"Kirby, it's not about you having nightmares," he said in exasperation.

"Then tell me what it *is* about. You've never given me any reason for leaving. Is it because you want to see someone else?"

"Of course not. I haven't even considered going out with anyone."

"I had decided that's what it was. I even thought maybe you had moved in with a woman."

"The boys have spent weekends at my place. Don't you think they would have mentioned it if a woman was living there, too?"

"Josh certainly would have. He blames everything on me and would do or say anything to hurt me these days."

"I've noticed he's more difficult to talk with lately."

"We can talk about Josh in a minute. Tell me why you moved out."

He stared at her as if he couldn't understand her not knowing. "I don't want to get into an argument with you."

"I don't want that either. So it's not that I have nightmares?" She knew it had to be more than this, but for some reason Russell was reluctant to answer her.

"Of course not. Everybody has nightmares. I'm not so selfish as to leave just so I can get a full night's sleep."

She waited.

"We've drifted apart." He glanced around. "Where are the boys? Can they hear us?"

"No, they've gone to Dad's. They're not expecting you to be here for half an hour. No one can hear us."

"We had stopped having sex almost altogether. When you did let me near you, you made me feel like a rapist!"

"I didn't!"

"You asked what was wrong. You're going to hear it. I don't know what's going on with you. You weren't like this when we married. For the past two years, maybe longer, you've held me at arm's length. You don't even like it when I hold your hand or put my arm around you when we're fully clothed."

"I can't help that. I just feel claustrophobic lately. I've started having panic attacks. I suppose that's why I don't like to be touched."

"You've never enjoyed making love. At first you pretended, but I've known for years that you don't like to go to bed with me."

"That's not true." She avoided eye contact. "I can't sleep when you're not in our bed."

"That's not the same as making love."

She stood and strode to the window. Still looking away from him, she said, "I don't know why you like sex so often. Maybe you're the one who's wrong, not me."

"This isn't a case of assessing blame. If you love someone, naturally you want to touch them and make love. It's what adults do, damn it!"

"So you left me because you want sex more often than I do?"

"No," he said with exaggerated patience. "I left because you hate for me to touch you. The last time I tried, you nearly shoved me out of bed! What if I had done something like that to you?"

"It's just like a man to center everything around sex." She glared out the window at the street.

"Don't do that! Don't lump all men into one category and label it as bad. That would be like me saying all women are hard to get along with and frigid."

His words hung between them like the icy barrier they implied.

"I'm sorry," he said to break the long silence. "I shouldn't have put it that way. It's just that I get angry when a woman starts any sentence with 'All men . . . ' I went too far."

"You think I'm hard to get along with?"

"We argue constantly these days. It's been getting worse for several years."

"And that I'm frigid?" She found it difficult even to say the word.

"Kirby, I don't want to fight. Maybe I should leave."

"No, we need to talk about this. *Am* I frigid?"

"I don't know. Yes, maybe."

"I think you're just oversexed."

"Kirby, please. If we can't discuss it rationally, I'm leaving."

"Now I'm irrational, and you're leaving. Well, you're good at that." She closed her eyes. "I'm sorry. Now I've gone too far."

"I want you to get into counseling."

"Why me? Maybe you're the one who needs it."

"You know it's not normal for a woman to have a panic attack every time her husband comes near her."

"Now you're an expert on panic attacks, too?"

"No, but if I were having them, that would be reason enough for me to see a therapist and do something to get rid of them. I've never had one, but they can't be pleasant."

She gave a mirthless laugh. "No, I wouldn't call them pleasant."

"I can find the name of a therapist for you. I'm sure there's one at the college that you could see."

"No, I don't want to do that."

"So what you're telling me is that you have no intention of changing? I'm not coming back under those conditions."

She strode back to her chair and sat down. "I'm not going to be forced to say I'm crazy to get you back."

"It's not crazy to have panic attacks." He frowned at her as if he couldn't understand her attitude. "It's certainly not an admission of insanity to see a therapist. People do it all the time."

"I can just see Dad's reaction if I were to tell him I was in counseling. He would be furious!"

"Then don't tell him! If you had the flu, he wouldn't care if you went to a doctor. This is no different. He never needs to know."

"I don't do things that I have to keep from him."

"Is that why you don't want to make love with me?"

Kirby shot him a glance. "That doesn't make any sense. Dad knows I'm not a virgin. I have two sons." She couldn't keep the sarcasm out of her voice. "Everyone is an amateur psychologist."

When Russell spoke again, he sounded tired, as if he knew he had lost the discussion. "How is Josh these days?"

"He's turning into a spoiled brat, frankly. If he were younger, I'd spank him."

"As bad as that? We never spanked the boys except in extreme circumstances."

"Maybe we were wrong about that. I never rebelled against my father like Josh does against me."

"No, but your father beat you with a belt. You were afraid of him."

"No, I wasn't," she said in confusion. "I love my father."

"Have it your own way. I just remember that the first time I spanked Josh, you reacted as if I was trying to kill him."

"This isn't about Dad."

"If it's any consolation, I'm having problems with Josh, too, during visitations. He wanders off without telling me where he's going. Last weekend, some of his new friends came by to see him. Have you seen the boys he's running with?"

"Yes. I believe a boy should be allowed to choose his own friends," she replied stiffly.

"So do I, within reason, but these characters are bad news. They smoke and one had a beer bottle. You wouldn't have wanted to hear the language they were using or how they were discussing girls."

"Oh?" She had seen some of the boys, but none had been drinking at the time and she hadn't heard their conversation with Josh. "I didn't eavesdrop on them."

"Stop it, Kirby," he snapped. "We aren't getting anywhere like this."

"Okay, so I didn't like the looks of the boys either. I told Josh to stop seeing them and he laughed at me. He doesn't even bother to hide the fact that he's disobeying me."

"I'll have a talk with him, but I don't think it will do any good." He paused. "I hate to mention this, but maybe he needs counseling, too."

"Why are you on this therapy kick all of a sudden? Does everyone you know need counseling?"

"It's hard on a kid when his parents separate. It's traumatic. Whether you agree or not, some kids need help at a time like this. Why tough it out when there's help to be had?"

"It sounds to me as if you've got the hots for some psychologist and are trying to send her some business," she said acidly.

Russell glared at her, then got to his feet. "I'm leaving. Tell the boys that I'll call them later tonight."

Kirby wanted to ask him to come back and sit down, but her pride couldn't let her. Talking to him brought out the worst in her these days. She couldn't believe some of the things she had said. The door at the far end of the house slammed. He was gone again.

Tears gathered in the corners of her eyes and she pushed them away. Russell made her so angry! She had hoped he would admit that he was lonely without her and that he wanted to come back. Then she could have been gracious and friendly. Instead, he had called her frigid! She didn't know why she wanted him to come back to her so badly.

Several minutes later she heard the boys come in. "Mom?" Cody called. "Is Dad here yet?"

"Did you see his car, stupid?" Josh said.

"Come in here," she called to them. When they entered the den, she tried to smile at them. "Did you have a nice visit with Grandad?"

"Sure. When is Dad coming?"

"He's already been here, honey. He left angry a few minutes ago." Cody's face showed his hurt before he remembered to hide it. She wished he were still small enough to cuddle in her lap. He needed comforting but was too old to accept it.

"You chased him off again?" Josh demanded. "What's with you anyway?"

"Don't talk to me like that," Kirby snapped. "No, I didn't chase him away. We had an argument and he left."

"He knew we were coming back, didn't he?" Cody asked.

"Yes, he did. He's going to call you tonight. He loves you boys very much and he misses you a great deal."

"So why did he leave? You hate him for loving us, don't you?" Josh stepped closer, his hands clenched into fists at his sides. "You're just jealous because he don't love you anymore."

"Doesn't," she corrected, staying calm only with great effort. Since Josh had changed friends, his grammar was slipping into street talk. She knew he was doing it to irritate her.

"I don't have to talk that way if I don't want to. You want me to sound like a dork like Cody."

"I'm not a dork!" Cody shoved his brother angrily. "You just leave me alone!" He turned and ran from the room.

"What a wimp!" Josh sneered.

"Josh, I won't have Cody treated like this! You apologize to him at once!"

"Forget it. I don't apologize to wienies."

"I won't have you talking to me this way. I'm your mother and I'm not going to put up with it!"

"Yeah? You don't have a hell of a lot to say about that, do you!" He gave her a glare filled with hatred and left the room. A few seconds later the back door slammed.

Kirby felt sick inside; for a moment she actually had been afraid of him. She started after him and from the kitchen window she saw him out in the backyard teasing the dog by holding her favorite toy just out of her reach. Kirby jerked open the back door. "Stop teasing her. You're not going to be mean to Abby just because you're angry at your father."

"I'm not mad at him! I'm mad at you!" he shouted at her.

Kirby glanced toward her neighbors' house and saw the husband and wife staring at them. They quickly turned away as if they hadn't overheard. "Josh, you're grounded. Come in the house."

He laughed and sauntered out of the yard, leaving the gate open behind him.

Kirby hurried out and caught the dog before she could make a dash for freedom. By the time she wrestled Abby to the gate and shut it, Josh was out of sight. Once she was back in the house, she realized she was crying.

She stifled her tears and went up to Cody's room. "Hey, honey. Okay if I come in?"

"Sure," Cody said disspiritedly.

She sat on the edge of his bed and ruffled his hair. "I'm sorry it worked out this way."

"It's not your fault." He sounded as if he had been crying, too.

"Josh didn't mean to call you names. You know how he is when he gets upset. He's taking this separation really hard."

"So am I, Mom." Cody rolled to his back and glared at the ceiling. "Just because I'm not having a temper tantrum every five minutes doesn't mean I don't miss Dad."

"I know." Kirby wished she could bear his pain for him. "I guess it's a case of the squeaky wheel getting the oil. Josh is so loud and so obviously angry that I tend to see his misery more. I'm sorry, Cody." She took his hand and this time he didn't pull away. "I wish you were still small enough to rock. When you were unhappy, I used to rock you and sing you a song until you felt better. Remember?"

He smiled faintly. "I remember. But I'm too big for that now."

"I know." She patted his hand. "Would you like to go back to Grandad's with me? I need company just now."

"Okay. Tara may be there by now. Her mom was going to bring her over while she ran some errands."

At least, Kirby thought, she had one son who gave her no trouble. She hoped that remained true.

When they arrived at the Walker house, Tara was playing in the front yard alone. Her face brightened when she saw Cody had returned. Kirby left them outside and went into the house.

"Hello, Kirby. I didn't expect to see you this afternoon. Is Russell with you?" Jane asked.

"No, he left. He didn't even stay to see the boys." She dropped her purse on the kitchen table and sank into a chair. "Josh is terribly upset. He thinks I drove Russell away again. He said some really nasty things to me."

"He was just upset."

"How does he behave here when I'm not around? Is he giving you problems as well?"

"Not really."

Kirby didn't believe her. Her mother always tried to white-wash the misbehavior of her grandsons, but the inflection of her words gave her away. "I don't know what I'm going to do with him. Russell seems to think he's running with a bad crowd. I agree, but I've told him not to see them again and he pays no attention to me at all."

"All children go through a rebellious stage. I'm sure he'll outgrow it."

The phone rang and Jane picked up the kitchen extension. "Hello?" Her face was suddenly somber as she glanced at Kirby. "He did? Is he there now?" There was a pause while she listened to the caller. "I see. Yes, his mother will be down to pick him up. Yes, right away." She hung up the phone, looking markedly pale and stunned as if she were in shock.

Icy fear washed over Kirby, then the searing pain struck her middle as if she'd been impaled by a hot poker. "What's happened? Is Josh hurt?"

"No, no. He's not hurt. He's . . ." Jane faltered as if she didn't know the words to use. "It seems he's been arrested."

"Arrested! I just left him! For what?" Kirby's mouth dropped open.

"He was caught shoplifting at Brennahan's. I'm sure there must be some mistake." Her face was crumpled as if she would burst into tears. "Josh has no reason to steal. I told them you'd be down to get him."

"Where is he?"

"At the store. They're holding him there."

"I'll be right back. Cody is out front with Tara."

Kirby grabbed her purse and hurried back to her car. Josh arrested! She took the corner too fast, squealing her tires, then forced herself to slow down. Wrecking her car would be one straw too many.

At the store, she was directed to the manager's office and found it without difficulty. Josh was sitting in sullen silence beside the desk. A uniformed policeman stood nearby. A man who was presumably the store manager sat behind the desk with his arms crossed defiantly across his chest. Kirby turned back to Josh. Until this moment, she had hoped it was a case of mistaken identity. "What did you do?" she demanded.

Josh glared at the floor and shuffled his tennis shoes on the carpet.

"He was caught stealing T-shirts." The man behind the desk gave her a measuring look as if she might be partly to blame. "He went to the dressing room and put on several tees under his shirt and was leaving the store when Officer Hayes stopped him. By the way, my name is Mr. Dupree. I'm the store manager."

"I'm Kirby Garrett." She couldn't stop staring at Josh. It was as if she no longer knew him. "Why did you do it, Josh?"

"It figures you'd take his word and not mine," Josh growled.

"These are the shirts," Hayes said, indicating several T-shirts on the desk. "There are three of them. From the way he did it, I think he may have done this before. He apparently knew what he was doing."

She stepped up to the desk and looked at the shirts. "If you wanted new clothes, why didn't you ask for them? I would have bought them for you." She was remembering the new clothes Josh said Russell had bought for him the week before. At the time she had been angry that Russell was buying clothes for one boy and not the other. "Have you done this before?"

He stared stonily ahead.

"I haven't read him his rights," Hayes said. "Because of his age and the relatively small amount of money involved, we thought it would be best to call you before I do anything official."

Kirby's first impulse was to have him arrested and taken to the jail for a few hours. "Thank you, Officer. Since this may be his first time, I'd appreciate it if you'd let him go." She turned to Dupree. "I'd be glad to pay for the T-shirts."

Dupree looked as if he would prefer to press charges but recognized her as a regular customer. "There's no harm done. But if he were my boy, I'd keep a close eye on him from now on. We know you and your family and that you shop here frequently. But I would rather him not come back into this store without an adult. I hope you understand."

"Yes. Yes, I do." Kirby didn't know what to think. She had never considered either of her boys would ever break the law. To Josh she said, "I'm going to tell you something in front of Mr. Dupree and Officer Hayes. If they ever catch you stealing again, they are to arrest you, take you to jail, and book you. Do you understand, Josh? I won't allow this to happen again."

"Yeah, right."

Hayes frowned at him and Josh flinched away. "You'd do well to listen to your mother, boy. You haven't seen the jail. I have and you sure don't want to be locked up there. If I book you, it will remain on your record until you reach legal age. You'd have a hard time getting an after-school job if you've been arrested for shoplifting."

Josh pretended not to hear him.

Kirby was becoming too angry to stay any longer in the

stuffy office. "Thank you for calling me." She opened her purse and took out a fifty-dollar bill, which she laid on the desk. Then she caught Josh's arm and pulled him up. He jerked away from her and jammed his hands into his pockets.

All the way out of the store, Kirby had the discomforting feeling that everyone was staring at her. How many of the personnel knew what Josh had done? She doubted she would ever be able to shop there again.

In cold silence she drove him to her parents' house. She didn't dare speak to him for fear of blowing up and saying more than she should. He had been caught shoplifting! Stealing from a store!

Josh followed her into the house. By the curious looks Cody and Tara threw them, Kirby knew they hadn't been told what had happened. Jane and Addison were waiting for them in the den. When Addison saw them, he got to his feet and stared furiously at his grandson.

"What have you done!" he roared.

Kirby flinched. She hadn't seen her father's rage in years.

"Nothing! They were lying when they said I was stealing! I was just trying those clothes on!" Josh ducked his head in sullen defiance.

"You're lying, boy!" Addison grabbed his arm and jerked him around. "Look at me when I'm talking to you!"

Josh gave a startled cry of pain and tried to pull away. Addison gripped him tighter and refused to let go. He shook him until Josh's head snapped back. "You're nothing but a common thief! Do you have any idea how much harm you may have done my career? How can I hope to get such an important appointment if my grandson is a goddamned thief! You've brought disgrace on the whole family!"

"Dad! Stop! You're hurting him!" Kirby rushed to her son's side.

"Shut up, Kirby. You're not doing so well in raising him. The boy needs a firm hand. You and Russell have done a damned sorry job on this one!"

"You leave my father out of this!" Josh shouted.

Addison slapped Josh so hard that he would have fallen if

Addison hadn't been gripping his arm. As he raised his hand to hit the boy again, Kirby shoved between them.

"No!" she screamed. Her body was shaking and she was drenched in cold fear, but she stood up to her father. "No! You're not going to hurt him!" She shoved Addison's hand away from Josh's arm. "Get in the car, Josh! Now!"

Josh didn't need urging. He fled the scene.

Addison turned on his daughter. "You shouldn't have stopped me," he growled furiously. "It takes a man to raise a boy right and you sure as hell are screwing him up."

"He has a father. I'll call Russell as soon as I get home." She refused to quiver and flinch away from him even though she was terrified.

"His father is a goddamned, liberal pansy! He deserted his family and his responsibilities, probably to shack up with some goddamned coed! What good can he do!"

Kirby backed away. From the corner of her eye she saw her mother cowering in her chair. "Don't talk about Russell that way! He's my husband!"

"No, he's not! You couldn't even hold on to him! You're a fine one to talk about knowing how to raise boys! You've never done a goddamned thing right in your whole fucking life!"

Kirby hadn't felt this way since she was a child. Addison had never dared talk to her this way in front of Russell and she had forgotten how terrifying he could be. Her knees were so weak from fear she wasn't sure they wouldn't buckle under her. She wanted to turn and run but was afraid Addison would grab her by the hair before she could escape and haul her back for one of the beatings she had thought she would never have to experience again.

"Go on!" he bellowed. "Get the hell out of my house! And don't come back until you're ready to apologize to me for interfering in Josh's discipline!"

It took all the willpower she could muster, but Kirby walked out of the house rather than running like the frightened child she felt. By the time she reached the car, Cody was in the back seat with Josh. She could tell by his silence that Josh had told him some of what had happened. Josh looked near tears and he had a large red welt on his jaw where Addison had struck him. Kirby prayed that it wouldn't bruise. The prayer was a familiar one from her own childhood.

No one spoke until she was parked in their own driveway. Before they left the car, Kirby said in a remarkably calm voice. "You're grounded for a week, Josh. Tonight you're going to write Mr. Dupree and thank him for not having you arrested and apologize for shoplifting in his store."

Josh made no objections.

The phone was ringing as they entered the house. She was tempted to ignore it, but couldn't bear the noise. "Hello?"

"Kirby?" Jane said. She was talking in a whisper as if she were afraid Addison might overhear. "Is Josh all right?"

"I think so. I don't know if it will leave a bruise or not." Numbness was settling in on Kirby. This, too, was familiar. Numbness had always followed her father's rages. "He's gone up to his room."

"Put ice on it, dear. That's best."

"I know. I will."

"And don't think badly of your father. He just lost his temper. He can't help it."

Kirby closed her eyes. How often she had heard this. Dutifully, she said, "Okay, Mom. I won't."

"Tell Josh not to be upset with him."

"But Mom, he hit Josh hard enough to leave a welt on his face! I can't tell him not to mind!"

"Hard feelings never helped anything. We have to forgive and forget. It says so in the Bible. Addison knows it's his duty as head of the house to administer discipline. I imagine it was as difficult on him as it was on you."

"Spare the rod and spoil the child," Kirby said as she sank down onto a kitchen chair. "I know. I've heard it all my life."

"There's truth to it. I'm sure there must be or it wouldn't be in the Bible."

"Mom, the Bible was written by men in a patriarchal society. In the past several thousand years we've learned a lot about not abusing children. The men who wrote that lived in a culture that was little more than barbarian. Didn't it ever occur to you the Bible might be wrong about this?"

Jane paused as if she was thinking. "Why, no, it didn't. I

don't believe it can be if it was written in the Bible. It wouldn't be in there if it was wrong."

"I have to go, Mom. Josh needs the ice pack."

She hung up and sat staring at the phone for a moment. Addison's actions had brought up a score of memories she had managed to blank from her mind. His rages had terrified her as a child and on many occasions she had been beaten—not only with his belt but with his fist. If she hadn't intervened, Josh would have had worse bruises than this one.

In the few seconds it took her to reach the freezer for the ice, she was already distancing herself from the event, making it more trivial than it had been.

By the time she took the ice pack up to Josh, she believed it had been no more than an admonishing slap and that Josh was making more of it than was called for.

And it never occurred to her that she was protecting Addison and not Josh.

Chapter Fifteen

As usual, Leon Zimmerman's assistant DAs and investigators were gathered about him in the conference room adjoining his office for a case briefing. Kirby was trying to pay close attention, but her mind was still on Josh having shoplifted. She was concerned that if the store manager had a change of mind, he could still press charges. However, instead of being worried about the impact on Josh, she was apprehensive about what this would do to Addison. He had been clear that having a grandson breaking the law would jeopardize the appointment he was anticipating. *Appointment?* Had he said appointment? Surely she had misunderstood him or maybe he had said appointment meaning getting elected to the appellate judgeship he had been appointed to previously. With the tendency to dirty political campaigning in Texas, anything that made Addison or his family less than lily pure in the eyes of his constituents could and would be used against him. And it could cost him the election.

Something Zimmerman was saying jerked her attention back to the briefing. "What do you mean the Chandler conviction was overturned?"

"The appellate court ruled against us on that one. I'm sorry, Kirby."

"I didn't even know it was being heard! I never even saw the defense brief."

"I know. I reviewed it and let my appellate section handle our response. Good thing I did, too, because the defense asked for the court to hear oral argument and, believe it or not, it was granted. And that doesn't happen often."

"But that was my case! You know I had a personal interest in the appeal! It didn't have to go to the appellate section. You told me yourself that you sometimes made exceptions."

"I know, but you were busy with the Ardella Turner murder. I didn't want you distracted from that. Besides, the waters got muddied a bit when Chandler changed lawyers and hired Jim Haufman from your former firm. Even though it wouldn't have been a breach of ethics for you to work on it for that reason, I felt it best to have someone look at how it went with a fresh pair of eyes, greater objectivity. After all, you did get a bit too emotionally involved with that one."

"Jim Haufman got him off? What was the court's rationale?"

"It was all pretty involved. I reviewed it and we don't have any basis for a retrial. It's over and done."

"But the man raped his own daughter as well! With this conviction overturned, we'll have even less chance of ever prosecuting him for sexual assault of Kayla. Doesn't anyone care about that?"

"We all do. But we have to follow the rules. We can't retry him for the Brooks girl's molestation and we don't have the resources to try him for raping Kayla—even if the grand jury would bring an indictment against him, which I seriously doubt. Forget it, Kirby. I shouldn't have given you Davies' name in the first place. You got too personally involved in this case."

"What does Davies—"

"I said it is over and done with."

"But my father sits—"

"Wait a minute, Kirby. That was all handled properly. Justice Walker properly recused himself. He was not present in any of the proceedings. You're not suggesting your father did something illegal, are you?"

"Of course not!" Kirby shifted uncomfortably in her chair. She had often heard her father say that the justices conferred on occasion and it was possible that he had some knowledge of the arguments for reversal that were discussed in committee. She hadn't thought about that when she mentioned to the room full of attorneys that her father sat on the Fourteenth Court of Appeals. She'd only been thinking aloud about anything that might invalidate the court's reversal of Chandler's conviction. She certainly didn't intend to suggest that her father had done anything unethical or illegal. He would never knowingly do anything like that. "I just can't get it out of my mind that Chandler has molested two little girls and he needs to be put away."

"I agree. But there's nothing more we can do about that now. You know that, Kirby."

"So now we have to sit around and wait until Chandler does it again?"

"We've done all we can for now."

"Damn!" She tossed her pen down on the scarred table. "We had him put away and now he's free to molest children again! He may even be able to use this to get his visitation rights with his daughter reinstated! If we ever get him up on charges again—assuming he hasn't become too smart from this experience for that to happen—I want to handle the case."

"We'll talk about it then." Zimmerman's voice was strained and it was apparent he was fighting hard to keep his temper in check. Without looking back in her direction, he moved on to a pending case of aggravated robbery.

Kirby was far from satisfied.

She had received the pornographic magazine from Connie Chandler and it was even worse than she had expected. She had intended to pursue Kayla's molestation and have that charge as a backup for Glenda Brooks to doubly ensure Chandler was kept off the streets. Now she would have to rethink her entire procedure.

For a moment she considered asking her father about the case, but then thought better of it. She couldn't risk doing anything that might interfere with the possible conviction of Chandler in the future. She knew the justices who sat on the court with Addison. They were close friends and many of them had visited at the Walker house. Even if they had talked about the case with Addison, her father had no reason to want Chandler released. He didn't even know the man. He would have been no more likely to do something like that than trying to influence the appeals court to uphold the conviction because his daughter was the prosecutor. Or would he? She shook her head to free it of the thought. What kind of daughter was she to suspect her own father of any wrongdoing?

Tara hurried to the school bus and sat in the seat Cody had saved for her next to him. Her mother had one of her frequent appointments today and had sent word to the school that Tara was to take the bus with her cousins and go straight to her grandparents' house. Josh was nowhere to be seen. Tara assumed he must be with his new friends. She didn't like them and was glad they weren't on the bus.

"Can I talk to you?" she asked Cody in a low voice.

"Sure. We talk all the time." He was busy drawing a winged dragon on his English book cover.

"I mean about something real important. You have to promise not to tell anybody."

"I won't." Cody added scales to the dragon's wing and looked up. "What's wrong? Is some guy bothering you in school?"

"No. I can take care of that myself. Unless the boy was real big," she amended. "This is something else."

"Well?" he prompted when she paused several seconds.

"Do you like going over to Grandad's house?"

"I guess so." He frowned slightly. "There's not much to do over there."

"I'm over there a lot. Mom runs a lot of errands and she doesn't like to take me with her."

"So take a book or a game with you. That's what I do. Grandad will usually play a game with me if he's not busy doing something else."

Tara bit her lip. "Does he ever, well, do weird things when you're around?"

"Weird in what way? You know how old people are. He just

sits and watches TV most of the time. Boring stuff, like the news."

"Does he ever want to play hide-and-seek?"

Cody laughed. "Hide-and-seek? With me? I'm a little old to play hide-and-seek, Tara. Of course not!"

"Oh." She sighed. Cody didn't understand what she was trying to say and she didn't know how to put it any plainer. She didn't know the words to explain how her grandfather's version of hide-and-seek was different from the one she and Cody had played when they were younger.

"Just tell him you're too old to play a baby's game. That's what I'd do." He went back to work on his dragon.

Tara stared out the window. No one understood what she was trying to say. Maybe she was acting like a dork to care about it at all. Next to Melissa Puricelli, Cody was her best friend, and if he didn't understand her, maybe no one could. Or maybe her grandfather was doing what all grandfathers did and there was something wrong with Tara for being bothered by it.

She and Cody got off the bus at the stop in their neighborhood, and after telling her goodbye, Cody went running off toward his house. Tara knew she was supposed to go to her grandparents' house, but after thinking it over, she decided instead to pretend she forgot and wandered off in the direction of her own home.

She was eight years old and that was plenty old enough to stay alone. Melissa had been staying home alone after school since the beginning of the semester.

Since she didn't have a key, Tara went around the house to her backyard and sat on the picnic table to wait for her mother to return. Leaves from the past winter littered the redwood surface of the table and an inch worm was measuring its way across the wood. Tara watched the insect until she was bored, then coaxed it onto a yellow leaf and put it in the flower bed. She wondered how long it would be before her mother got home.

The day was hot for May. Spring in Houston was almost as brief as the winter season. Soon it would be so hot that little shimmers of heat would rise from the streets and the air would seem brassy and the afternoon rains would begin. Tara loved being out of school, but she also dreaded the coming of summer. When her mother ran errands or had appointments, she would have to go to her grandfather's house more often.

She climbed onto the tabletop and lay there staring up at the clouds, building high above her back fence and seeming to be no farther away than the tops of the trees. Several birds circled and dipped lazily in the blue of the sky. She heard the hum of a flying insect near her ear and batted at it instinctively. What would her mother do to her if she refused ever to go to her grandparents' house again?

After what seemed like hours, Tara heard the sound of a car turning into the drive. She rolled to a sitting position and jumped off the table to meet her mother.

"Tara? What are you doing here, honey?"

"I rode the bus home from school." She tried to look innocent, as if she had forgotten all about her mother's instructions for her to go to her grandparents' house. "I've been playing in the backyard."

"You were supposed to go to Grandad's house. Grandma must be worried about you."

That hadn't occurred to Tara. She loved her grandmother. "I guess I forgot. I heard the phone ring a few times. Maybe that was her. I couldn't answer it because I couldn't get in the house."

The look on her mother's face told Tara that she was a little upset that Tara had not figured that she was supposed to be at her grandparents' if she was locked out of her own house. Tara smiled sweetly, hoping it would improve her mother's mood. She wasn't afraid of her mother punishing her, for she seldom did, but she was always concerned when her mother didn't look happy.

"Come on in. I'll call Grandma and tell her what happened and that you're safe."

Tara followed her mother into the house, and while her mother went to the phone, she got a bottle of orange juice out of the refrigerator and poured herself a glass.

Mallory dialed the number and waited. "Dad? I'm home.

Apparently Tara forgot she was supposed to go to your house after school. Has Mom been worrying?"

Tara couldn't hear what was being said on the other end of the line. She reached for the cookie jar and helped herself to two cookies.

"I'm sorry she worried you. At least Mom wasn't there to be upset."

Tara listened without appearing to be paying attention. If she had done what she was supposed to, she would have been all alone with her grandad all this time. She was glad she hadn't gone.

After her mother hung up the phone, she said, "Grandad is a little upset with you. You have to use your head, honey. If I'm not home and the house is locked, you're to go to their house."

"Can I go to Cody's instead?"

"No, he and Josh are alone there most days, and if you started roughhousing and got hurt, there would be no adult around to help you."

"Josh is nearly an adult."

"Not lately, he isn't."

"Could I go there on the days when Ellen is cleaning?" Recently Cody had told her that his mother had asked Ellen to come only a couple of days a week.

"Ellen has enough to do without having another child to watch over."

"Mom, can I talk to you for a minute?"

"Sure, honey. What's going on?"

"I don't like going to Grandad's."

"Of course you do," Mallory said with a laugh. "You've been going over there all your life."

"I know." She fell back on Cody's excuse. "There's nothing to play with over there."

"Take some of your books or toys with you next time and leave them there. Grandma won't mind."

Tara frowned. "I don't like staying there." She ducked her head. "Sometimes Grandad scares me a little. When you and Grandma aren't around," she added, hoping her mother would understand.

Mallory stared at her. "How could you possibly be afraid of Grandad? He adores you. Why, before you were born, he hoped you would be a girl. He used to say, 'Kirby has a house full of boys. I'm counting on you and Derrick to give me a granddaughter.' Remember me telling you about that?"

"I remember." She crumbled the cookie onto the kitchen table.

"Don't make a mess," Mallory scolded mildly. "Either eat the cookies you get out of the cookie jar or don't get them in the first place."

"Mom, can I start staying here alone when you run errands? You could hide the house key like Melissa's mother does. She puts it under a flowerpot on the side porch. I could let myself in and watch cartoons until you come home."

"No, you might be afraid here all alone. I'd worry about you if an adult wasn't with you to supervise. What if a stranger came to the door?"

"I know not to let strangers into the house. I'd pretend I wasn't here. I'd hide upstairs until they left."

Mallory shook her head. "You have an answer for every thing, don't you? Maybe you'll be old enough to stay alone next year."

"Mom, I'm eight years old!" She tried to make it sound ancient. "Why don't you listen when I tell you I'm afraid of Grandad?" Tears rose in her eyes and she let them roll down her cheeks. Sometimes this worked.

"Because it's silly for you to be afraid of someone who loves you as much as Grandad does."

"He's not the same when you aren't there." Tara rested her elbows on the table and moved the cookie crumbs around with her fingertip.

"I'm not going to argue with you, Tara. You're lucky to live in the same town with your grandparents. Not many little girls do, you know. Now I'm not going to hear any more about it. When I can't be here, you're to go to their house and don't forget it again." She left the room.

Tara drew in a deep breath and blew the crumbs across the table. She had known her mother wouldn't understand. No one did.

* * *

Kirby turned up the heat under the pot of pinto beans she was cooking. With Russell gone, she found it hard to decide what to prepare for dinner. She hadn't realized how often he had dinner started by the time she came in. Lately she had been so depressed she hadn't wanted to eat at all. Food seemed to have no flavor, and dinnertime was usually unpleasant with Josh's new rebellious behavior. She was still haunted by the embarrassment of his shoplifting episode at Brennahan's.

"What are we having?" Cody asked as he passed through.

"Red beans and rice."

"Again?"

"It's good for you." She went to the freezer and took out a box of fish sticks. The boys needed meat. She put a skillet on the stove.

"I hate fish sticks."

"You've always loved them before," Kirby reminded him.

"No, I don't. Dad likes them."

She sighed. "Well, I knew someone did. We need to eat them up, I suppose."

Cody was muttering under his breath as he left the kitchen. She poured a little vegetable oil in the skillet, and when it was hot enough for frying, she tossed in enough fish sticks for the boys. Swallowing beans and rice would be difficult enough for her. Fish was out of the question.

"Mom, did Cody come through here?" Josh asked, banging the door behind him.

"You just missed him." She looked at her older son. "Why don't you help me cook supper? I miss talking to you."

She had read somewhere that rebellious teens could be reasoned with best over chores in the kitchen. Lately she didn't look forward to relating with Josh and that disturbed her. She had to find a way to rediscover the loving boy he had been before the separation. He hadn't talked to her about the shoplifting incident or even the emotional explosion at Addison's house. She had no idea what he was thinking these days.

"Cooking is women's work."

"That's news to me. I've seen your father cook enough

times," she said dryly. "But since you're determined to be sexist, you can mow the grass." She tried to keep her tone of voice light, but failed.

"No way. I mowed it last time."

"No, you didn't." Every conversation she had with Josh these days degenerated into an argument between them and she couldn't bear the thought of another. Already she was almost too tired to push the fish sticks around so they wouldn't stick to the pan.

"I hate fish sticks."

Consciously deciding not to let him prod her into conflict with him, she smiled and said, "You and Cody can form a club. He's already registered a complaint."

Josh leaned his elbows on the counter that flanked the stove. "I hate beans and rice, too."

"Maybe you should go watch TV. You're only going to get in trouble in here."

"God, Mom! I'm not a baby!"

Kirby tensed, fearing she would lose control, and turned back to the stove. Suddenly she was in the middle of a flashback. Her breath came in sharp gasps as she felt, rather than saw, a man coming up behind her. They were alone in the house and she was trapped in the kitchen. There was no escape, no place to hide. With a strangled cry, she shoved herself back from the stove.

"What's wrong with you?" Josh asked suspiciously, not knowing whether to be alarmed or not.

Kirby couldn't answer. The smell of the fish sticks and red beans was overwhelming. The same smell had been woven into the flashback. Nausea filled her and the kitchen swam dizzily before her. For a terrible moment she couldn't be sure whether she was in her own kitchen with Josh or still in the kitchen of the flashback. "Panic attack," she managed to murmur.

"You look like you're going to throw up or something."

"Josh! Get out of here!" she screamed.

He jerked upright, looking startled, but a moment later the sullen expression was back on his face. He shoved a kitchen chair out of his way as he stormed from the room.

Kirby leaned over the sink and splashed cold water on her

face. That helped some. She washed her hands as if they were too dirty ever to be clean again. She was trembling so violently she almost couldn't turn off the water.

The smell of smoking grease pulled her back into the present. Hastily she turned off the heat and pushed the skillet off the burner. The kitchen was filling with acrid smoke. A few seconds more and the grease would have caught fire. How long had she been washing her face and hands? The fish had barely started cooking when she backed away from the stove.

She leaned against the counter and buried her face in her hands. What was happening to her?

"Mom? Are you okay?" Cody asked. His voice was small and worried.

She lowered her hands and forced a smile. "I'm fine, honey."

"Josh said you're acting weird."

"He says that about everybody." She didn't meet Cody's concerned stare. "Supper is almost ready."

"You burned the fish."

Unconsciously, she snapped back at him. "You said you hate it, so why do you care?" Then realizing what she'd done, she softened her voice and said, "I'm sorry. I'm not feeling well. Tell Josh to come to the table. I'll set the table, but then I'm going to go up and lie down for a while."

"You're not eating again?"

"Don't you get on my case, too." She ladled up the food and salvaged the least burned fish. The kitchen suddenly seemed dangerous and she was eager to be out of it.

As she was putting the food on the table, the boys came in. "Cody, it's your turn to do the dishes after you two finish eating."

"It's not my turn. It's Josh's," he protested.

"Josh is going to mow the yard." She saw Josh open his mouth to argue and she glared at him. "Not a single word, Josh. I mean it!"

He dropped into his chair and glared at the food. Kirby hurried from the room.

She didn't slow down until she was in her bedroom with the door shut. As she had done when she was a child, she threw herself across the bed and curled into a fetal position. She still felt shaken and sick. What had happened to her? In the past few weeks she had been reading up on panic attacks and nowhere did it say that the attacks came with a scenario that seemed to be a terrifying memory.

For a long time she lay there, listening to the faint sounds of the boys rattling dishes in the kitchen, then the low hum of the lawn mower. Over and over she told herself that she was safe. No one was trying to hurt her. No one could get into the house and do terrible things to her. She had no idea what the terrible things might be, but she felt they were hiding there in her brain and refusing to be seen.

When she could sit up without shaking, she looked up the number of the psychiatrist recommended by Dr. Nichols and wrote it on a piece of paper. She put it in her purse and hugged the purse to her breasts. In the morning she would call for an appointment.

Several times during the intervening three weeks she had had to wait to get in to see Dr. Jacobs, Kirby had been tempted to cancel her appointment. There was nothing wrong with her, she'd argued to herself, and it would be a waste of money and time to go. However, the recurrent, horrible nightmare that had so often robbed her of sleep had come again the night before, dispelling any question in her mind as to the need to seek help.

She arrived a few minutes early and took a seat alone in the tranquil ambiance of the waiting room. Surrounded in pastel shades of blue and gray, rather reminiscent of her mother's decorating scheme, she thought that her mother would have felt perfectly at home here. Even the magazines scattered about were many of the same ones Jane had subscribed to for years. Rather than these things putting her at ease, however, Kirby found herself shifting uncomfortably in her overstuffed chair and wanting to leave. Pride, however, anchored her to the chair.

"Mrs. Garrett?" a friendly voice said.

Kirby jerked her head up. She hadn't heard the woman come down the carpeted hall. "I'm Kirby Garrett."

The woman smiled and extended her hand. "I'm Lauren Jacobs. Would you like to come into my office so we can get acquainted?" The woman was slender and blond, and looked both competent and friendly.

Kirby repressed the sudden urge to run away and followed her down the hall. Unlike the waiting room, the office was done in forest green with cream accents. The furniture could as easily have been that of a tastefully decorated living room except for an oak desk with a computer on it. She sat on a love seat near the door. Lauren Jacobs took the overstuffed chair beside a lamp.

"Dr. Jacobs," Kirby said uncertainly. "I'm feeling really ill at ease here. I think maybe I'm wasting both your time and mine."

"Please, call me Lauren. Do you mind if I call you Kirby? It's so much easier to get to know one another that way."

Kirby realized she was clutching her purse in her lap, so she released her grip and tried to appear more comfortable. "I probably have no reason to be here at all. It's just that I've been having panic attacks and my medical doctor suggested that I see you."

Lauren glanced at the papers in her folder. "Warren Nichols is an old friend of mine. How is he doing these days?"

"He's fine. If you could just write me a prescription for something to control the panic attacks, I'll be on my way."

"Will you describe them for me?"

Kirby swallowed nervously. "Well, they happen at the oddest times. I never know when one will crop up." She tried to laugh to cover her nervousness, but that made it worse. Forcing herself to continue, she said, "One even overtook me in the kitchen."

"What was it like?"

"It's really strange. It's as if I'm a child again and someone is about to hurt me." Kirby watched the psychiatrist closely to see what effect her words were having, but couldn't read any changes in the woman's calm face.

"You seem to be a child?" Lauren jotted several quick notes then looked back up. "Who is it that hurt you?"

"No, I said someone seemed to be about to hurt me. Certainly nothing like that ever happened to me as a child. These aren't memories, even if they do seem to be. No, I was loved and protected as a child. No one ever hurt me at all. Not ever."

She realized she was protesting too much and pursed her lips firmly. Thoughts of the beatings her father had given her over the years rushed by, but she refused to consider them hurtful. All fathers disciplined their children. Besides, these flashes of panic didn't seem to have anything to do with his rages or beatings.

"I see. Did you grow up here in Houston?"

"Yes, I'm one of that rare breed—a Houston native. Almost no one is these days. People move around so much. My father is Addison Walker, the judge."

"I've heard of him. I read about him in the paper from time to time. I believe he hosted a party for Raymond Stansfield's presidential campaign."

"That's right. He and Mr. Stansfield have been friends for many years."

"And your mother? Is she still living?"

"Yes. Didn't I mention her?"

"No, only your father."

"I've always been closer to him. I guess you'd say I was a Daddy's girl when I was growing up."

"In what way?" Lauren smiled as if they were having nothing more than a pleasant conversation.

Kirby squirmed, though she was unaware she had. "I was his favorite. I guess that sounds conceited, but my sister is more like Mom. I'm an attorney like Dad and was with his law firm for a number of years. I'm working in the district attorney's office now. Not that Dad and I had a falling-out. Nothing like that. I just don't care much for my brother-in-law and didn't want to work with him." She heard herself saying far more than she had expected or intended. How did Lauren have that effect on her?

"Your brother-in-law is also a lawyer?"

"Yes. His name is Derrick McKinsey. He and Mallory, my only sister, have been married a number of years and have a daughter named Tara."

"Are you married, Kirby?"

"Yes. But we're separated. I'd rather not talk about that."

"If you'd rather not, we won't, but it might have something to do with these panic attacks."

"From what I've read, panic attacks come on for no reason at all. My separating from Russell has nothing to do with it. Besides, I was having them before he left."

Lauren made more notes. "In all your panic attacks, are you seemingly a child in danger?"

"They aren't all identical, if that's what you mean. I do feel as if I'm a child. That part is right. The same thing doesn't seem to be happening every time, though. In fact, I'm not sure what *is* happening. Only that I feel frightened and as if I'm in danger."

Lauren put down her pen. "I'll be honest with you, just as I expect you to be with me. What you're describing doesn't sound like a panic attack to me."

"No?" Kirby asked in a small voice. Part of her had known this.

"They sound more like flashbacks."

"I don't understand. What are flashbacks?"

"It's when you live through a traumatic event and years later have memories so vivid it's as if you're back in danger again. Unlike regular memories, flashbacks seem as if you're the age you were at the time of the trauma and in the same locale. It's as if you're reliving what happened, not just remembering it."

"That's not possible," Kirby said flatly. "I had a perfect childhood. My parents loved me and protected me. There's no way these are memories of something that happened to me."

"Perhaps I'm wrong. Why don't you tell me about what you've experienced in greater detail?"

Kirby drew in a deep breath. "This isn't easy to do. Okay, I was cooking supper a few weeks ago. The evening before I made the appointment with you, to be exact. I felt as if I was trapped in a kitchen somehow. The type of food I was cooking, the smells, seemed to be part of the panic . . . whatever it was. I felt as if a man had trapped me and there was nowhere I could hide."

"Was it as if you had come into the kitchen to hide from him?"

"Yes. I suppose you could put it that way. I felt as if I were a small child. Much younger than would be cooking supper."

Kirby suppressed a shiver. "Even talking about it makes me uneasy. It's almost as bad as my nightmare."

"Nightmare?"

"That slipped out. I didn't mean to say that. It's just a nightmare. I've had it for years."

"It's recurred for years? The same nightmare?"

"Everybody has them," Kirby said defensively. "In mine, I'm a child standing in a long, blue hall. Your waiting room reminded me of the color. I guess that's why I mentioned it. Anyway, I seem to be looking for something but I don't want to find it and I know whatever it is will be in the room at the far end of the hall." She paused. "This is really difficult to talk about. I've never told anyone but Russell about this dream."

"Just take your time. Would you like some coffee?"

"Yes, thank you." She watched Lauren go to the coffee pot and begin pouring a cup for each of them. She thought it would be easier to talk when Lauren wasn't looking at her, so she continued. "In the dream, I finally open the last door. I see a man lying on the bed. At first it's as if he's asleep." Her voice faltered as Lauren turned around and started back to her.

Lauren handed her the cup. "Careful. It's hot." She sat back down. "What happens next?"

Kirby couldn't answer for a moment. Then, hoping to dismiss the subject, she said, "I suppose that's pretty much all of it."

When the psychiatrist remained quiet, Kirby sighed, concluding she wasn't going to be let off the hook so easily. She knew if she wasn't going to talk, nothing would be changed. And even though it was only a nightmare, she wanted to be rid of it. "Lately the dream has a new part added. The man is, well, touching himself."

"Touching himself?" Lauren's voice was still calm and gentle as if she weren't at all shocked.

"He's touching his penis." Kirby said it almost angrily. "I'm embarrassed. I didn't intend to tell you all this! I only came for medication for panic attacks!"

"I know. This man—is he anyone you recognize?"

"Of course not. I wouldn't dream some acquaintance of mine was masturbating! I don't have dreams like that!"

"Do you need cream or sugar for your coffee? I forget to

ask." Lauren smiled as if she discussed nightmares of strange men masturbating every day. It struck Kirby that perhaps she did.

"No. Dad and I drink it black."

"Did you say 'Dad and I' for some particular reason?"

"No. Of course not! We just drink coffee alike. That's all I meant. Mother and Mallory put cream in theirs."

"And your husband?" She consulted her notes. "Russell?"

"He drinks it black, too. What difference does it make how anyone drinks coffee?"

"It doesn't. Why does the question upset you?"

Kirby frowned at her. "I'm not upset! Okay, so I am. But it's not easy coming in here and talking to a perfect stranger. I feel stupid telling you things like this!"

"Do you usually find it difficult to discuss things of a sexual nature?"

"Russell would tell you I do." She frowned into her coffee cup, then grimaced to show how foolish the idea was and added, "He says I'm frigid!"

"Are you?"

"No, he's oversexed. That's why he moved out, I think. We aren't sexually compatible."

"You're not sure why he left? How long has he been gone?"

"Several months. We have trouble communicating. Yes, I think—okay, I'm sure—that's why he left. He's the one who should be in here, not me."

"Frequency of making love isn't as important as whether the two people agree on it. For some couples, once a month is plenty. For others, it's every night."

"God, I couldn't stand that!" Kirby blurted out, then put a fingertip to her lips. "I shouldn't have said that."

Lauren shook her head. "You can say anything in here. This is a safe place. For some of the people I talk to, it's their only safe place. I won't judge you or repeat anything you say. I'm here to help you resolve your own issues. I have no magic answers."

Kirby felt strangely touched. A safe place. How often she had wanted one! "If you don't think I'm having panic attacks, does that mean nothing can help me?"

"Not at all. Have you ever heard of repressed memory syndrome?"

"No. But these aren't memories."

"I understand that. Whatever they are, you don't want to continue having them, do you?"

"No. Lately they've been happening more often. I'm having the nightmare at least twice a week. And I'm so depressed I have trouble getting through all I have to do in a day."

Lauren reached for a prescription pad. "I'm going to give you something to calm you down and help reduce the level of anxiety. For the next three weeks, take one three times a day. Then we'll taper off until you reach a comfortable, short-term maintenance dose. I'm also prescribing a different depression medication that may be more effective than the one you've been taking. Take one in the morning and two at night. It will take a couple of days before you see a change in the depression, but after that, you should feel better." She opened her appointment book. "Is this a good time for you to come to see me next week?"

Kirby almost told her she wouldn't need to return. Then she remembered what Lauren had said about this being a safe place. It would be wonderful to have a place to unload all the tensions and concerns and troubles without having to justify any of them. "Yes. This is a good time for me."

"Then I'll see you next week." Lauren gave her a friendly smile. "I'm looking forward to working with you. Together, I'll bet we can get rid of that nightmare as well as the panic attacks, or whatever they are."

Kirby felt a sense of relief as she left the office. Although she knew the panic attacks were that and not memories of any kind, repressed or otherwise, it had helped to talk about them. Maybe Lauren could also help her figure out a way to get Josh to behave. She might even have some advice about how she could convince Russell to come home. She reached in her purse and touched the folded prescriptions. Just knowing there was help to be had was comforting.

Chapter Sixteen

"Hi, Kirby. How's it going?" Russell cradled the phone between his cheek and shoulder.

"Okay, I guess. Did you want to speak to the boys? Neither of them are home, but I'll tell them to call you when they come in."

Russell heard the distance in her voice and it hurt him. He knew Kirby so well. When she sounded like this it was a sure sign she was unhappy. "Okay, have them do that. How are you?" This was worse than talking to a stranger. Every word he spoke carried a potential pitfall.

"I'm well."

"You don't sound happy."

"I said I'm healthy, not that I'm happy." There was a pause. "I started seeing a psychiatrist."

"You did?" He couldn't keep the surprise out of his voice.

"Her name is Dr. Lauren Jacobs. Dr. Nichols recommended her to me."

"I'm so glad you're doing this!"

"You don't have to sound so thrilled. I'm only going to get rid of the panic attacks. Not because you told me to go."

"Don't get defensive. We're only having a conversation."

He heard her sigh. "I'm sorry, Russell. Lately I'm a bundle of nerves. I'm having nightmares almost every night now and the panic attacks are coming more often. I find myself creeping around the house in fear of the next one."

"Did you tell Dr. Jacobs about this?"

"Of course. She says they aren't actually panic attacks. She calls them flashbacks. I can't seem to convince her that I've never had any unpleasant experience to cause them."

"I can think of several off the top of my head. Are you forgetting how afraid you used to be of your father?"

"I was never afraid of him! How can you even say such a thing?" She was angry. "Dad is a perfect father. He never spanked me unless I needed it. I was his favorite!"

"I can remember seeing bruises when you came back to college after a weekend at home. You have a very selective memory when it comes to him."

"You've never liked him. I'm not going to sit here and defend him to you."

"Kirby, I'm only asking you to keep an open mind. Maybe the flashbacks are about him 'spanking' you." Russell had learned not to refer to the beatings as such. "Isn't that possible?"

"Maybe." She sounded tired. "I'll ask Lauren at my next appointment. I've been seeing her once a week for almost two months now."

"Would it help you if I also talk to her?"

"Why would you want to do that?"

"I want us to get back together." He moved the receiver to his other hand. "I miss you, Kirby."

"I miss you, too." Her voice broke as if she was fighting to hold back her feelings. "It seems as if you've been gone forever."

"I know. It feels that way to me, too." Lately he had been hard-pressed to remember that he had left home because conditions there had been so difficult. "It's especially tough after dinner. I miss hearing the boys running up and down the stairs or playing one of their games. It's very quiet here."

"Is it only the boys you miss?"

"No. You know better than that."

"No, I don't."

"I've never stopped loving you. I don't think that I ever will."

"Come home, Russell."

He closed his eyes. It was hard to resist her. "Maybe I will soon. I want us to talk to Dr. Jacobs together and work out our problems first."

"She prefers to be called Lauren. I suppose we could do that. Are you going to tell her that you think I'm frigid?"

"Don't get angry with me all over again. I've apologized several times for saying that. I was upset. But if I come back, I want us to be lovers as well as husband and wife."

There was a long silence on the other end of the phone.

"I guess that's my answer." He sighed. "Well, Kirby, let me know when or if you want me to make an appointment with Lauren. I want us to get back together but not the way we were before."

"I think I need to get off the phone now. I'll have one of the boys call you."

Kirby hung up, but Russell held the receiver for a moment before doing the same. He looked around his apartment. It was small and clean but it was much too quiet and too empty. He liked being married and having a family and he wanted to be back in his own home. He knew, however, that he had to hold firm. If he went back into home life as it had been when he left, he would still be unhappy and eventually he would leave again. He had no intention of spending his life moving in and out of his own house.

What would his life be like without Kirby on a permanent basis? He didn't like the prospect. It wasn't that he didn't think he could make a new life for himself. A number of women on the faculty had openly or covertly asked him for a date. He had turned them all down. In his mind he was still married and he was monogamous by nature. But he was so lonely he dreaded waking up every day.

Celibacy hadn't been easy, whether he felt he was still married to Kirby or not. He couldn't remember the last time they had made love, only his last attempt. She had acted as if he were trying to rape her.

Russell couldn't understand it. Kirby had never enjoyed sex

but he had no idea why. When they married, she had said she was a virgin. Russell hadn't had all that much experience himself but he had no reason to disbelieve her. He was as positive as a man could be that she had never had an affair, nor had she been threatened with an actual rape. There simply was no explanation for her growing aversion to sex.

If only he understood it, he felt sure he could handle the situation better.

Tara sat on the tall kitchen stool in her grandmother's kitchen watching Jane crimp the edges of the pie crust. The heat from the oven was making the room too warm but she wasn't about to leave the protection of her grandmother's side.

"I think you're going to be a wonderful cook," Jane said. "I've never seen a child more interested in watching me bake."

"If the pie is done before Mom comes after me, can I have a piece?"

"I suppose it wouldn't hurt just this once. You're welcome to stay for dinner, you know."

"Mom would miss me." She heard a door close in the other end of the house and knew it was her grandfather. She had hoped he would stay out in the yard until she went home.

"I'm sure she would." Jane smiled at her and dabbed at Tara's nose with the hand towel. "Your nose has flour on it."

Tara smiled and rubbed it herself.

"Now we put some butter on the top crust and sprinkle it with sugar and cinnamon to make it brown nicely, and cook it."

Tara picked up one of the long spirals of apple peeling and began to eat it. Her grandmother was the only person she knew who could peel an apple so that the entire skin was together in one long spiral. Jane had told her once that her own grandmother had thought it was bad luck to break it. When no one was around to make her grandma shy, she had many stories to tell Tara.

The thud of heavy footsteps crossing the dining room floor signaled Tara that Addison was coming to the kitchen. She leaned against Jane's arm.

''Sit up, honey, You'll fall off the stool when I put the pie in the oven.''

Tara straightened.

''There you are!'' Addison said. ''I thought you'd like to come out and see the flower bed I'm weeding. It's got all your favorite flowers in it.''

''I don't like flowers anymore.'' Tara watched him cautiously.

''Not like flowers?'' Jane asked with a laugh. ''Tara, you say the funniest things.''

Addison held out his hand. ''Come on, baby. I'll show them to you.''

Tara drew back. ''I don't want to. It's too hot outside.''

''You're not getting lazy, are you?'' Addison's voice was still jovial but his eyes were losing their humor. ''A little girl shouldn't mind being outside in the summer.''

''There's plenty of shade out there,'' Jane said, giving Tara a gentle nudge. ''Let him show you the flower bed. He's worked so hard on it.''

''I'm helping you bake a pie.''

''The pie is finished except for putting it in the oven. There's nothing more to watch. I'll call you when it's done.''

With no more excuses to protect her, Tara slid off the stool and followed her grandfather out of the kitchen.

When they were in the backyard, Addison said, ''You've been avoiding me. I don't like that. I thought you were my best girl.''

Tara shrugged. The sun was hot on her head and waves of heat seemed to rise even from the grass. Dutifully, she gazed at the flower bed. Addison had planted all her favorite flowers, just as he had told her he would. There were roses and zinnias and bright red mounds of ruby begonias. She knew he had worked hard on the flower bed.

''Do you like it?''

''It's pretty,'' she admitted.

''Don't you think I deserve a kiss for all my hard work?''

This was what Tara had dreaded. All Addison's gifts had a price tag. She turned away and kicked at the thick grass.

''Come over here.'' Addison glanced at the windows of the house and drew her to the side fence where no one inside could see them. The yard was surrounded by a high wooden privacy fence that completely concealed the yard from the neighbors.

"I don't want to."

Addison took her hand and led her into the shade of the live oak tree. He lifted her and put her on the lowest limb. That made them the same height. "You've always been my favorite, Tara. I love you even more than my own girls. You're special."

She watched him silently.

Addison ran his finger along the curve of her cheek. Tara wanted to pull away but her position on the tree limb was too precarious. "You have such pretty eyes. I've always been partial to brown eyes."

"Mom says I have her eyes." Maybe if she could keep him talking, the other things wouldn't happen.

"Yes, you do. All your grandmother's family have brown eyes and dark hair, just as mine have gray or blue eyes. There's not a single blond in the whole family. Did you know that?" He traced his finger down her neck and along the front of her T-shirt. "It won't be long before you turn into a young lady. You won't be a little girl much longer. I'm looking forward to watching you develop."

Tara moved uneasily. The ground was a long way down and the bark was rough against her skin below her shorts. If she slid off the tree, she would hurt herself.

Addison rested one hand on her bare leg and put the other behind her back. "I don't want you to fall," he explained. He was getting that odd look in his eyes. "I think you owe me a kiss for making you such a pretty flower garden."

"I didn't ask you to make it. That was your idea."

"Now don't get sassy. Little girls aren't pretty when they talk back to their elders." He smiled at her. "Just one kiss."

Before Tara could think of a way to avoid it, Addison put his lips on hers. She stiffened and felt his fingers slide under the hem of her shorts and up her leg.

With a strangled cry, Tara kicked out as hard as she could and he stepped back in surprise. She slid off the tree limb, feeling the searing abrasion of the skin on the backs of her legs. As soon as she hit the ground, she scrambled to her feet and ran as fast as she could. She knew this house offered no protection, so she ran home.

Seeing that her mother's car wasn't in the driveway, she let herself into her backyard and hid behind the garage. Her heart was hammering and she felt sick at her stomach. Was he coming after her? She tried to breathe silently so she could hear if the gate opened.

The back of the garage was a tangle of ligustrum that had reached tree-like proportions and the deep shade made them bare of leaves on the lower branches. She knew from experience they weren't strong enough to climb, but they made a maze of limbs as thick as the garage was wide. Carefully she weaved her way through to the fence. If he was after her, he wouldn't be able to catch her easily.

The backs of her legs were hurting and when she gingerly touched them, her fingers came away sticky with blood. In getting off the limb, she had given herself a bad scrape on both legs. Tara felt like crying but she was afraid of making any noise. She had no idea where her mother had gone or when she would be back. If her grandfather was following her, she couldn't be positive he wouldn't be able to get to her. If he commanded her to come out of the maze of branches, she might be too afraid to disobey.

Tara couldn't keep the tears back. She knew she needed help but there seemed to be no place to get it. No one understood when she tried to tell them what Addison was doing to her. Did that mean he wasn't lying when he said all grandfathers did this to show how much they loved their granddaughters?

She had been hiding among the twisted ligustrum branches for a long time before she heard the sound of her gate opening. Tara held her breath and tried to crouch out of sight.

"Tara? Are you here, honey?"

"Grandma? Is that you?" she called in relief.

Jane hurried to the back of the garage and peered through the branches. "Tara? What are you doing back there?"

"Nothing." She looked past Jane to see if Addison was with her. "Are you by yourself?"

"Yes. Come out of there, honey."

Slowly Tara worked her way out of the tangle. She gazed

up at her grandmother fearfully. She knew she had been disobedient to kick Addison and run away. She was supposed to stay at their house until her mother came for her. Addison would be really mad this time.

"Why did you come over here? Did you think your mother had come home?" Jane hugged her. "She told you to stay at our house."

"I'm big enough to stay alone."

"You'll have to talk to your mother about that. Come along now. My goodness, you're as hot as a firecracker. Let's go back to my house and get in out of the heat."

"No!" Tara backed away.

"Why not?" Jane stared at her in surprise. "Don't you want to come with me? We have such fun together."

"Grandad is mad at me."

Jane tilted her head to one side for a moment as if she was thinking. "Do you have any idea why he would be mad?"

Tara nodded. "I can't tell you though."

"I'll tell you what. Let's go on the porch and sit in the shade and you can cool off there."

Tara doubted the porch would be much cooler than the huge ligustrum bushes, but she followed Jane to the group of rattan chairs. Jane turned on the ceiling fan that cooled the deep porch and patted the chair beside her for Tara to sit down.

"I don't want to sit down. My legs hurt."

"Your legs hurt? What do you mean? Come here and show me." Jane turned her around. "My goodness! What happened to you!"

"I slid off the tree limb."

"Why, honey, you scraped all the skin off! You need to come home with me and let me doctor that!"

"No! Grandad will hurt me!"

Jane's mouth turned down and she got that puzzled look on her face that meant she didn't understand. "Hurt you?"

Tara nodded and ducked her head.

Jane pulled her into her lap. The silky fabric of her grandmother's skirt felt good against the undamaged skin on Tara's legs, but even as soft as it was, it made the scraped parts burn. Tara, however, didn't complain; she wanted a hug more than anything. Jane kissed the top of her head. "Sometimes grown-ups get angry and say things they don't mean. Grandad loves you but at times he gets so mad he can't stop hurtful words from coming out. Did he say he was going to spank you?"

Tara shook her head. "I know he will though." He had spanked her once before, using his belt, and Tara thought she would die if anyone hit her with anything on her scraped legs. They hurt something awful as it was. The last time it happened, her daddy had been really upset and said he didn't care if Tara broke every glass over there, no one was going to spank her. But later her mom had told her that she had to be extra good at Grandad's house and not make him so mad. Tara knew she could be spanked before either of her parents knew what was happening. She was never struck at home and it terrified her.

"Well, then, let's stay here and wait for your mother." Jane cuddled her as if Tara were still a small child and not in third grade.

After a while, Tara felt better and wasn't as afraid. She got out of Jane's lap and snuggled in the chair beside her. Jane asked finally, "Do you know why Grandad would want to spank you?"

"I didn't want to kiss him."

"I don't understand."

"He said I should give him a kiss to thank him for making the flower bed look nice since he used all my favorite flowers."

"That's not a very big price," Jane teased gently. "What could one kiss hurt?"

"He put me in the tree and kissed me. I slid off the limb and ran over here."

Jane thought for a moment. "I still don't see why that would make him angry."

"Nobody ever understands! It's like I'm not talking English or something!" Tara was close to tears again.

"Now, now. Don't get upset," Jane said soothingly. "Explain it to me again. Maybe I missed something."

Tara drew in a deep breath. "He showed me the flower garden and said I owed him a kiss for making it. Then he put me on the tree limb and kissed me. Like a grown-up kiss."

Jane was quiet for a long time. "Like a grown-up kiss?"

"You know, on the mouth. And he touched my leg under my shorts."

Even though her grandmother's expression didn't change, Jane was silent so long Tara thought she had made her angry, too. Finally Jane said, "I think maybe this should be our secret. It would just upset your mother if she knew and your daddy wouldn't understand at all."

"Will you talk to Grandad and tell him not to do things like that?"

"I'll tell you what I'll do. When your mother has errands to run, I'll come over here and stay with you. When I can't, you can stay right beside me all the time. How will that be?"

"I guess that would be okay." Tara lay her head on her grandmother's shoulder. She had hoped her grandmother would be able to stop him altogether but thought she understood why she couldn't. Tara had seen her grandfather in a rage, so it made sense to her that Jane didn't want to make him angry. "I don't want to go back over there today though."

"No, we'll stay right where we are. Grandad can take that pie out of the oven as easily as I can."

Tara was relieved that everything was finally going to be all right.

"I've been coming to see you for two months. Can you tell me when the panic attacks will stop?" Kirby waited.

"I'm not sure. Is the medication helping?"

"Yes, but I don't want to stay on medicine all my life."

"No," Lauren agreed. "I don't want that either. Depression doesn't go away overnight. It can be treated, but it takes a-while. We have to get to the cause and work our way up from there. When the depression begins to resolve itself, I have hopes that the panics will start to go away."

"I talked to Russell the other night. He volunteered to come in with me."

"I think that would be helpful. How do you feel about it? After all, this is your safe place."

"I've thought about that. Frankly I don't know if marriage

counseling works. I want to be with him, but I wasn't happy before. Maybe I wouldn't be any happier if he came home."

"That's possible."

"He still thinks I'm frigid." Kirby hoped Lauren would dispel her fears.

"Frigid is a term that's used rather loosely. Tell me, Kirby. What is it about making love that upsets you so much?"

Kirby thought for a minute. "You ask hard questions. I don't know. I feel trapped. I can't breathe. I know Russell would never hurt me on purpose, but I'm afraid he might by accident. I feel completely powerless."

"Have you tried different positions? Sometimes that helps. Is your husband a large man? If he outweighs you a great deal, it's understandable that you might feel squashed and unable to breathe."

"No, Russell is slender. He's tall, but not overweight. We used to try different positions but I didn't like to experiment. I would rather just get it over with." She laughed nervously. "I hate talking about this."

"I know it's not pleasant. We can stop if you'd like."

"No, I want to reach some sort of conclusion. I suppose talking about it is the only way."

"That's been my experience. Most of the women I talk with feel more secure if they can put their feelings into words. It works for men, too."

"I can't imagine a man needing to feel more secure," Kirby said bluntly. "They have so much power as it is!"

"You feel men are more powerful than women?"

"Of course I do. They're larger and stronger. If a man wants to hold someone smaller down, he can't be stopped."

"Who are you talking about?"

Kirby looked at her in confusion. "Men. In general."

"Has any man tried to hold you down and do something you didn't want to have done to you?"

"No!" Kirby rubbed her temple. A headache was suddenly building. "I'm sorry. I didn't mean to snap at you like that."

"It's okay. You can get angry if you want to. That's what safe places are for. Does it make you angry to think about a man holding you down?"

All at once Kirby could feel a man's hands pressing her down, and instead of Lauren's couch beneath her, she felt the slick, polished cotton of a bedspread. The smell of carnations filled her nostrils and almost gagged her.

"What's happening?" Lauren asked. She was eyeing Kirby intently.

Kirby drew in a ragged breath. She felt as if she couldn't get enough oxygen into her lungs. "It just happened again! A panic attack!"

Lauren leaned forward. "Tell me about it. What exactly happened?"

"I felt as if a man were holding me down. I could feel hands on my arms. And a bed under me. I smelled carnations or something like that."

"Could you see his face?"

"No! I don't know!"

"It's okay. You're here and you're safe. Look around. See the pictures on the wall. The carpet on the floor. This is the present, not the past. You're here safe in my office."

Kirby glanced around. The panicky feeling subsided a bit. "Yes. I'm okay now."

"Could you see anything in the room?"

"No." Kirby's voice was little more than a whisper. "There's something about the room, but I can't remember." Her headache was raging.

"What about a taste?"

"No. No taste at all. Just that awful smell."

"Could you hear anything?"

"I'm not sure. It was almost as if I could hear someone breathing, but it could have been me."

"Do you smell anything other than carnations?"

Kirby thought for a minute. "There was something. Like an after shave. But the carnation smell was stronger."

"Think about the bed. Were you on sheets?"

"No, the bedspread. It felt slick like polished cotton."

"Do you have polished cotton spreads in your house?"

"No. I don't own anything like that."

"Does anyone you know?"

"No, Mallory has quilts she uses as bedspreads. Mom has a woven spread on their bed."

"Do you remember a bedspread like that when you were a child?"

Kirby nodded her head. "Of course. A lot of people had polished cotton bedspreads back then. I think Mallory and I had them in our rooms."

"Could this have been your bedroom when you were a child?"

"No. I never had flowers in my room. I don't like the smell. Now that I think about it, Mallory and I had those ribbed spreads, not polished cotton. I remember now. Mine was green and hers was yellow. Our room was the only one in the house that wasn't done in Mom's favorite shade of blue."

"Do you remember a color from this panic attack?" Lauren called them by the designation Kirby had chosen.

"Blue. I remember something blue." Kirby shrugged. "It's gone now. They always go away after a while."

"Do you remember what we were talking about just before it happened?"

Kirby searched her memory. "We were discussing what it feels like for a man to hold me down."

"I find it interesting that you phrased it like that."

"How would you have put it?"

"I wouldn't have personalized it so much. Did the panic come back when you answered me?"

"I hate the idea of a man overpowering me, but the panic didn't return." She watched Lauren closely. "Why would that cause me to have an attack?"

"I think your mind is trying to tell you something."

"Such as?"

Lauren shook her head. "You have to find your own answers."

"You're a big help." Kirby grimaced and searched for an explanation. "I think all women would hate that."

"Probably. But you seem to feel it so strongly."

"No one ever held me down. Russell wouldn't do such a thing. He's gentle with me."

"Maybe it wasn't Russell."

"He's the only one I've ever had sex with."

"Interesting you would put it that way. Most people refer to it as 'making love.'"

"I meant to say that."

"Do you have any reason for why you dislike sex so much?" Kirby shook her head. "I've never been fond of being touched. Not ever. I've wondered if the problem with Russell came to a head that night because I had been so steeped in the incest case I was working on. I was spending long hours studying incest cases to use in prosecuting a man named Gary Chandler. Maybe that affected me more than I thought it would."

"You don't strike me as the obsessive type. Not to the extent of ruining your sex life just from reading about incest cases. Is there anything about your relationship with Russell that would remind you of those cases?"

"Not a bit."

"You've already told me that the problems between you and your husband had been growing worse for a long time."

"Yes. I was just hoping for an easy explanation." Kirby rubbed her temples again. "Could I have a glass of water? I need to take something for this headache."

Lauren went to the small table that held the coffee pot and poured water from a pitcher. She handed the glass to Kirby. "Do you have many headaches?"

"Not many. I've had more lately than ever before. They seem to come when I think about the panic attacks or Russell." She managed a smile. "Maybe my headaches are trying to tell me Russell is a pain in the neck."

Lauren laughed. "Maybe."

"He's not really," Kirby admitted softly. "Actually he's very nice. He's the only man I've ever loved. Other than my father, of course."

"I'd like to meet Russell if you wouldn't mind. Maybe he could come with you next week?"

"I'll ask him. He seemed eager to get in on this. But you're not to believe him if he says I'm awful and that I'm frigid."

"I form my own opinions. I don't think it's likely that you're frigid. That's not a common problem."

"You'll probably find Russell is oversexed." She watched

for a reaction from Lauren that might show she'd been thinking that already.

"I doubt that, too." Lauren smiled at her. "Are you mind reading again?"

Kirby laughed. "It's an old habit. I always try to figure out what people are thinking and what they're about to do. It's all a part of being a lawyer."

"Perhaps. I've seen it before—usually in survivors of child abuse."

"I wasn't abused. Not in any way. My dad was a perfect father."

"Why do you always assume I'm thinking about your father? Your mother was there, too."

"It's even more unlikely that Mom would hurt me. You should see her. She wouldn't harm anyone at all."

"All right."

"I'm serious. My parents are wonderful people."

"I believe you."

Kirby frowned. "Why do I think you don't?"

"You're mind reading again."

"One of these days you're going to see I'm right and that I had a childhood that anyone would envy."

"I hope so. Far be it from me to argue with you about it. I wasn't there. You were."

"Okay. So Dad has a temper. Everyone does."

"You've never admitted it before."

Kirby glanced at her watch. "Time's up." She felt as if she had received a reprieve. "I'll see you next week. Maybe Russell will be with me."

"Take some time before next week to think about what we've discussed. We'll pick up where we've left off. I'll see you then."

Kirby was glad to escape into the waiting room. She didn't make eye contact with anyone else as she hurried from the building. When she reached her car and drove away, her mind was whirling over possibilities. Kirby was an intelligent woman, and she was trained to listen to verbal slips that would affect the leverage in her legal battles. She had made a dozen slips in the past hour.

What was she trying to tell herself, assuming Lauren was right? She had been a loved and protected child and her father was the perfect dad. Kirby frowned. Lauren was right; she almost never referred to her mother and spoke of her father as if he were a saint. She thought about Addison's violent and unpredictable rages. He had beaten Mallory and her with his belt and his fists—and her mother as well!

Kirby pulled into a parking lot, too shaky to continue driving. She opposed hitting a child for any reason, and thus, she had never spanked her sons. So why was she so adamant that Addison was a perfect father? No child was so bad that he deserved being beaten. And as Russell had recently pointed out, the beatings she had suffered had continued through college and ended only when she married.

No! Kirby struck the steering wheel with the heel of her hand. She wasn't going to think like this! She loved her father and he loved her. It didn't matter how many Freudian slips she made or how Lauren interpreted them. Lauren was simply wrong. Had she known Addison better, she would have seen that.

Feeling somewhat better, Kirby drove back into the stream of traffic.

Chapter Seventeen

"I'm so glad you came over," Kirby said to her sister. "I really need to talk to someone."

"Is it about Russell? He hasn't filed for a divorce, has he?"

"No. He says he won't file and I guess I have to believe him. One condition for him coming back home is that I see a counselor."

"What! You're not crazy, Kirby."

"I know I'm not. But I've been terribly depressed since he left." She sighed. "That's not entirely accurate. I was depressed before that as well, but I was hiding it. I started having those panic attacks. Remember?"

"I remember you telling me about them. Aren't they any better?"

"They started happening more frequently. Dr. Nichols recommended that I see a psychiatrist and recommended Dr. Lauren Jacobs."

"A psychiatrist? What on earth would Dad say if you went to see her? You know what he thinks about psychiatry."

"I've been seeing Lauren for two months. Dad doesn't know and I'm not going to tell him. I don't want you to tell him either."

Mallory's mouth dropped open. "You're actually going in for counseling? I can't believe you'd do such a thing!"

"It's not the Dark Ages," Kirby said a bit sharply. "A lot of people go to therapy these days. I'm on depression medicine and she gave me something to take for the panic attacks. I'm doing much better now. I'm even sleeping at night."

"I don't know," Mallory said doubtfully. "A psychiatrist!"

"Lately I've found myself saying things to her that I don't understand. You know, verbal slips. Once she pointed it out to me, I've noticed I do it quite often. Have you ever noticed we never refer to Dad's house as also belonging to Mom? And that we weigh everything on what Dad would think?"

"So what? We're his daughters and we love him."

"We love Mom, too. As adults, we shouldn't still have him on a pedestal the way we did as children. Our lives should be measured by what *we* think, or maybe our husbands, but not our father."

"I couldn't disagree more. Dad has twice as much brains as Derrick. Derrick will never be the man Dad is."

"Then why did you marry him? Didn't you love him? You told me you did."

"I thought I did at the time." Mallory lifted her cup of coffee and sipped it carefully. "I don't still love him. That's for sure."

"Then why don't you divorce him?"

Mallory laughed. "Come on, Kirby. Get real. Why haven't you divorced Russell?"

"I love Russell. I'm trying to get him to come home."

"That's not Dad's opinion. You should hear the things he says about Russell."

"I can imagine." Kirby gazed into her coffee as if she were trying to read her future there. "I would just as soon not know."

"I assume your psychiatrist doesn't approve of you still loving Dad?"

"No, that's not it. She's only wondering why Dad is still of such importance in my life."

"Next she'll be saying he molested us."

Kirby jerked her head in Mallory's direction. "Why did you say that?"

"Because it's all you hear on TV these days. It's the vogue for children to claim their parents molested them. It's on every talk show. I'm sick of hearing about it."

"But some parents *do* molest their children. Surely you don't deny that."

"No, but it doesn't happen to people we know. Can you name a single person we knew in school who said her father was molesting her? I can't."

"So you've thought about it?"

Mallory stood. "Is it okay if I get more coffee?"

"Sure, help yourself." She watched her sister cross the kitchen to the coffee pot and pour herself another cup.

"No," Mallory said as she added cream to her coffee. "I think the people making these claims are either making it up or their therapists are leading them to say it. That's what the talk shows are saying."

"Lauren doesn't lead me to say or think anything. I have to figure it out for myself."

"Then why pay her to sit in her office? I'm telling you it's a rip-off."

"No, it's not. I feel much better since I started going. And not only because of the medication. There's a difference in my life."

"Whatever you say."

"Mal, I asked you over to talk to you about something that's bothering me. Is it possible that someone molested me as a child?"

"How should I know?"

"You were there. We lived in the same house. Did we ever have any cousins that stayed over or maybe friends of the family?"

"Never. Not unless we had a houseful, like at Christmas. You know we rarely had overnight company at all."

"I didn't think so."

"Why would you think someone molested you? You've asked me this before, you know."

"I know, but it's still bothering me. I thought since time has passed that you might have remembered something."

"There was no man around except Dad. Why do you think you were molested?"

"Lauren says I shouldn't be upset if I discover that I was. I think she's trying to prepare me."

Mallory rolled her eyes. "There! That's just what I'm talking about. Counselors plant that garbage in people's minds to tear families apart. It's bullshit!"

"I don't think so. Lauren has no interest in ruining my life. She doesn't even know Dad. I've been listening closely to what I say, and I think she's right. She's explained about repressed memory syndrome. I looked it up and I have all the symptoms."

"Yes, and when a person studies medicine, they think they have all the diseases. That doesn't mean a thing."

"I think it does this time."

"So what are you saying? That Dad molested us?" Mallory stared at her.

"I don't know about you. I can't remember. It's not normal for a person to forget eight years of her life! You and Mom both said that. Remember?"

"Yes, but that doesn't mean somebody was molesting you! There are probably a dozen other reasons why that would happen."

"Name one."

"Besides, I remember those years and nothing happened. I would have been, let's see, four years old to twelve. I remember those years perfectly."

Kirby leaned forward. "What was Dad like? Toward me, I mean."

"The same as he was toward me. Dad loves us. It's natural for a loving parent to kiss his children and hug them. If you're smart, you'll stop seeing this quack and get on with your life."

"How did he kiss me?" Kirby had never told Mallory that she hated to be kissed for as long as she could remember.

She shrugged. "Like he kissed me. I remember sitting on his lap and thinking I was the most special little girl in the world. No one will ever convince me that Dad did anything wrong."

"Don't you think twelve is a bit old to be sitting on your father's lap?"

Mallory frowned at her. "Don't do this, Kirby. Don't try to turn me against Dad!"

"I'm not doing any such thing! I'm only trying to find out what happened during those missing years."

"He loved you and took care of you and taught you the things you needed to know to be an adult. He did what fathers are supposed to do!"

"I love Dad as much as you do. What did he teach us that trained us to be adults?" At least Kirby was learning what questions to ask. "Was Mom around when these lessons took place?"

"I don't know. I don't remember Mom being around much at all, if you want to know the truth. She's always had meetings and committees to attend."

"Mal, that's not true. She's always at home."

"I don't know where you grew up, but I remember it differently."

Kirby frowned as her thoughts raced. "We grew up together but we seem to have very different memories of what it was like."

"I don't know why you can't remember those years, but that's no reason to blame Dad for something he would never have done."

"You have a daughter," Kirby said bluntly. "If something happened to us, it could happen to her, too. One of the facts that I've uncovered in my research is that if a person begins molesting children, he doesn't stop at one victim. Whoever did it may still be hurting children."

"Are you sitting there and telling me that you think our father, who is the best man I've ever known, is molesting my Tara?"

"No, I didn't say that. I don't think Dad—"

"Let me tell you something, Kirby! You can just take that bullshit and shove it! Dad loves Tara just like he loved us and this nonsense about Tara not wanting to stay over there with him is just ridiculous! When I heard what she did, I grounded her from TV for a week! She must have hurt him deeply, rejecting his affection like that. I certainly won't sit here and listen to you do the same thing!"

"What are you talking about? Tara doesn't want to go to Dad's house?"

"Don't pretend you don't know about it. I'm sure Tara or Mom told you all about it. Tara's given me no reason at all but

she's decided she's afraid of Dad and that she's not staying
there anymore. Mom asked if she could come to my house and
watch her on the days when I have errands to run! Can you
imagine Tara asking Mom to do such a thing? I was furious!"

"Maybe Tara has a good reason."

"Just shut up!" Mallory jumped to her feet. "I know what
this is all about! You found out that Dad was the one to make
Derrick head of the law firm and you're jealous. You're trying
to say ugly things about him out of spite!"

"I'm not doing any such thing!" Then Mallory's words sank
in. "Wait a minute. *Dad* moved Derrick into the head of the
firm, not Hershal Glassman? He can't do that! It's a breach of
ethics and a conflict of interest! How do you know he did
this?"

"Derrick told me. You know how he brags when he's had
too much to drink. His tongue runs away with him. He told
me that when Hershal died, Dad called him and told him Hershal's job was his. He was making him the new head of the
firm." Mallory lifted her head defiantly. "Don't tell me you
didn't know about it. Derrick says that's why you left the firm.
Because you were jealous. I'm ashamed of you for saying these
awful things for such a petty reason." She angrily stormed from
the room.

Kirby sat there in stunned disbelief. Had her father been
so unscrupulous as to violate the judicial code of ethics that
prohibited him from having any influence over the law firm he
had headed before his judicial appointment? And he had picked
his son-in-law over his own daughter to succeed Hershal Glassman? She was going to get to the bottom of this. All her life,
Addison had been on a pedestal and now she could feel it
toppling.

Mallory was so angry when she left Kirby's house after
their argument that she headed straight for the nearest bar. She
ordered a stiff drink and tossed it down with practiced ease. How
could Kirby even suggest that their father had done something
wrong?

Mallory remembered her childhood perfectly. Addison had

been affectionate toward them both, although he had told her she was his favorite. He was more demonstrative than any of her friends' fathers so he had told her it would be best not to make them jealous by telling how much he loved her. This had made sense to Mallory so she had complied.

She could remember kissing her father. It was a perfectly natural thing for a daughter to do. Addison had told her so himself. As for the other, it was a father's job to teach her the things that would someday make her be a good wife. Addison had been very clear about that. Even though she hadn't liked these lessons, she had been too obedient to tell him so. In the long run, he had been right. Mallory had no doubts that she was unusually talented at making love.

The fact she could rarely be satisfied sexually by her lovers was a small difficulty. The important thing was that she was good at sex.

Against her wishes, she recalled her favorite fantasy. The one where she was a small child being instructed in the art of lovemaking by a father figure. Just thinking about it made her pulse quicken. She had never questioned this fantasy before. It was the only fantasy that brought her surcease from her almost constant appetite for sex. She was positive other women must have this same turn-on but she had never had a friend close enough to ask. From the reaction of her lovers when she acted it out, she was beginning to wonder if it was an unusual one or if other women simply didn't indulge in sexual role playing.

Her conversation with Kirby brought all of this into question.

Mallory loved, idolized, her father. She was thoroughly convinced that nothing he did could be wrong. But she knew Derrick never instructed Tara in sexual matters. Since Tara had reached the age where Mallory's own instruction had started, she had wondered about this. Was it only that Derrick didn't like sex or had she been wrong all these years about this being something all fathers did?

Addison had said they did.

She had always refused to think about it too closely and never had questioned it.

Mallory thought back to the girls she had known in school.

None of them had ever referred to things like this that their fathers had taught them. And a few of the girls had been completely uninformed as to what happened between a husband and a wife until Mallory explained it to them.

A chill passed through her. She didn't like to think about those lessons. They had always felt wrong in a way Mallory hadn't been able to understand. And Addison had told her she must never tell her mother about the things he was teaching her. Thinking about it now, Mallory wasn't certain that Kirby knew about them, though at the time, Mallory had assumed Addison also had taught the same lessons to her.

A cold sweat dotted her forehead, even though the room was cool. There had been nothing wrong with it! Nothing at all! Her dad would never do anything wrong. He had taught her about sex because he loved her!

As always when she found herself thinking too closely about her childhood, Mallory clicked off that part of her brain. She was quite good at it; she had been doing it for years.

Mallory signaled the waitress to bring her another drink. Across the room she saw a man watching her. She crossed her legs, letting her skirt edge up her thigh, and gave him a smile. Sex always enabled her to channel her mind into more pleasing subjects.

Kirby found her father in the lobby of the criminal courts building. When he saw her, he smiled in welcome. Kirby tried to view him dispassionately as a man and not her father. He was tall and slender, with thick silver hair and gray eyes. Addison was as handsome a man in his later years as he had been when he was younger. His smile was engaging and absolutely sincere. His voice reassuringly deep. As a judge he portrayed the image of a kindly and just father, meting out justice fairly and with no shadings of prejudice.

"Kirby, what are you doing here? I had forgotten you're off this afternoon. Do you have time for a drink with me?"

Kirby wasted no time with formalities. "I have to ask you something. I just heard you were responsible for Derrick becoming the head of the firm. Is that true?"

''He's a good lawyer. I know you have your differences, but it made more sense to me to have the firm headed by a man. It wasn't slanted against you.''

''Then you did do it? It wasn't Hershal Glassman's decision, but yours that Derrick was put in control of the firm? You're a judge! You can't do something like that! What about judicial ethics?''

Addison glanced around. ''Lower your voice. We aren't alone here.''

Kirby didn't care that several people were glancing in their direction. ''You can't have any input or influence in the firm as long as you're on the bench. You know that! What were you thinking?''

''I didn't intend for you to know. If I had wanted you in on it, I would have told you. I gather Derrick is responsible for telling you?'' He waited for a reply.

''It doesn't matter where I heard it.'' She wasn't going to betray Mallory's confidence.

''It was all done unofficially.'' He darted his eyes around as if he was growing increasingly nervous about having this conversation in a public place. ''Hershal never made the decision. His death was so unexpected. Someone had to do it, so it was up to me.''

''But Derrick told me Hershal had made the decision and put it in writing in case anything happened to him. That's not true, is it?''

''Don't be so upset that I didn't put you in charge. I built that firm with years of sweat and hard work and wasn't about to let it lose any of its prestige due to poor leadership. That's why Glassman took over when I left. I knew he'd listen to me. And Derrick has always respected my judgment and direction as well. How would it have looked if my daughter had succeeded Glassman? People would have thought I'd used my influence to put control of the firm back in my family. Nepotism is an ugly thing to be accused of.''

''So is conflict of interest and breach of ethics. And I don't see much difference in a son-in-law and a daughter when it comes to nepotism. How could you compromise yourself like this?''

"I don't think this is the time or place to be having this discussion." A vein was throbbing in his temple. It was a sure sign of an impending rage.

"I think this is the only place to discuss it. I want to be heard, and when you get angry, you never hear anything anyone else has to say."

His eyes were icy and in a dangerously low tone he said, "Kirby, I'm telling you one more time to keep your voice down."

"I just wanted to hear from you that it's true." She was so angry it was all she could do to keep the volume of her voice at a conversational level.

"So now you know. Surely if you think about it logically, you'll see I had no choice but to step in."

"No. I don't see that at all. You should never have made a decision about this at all. And you shouldn't have given Derrick preference over me simply because he happens to be male."

"We'll talk about this another time." Addison turned and stalked away.

Kirby started to go after him but she realized a number of people were frankly staring at them. Embarrassed, she left the building.

In her car, she cursed herself for making a foolish mistake. She should have waited until Addison was in his private chambers or at home. She should have telephoned. She had been too angry to think.

That worried her. Was she starting to rage as he did? She had so often seen him do or say something in anger that a prudent person wouldn't have done or said. And she had upbraided him in a public place! That was a cardinal sin in the Walker family. What happened at home was never, absolutely never, to be addressed in public. She found herself gripping the steering wheel so tightly that her knuckles ridged white.

Her first instinct was to call Lauren but she refrained. The fear she was feeling was an overreaction. Addison couldn't hit her. She was in no physical danger. He was in his own car on the freeway by now and she was safe in hers. She didn't have to go home and be beaten as would have happened when she was a child. He wouldn't come to her house and strike her.

These were old tapes playing in her head from her childhood and no longer real signals of impending danger.

All the same, now that her anger was subsiding, she was terrified.

She pulled into a parking lot and waited for the panic to pass. As Lauren had instructed her, she grounded herself to the present. She concentrated on the color of the car seat, the wood grain of the dashboard, the blue of the sky beyond the windshield. She wasn't a child in danger of a beating; she was an adult in control of her own life. After a few minutes, Kirby felt safer and again entered the flow of traffic.

She had always hated being afraid. Fear made her feel weak and vulnerable.

Again her mind filled with the confrontation with Addison. He must be furious with her! For a moment, she considered not going straight home in case he was waiting in a rage for her to arrive. Then she remembered her sons would also be there and pressed harder on the accelerator.

It occurred to her as she exited the freeway and merged with the traffic on the feeder street that she had accomplished something that day she wouldn't have attempted before. She had spent most of her life running interference for herself and others to keep Addison from becoming angry. Today she had openly—perhaps too openly—confronted him, and although she had been afraid of the consequences, no bolt of lightning had obliterated her.

Realizing the courage it had taken, she felt rather proud of herself and smiled all the way home.

Chapter Eighteen

Sunday without Russell was the worst day of the week. During the week they had gone their separate ways more often than not and on Saturday one or the other frequently had to work overtime or take the boys to ball practice or whatever. But on Sunday, they had always been together.

Kirby looked through the doorway to her den. Josh was sitting in front of the TV watching some sports event. These days when he was home he spent most of his time in front of the TV. She had told him three times to mow the grass, but he hadn't made a move to do it. That had also become a habit. If Josh's chores got done at all, Kirby or Cody had to do them.

It was difficult for her to admit or even to believe that she had completely lost control of her son.

A car honked out front and Kirby heard a muffled shout. Josh pulled the blinds open to look out, punched the TV's remote control, and headed for the door.

"Where are you going?" she called after him.

"Out."

Anger boiled up in her and she considered going after him and pulling him back into the room. The only problem was that she wasn't sure she was physically strong enough to do it and she didn't want to look like a fool.

"Josh! Come back here. You're not going anywhere until the lawn is mowed!"

"Yeah, right," he tossed back at her and kept going.

Kirby was so angry that her hands were shaking. She told herself to calm down as she heard the door slam. She went to the window in time to see the car full of boys screech away from the curb.

She had lost all control of Josh and he knew there was nothing she could do about it.

As much to work off her anger as to get the grass mowed, she went to the garage and dragged out the lawn mower. Before Russell left, she had never so much as touched the mower. She knelt and checked the gas. There was probably enough in the tank to do both front and back yards.

"I thought Josh was supposed to mow this time," Cody said from behind her.

She glanced up at him and saw Tara was standing behind him. She smiled at her niece. "He was. Looks like it's my job again."

"I don't know why you let him get away with that," Cody said angrily. "He takes advantage of you and you just let him!"

"What else could I do? He was out the door before I knew he had anything planned." She hated defending her actions, even to Cody. "I don't mind. The exercise will do me good."

"It's too hot. I'll do it for you."

"No, you and Tara go in where it's cool. Both of you look hot enough to melt."

"Can I have a drink of water?" Tara asked.

"Sure you can, honey. You know where the glasses are."

Tara turned and trotted into the house.

Cody watched until the door closed behind her. "I think something is wrong with Tara. Can you talk to her?"

"Wrong in what way?" She sat back on her heels and shaded her eyes so she could look up at him. "Is she feeling ill?"

"No, she just seems different. Like she's sad or something."

"Maybe she's dreading the start of school."

"Not Tara. She loves school."

"I don't know. Ask her if anything is wrong. She's always

confided in you." She pulled on the starter rope and the mower coughed despondently but didn't start.

"I did ask her, but she wouldn't tell me."

"Maybe that's because nothing is bothering her." Kirby knelt on the grass and looked in the direction Tara had gone.

"It's more like she's keeping something from me. I'm really worried about her."

"Cody, you may as well get used to the idea that people are going to keep things from you from time to time. If Tara doesn't want to talk about whatever it is, don't pressure her."

"Mom, would you just ask her?" he persisted.

Kirby jerked on the rope again. "Damn this thing! It's so hard to start!"

Cody moved her aside and pulled the rope. The mower purred into action. "I'll do this. You talk to Tara. Okay?"

Kirby sighed. "Okay."

Tara was in the kitchen when she entered. At the sound of Kirby's footsteps she jumped and whirled around, a frightened look on her face. "I'm sorry. I thought you heard me come in."

"You just surprised me. That's all." Tara finished the glass of water and put the glass in the sink. "Is Cody mowing?"

"Yes. Why don't you sit down and visit with me awhile? We never seem to talk anymore. You're growing up too fast."

Tara ducked her head and dropped into a kitchen chair. "I don't like growing up."

"You're a little too young to worry about your age," Kirby said jokingly. "You still have a few good years left."

Tara pushed the salt shaker between her hands and was silent.

"How are things at home?" Kirby knew Derrick was drinking more than ever and that Mallory was gone frequently. Mallory seemed to have more to do away from the house than anyone Kirby had ever known.

"Okay, I guess."

"Are you ready for school to start?"

"I sure am," Tara said with feeling. "Then Mom has all day to run errands and go places."

"Are you lonely? Is that what's bothering you?"

"Who said anything is bothering me?" she demanded.

"No one. I was just guessing." Kirby looked at her in surprise. Tara had never been one to lose her temper easily.

She glared at the salt shaker. "Well, nothing is bothering me."

Kirby began to see why Cody was concerned. "Honey, I don't believe you."

Tara jumped to her feet. There were tears in her eyes. "Nobody believes me! Nobody ever does! You all think I'm a big liar!" She ran from the room and out the door.

Kirby went to the window and watched Tara run in the direction of her house. Concerned but not knowing just what to do, Kirby went to the sink and washed the glass Tara had used. Something was very wrong. After thinking a moment and concluding that Mallory probably by now had forgotten their recent argument, she dialed Mallory's number.

"Hello?"

"Mal?" Kirby began tentatively. "Tara is on her way home."

"So soon? I was just about to leave."

From Mallory's tone of voice, Kirby was sure she'd forgotten their argument or had decided not to be mad over it. "I think you may want to have a talk with her. Something is bothering her and she won't tell me what it is."

"I haven't noticed anything different about her."

Hoping to avoid another angry exchange with Mallory, Kirby refrained from pointing out that, in her opinion, Mallory saw her daughter too seldom to notice. "I asked her if something was bothering her and she ran out of the house. She was very upset."

"I see her coming across the yard. I'll ask her what's wrong."

Kirby hung up but she couldn't stop worrying about her niece. Tara's odd behavior reminded her of something but she couldn't put her finger on it. Thinking back, she remembered Tara was quieter than usual and she avoided Josh. Had he said something cruel to her or frightened her in some way? Kirby hardly knew him anymore. She was a fine one to throw stones at Mallory for not spending more time with Tara. On the other hand, she reminded herself, Josh was the one who was avoiding her, not the other way around. Nevertheless, she still felt guilty.

She went out and waved at Cody until he noticed her and

stopped the mower. "I tried to talk to Tara but she became upset and ran home. I think you're right. Something is wrong with her."

"She went home? We were going to watch that movie I checked out this morning."

"Maybe if you call her, she'll come back over. Could it be that Josh has been mean to her?"

"Not that I know of. He usually saves all of that for me." Cody scowled at the mower. "Tara doesn't have much to do with him these days. She says he's getting too grown up."

"I guess she's right. He's a teenager now and he looks older than he is." She nudged Cody away from the mower. "Go call Tara and see if she'll come back over. I didn't mean to chase her away. I'll finish here."

Cody started the mower for her and ran into the house to call Tara.

Kirby paced behind the mower, feeling the sting of grass hit her bare legs and knowing she should have worn long pants, but the heat was too stifling. She considered hiring someone to mow the lawn this time, but that would give Josh reason for not cutting it himself next time and would undermine her efforts to teach both boys about responsibility by having them do regular household chores. Still, it was tempting. At the moment, she had money in savings to pay to get some things done, but she wasn't sure if she would need all that money later to help make ends meet. When she left the firm for the job in the DA's office and took that big pay cut, she had had Russell's salary to depend on as well, and even though he was still helping by paying most of their bills, she couldn't expect him to continue that if he never came back home.

She cut the grass with a vengeance. She was so tired of being out of control of her life.

That night she had the nightmare again. Once more she was a little girl walking down the long blue hall. Pictures hung over her head and she passed several closed doors. She knew she had to open the door at the end of the hall, no matter how long she might dawdle in getting there.

She found herself at the door, her small hand on the knob. With a racing heart, she opened it. The man lay there on the bed. He turned his head and looked at her with a sickening smile on his face. As always, his face was a blur. It was as if she refused to see it. As frequently happened in the dream lately, he wore no pants and was touching himself. His penis was enlarged and angry looking and she couldn't stop staring at it.

He motioned for her to come closer and little Kirby knew she had to obey. She didn't want to touch it—she had no real name for it. He called it his Secret. She knew she had no choice. The cloying scent of carnations seemed to suffocate her.

Suddenly the dream varied. The man grabbed her as soon as she was within reach and pulled her onto the bed. Kirby tried to scream but she was unable to make any noise at all. She struggled as he pulled her under him and started to force her legs apart. No one could hear her! No one was at home but the two of them! She continued screaming as she felt a burning pain between her legs. Suddenly she saw his face clearly!

Shocked by the recognition of him, she screamed aloud. His face came nearer, nearer, threatening to smother the life out of her! And the worst part was that she recognized him!

"Mom! Mom!" Cody was shaking her frantically.

Kirby sat up. Her skin was drenched with perspiration and she was terrified. Her throat was sore from screaming and her breath came in rasping gulps.

"Mom, wake up!"

Her eyes darted around the dark room fearfully. Where was he? Had it been only a nightmare? It was so real! She could still feel the blind terror and the burning pain.

"Mom? Are you awake?"

"Cody? What's happening?" She caught his wrist so he would stop shaking her. "What's going on?"

"You were screaming. I didn't know what was wrong."

Josh was standing just outside the doorway, lit by the light from the hall. He was trying to look as if he couldn't care less what was wrong, but she could tell he was frightened. "I'm okay. It was a nightmare. Just a nightmare." Already it was fading from her mind. She had seen and recognized the man's face. Who was it? She tried frantically to recall the dream.

"You were screaming really loud!" Cody said.

She hugged him. "I'm sorry I woke you both." Her hands were shaking.

"Do you want me to get you a glass of water or something?"

"No, thank you." She stroked his rumpled hair. "Go back to bed. The excitement is over for tonight." She watched Josh push away from the door, his usual sullen expression locked into place again. "Thank you, boys, for coming to see about me." Josh made no acknowledgment.

"Are you sure you're okay?" Cody asked, his young voice filled with uncertainty.

"Yes. I'm fine. You know how it is when you have a nightmare. At the time it seems so real. I'm awake now and can hardly remember it." She kissed his cheek. "Good night."

He smiled as he went to the door. "Good night again, Mom."

Kirby sat curled up in bed. When Cody turned off the hall light, the room was too dark for comfort so she snapped on her bedside lamp, bathing the room in a comforting rosy glow. Unlike her mother, Kirby preferred shades of pink to blue. Russell had sometimes teased her about having rose hues in a household that was predominately male.

She reached for the notebook she kept beside the bed. Lauren had encouraged her to write down her dreams and to keep a journal of any insights that might come to her. At first Kirby had felt silly writing down her thoughts and dreams. She had never kept a diary, even as a girl. Lauren assured her it was important, however, so she had started one.

She wrote the details of the nightmare. Most of it was repetition. All but the ending. She didn't have to be a psychiatrist to know she had been raped in the dream. Even though she was fully awake, she could still remember the searing pain of her tender flesh tearing. How old had she been in the dream? Eight? Maybe nine?

She had seen his face. She had recognized it! But now it was gone again! Why couldn't she remember? Kirby closed her eyes and willed her mind to show it to her again. No picture appeared.

Why couldn't she remember something so terribly important? Kirby felt angry frustration mounting in her. She had to know who it had been! Dream or no dream, it was of vital importance. Maybe once she remembered that, she would stop having the nightmare.

The memory refused to resurface. In frustration, Kirby closed her journal and leaned back against the headboard. What was going on? Had she really been raped as a child? She was a reasonable adult and knew the nightmare was telling her something. But if she had been raped at the age of eight or nine, why couldn't she remember it?

She thought back to her wedding night. Russell had been so tender with her, so caring. Although she had been terrified, she hadn't been hurt. At the time, she had attributed the lack of pain to the fact that he had been so gentle. Wasn't it possible that it hadn't hurt because she no longer had a hymen to impede his penetration?

It made so much sense.

Other things fell into place if she accepted the fact that she had been molested as a child. She had no brother or male cousins or boys in her neighborhood, but she had always known what a penis looked like and felt like. To her, they felt as if they were plastic and not a real part of a human body, but she had known this as a teenager, when she had never touched a penis in her life so far as she knew. Until now she had never questioned this.

It had bothered Russell that she didn't like to touch him, but this made sense if her nightmare had happened in real life. Being raped, especially at such an early age, would have damaged the way she thought about sex for the rest of her life. It even explained why penises seemed plastic to her. She was making them unreal so her mind could pretend the rape hadn't actually happened. A plastic penis couldn't rape anyone.

She picked up the receiver to call Lauren, then noticed what time it was and put it back. No one would welcome a call at four o'clock in the morning, no matter how earth-shattering the breakthrough.

Kirby lay down, but left the bedside lamp burning. She had a lot to think about. Accepting that this had actually happened to her changed so many things. It even changed the way she thought about herself because it irreversibly altered her personal history.

She was a little surprised that it had taken her this long to realize what had apparently been clear to Lauren from the beginning. Everything pointed to her having been molested, now that she thought about it. There was her fear of the dark, of men, or being held down, of sexual intimacy. No wonder she was frigid—it was remarkable that she was able to have sex at all! If her memories had been complete all along, maybe she couldn't have.

But who could it have been?

According to the nightmare, and this never varied, she was in a house. That would seem to preclude a yard man or someone making deliveries. Maybe there had been some cousin who came to visit that she and Mallory didn't remember. The blue of the long hall suddenly made sense. When she was a child, her mother had painted the hall blue. Now the hall was white, but the same shade of blue was predominant all through the house. Why hadn't she thought of that before? Wedgwood blue was her mother's signature color.

She had to talk to someone. This realization was too huge to bear alone.

She closed the door to the hall so the boys wouldn't hear her and dialed Russell's number. He answered on the fourth ring, his voice groggy with sleep.

"I'm sorry to wake you, but something just happened."

He seemed to be awake instantly. "Are you hurt? What about the boys?"

"We're fine. At least I think I am. I had the nightmare again."

"God, Kirby, do you know what time it is?"

"Yes, I do. I wouldn't have called you at this hour if it wasn't important."

"Okay. What about the nightmare?"

She could picture him dropping back onto his pillow and closing his eyes. "I was molested as a child. That's what the dream was trying to tell me!"

"It's just a nightmare. Not a revelation."

"Don't you see? That's why I've had it over and over. It's

not just a dream, it's a memory trying to surface! The hall is blue, just like it was when I was little! It explains everything if it's true."

Russell was quiet for a long time. "You were molested? Who did it?"

"I don't know. This time I saw his face, but I can't remember who it was. Cody woke me up because I was screaming and it happened so suddenly I forgot it again."

"You're sure about this?"

"As sure as I can be. I mean, I don't have a memory of it having happened, but look how much it explains! I've heard of repressed memory syndrome. Haven't you?"

"Yes, but I wasn't sure if it was valid." He seemed to be speaking carefully as if he were afraid he would say the wrong thing. "I thought you didn't believe in it."

"I do now. Russell, if that's what happened to me, I can change the way I am. You know, the frigidity." It still pained her to say the word.

He was quiet again.

"Are you awake? Don't you dare go to sleep at a time like this."

"No, no. I'm wide awake. I was just thinking. What are you going to do?"

"I don't know. I guess I'll call Lauren tomorrow and ask her to work me in. My appointment isn't until Thursday and I can't wait that long."

"Do you want me to meet you there?"

"No," she said. "I have to talk to her alone. I'm not used to this idea and I'd be afraid to say it out loud if you're there." She paused. "I guess that sounds silly."

"No, it doesn't. I agree it's best for you to go alone. Will you call me as soon as you talk to her?"

"Yes. I'll call you."

"Kirby?"

"Yes?"

"I love you."

She gripped the phone. Tears stung her eyes and this time she didn't fight them back. "I love you, too, Russell." She hung up gently and gazed up at the ceiling. The hours until

morning would be tediously long and she knew she wouldn't
go back to sleep. There was too much to think through.

The next morning Kirby called Lauren's office and was told
Lauren could work her in at nine o'clock. To keep from having
to explain to Zimmerman about being in therapy, Kirby called
in sick and planned to go into the office that afternoon.

She had been awake the rest of the night and was tired, as
well as filled with surges of conflicting emotions. On one hand,
she still refused to believe the nightmare was an emerging
memory; on the other, it would explain many of the inconsisten-
cies in her life if it was true. She still had no idea who the man
could be. Several times she had wondered if it could have been
her father, but each time she pushed the thought away. Not
Addison. Anyone but him!

Incest had always been particularly revolting to Kirby. The
Chandler case had haunted her for months and she barely knew
the people involved. She thought any man who was capable
of sexually molesting his daughter didn't deserve to live and
should be made to die slowly and painfully.

How could it be her father? The man she had revered all her
life? The man who had told her time and again that she was
his favorite, his princess?

The implication now made her sick. Maybe he meant much
more by "favorite" than she had ever guessed.

How could she have forgotten something that would shatter
her life?

How could she *not* have forgotten?

She dressed and then sat on the bed to read her journal entry
once more. She was glad she had taken the time to write it
when the nightmare was still fresh. In the light of day it had
an aura of unreality. Reading the words made it all come back
again. There was still something that was eluding her. Perhaps
Lauren would know some psychiatric trick that would make it
all clear. Maybe hypnotism would give her greater recall.
Maybe it would even give her a different suspect.

She put the journal under her arm, took a deep breath, and
was on her way. As she maneuvered her car through Houston's

tangle of morning traffic, she found herself going back to the dream. What was it that she could sense lingering just out of her reach? Again she thought about the words she had written. She was missing something.

Suddenly she remembered. The scent of carnations! Kirby's mouth dropped open. Why hadn't she remembered this at once? Her mother loved the smell of carnations and kept bowls of carnation potpourri all over the house. The aroma was especially strong in the guest bedroom because that was where she mixed the carnation scent with rose petals to make the blend she liked. The guest bedroom.

A room with a polished cotton bedspread in the exact colors she remembered from her nightmare.

The room at the end of the long blue hall. The room where her father had waited for her in their frightening game of hide-and-seek.

The thought struck Kirby so forcefully she swerved into the oncoming traffic. Alarms went off in her brain as she tried desperately to get back in the correct lane. A dump truck was barreling toward her. She could see the shocked expression on the driver's face and steered hard to the right. For a moment she thought it would miss her. Then she felt the impact.

Her car bounced off the truck's side and slid into the median, where it came to rest against one of the rain trees that had been planted there. The driver of the truck was already out and running toward her.

Dazed, Kirby tried to open her car door but the tree held it shut. She stared at it, not able to understand that she couldn't get out that way.

"Lady! Are you hurt?" the man shouted as he yanked open the passenger door.

Kirby shied away from him.

He bent into the car. "Are you hurt? Is anything broken?"

Kirby shook her head. "I don't think so." She saw a patrolling police car turn on its lights and make its way past the traffic that was starting to back up. Gingerly she moved. She hurt all over but not worse in any one place more than another. "I think I'm all right."

''Maybe you'd better get out of the car.'' He jerked his head toward the rear. ''Your tank is leaking gas.''

His words didn't make much sense, but Kirby did as he said. She slid across the seat and out the door. She would have fallen if he hadn't caught her arm. To her embarrassment, several cars were stopped and the passengers were gawking at her. For a horrible moment she thought she was going to be sick. The smell of gasoline was everywhere.

The policeman called for a fire truck as soon as he saw the spreading liquid under her car and hurried over to see if she needed assistance. Kirby let him put her in the back seat of his car while he ran across the median to direct traffic away from the spilling gasoline. The driver of the dump truck stood at his vehicle, ready to move it if the gas should ignite.

Everything seemed to be happening to someone else. Kirby saw it as if it were all far away. She heard the wail of the ambulance siren but didn't connect it with herself until it parked and two EMTs jumped out and hurried to her.

She touched her forehead and her fingers came away sticky with blood. She still didn't feel the cut. Because the EMTs looked concerned, she let them take her to the emergency room of Ben Taub Hospital. She assumed the police would take care of having her car towed away.

At the hospital she told someone to call Russell and how to find him. She was glad to comply with the instruction she was given to lie still until a doctor came to see about her. Instead of feeling better, she was becoming dizzier and she tried to tell him so, but she couldn't seem to get the words out. Blackness replaced the doctor and she felt as if she were falling from a great height.

When she woke, she was in a hospital room. Russell was sitting in the chair beside her. When she moved, he stood and leaned over her.

''Russell?'' she whispered in a dazed voice.

''Hi, honey. Don't try to sit up. Just be still.''

''What happened?'' She looked around in confusion. It all came back to her. ''Was I in a car wreck?''

''I'm afraid so. The car was totaled.''

''I didn't hit the truck that hard.''

"No, but you hit hard enough to rupture the fuel tank. It caught on fire. Don't worry. The insurance will cover the cost of another one."

"My car burned?" She touched her forehead and found bandages. "Why am I bandaged?"

"You cut your head. It's not bad. Most of it's in the hairline so you probably won't even have a noticeable scar."

"I don't remember coming up here. The last I remember was telling some woman to call you and seeing a man that I think was a doctor. Am I injured badly?" Now that she was more alert, she hurt from the inside out.

"You have some internal bruises as well as some outer ones, but no broken bones. It could have been a lot worse. It's a good thing you were wearing your seat belt."

"Where are the boys?"

"They've gone to your parents' house. I told them you'd be all right. The doctor wants to keep you overnight just to be sure."

"I can't stay all night. The boys have school tomorrow."

Russell lifted her hand and kissed it. "Quit worrying. I'll stay with them and be sure they're out the door in the morning."

"You'd do that?" she asked with relief.

"Of course. Kirby, I've had several hours to think while I waited for you to wake up. I want to come home."

"You do?" she asked in a voice that quavered with the emotion his statement had evoked.

"I love you. When I saw you lying here with that bandage on your head, it occurred to me just how short life is. I want to spend the rest of my life with you. It doesn't matter that we have our differences and that we still have issues to resolve. I want to come home. I want to be with you."

Kirby caught his hand and gripped it tightly. "I want you with me. I love you, too, Russell."

He leaned over and brushed her lips with his kiss.

"Will you call Lauren? I was on my way to her office. Tell her I remember who the man was in my nightmare. Tell her it was Dad."

Russell stared at her for a minute. "Your dad?"

Silently she nodded. She wasn't able to say any more about it. But she knew it was Addison beyond a shadow of a doubt.

For a moment, Russell stood there staring at her. Then the muscle in his jaw flexed and he nodded. "I'll tell her." He left to find a phone.

Kirby was glad he hadn't used the phone by the bed. She needed time alone, just as Russell apparently did. Saying the words aloud was much worse than merely thinking them. Hot tears gathered in her eyes and spilled over onto her cheeks. She felt too weak and shaken to blink them back.

All her memories, all her personal history was altered the moment she consciously remembered Addison molesting her. Everything she had believed to be true about herself was suddenly in question. This revelation clouded everything. If she had forgotten something like this, what other horrors might be lurking in her mind? How could she ever hope to cope with this?

Then she remembered Russell and that he loved her. And Lauren would believe her and help her.

Somehow, some way, Kirby would survive.

Chapter Nineteen

Kirby's doctor kept her in the hospital longer than she had expected, but she was glad he did. By the day after her accident, she hurt worse than ever and would have found it difficult to get into Russell's car, much less up the stairs to their bedroom.

When she was finally released from the hospital later that week, Russell came after her and tucked her carefully into the car. As he pulled out into traffic, she was seized with an unexpected fear.

"Are you okay?" he asked.

"I guess so. No. I'm afraid. I'm afraid of having another wreck."

He took her hand. "It will be okay. You know I'm a safe driver and we'll take it nice and slow. You can't avoid being in cars. Not and live in Houston."

"I know. I'll work through it." All the same, she was glad when he turned into their familiar driveway. Both boys were there to meet her. As soon as she was on her feet, Cody put his arm around her.

"Hug her easy, son," Russell advised. "Don't break her."

Cody immediately moved away.

Kirby pulled him back. "I won't break that easily." She reached for Josh as well, but he drew back. Her eyes met his and she saw that nothing was changed.

"I guess now that you're back, Dad will be leaving," Josh said as he shoved his hands into the pockets of his worn jeans.

"No. I'm staying." Russell frowned at him. "I don't think that's any way to welcome your mother home from the hospital."

"Welcome home." Josh made it sound like an insult. Before she could answer, he turned and walked across the yard and away from the house.

"I'm going after him," Russell muttered, handing Kirby's travel bag to Cody.

"No, don't. I'd rather you help me up the stairs. I'm not as spry as I used to be, as my grandmother used to say."

Cody opened the kitchen door and Russell held Kirby's arm to steady her. She wouldn't have admitted it, but each step hurt. She tried to smile so Cody wouldn't worry. "Are you ready for school to start on Monday?"

"I am. Josh is still bitching about it."

Russell gave him a warning look.

"Is there something I don't know?" Kirby asked, looking first at her husband and then her son. "What's going on?"

"Nothing I can't take care of. You don't need anything else to worry about." Russell helped her take the stairs to the bedroom one at a time, very slowly.

Kirby knew what Josh was up to. One evening the previous week she had overheard him telling Cody that he was going to drop out of school. He seemed to think thirteen was old enough to make this decision. She was glad not to have to deal with this newest crisis alone. Just getting into bed was trial enough.

A large basket of flowers awaited her in her room. "How pretty!" she exclaimed.

"They're from your office. They arrived just before I came to get you."

Cody brought her the card as she sat on the edge of the bed. She recognized Mrs. Parsons' firm handwriting. "Come back soon. We all miss you," she read aloud. "How nice of them."

"I didn't get you any flowers," Russell said apologetically. "It wasn't because I didn't want to give you any. I just plain forgot."

Kirby smiled. "I know. You'd misplace your head if it wasn't screwed on tight, Mr. Absentminded Professor."

He grinned. "I was afraid you'd think I didn't care. But until these arrived, I just never thought about it."

"You're home. That's better than any flowers." She knew his forgetting to buy flowers didn't mean he no longer loved her. Russell had never been one to send flowers. She had always taken care of that.

"Run along, Cody," Russell said. "Your mom needs to put on her gown and get into bed." When Cody left, he closed the door and turned to Kirby. He seemed self-conscious. "If you want me to leave, I will."

"No. I need you."

Kirby let him help her out of her clothes and tried not to show how embarrassed she was to be naked in front of him. Russell understood. She had never been comfortable when she was undressed, even without the assortment of bruises. He carefully looked away to make her feel more at ease.

When she was in bed, he sat beside her. "I need to ask you some things. We need to set the ground rules. Do you want me to sleep in here or not? I've been thinking and I could put a sleeper sofa in the den."

"No. I want you to sleep in here." She touched his arm with the tips of her fingers. "I've missed you so much. I don't want us to ever sleep apart again. I'm going to try harder, Russell. Lauren thinks I can work through this . . . unwillingness to have sex."

" 'Make love,' " he corrected. "I don't want to just have sex either."

"All right. Make love. Whatever. I'm going to work through it and be the wife you want me to be."

"Don't do it for that reason. Do it because you love me and want us both to be happy. Otherwise it won't work."

She smiled. "How did you get to be so wise?"

"I've been reading a lot of psychology books in the past eight months. What else has there been to do?" He kissed her lightly.

Kirby firmed her resolve. Lauren said it was possible to enjoy sex and somehow she was going to learn to do it.

As she began to relax and get comfortable in bed, she watched Russell move about the room as he unpacked her small suitcase from the hospital. It was so good to see him, to hear the sounds of another person in the room—especially when that person was Russell. Judging by the articles belonging to Russell that were on the dresser and that his robe was hanging on the closet door where it had always hung, she knew he had already moved back in.

"It felt so good to move my things back," he said, as if he were reading her thoughts. "I can't tell you how miserable I've been without you."

She nodded and felt her eyes fill with tears. "I know exactly how you felt. I don't think I've laughed since you left. I was so afraid I had lost you forever." She pushed away the tear she couldn't blink back.

He sat beside her on the bed. "You're crying. You almost never do."

"I hate to cry."

He hugged her gently and Kirby put her arms around him. He smelled so clean and familiar. Beneath his shirt she could feel the strength of his muscles. Every inch of his body was familiar and reassuring. Kirby felt whole again for the first time in months. She was in no hurry to release him. This, too, was new.

After a while, Kirby's body rebelled and she lay back on her pillow. Russell still sat there, holding her hand and rubbing his thumb over her wrist. Their eyes met in a communication that needed no words.

At last she said, "I'm so glad you're home. I love you."

He smiled. "I love you, too. I'll never leave you again." He kissed her on the forehead. "Get some rest. I'll be downstairs if you need me."

Kirby closed her eyes but found she was still smiling.

When Kirby was able to resume her weekly counseling sessions with Lauren, she found herself actually looking forward to them. "I never thought I would," she confessed. "Until now, I haven't enjoyed coming in to see you."

"Most people don't. It's no fun to dig up all the unpleasantness and work through it. It shows you're making progress."

"It's been great having Russell back home, too. It's amazing how much smoother everything runs. Josh doesn't give me nearly as much trouble with his father in the house. Cody is happier, too." She grimaced. "Josh even tried to quit school. Russell told him thirteen-year-old boys aren't allowed to make that decision and showed him the law that proves it. Josh actually backed down!"

"How are things between you and Russell personally?"

"Much better than they were. I think we both realize now what we stand to lose if we can't work out our problems. We're both trying harder."

"Don't take this as prying, but how are your intimate relations?"

Kirby glanced away. "Better. Still difficult."

"The idea is not for you to get better at hiding your true feelings, but to enjoy making love."

"I know that, but it's not easy. At least I haven't had another flashback during sex."

Lauren leaned forward. "You never told me much about your wreck. What happened to cause you to drive into the oncoming traffic? Russell came in to see me, as you know, and he said nothing was found to be wrong with your car."

"No. The car was in perfect working order." Kirby bit her lip nervously. "This isn't easy to talk about."

"If it makes it easier, Russell gave me your message from the hospital. You said you recognized the man in your recurrent nightmare and that it was your father."

"Yes. As I was driving to your office, I remembered the smell of carnations in the dream. Suddenly I remembered that Mom uses a potpourri that smells exactly like the one in my dream and that she mixes it herself in the guest bedroom. A room at the end of a long hall that was painted blue when I was a child. And I remembered Dad waiting for me in there." She tried to laugh. "At least that's what I was thinking. You can see why it made my concentration waver from the traffic."

"So it was your father," Lauren said thoughtfully, as if she had never considered it could be him until Kirby revealed it.

"No, I only thought it was. It couldn't be. I've had a lot of time to think about it and Dad wouldn't have done such a thing."

"Why did you believe it that morning?"

"I was putting all the pieces together. The color of the hall, the smell, the color of the bedspread Mom had in there when I was a girl. The game of hide-and-seek. I never even liked that game! It was always scary to me. I wouldn't have asked him to play it with me."

"Maybe it was his idea."

Kirby laughed. "You don't know my father. He's not the sort to play tumbling games with little girls. He's very serious and studious."

"Hide-and-seek is a 'tumbling' game? I remember it differently."

Kirby faltered. "No, of course it isn't. But Dad wouldn't play it. I can't imagine him doing that."

"What else were you thinking?"

"I have no reason to be afraid of the dark, but I would have if I was afraid that someone would come in at night and hurt me. And when Russell and I married, our wedding night was painless for me." She hoped Lauren would understand and not ask her to be more graphic.

Lauren nodded. "You think you weren't a virgin."

"I was thinking that, yes. Now I'm not so sure. I mean, all women don't bleed when they lose their virginity, do they? There could be other reasons they wouldn't. I used to ride bicycles and horses a lot as a child. I've heard both can tear the hymen."

"I've heard that, too, but I can't honestly see how. Can you?"

"I never thought about it." Kirby didn't want to have to defend her denial. It wasn't firmly in place yet.

"Anything else?"

"I hate to be held down. It's a very real problem with me. I panic and I feel as if I'm suffocating. If I were arguing the case in court, I would use that as evidence that someone held me down and did something unpleasant to me, possibly smothering my screams as he did, causing a suffocating sensation."

Lauren smiled. "I would say exactly the same thing."

"But then I'm trained to argue a case whether there's a genuine crime committed or not." Kirby smiled back. She had Lauren there.

"Yes, but these are symptoms that are real. You manifest them yourself and you know they are true. There aren't a huge number of things that would cause fear of sexual intimacy, darkness, and being confined. They occur frequently, however, in cases of child molestation. So do bed wetting, mood swings, withdrawal or acting out, sexual play-acting with dolls, and a number of other behaviors."

"I know. I read up on molestation and incest to prosecute the Chandler case. The fact so many traits fit me and my childhood behavior are merely coincidental."

"Did you also read about denial? That's a common part of accepting what really happened. Everyone goes through some form of it. 'He didn't mean to' or 'He only did it because he loved me.'"

"But maybe he really *didn't* do it."

"If he didn't, who did? I don't want to blame an innocent man any more than you do. At the same time, your symptoms are classic for an adult who was sexually abused and my first priority is to support you and to help you feel happier and safer."

"But you think it was Dad!"

"No, I only form opinions based on what you tell me. I don't even know your father and I have no reason to malign him. I hope we're wrong and nothing at all happened to you. However, I wouldn't be truthful if I led you to believe that's likely. I've talked to too many women—and men—with your symptoms."

"Men, too?"

"Little girls aren't the only ones to be sexually molested. Research shows that a child molester is interested in children, not necessarily a child of a particular sex."

Kirby hadn't realized this. None of her research had given her this information. But then, she had only looked for files that would help her with the Chandler molestation case.

"Whether or not a matter is strictly factual, it might as well be true if you believe it to be. In other words, if we assume you were sexually violated by someone, we have a way of attacking your problem. You don't have to know who hurt you or have proof that it happened, as long as you think it did. But we have to have some thread to work on or nothing will change in your life."

"I think I understand."

"Frequently when a person starts to work on getting his life back into order, the face of the perpetrator will come back to him clearly. On the other hand, it doesn't happen to everyone. You may never know for certain."

"I don't know. I'm used to dealing with facts. Hard evidence. I can't take something this abstract and proceed as if it were true."

"No? I'll bet you do that on cases in court all the time."

Kirby frowned. That was true. "You're not a comfortable person to talk to at all times."

Lauren smiled again. "I know. But do you have anyone else you can say these things to?"

"You know I don't. I certainly can't talk to Mallory. She nearly bit my head off when I asked if it was possible someone molested me. You'd have thought I was attacking her!"

"Maybe it happened to her, too."

Kirby stared at her. "I wondered that myself! Is it possible?"

"It's even probable. A child molester rarely stops with hurting only one child. It usually goes on until he's caught or dies."

"I read that. I even used it in court against Chandler." She tried to assimilate all this. "I never thought about it in terms of it happening to Mallory, though."

"It might explain why she was so defensive. Maybe she remembers."

"She would tell me!"

"She may have worked it out in her mind so that nothing wrong took place. It's possible to remember the event but sugar-coat it until the emotions generated at the time aren't remembered with any accuracy at all. She may have convinced herself it was no big deal and that it didn't matter."

"Not matter if she was raped?" Kirby looked at her with defiance. "No way!"

"She was a child, too, remember. Children are amazingly resilient. They can bounce back from things we adults couldn't began to cope with. They bury their scars and the results may not surface for years. But molestation, and especially incest, wrecks lives. Every time!"

"Mallory is fine. She's married and has a little girl. God knows she loves sex! She has no problem talking about it, either. I've heard more than I ever wanted to know about her personal life, I can tell you!"

"The other side of the frigidity coin is promiscuity."

Kirby stared at her. "I have to think about this. I don't know what I think anymore. At one time I thought Mallory was promiscuous, but now . . . she's married."

"That doesn't matter. When a child is hurt sexually, there are negative results, to put it mildly. Not a single one is unscarred. Not one. No matter how they may argue about it as an adult."

Kirby was silent for a long time. "You said a child molester rarely stops at hurting only one child."

"That's right."

"And Mallory might also have been molested."

"If you were, I'd say it's probable."

Kirby bit her lip. "I'm wondering if anything like this is happening to Tara, my niece. She's the age I was when I stopped remembering the details of my childhood."

Lauren didn't hide her concern. "Does Tara see your father often?"

"Of course. She lives only a block away from them. But we don't know it was Dad! It could have been some cousin or family friend we don't see anymore."

"Maybe."

Kirby sighed. "I know, I know. But what if it *is* Dad? Tara is there all the time."

"How has she been behaving? Have there been any changes in her personality or openness?"

Kirby drew her breath in sharply. "Yes. There have been. Even Cody has worried about the changes he's noticed. Several times I've had the impression Tara wanted to confide in me but didn't." She felt the blood run from her face. "My God!

Could *that* have been the secret she knows that Dad told her not to tell?"

Lauren's frown deepened. "She told you that?"

"Yes, weeks ago. I didn't think much about it at the time. I thought she did something wrong and Dad was covering for her."

"Would he do that?"

Kirby tried to answer but no sound would come out. She shook her head.

"I don't want to alarm you, but I think you should look into this. Talk to Mallory and tell her what you suspect."

Numbly Kirby nodded. How could she ever suggest such a thing to Mallory, who adored their father? What about Josh and Cody? They often went to his house, too.

Kirby stood and clutched her purse tightly. "I'm tired. I really have to be going."

"Of course. I don't want to tire you on your first day out alone. I'll see you next week."

When Kirby got home, she was relieved to see Russell's car was already in the drive. No matter how often she saw it there, she felt thankful. She had come so close to losing him. She found him in the kitchen preparing dinner.

"Hi, honey. How did it go?"

"Where are the boys?"

"Upstairs. Supposedly doing their homework." Russell looked at her closely. "You look upset."

"I want to ask you something and I want an honest answer. Do you think my father molested me? I know you don't like him, but I want your opinion."

Russell thought for a minute. "To tell you the truth, I can't imagine him having any passions that didn't involve law. I assume it takes a passion of sorts to molest a child."

"That's exactly what I think. He couldn't have done it."

"You told me he did when you were in the hospital. You seemed certain of it."

"That doesn't count. I had just been in a car wreck. I was hurting."

"You weren't hurt so badly you were talking out of your head or anything like that. You told me that was why you swerved into that truck. That you remembered him hurting you."

"No. I couldn't have said that. I meant he was the man in my dream. It's only a nightmare. Nothing more."

"You don't have to convince me. I'm not judging this."

"Sorry." She forced a smile to her lips. "I didn't mean to come on so strong."

"You don't have to go around apologizing all the time. Have you ever noticed how often you do that? So does Mallory."

"I guess it's just a habit. I don't want you to be upset with me or to think I was picking an argument with you."

Russell went to her. "Kirby, I'm going to love you, no matter what memories you discover. A bad memory can't chase me away. Those months away from you were hell. I'm not leaving you again."

"You won't? Not even if I stop going to counseling?"

"You aren't going back? Why not?"

She looked away. "I don't know. I don't seem to be getting anywhere with it. I don't want to sit in Lauren's office and guess what might have happened twenty-eight years ago. What if I'm wrong? There's such a thing as bearing false witness, you know. I certainly don't want to be guilty of telling Lauren such an awful thing about Dad and it turn out not to be true. That would be terrible!"

"Who would ever know? Other than you and Lauren, that is."

"Well, that's two too many. I think it's best if I stop therapy and get my life in order on my own. I can do it. We've always said that together we can whip dragons."

"I know, but I'm not sure it's a good idea for you to stop counseling. You're doing so much better. The darkness doesn't bother you as much as it once did and you don't jump out of your skin if I come up behind you unexpectedly."

"Then it's been successful. I'm going to break my next week's appointment."

Russell shook his head. "I think that would be a mistake."

She tiptoed up and kissed him. "I know what I'm doing."

She went upstairs to be certain the boys were studying. It was easy to convince herself that she had made the right decision. How terrible it would have been to tell Lauren or anyone else such awful things about a wonderful man like her father. She felt dirty and guilty for suspecting that he might be molesting Tara. Or Josh and Cody!

That he had hurt her sons was unlikely. Cody had always enjoyed going over there and that hadn't changed, and Josh was so determined to hurt her lately that he would probably blurt it out at the dinner table if it was happening to him. No, Addison was not committing incest with his grandsons.

As for the changes in Tara, there must be some other explanation. Something at school could be upsetting her. As for the secret, it could be anything at all. Mallory would never leave her daughter with someone who would hurt her.

All the same, Kirby knew she had to broach the subject with Mallory on the outside, remote possibility that her terrible suspicions were true.

Kirby dreaded the revelation with all her heart.

Like most of America, Addison spent the night of the November elections glued to his TV. Jane was trying to pretend an interest, but he knew she probably couldn't care less who won the Presidency. Jane wasn't an intellectual giant.

He gave her a sidelong glance and wondered why he had ever married her. She was pretty, or had been when she was younger. Now her face was showing signs of sagging into middle age and a fine webbing of lines was forming at the corners of her eyes. She still wore the same dress size, but somehow dresses didn't look the same on her. Jane was growing old.

He touched the skin under his jaw. No sag, no puckers. His skin was looser than it had been when he was a young man, but he was aging well. Addison thought he looked better, if anything. He still had a thick head of hair, which had turned from black to silver at an early age. He could tell by the way women looked at him that he was still desirable to them.

Not that he had ever had an affair with one.

Ever since he met Raymond Stansfield, he had had one dream. Addison wanted to be on the United States Supreme Court. He wanted the power and he wanted the prestige. Raymond understood that kind of ambition and together the two of them had decided long ago that together they would go to the top. The Supreme Court for Addison, the Presidency for Raymond.

Raymond had made all the right moves. He had entered into a brilliant marriage. Virginia was the daughter of a former Secretary of State. Everyone in Washington admired her family, and in politics, who you knew counted. The people might think they elected their government's officials, but those choices were decided by the powers in Washington, D.C.

The numbers flashed and a cry went up in the Republican Headquarters. Raymond had surged ahead by a huge margin. Within minutes, the Democratic nominee called and conceded the election to Raymond Stansfield.

Jane stretched and put down her needlepoint. "I'm almost falling asleep. I'm going to bed. Will you be long?"

"Not long." He didn't even glance at her as she left the room. Her presence didn't matter much to him one way or the other.

Hats were sailing in the air and balloons were being released as Raymond's theme song blared out, eclipsing all but the loudest noises. Addison grinned and leaned back in his padded wing chair. Raymond Stansfield was heading for the White House. His future was assured.

Addison looked around the den at the house he and Jane had lived in over half their lives. It wasn't grand enough by half. When he bought it, he had dived in well over his head financially, but that had been many years ago. Addison was now a wealthy man. He had only been biding his time until Raymond could convince the Republican Party to nominate him for President. After that, everything had rolled exactly the way they had planned.

An hour later the newscasters were still summing up the elections and predicting what the Stansfield Presidency would be like. Addison was almost ready to go to bed, too, when the phone rang.

He answered it and grinned when he recognized Raymond's voice. "Congratulations, Ray!"

"Thanks," boomed Raymond's voice. He was hoarse from the celebrating. "Got your bags packed?"

"Not yet."

"Well, start planning to move north. I have it on good authority that a judge is about to retire for medical reasons. It should happen soon after my inauguration."

"I'll be ready."

"We did it! We really did it! Just like we planned!" Raymond sounded as excited as a boy. "Damn! Who would have thought it?"

"I knew you had it in you."

"Tell Jane to get ready to move. She may not be happy about leaving those grandchildren."

"She'll be ready." Addison had never wondered if Jane would be in favor of moving to Washington. He was going whether she did or not. If it wasn't for the way it would look, he would rather have her stay here. Sometimes he was embarrassed that she wasn't a more intelligent woman, and because she looked every year of being middle-aged, he was branded as being older than he looked. "You just let me know, Ray."

"We have to take things in order. First I have to hear about the judge's decision to retire—I'd rather not say which one it is."

"I understand. I can already figure it out."

"Then I have to give your name to my selection committee along with two or three others that no one in their right minds would want appointed. Then Senate confirmation, merely a formality in your case. It's just a matter of time."

"I'll be ready."

After congratulating Raymond again on his victory, Addison hung up. He sat there for a while, gloating over his coming triumph. Nothing could stop him from getting the appointment. He was going to be a justice on the United States Supreme Court! An appointment for life. And Addison knew the appointment was only a formality. He was in!

* * * *

Kirby lay awake listening to Russell's rhythmic breathing. She had become more adept at faking pleasure and could even convince him she had had an orgasm. It was no more than she had done in the earlier years of their marriage. Now it was important again.

Still, she couldn't help but wonder if Lauren could have really helped her get to the point of having an orgasm for real. Kirby had never had one during sex and she wondered what it would be like. Faking it wasn't so difficult.

She shifted in the bed. Was Russell sound asleep? She wasn't sure so she waited.

For a while after she quit therapy, the nightmare had left her in peace. Lately it had returned. So had the flashbacks. They were coming frequently, though she hadn't told Russell. It was getting more and more difficult to pretend not to know what they were showing her. She was, however, skilled at pretending nothing was wrong. She could have a flashback while watching TV and no one else in the room be aware it had happened. This gave her a sense of power, but she would rather not have them at all.

Below in the darkness, the grandfather clock rang out the hour. Surely by now Russell was asleep.

Kirby leaned up on one elbow and looked at him closely. A lock of his hair had fallen over his forehead and made him seem years younger than he really was. If it wouldn't have awakened him, Kirby would have hugged him.

Quietly she got out of bed and tiptoed to the bathroom. She shut the door and turned on the shower. As she waited for the water to heat up, she looked in the mirror. She was wearing her nightgown, of course. Russell never asked her to take it off when they made love and she appreciated that. Her eyes had a haunted look deep in them that she never let Russell see. The only time she wanted the bedroom dark was when they made love. Then she didn't want so much as a sliver of light to show. She didn't want to see him above her or, worse, to

have him see her. Kirby wasn't always sure she could keep the
expression on her face controlled.

She didn't like lovemaking any better than before. If anything, it was more difficult for her. And she would have died
before letting Russell know that. If she could keep him by
pretending to enjoy sex, she would do that.

As soon as puffs of steam drifted from the shower, Kirby
slipped off her gown and stepped under the water. Whenever
Russell made love to her, Kirby was left with a feeling of
shame and uncleanliness. As soon as he was asleep, she always
took a shower, the hotter the better. Only after she had scrubbed
her body over and over did she feel clean again.

As she stood there letting the near-scalding water sluice over
her body, she realized what she was doing. Her cleansing ritual
had nothing to do with Russell. She loved him and it made no
sense that contact with him would make her feel dirty.

On the other hand, she recalled other hot baths and showers
as she was growing up. Images of herself as a girl, scrubbing
her skin almost raw, came to her. If the molestation hadn't
occurred, why had she taken all those baths and showers, some
of them in the middle of the night?

Suddenly it struck Kirby that she was recalling memories
from those missing years.

She turned off the water and stood in the quiet shower, trying
to dredge up a memory that would spell out why she felt so
dirty and degraded. A memory to explain why she felt this way
after touching the man she loved. She buried her face in her
hands and began to silently cry.

Chapter Twenty

"Where are you going?" Russell asked Josh.

"Out."

Kirby looked up from the book she was reading.

"That's not what I asked you. I can see you're heading out the door." Russell kept his tone calm but he wasn't going to continue letting Josh behave like this.

"I'm going out with my friends. Okay?" His manner was sullen and angry.

"What friends?"

"What difference does it make? Just some friends!"

"If it's the ones I met at my apartment, you're not going."

"Then it's some different ones." He yanked the door open.

"I don't believe you," Russell said quietly. "Come have a seat. We need to talk."

"No, we don't. I'm not a baby like Cody," he sneered.

Russell went to him. Through the open doorway he saw a dented, white car packed with teenage boys pull up out front. He also saw the beer bottle one of them hid when they recognized him as a parent. "You're lying to me. Those are the ones I met and they're drinking."

"Sure, root beer. They make root beer in long-neck bottles now."

"Let's go out to the car and you can prove me wrong."

"Okay, come on," Josh bluffed.

Russell led the way. The boys in the car looked nervous and were considerably quieter as he crossed the yard. He also saw one palm a cigarette that looked homemade. As he drew closer, he smelled the unmistakable odor of pot.

He put his hand on the rolled-down window and leaned down so the boys could hear. As he looked at their faces, he said, "I don't want you boys to come over here again. I don't even want you driving down this street. If I ever hear you're talking to my son at school or anywhere else, I'll report you for smoking pot and drinking. Got it?"

The boys were dead quiet, though rebellion was about to break out.

Russell had taught high school before getting his graduate degree and moving up to college professorship, and the skills he'd learned for handling teenagers in class had stayed with him. He knew how to time pronouncements such as the one he had just made. Before any of them could react, he straightened and jerked his thumb signaling the driver to leave.

Josh bellowed out in rage and tried to get into the car. Russell grabbed his shirt collar and hauled him back. The car took off in a squeal of rubber. Russell read the license plate and filed it away in his mind.

"You can't do this to me!" Josh shouted. "Who the hell do you think you are!"

"I'm your father and you're a thirteen-year-old boy. I can and will do whatever it takes to raise you safely and properly."

Josh tried to jerk his arm free but Russell was stronger. "You let me go! I'll report you for child abuse!"

"Go ahead. Want me to look up the number for you? All I have to do is call a friend of mine at the police station and have your friends picked up for driving while intoxicated, alcohol possession by minors, and possession of a controlled substance." He paused. "Well? Want to make that call?"

"Leave me alone!"

"I've needed to have a talk with you for a long time. I didn't plan for it to be here, but you picked it." He saw the neighbors next door step out on their porch to see what the trouble was.

"You're not going to run with that gang and you're going to stop skipping school."

"Who said I'm cutting school? Was it Cody?" Josh pulled against Russell's firm grip.

"No, it was your teachers. I wouldn't put Cody in that position. I intend to keep checking. I know boys, Josh. There's not anything in your head that I haven't seen at the college or at frat houses. I deal with boys that are a lot tougher than you are every day so you might as well straighten up and start behaving again."

"Let me go! You're hurting me!" Josh had also seen he had an audience and was playing the injured child to the hilt.

Russell ignored him. "You're also going to stop treating your mother like shit. She deserves your respect and you're going to give it to her."

"I'll run away!"

"If you do, I'll have you arrested. It's against the law for a thirteen-year-old to run away."

"You'd have me arrested?" Josh made certain his voice was carrying to the neighbors, then added, "I'm going to report you for child abuse!"

"You're also grounded. Starting tomorrow, I'm taking you to school and I'm picking you up. If you're five minutes late, I'll come in looking for you. If I hear you're cutting class, I'll go to class with you until you stop."

"You can't do that! You have a job."

"I'll work around that." Russell started leading the boy back to the house. He nodded to the neighbors and they looked embarrassed to be caught eavesdropping. "Josh has started running with some boys I don't approve of," he called to them. "If you ever see that white car here again, I'd appreciate a call at the college." He didn't wait to see if they nodded. That shot had been mostly for Josh's benefit.

When they were in the house, Russell turned him loose. "I think you'd better go to your room until you cool off."

Josh gave him a long glare, but then he thundered up the stairs.

When he went back to the den, he found Kirby standing in the doorway. "Is he okay?"

"Of course. What did you think I was going to do? Beat him up?"

She turned away and he realized that was exactly what she had thought. He went to her and caught her arm. "I don't hit kids. You know I don't."

She nodded without speaking. Her silver eyes held that haunted fear deep in their depths.

"All I did was chase away his buddies and embarrass him. He's not hurt. I'm going to start driving Cody and him to and from school for a while. It'll mean a crunch in my own class schedule, but it's worth the trouble. We have to get him out of that gang."

"It's a real gang?"

"They were wearing jackets with that picture Josh painted on his the other day. It was a gang or close enough to it."

She looked stricken. "What are we going to do? He's always been strong-minded, but lately I can't control him at all."

"I know. I'm home now and I'll help you get him back on the right path. He's a good boy at heart. He's just running with a rough crowd."

"I hope you're right." She sat on the couch, leaving room for him to sit beside her. "God, when I think what Dad would say, I go cold all over!"

"Kirby, this doesn't involve your father. Josh is our son. Not his."

"I know that, but Josh's actions might negatively impact Dad's career. He has to keep a good image."

"Relatively speaking, yes. But his grandson's behavior isn't that crucial to Addison being an appellate court judge. They don't even live in the same house. You're blowing this way out of proportion."

She shook her head. "I'm not. You didn't see how furious Dad was when Josh was caught shoplifting. It was terrible! If he heard half that goes on between Josh and me . . ." She didn't finish the sentence.

Russell put his arm around her. Although she checked the instinct to draw away, he felt it and removed his arm. "You're having nightmares again, aren't you?"

She nodded. "I don't mean to wake you."

"That's not the point. I want you to go back to see Lauren."

"No, I don't want to do that. She was putting all sorts of ideas in my head."

He rested his forearms on his knees. "I've been thinking. Remember when you asked me if I thought it could be true that your father molested you? I said no, but since then, I've had time to think about it. I could believe it."

"Russell, how could you?" she exclaimed. "My dad—"

"Is perfect. I know. You've told me that for years. But I've seen his temper. I might not have been there when he tore into Josh, though I sure wish I had been, but I've seen him rage on other occasions. Your father has two distinct parts to his personality. There's the face he shows to the world and the one his family knows."

"Don't tell me these things."

"You know they're true. Don't lie to yourself, honey. If you don't want to see Lauren, go to someone else. Houston has plenty of psychiatrists and psychologists. You need to get some help. I hate seeing you so miserable."

She was silent for a while. "I guess it wouldn't hurt for me to make a few more appointments with Lauren. She already knows my history so I wouldn't have to start over. But that's not an admission that Dad did anything."

He smiled at her and gave her a brief hug that wouldn't alarm her. "I think I'll make an appointment for myself. If you're going to get back into counseling, I want to be with you every way I can and Lauren can help me know what to do and say."

Kirby slipped her hand into his. It was rare for her to make any physical sign of affection and he was touched. "Thank you, Russell. You're very good for me."

He refrained from hugging her again.

As she went back to her book and he picked up his, he was thinking about Addison and what he might have done to her. If he was indeed guilty, Russell knew he would need counseling to keep from going over and smashing Addison's face in.

Russell knew about Kirby's midnight showers. Because she had done this all their married life, he seldom thought much about them. It had only been since he moved back home that he had seen a connection between the showers and their love-making.

He had been concerned when Kirby stopped seeing Lauren. In his opinion, Kirby still had a long way to go before she would have her life happy and in order, but that wasn't something he could say to her.

He glanced at her over the top of his book. She personified all he had ever wanted in life. Her agreeing to marry him had been like a gift from heaven. There was nothing he wouldn't do for her and no danger he wouldn't brave for her sake, but he couldn't make her happy.

Had Addison molested her? Russell honestly didn't know. If he ever became convinced that Addison had, he wasn't sure what he would do. Merely thinking that Addison might have molested the woman he loved sent waves of anger rushing through him. The fact that there never had been any love between Addison and himself only added fuel to the fire. What would he do? What would Kirby want him to do, or rather not do? Yes, Russell thought, he definitely needed to talk to Lauren.

Jane sat in her silent den, placing one stitch in her needlepoint after another. Addison sat opposite her, paying the month's bills. She would have been glad to do that chore, but a long time ago he had said she would do it wrong, so she never offered again. Once Addison had his mind made up, there was no changing it.

From across the hall, she could see the rosy glow of their Christmas tree. Although they almost never went into the living room unless they had company, Addison liked to have it lit every night so people passing down the street would know they had one. It was one of his eccentricities that he wanted the tree lit, yet would complain if she stayed up too late reading because it used too much electricity. Jane supposed it was one more thing she didn't understand.

Since her talk with Tara several months before, Jane had been troubled. She was pretty sure she understood what her granddaughter was telling her about Addison, but there was nothing she could do about it. To keep from being placed in the position of letting Addison know that Tara had told her what he was doing, Jane usually took Tara shopping when Mallory dropped her off in the afternoons. Tara had responded by becoming more like her old self.

It bothered Jane a great deal that Addison would do something inappropriate to their granddaughter. That was how she thought of it. One of Jane's uncles had done much the same thing to her one summer when she was starting high school. She had never told anyone but had avoided being alone with him after that and the incident hadn't repeated itself. All the same, she could recall every frightening moment of that summer afternoon.

There was the chance that Tara had misinterpreted what had happened. There was so much sex and violence on TV that it was no wonder a child might be confused over what might have been only a grandfatherly display of affection.

But in the back of Jane's mind she was suspicious. Tara's behavior reminded her of Kirby when she was about Tara's age.

Jane remembered quite distinctly when Kirby had started to change from a happy, demonstrative child to one who was shy and withdrawn. It had started the summer Kirby was eight. Jane had never figured out what was wrong and Kirby never gave her any hints.

Jane didn't think for a moment that Addison had or would go beyond an inappropriate kiss and perhaps fondling. She reassured herself it wasn't really sexual molestation unless intercourse was involved. And Addison would never do that! Unwillingly she recalled the day her uncle had kissed her and groped at her body and how terrible that had been. Even though it only happened once, she had felt soiled for years.

When Kirby had become withdrawn, Jane had tried to bring her out of it by spending more time with her. Quality time, as they said these days. She had been involved in so many organizations and charity projects, she hadn't been able to be with the girls as much as she would have preferred. Addison had wanted her to be involved in the community and in activities that would reflect favorably on his career. Jane had always wished, however, that she had spent more time with her daughters. At least, she thought, Mallory could do that with Tara. Mallory belonged to no clubs or service organizations, and except for her prolonged shopping expeditions, she was at home.

Jane wondered if she should have told Mallory what Tara told her, but had decided against it. Whatever Addison had done and however he had intended it, the deed was done. In time, Tara would forget it, just as Kirby had apparently forgotten whatever bothered her at this age.

She didn't want to believe Addison had done anything that was actually wrong.

She looked over at her husband. He was still a handsome man. He had been the most handsome and popular boy she had ever dated. When he proposed to her, Jane had thought she was hearing angels singing. They were married before she ever put two and two together and saw that Addison had a great deal to gain by being her father's son-in-law. Jane had more or less taken it for granted that her father had been mayor of Houston for a number of years. Addison had used it as a step up the political ladder, she had finally realized.

She put aside her sewing and went to the bookshelf to get one of the photo albums from the years when she was younger and her daughters were little. Going back to her chair, she opened it. There was Kirby with her front teeth missing and a shy smile and Mallory flirting with the camera even though she wasn't old enough to go to kindergarten. They had been such pretty children. Addison had doted on them.

There was one she had snapped in the backyard. The trees looked comically small compared to their size now. Addison was kneeling between the girls. He was smiling but both girls had their arms crossed and were leaning slightly away. Mallory's smile was wavering and Kirby was frowning. The picture had always bothered her but she had never been able to figure out why. In view of what Tara had said, it made more sense. If Addison had been molesting the girls, naturally they wouldn't want to hug him.

What was she thinking of? Jane looked across the top of the album at her husband. Addison would never hurt a child! Not in that way! He had beaten them and she had hated that, but children had been punished for misbehaving for as long as families had existed and they survived. The girls hadn't seemed to hold a beating against Addison once it was over. This was one of the reasons Jane had used to rationalize staying with him. It had been the same for herself. After the bruises faded and he explained how she had goaded him into striking her, she had always forgiven him.

No, incest was a different matter entirely. Surely if it had happened, Kirby and Mallory would have turned against him. Yet they both clearly loved and respected him. Jane told herself this was proof it hadn't happened.

Tara had been confused about Addison's intentions. Nothing else. Not doubt TV was to blame. Addison was a decent man, a good person. He wouldn't touch a daughter or grandaughter in that way. Of course he wouldn't.

He sighed heavily and said without looking up, "Why do you keep staring at me?"

Jane averted her eyes. "I'm sorry." A few minutes later she found herself unable to keep from glancing at him again.

"You're doing it again. You know how I hate for you to stare at me." He slapped his pen down onto the table and scowled at her. "What's wrong now?"

"Nothing." She couldn't possibly tell him what she had been thinking. "Did you know Kirby is seeing a therapist? A psychiatrist."

"What? A psychiatrist!" He shifted to face her. "Why would she do a damned fool thing like that?"

"Why, I don't know," Jane stammered. She had chosen the wrong subject. "I suppose she felt she needed counseling. She and Russell are back together, but I don't know if they're happy or not."

"Counseling is a pile of bullshit." He turned back to the bills he was paying. "Tell her I said to stop."

"I can't do that!"

"Tell her the order came from me."

Jane stared at him openly. "What does it matter if Kirby is in counseling? A lot of people are."

"Not in my family. Use your head, Jane. Try thinking for a

change. My political opponents would have a field day over my daughter seeing a shrink."

"It's quite confidential, I'm sure. At least I hear it is," she added doubtfully.

"Look," he said with exaggerated patience. "I'm important in this town and I'm about to become a hell of a lot more important. People are going to be analyzing every move I make. I can't have anyone saying my daughter is insane."

She tried to laugh. "Kirby isn't insane. That's just silly."

"Maybe the press needs a great brain like you to explain that to them."

She hated it when he was sarcastic. It made her feel even more foolish. "I'm sorry, Addison."

"If there's anything wrong with Kirby, it comes from your side of the family. I still remember Rachel Ann. She's as nutty as a fruitcake."

"I have to admit Rachel Ann is a bit odd," Jane said carefully, "but I wouldn't call her insane."

"Well, I doubt you'd be considered much of an authority, now would you," he said dryly.

"I suppose not," she said unhappily.

"Tell Kirby to stop seeing the psychiatrist. That's easy enough even for you to understand."

"Yes, Addison." She sat there, gripping the photo album while he went back to writing checks. The reprimand was over.

Jane took a grateful breath of air. She hated for him to be upset with her. In her family, no one had ever raised his voice, and Addison had always frightened her when he was angry and loud. His rages terrified her. As silently as she could, she took the album back to the shelf and headed toward the door.

"Stop sneaking around!" Addison shouted as he angrily crumpled the paper in front of him. "I hate it when you creep about like that! Are you deliberately trying to provoke me?"

"No, Addison. I'd never do that!"

"Get out of here. I don't want to be in the same room with you."

Jane hurried out before he could change his mind. Paying bills always upset him and she should have known better than to sit in the room at such a time. It was her own fault that she got into so much trouble.

Instead of going to her bedroom, she went down the hall to the guest room. For years she had wished she had the courage to suggest that she move in here, but she dreaded the explosion that surely would take place. It was a shame. She would be much happier in the smaller, cozier room. Away from Addison.

She went to the closet and took out the dried flower petals she stored there. Jane had made her own potpourri for many years. She loved sweet smells, and none of the commercial mixes suited her taste exactly. She poured a plastic bag half full of the petals she had gathered from her garden in the summer and dried. Measuring carefully, she dropped essential oil of rose and twice that amount of carnation into the bag. She fastened the top and shook it to mix it all together. It would have to season for a week or so, then she would refill the dishes of petals around the house.

Being in the room reminded Jane of the day some months ago when she had sent Kirby in here to get something and it had taken her practically forever to return. That was the same day Kirby had told her she couldn't remember eight years of her life.

That was so remarkable that Jane had thought about it often.

Kirby was about eight when Jane had started to wonder if Addison was having an affair. He had been distant, as if his mind was on someone else and he had yelled at her if she came unexpectedly into a room. Had Kirby seen him with another woman? Was that why she couldn't remember? If that was the case, Jane hoped her daughter would never recall those years. She had always wanted to spare her girls from unpleasantness.

Raising them hadn't always been easy. She could remember when Kirby and Mallory were both out of sorts for months on end. Those times fell in the years Kirby couldn't remember, too. The time when Kirby had become withdrawn and sulky. A couple of years later, Mallory had turned into a rebel practically overnight. Jane had told herself that their shift in behavior was only her payment for them having been so delightful as toddlers and sailing through the terrible twos and ferocious fours so easily.

Once Kirby had tried to tell her Addison was doing something he shouldn't. It had happened much like the incident with Tara. As with Tara, Jane had told Kirby to put unpleasantnesses out of her mind and to leave well enough alone. Jane had assumed at the time that Kirby had discovered her father was having an affair. She had read Kirby a story with religious overtones about a little girl who said bad things about her father and how it had backfired on her. After that, Kirby had never brought up the subject again. Jane had congratulated herself on having handled something right for a change. Now she wondered if she had merely swept it under the carpet.

There was so much on TV about incest and child abuse! Jane assumed it was simply getting more prevalent in society, but Freddie Rae Powers had told her it had always been around, just not talked about.

Could that be what Kirby had been trying to tell her? Was it what Tara had meant? Jane simply didn't know and had no one to ask.

Jane wished she was smart enough to figure this out. Just when she needed to think the most, her mind seemed to wander off into a wilderness and desert her. If someone, anyone, was harming Tara, she had to do something about it. But if this was only another foolishness of hers and Addison found out, he would half kill her.

He hadn't hit her in a long time and she didn't intend to provoke him into doing it again. Not that he had ever been as rough on her as with the girls. Jane was positive that he would never have hit her if she hadn't provoked him.

She opened the bag and breathed deeply of the sweet aroma. As always, it soothed her.

But just as quickly, guilt crept back in. Thinking such things about Addison was sinful of her. She was positive of that. If Addison had ever overstepped the bounds of propriety with their daughters, they hadn't been harmed by it. Both had made good marriages, even if Addison didn't like Russell, and Kirby was a brilliant lawyer. Both girls adored their father.

She decided it would be best not to think about it anymore.

* * *

Down in the den, Addison put down his pen and was no longer writing checks. Kirby was seeing a psychiatrist. That was bad. He had never gone to one himself, of course, but he knew those people could worm their way into matters that were better left alone.

He hadn't touched Kirby in years. Why would she start causing trouble now?

He remembered how she had been as a child. Whereas Mallory had been like a bright butterfly, Kirby had been serious even then. She was quiet and shy and obedient. It had torn him apart when they got old enough to date. He could imagine every boy they went out with pawing at them, using them in ways that Addison considered exclusively his own.

All that crap on TV was misleading. Nothing he had ever done had damaged his daughters. If anything, it had probably made them better able to satisfy their husbands. It hadn't caused any lasting effect in either of them. Mallory had never had much ambition when it came to a career, but that was just Mallory's way. Kirby was as hard-driving a lawyer as any he had ever seen. No matter what the supercilious talk show hosts might claim, nothing he had done was harmful to anyone.

He hadn't done anything that wasn't considered normal and a father's prerogative in some cultures in the world.

Calling it incest gave it a bad name. He was willing to bet a lot of the talk show hosts were into it, too, if the truth were known. He honestly believed most fathers were. If not, they were missing something.

Nothing was softer than a little girl.

All that aside, he didn't want anyone to know what had gone on in his house. He wasn't ashamed of what he had done, but it would look bad to the press. That was guaranteed. If it became public knowledge, it would ruin his career.

He rubbed the bridge of his nose, taking care not to shift his contact lens. Kirby had to be silenced. Would Jane have enough sense to prevent her from seeing the psychiatrist? Addison should do it himself, but he was reluctant to talk to Kirby about it. It was almost as if they had decided to keep all that had happened between them a secret, even between the two of them.

At times, he had wondered if Kirby remembered it at all. If she had, why had she been so shy about her marriage? He hated thinking about that time. She was the first daughter he had lost. Mallory hadn't been far behind her. Even though they both lived close by, Addison had never touched them again. They belonged to their husbands now and he was an honorable man.

But it had been as if Kirby hadn't known exactly what would happen on her wedding night.

He had been jealous of Russell. That was the main reason he disliked him so much. From the beginning Addison had known Russell had been more than a mere date. When he and Kirby started dating each other exclusively, Addison had been convinced they were going to bed at every opportunity. The fact that Kirby never came to him and confessed only made it that much worse. He had told her to tell him everything that happened when she started going out on dates. Mallory certainly had.

Thinking of Mallory put a smile on his face. She was like a sexy little kitten. So cuddly and playful. She would have done anything at all for the right bribe. It had excited him seeing just how outrageous she would become by offering her a new sweater, a toy, a trip to the zoo. After she started dating, she had dutifully reported everything she had done. And there had been a great deal to report. Jane's hair would have turned gray overnight if she had heard a fourth of it. He and Mallory had enjoyed a particularly close relationship.

Until recently he would have said the same about Kirby.

She was changing, Kirby was. There was the time, for instance, when he had tried to discipline Josh for stealing. Kirby had actually stood up to him! She had refused to back down and had taken the boy home! Addison was still angry over that. And the time when she had confronted him in the lobby of the criminal courts building over his breach of ethics in seeing to it that Derrick succeeded Hershal Glassman as head of the company. He'd been furious with her for bringing that up in a public place. She had changed, indeed.

Lately, though, she was avoiding him. It had started shortly before her car accident. He had wondered about it at the time, but decided it was because her marriage was breaking up. She hadn't admitted that a divorce was likely, but he had feared it was. He didn't like Russell and didn't want him in the family, but Russell was already one of them and they had to present an unbroken front to the public.

He wondered how soon he could expect to officially hear that the Supreme Court would need a new judge. It wasn't the sort of thing he could call Raymond and ask. As far as everyone else was concerned, the appointment had to seem as much a surprise to Addison as it would be to the other candidates. He knew how to play the game. It wouldn't do to get impatient.

All the same, he wished it would come soon and the confirmation hearings get under way before Kirby did something to screw it up.

Chapter Twenty-One

"Kirby, I'm glad you dropped by," Mallory said. "Do you want a cup of coffee?"

"No, I'm nervous enough as it is. I have an appointment this afternoon with Lauren Jacobs."

"Your psychiatrist? I thought you had stopped going."

"I had, but I'm starting to backslide." She smiled nervously. "Sometimes I feel as if I'm coming apart at the seams. Do you know what I mean?"

"Yes. I do." Mallory poured herself another cup of coffee and sat opposite Kirby at the kitchen table. "I've missed you coming by. I guess you've been really busy since Russell is back home."

Kirby nodded. "I've missed talking to you. We used to drop in to see each other almost every day. I wish we still did."

"We could, you know. Is Josh still giving you trouble?"

"By the boat load. Thank goodness Russell is there now to help keep him under control. I don't know what's gotten into him. One day he was a loving, wonderful child, now he's a surly teen."

Mallory laughed. "It's hormones. Don't you remember how we were at that age?"

"I was never that rebellious!"

"No, but I was."

Kirby had to laugh. "That's true. You were as touchy as old Russian royalty for a while there. I had forgotten. Maybe I will have a cup." She got up and poured it for herself.

"It's a phase. Josh will grow out of it. I did."

"That's true. Maybe I'm worried over nothing."

"It's how kids cut the apron strings. If he stayed as sweet and loving as he was as a little boy, he would never want to move out and get on with his life, and you'd never be able to let him go."

"I suppose that's true. You've always been so insightful when it comes to things like this. I still say you should have gone for a degree in psychology."

"I can just see me as a counselor." All the same, Mallory couldn't keep the wistfulness out of her voice.

"You could go back to school. It wouldn't take you all that long."

"You think so?" Mallory sipped her coffee. "Now that Tara is in school all day, I don't have that much to occupy my time. I didn't want to work when she needed me here, of course. And Derrick wanted me to stay home. You know how macho he can be when it comes to something like that."

Kirby wisely said nothing.

"Do you think I could sign up for some courses at U of H?"

"Certainly you could. I'll ask Russell to bring home a copy of next semester's courses."

Mallory sighed. "Who am I kidding? You're the one with all the brains. I'm not smart enough to be a counselor."

"I don't know where you got that idea. You're as intelligent as I am."

Mallory rested her cheek on her knuckles. "Imagine me going back to school!" After a brief pause, she said, "Yes, ask Russell to bring me the schedule. I have way too much time on my hands."

Although she didn't want to mention it to Kirby, she was starting to worry about her obsession with sex. She had never given it much thought, but the week before, she had seen a talk show about people who were addicted to sex, and the symptoms they described had fit her too closely. She was beginning to wonder if she was fooling herself about her affairs. Like the women on the program, she didn't get that much pleasure out of making love; she only wanted to be held and couldn't stop the need to prove her desirability over and over.

"You know," Mallory said, "I've been wondering if I should see a psychiatrist myself. Not that anything is really wrong," she added quickly, "but I have some problems that I'd like to talk over."

"You can talk to me about anything. You know that."

"I think I need an unbiased opinion."

"I'm sure Lauren would take you as a client. Do you want her number?"

Mallory nodded. She watched as Kirby wrote the phone number on a paper napkin. Mallory folded it and put it under the cookie jar on top of the refrigerator. She didn't want Derrick to see it. If she did this, it had to be her secret, at least for a while. At least until she found out if her sexual needs were out of bounds.

"How is Tara doing?" Kirby asked.

"I don't know. Her grades have dropped out of sight. I try talking to her but she just closes off. It's like talking to the wall."

"She's a bit young to be a victim of raging hormones like Josh."

"I know." Mallory sat back down at the table. "Kirby, can I ask you something?"

"Of course."

"You told me once that you thought Dad molested us. Did you mean that? You weren't just exaggerating?"

"I'd never say a thing like that unless I thought there was a basis for it. Surely you know that."

Mallory nodded. "I remember those years you've forgotten. But how do we know if what happened was really molestation or if it was natural? Maybe it happens in all families. Do you see what I'm saying?"

"I'm trying to."

"Maybe Dad didn't do anything deliberately to hurt us. Maybe he thought he was doing the right thing. You know, teaching us." She felt her cheeks grow red. She had never even allowed herself to consider that Addison had touched her or Kirby in a way that was abusive. Certainly she had never admitted it to anyone, not even Kirby.

"Mal, you and I both know fathers don't show their daughters how to have sex." Kirby drew back abruptly. "Why did I put it that way? It just fell out of my mouth!"

Mallory watched her closely. "You don't remember Dad saying those words to you?"

"Certainly not! If I did, I'd know right away that he was a perpetrator! That's classic in incest cases. The father frequently says he's doing it to instruct his daughter or because her mother won't be sexual with him and the girl owes it to him. That sort of thing. It's bullshit, but it's done frequently."

"Of course it is . . ." Mallory's voice trailed off. She was remembering how often Addison had explained his conduct toward her in that way. "Is it ever true?"

"Mal, what would you say if anyone said that to Tara and molested her?"

Mallory's answer was immediate. "I'd kill him." She put her fingers over her mouth. "I can't believe I just said that!"

Kirby looked at her sister thoughtfully. "Mal, something has occurred to me. I can't remember the years from the time I was eight until I was sixteen. Tara was eight when she started becoming withdrawn." Her eyes met Mallory's. "Is it possible this isn't a coincidence?"

"No! No, I'm sure it is. Nothing is happening to Tara. She would tell me." Mallory tried to sound convinced. Several times Tara had tried to talk to her and had seemed upset, but she had picked such inopportune times. She only wanted to talk when Mallory was busy or had her mind on other things— usually men, she realized with a flush of guilt. "Has she said anything to you?"

"That's just it. I'm not sure. She was trying to tell me something, but I couldn't figure out what she meant. She became upset and ran home. Remember? I called to see if she got home safely."

"I remember." Mallory absently drank her coffee. "I do remember. And she hates to go to Dad's house." Reluctantly she met her sister's eyes. "What should I do? I can't confront him with something like this unless I'm positive it's happening!"

"Keep her away from there. Don't leave her alone with him."

"I never do. Mom is always there, too."

"She was there when we were little, too," Kirby reminded her.

Mallory felt sick deep inside her. "Yes. Mom never worked. She was there." She shook her head. "That proves it couldn't have happened. Mom wouldn't have let anything happen to us."

"Can you honestly imagine Mom standing up to Dad over anything? And she wasn't with us constantly, not any more than we're with our own children every minute."

"I don't like thinking this way." Mallory turned away. "Do you want more coffee?"

"No. I have to be going. I don't like thinking it either, Mal. But if it's true, we have to know about it. You can't let it happen to Tara, too." She stood and picked up her purse. "Will I see you tomorrow?"

Mallory nodded. Her mind was whirling. "Tomorrow. Drop by on your way home from seeing Lauren if you'd like. I'll be here."

After Kirby let herself out, Mallory went to the kitchen sink and poured out the remaining coffee. She couldn't swallow past the lump in her throat. How could she have thought for a single instant that what Addison had done to her wasn't harmful? How could she have actually believed him all these years about it being his duty to teach her about sex? Tears welled in her eyes and spilled onto her cheek. She was barely aware of crying. She had thought she was the only one. That he wasn't touching Kirby the way he was her. He had said he was doing those things only to her because she was his favorite and it was their secret.

Was he now doing the same things to Tara?

"No!" she cried out, throwing her coffee cup against the wall.

The cup shattered and pieces of it scattered over the kitchen floor. Mallory stared at it, her fists clenched at her sides. It couldn't be happening! Not to Tara!

Mallory did nothing but worry until Tara came home from school. She saw her crossing the yard and met her at the door.

Tara stopped. "What's wrong? Am I in trouble?"

"Of course not, honey." Mallory made an effort to smile naturally. "How about some hot cocoa? That should warm you up."

Tara warily followed her into the kitchen. "Sure, Mom. I'd like that."

Mallory wasn't sure how to open the subject. It wasn't something she could just blurt out. She put some water in a cup and turned on the microwave. "How was school today?"

"Okay."

"Any homework?"

"I have to learn a bunch of words for a spelling test. Mom, why are you acting weird?"

Mallory sighed. "I've been curious about something. Why don't you like going to Grandad's anymore?"

Caution leaped into Tara's eyes. "I don't know." She broke eye contact and continued looking down as she kicked her heel against the chair rung. "I just don't."

"Honey, if anything . . . odd . . . happened, you'd tell me, wouldn't you?" Mallory sat in the chair opposite so they were more the same height. "You can tell me anything."

Tara continued to avoid her mother's eyes. "Okay."

The microwave dinged and Mallory took out the cup. As she stirred instant cocoa into it, she realized she was frowning but couldn't seem to stop. Tara was holding something back. She dropped a few miniature marshmallows into the cocoa and put it in front of Tara.

"Thank you," she said dutifully.

Mallory sat back down and slid the cookie jar within Tara's reach. Tara studied her speculatively. Mallory tried again. "When I was little, I liked to tell my mom when something was bothering me. Somehow she always knew how to make me feel better." This wasn't exactly true, but she thought the ploy might work.

"Grandma did?" Tara looked doubtful.

"Mothers love their children and want to know if anything is bothering them. I think something is worrying you, and I want to help."

Tara had taken a cookie from the jar, but now she pushed it away. "I guess I'm not hungry after all."

Mallory decided she'd have to use a direct approach. "Tara, has something happened at Grandad's that I need to know about?"

Tara stood up so fast her chair nearly toppled over backward. "No! I don't want to talk about it!" She bolted from the room.

Mallory dropped the untouched cookie back into the jar as she listened to Tara run through the house and into her room, slamming the door behind her.

"I handled that well," Mallory said wryly. One thing seemed certain. Tara was hiding something.

Unfortunately, Mallory was no closer to finding out what it might be than she was before. She started to pour out the abandoned cocoa, but she decided to drink it instead. As when she was a child, the cocoa was soothing.

She wondered if she could tell Derrick but instantly decided against it. He either wouldn't believe her or he would confront Addison. Mallory wanted neither to happen until she was certain Addison had done something to Tara. She shuddered to think what Addison would say and do if he were falsely accused. Mallory loved her father, but she also feared him.

She finished the cocoa and stared into the bottom of the empty cup as if she were reading tea leaves to determine her next action.

For one thing, she had to stop leaving Tara at Grandad's house. This would be terribly inconvenient for everyone. Either she would have to take Tara with her on errands and give up seeing other men, or her mother would have to come babysit here.

She was getting a headache. Why did this have to happen? Other families didn't have to worry about leaving a daughter with her grandfather. Surely, Mallory thought, other mothers were spared this problem. Wasn't it enough to have to worry about drugs at school and whether anyone was bullying her child and all the usual parental worries?

Regretting the situation didn't help. When it came right down to it, Mallory had to keep Tara safe at all costs, whether it was convenient or whether it hurt feelings in the family or not. Just thinking that Addison might hurt Tara made her blood boil.

Yes, Tara had to be protected.

"I guess you thought you'd never see me again," Kirby said as she entered Lauren Jacobs' office.

"I've missed you."

Kirby wondered if that was true. She had never made friends easily, as Mallory had. Her shyness as a child and her later reserve had stood in the way. It made her feel warm inside to think Lauren might have missed her as a person and not just in the professional sense.

"Yes?" Lauren prompted, motioning for Kirby to take a seat.

Kirby obliged. "I was just thinking that I've rarely had a best friend."

"Why is that? You're an interesting person and you're friendly. I would think you'd have an abundance of friends."

"I have friends, but not any one that's closer than another. I guess Mallory has always been my best friend as well as my sister. I didn't like to bring anyone home with me from school."

"No?"

"I was never sure if Dad would be home. Of course I had classmates over in high school, but not in the earlier grades."

Lauren picked up her pen. "Are you aware you just had a memory of the years you had forgotten? You remember not having friends over before high school."

Kirby stared at her a moment. "Yes. I guess you're right. How odd."

"What would have happened if a friend had come over and your father was there?"

"He might . . . I don't know. I don't think I ever considered the consequences. I simply never did it."

"What did you start to say? What was your first thought?"

"It was that he might play the games with them."

"Games?"

Kirby found herself clenching her hands together so tightly that they ached. "The games. Hide-and-seek. You know."

"No, I don't. You've never told me your father played games with you." Lauren was intent upon getting the answer. "How did he play hide-and-seek?"

"You know how the game goes. He would hide and I was supposed to find him." She frowned and rubbed her forehead. "I don't understand what's happening. I seem to have a memory of events that couldn't have taken place. They couldn't have happened. I wouldn't have forgotten something like this."

"Just tell me the memory."

"Dad would hide in the same place every time. In the guest bedroom at the end of the hall. Like in my nightmare."

"Where was your mother?"

"I don't know. I guess in the kitchen at the other end of the house, or maybe she was out running errands. She didn't work outside the house. Mallory and I were talking about that this morning."

"So your father hid in the guest bedroom?" Lauren prompted.

"Yes." She found herself unable to go on. She could feel sweat beading up on her forehead. Although she tried to speak, no sound came out.

"It's all right, Kirby. This is a safe place. You can tell me anything. No one else will ever know."

"I know." She wet her lips and tried again. "He would be there," her voice faltered for a moment, then she pushed on, "with his pants unzipped. Sometimes he wouldn't have them on at all." She shook her head from side to side. "I can't say these things."

"I'm not forcing you to. If it's too uncomfortable, you don't have to tell me." Lauren's voice was gentle.

"He would have me . . . touch him." Kirby felt tears stinging her eyes and she stopped and gulped in air, fighting to keep from crying.

"Just take your time."

Kirby drew in a shaken breath. "I don't think I can say these things out loud. Not ever."

"Would it be easier for you to write them in your journal?"

Kirby shook her head again. "No. I have to do this." She closed her eyes to compose herself. "I didn't want to touch him, but I knew I had to do it." Hot tears began rolling down her cheeks but she made no attempt to brush them away. "He made me touch his penis." Her voice broke and she gulped in air to try to control the overwhelming emotions.

"Did this happen more than once?"

"Yes," Kirby whispered. "It happened often."

"Did it go farther than you touching him?"

Kirby buried her face in her hands as she nodded. "It progressed as time went on. First with me touching him, then he touched me. We . . . Before long we were having intercourse."

"How old were you when this happened?" Lauren's voice was gentle and she sounded neither shocked nor disgusted.

"The touching started when I was eight. The intercourse . . ." Her voice quavered and she had to pause. "It started when I was about twelve. I think." She couldn't meet Lauren's eyes. "I was starting to develop breasts when it happened. I think I was twelve."

"It wasn't your fault."

Kirby finally looked at her. "It must have been. I touched him first. Remember? God! How could I have done that!"

Lauren moved closer and took Kirby's hand comfortingly. "He was the one who unzipped or removed his pants. You didn't want to touch him—you just told me all these things."

Kirby gripped Lauren's hand as if it were a lifeline. "But I did do it! And I never told Mom or anyone else. That makes me an accomplice!"

"No, it makes you a little girl who was trying to stay out of trouble. I'm sure your father must have told you not to tell. It's not uncommon for perpetrators to use threats to protect themselves. Some of the women I've talked to about these issues were told their parents would divorce, or even that their mother or a sibling would be hurt or killed if they didn't comply."

"God!" Kirby whispered. She reached for a tissue. "Maybe

that's why I was so sure Dad would go away and never come back if I told!"

"It seems likely."

"This is so unbelievable! Once I started talking about the game, it all fell into place."

"Sometimes it happens that way. Other times, the memories are buried deeper and it takes longer."

"I've been remembering bits and pieces for months. I never tried to put them into a real thought until now. God! I actually remember that happening!" She stood and paced to the window and stared out at the parking lot. "He did those things to me! I was just a little girl." She felt a dampness on her cheeks and realized she was still crying.

"You've accomplished a lot today."

"This has been a day for the record books." Kirby dabbed at her eyes. "I hate to cry."

"I know, but it's good for you."

Kirby almost laughed. "Every time something seems to be ripping my insides out, you say that."

Lauren smiled at her. "It only hurts to cry because you fight so hard to suppress it. Maybe it'll get easier with time."

"Before I came for my appointment, I found myself telling Mallory that it's not normal for fathers to teach their daughters to have sex." Kirby remembered the frightened expression in Mallory's eyes.

"You're right. It's not."

"Mallory seemed to know what I meant. The words just fell out as if they were something I had learned by heart years ago."

"They probably were. That's most likely the reason he gave you for his behavior."

"He must have done the same thing to Mallory." Kirby looked at Lauren. "I also told her it's too great a coincidence that I forgot the years starting when I was eight and that her daughter, Tara, started becoming withdrawn last year—when she was eight."

Lauren frowned. "I had forgotten that you said Mallory has a daughter."

"Tara is nine now and she's changed a lot in the past year.

She's gone from being openly affectionate to pouting and avoiding hugs.''

''Is she around her grandfather very often?''

''Of course. They only live a block from my parents.'' Kirby felt the pulse racing in her throat. ''Tell me I'm jumping at shadows. Tell me Dad wouldn't hurt her.''

''I can't tell you that. I don't know,'' Lauren said carefully. ''In virtually every case that's been studied, if a person molests a child once, it happens again and again, usually with whichever children he or she has access to most easily.''

Kirby was glad she was still sitting down. She felt weak all over. ''I didn't expect all this to happen today. I thought I would just come in and talk, touch base. That we wouldn't have anything to work on for several weeks. Not until I got used to coming again.''

''I guess your subconscious couldn't hold the memories back any longer.''

An anger was starting to build deep inside Kirby. ''My father molested me! I remember enough to know it happened!''

''I know this is difficult for you.''

''How could I have forgotten something so horrible?''

''You forgot because it *was* horrible. It's the brain's way of coping. That's why rape victims often report they can't remember what the rapist looked like. Their minds are trying to protect them.''

''Will I get back all my memories? All the details?'' Kirby was surprised how tight her voice sounded. It was as if she were borrowing someone else's vocal cords.

''I don't know. You probably won't remember every detail of every time it happened. Most people's memories don't work that exactly. But you'll probably remember enough to know the important facts about what took place. Either way, you'll be empowered again.''

Kirby looked at her as if she wasn't fully comprehending what she was hearing.

''That's why we use the phrase 'survivors' and not 'victims' to describe people who have lived through incest. To remember and to get angry about it gives you back the power you didn't have as a child. None of it was your fault.''

"But I played the game!" Kirby repeated in anguish. "I knew where he was waiting for me and I went looking for him! That makes me an active participant."

"No! That makes you a child. An adult, your own father, told you to find him and you did as you were told. Any child would."

"But . . ."

"No. This is important for you to understand. Even if you didn't fight against him; even if you brought him a condom when he told you to; even if you pretended to like it—it wasn't your fault. You have to understand and believe this because it's true. The adult is always at fault in child molestation. He had all the power and all the authority. You had none."

Kirby stared at her. "Even at sixteen? I don't remember those years either and I was certainly too old to play hide-and-seek. Too old not to know he was doing something wrong."

"You still had no choice. We do what we have to do to survive. No matter what it is. I don't know why he stopped hurting you at sixteen. Maybe he only likes little girls, maybe he thought you were about to tell."

"And Tara? What do we do about Tara?"

"She shouldn't be left alone with your father. Not for any reason."

"I'm going back to Mallory's house after I leave here. I'll tell her what you said."

"I'm not saying he's doing anything to Tara. We don't know that. Kids go through all sorts of phases and this withdrawal could be perfectly natural and without cause. But I wouldn't bet on it."

"Until I learned that Dad overstepped the bounds in appointing Derrick head of the law firm, a direct violation of the judicial code of ethics and a conflict of interest, I would have said that he couldn't and wouldn't do anything wrong." Her eyes implored Lauren to tell her the truth. "Is it possible that I'm somehow making up these memories in order to justify my anger at him?"

"I'd say that would be an overkill. Wouldn't you? Incest isn't in the same ballpark with conflict-of-interest issues."

Kirby nodded. "I just had to ask."

"Do you think he was molesting Mallory, too?"

"From the questions she asked me, I'd have to say yes. She was the one who brought up molestation and the idea that he could have been teaching us about sex."

"I'm glad you have each other. It's particularly helpful in instances where repressed memory syndrome exists. As you recover the memories, it will be good for you to have someone to talk to who was there at the time and who can verify things for you."

"I gave Mallory your number. She asked for it. I think she's going to make an appointment with you."

"Good. I'm looking forward to meeting her."

Kirby glanced at her wristwatch. "The hour is gone. How did it go by so quickly?" She stood and Lauren walked her to the door. "I could understand it if we were having a pleasant conversation, but this has been anything but pleasant."

"I know it's hard to talk about it. When the memories are elusive and you're just starting to feel the emotions, it's particularly difficult. It'll get easier."

"It will have to if it changes at all," Kirby said wryly. At the door she paused. "Thanks, Lauren. For not trying to convince me months ago that Dad did this and for not saying 'I told you so' today."

Lauren smiled. "I'll never do either of those things. See you next week?"

"Next week and a lot of weeks beyond that, is my guess."

Kirby left the office and went to her car. For several minutes she sat behind the steering wheel, trying to assimilate her thoughts. Whether she liked it or not, she did remember. The memories had been overpowering and they were unmistakable.

She drove to Addison's office. Even though it was late in the evening, his car was still in its parking space. Summoning her courage, she went straight to his office and tapped on the glass in his door. A moment later, he opened it.

"Kirby! I didn't expect to see you. Did we have an appointment that I forgot?"

"No, Dad. I was driving by and saw your car here and thought I'd drop by to say hello."

"What are you doing in this neck of the woods? The DA's office isn't near here."

"This is my afternoon off." She went to a black leather chair and sat down. She could remember helping him choose this furniture. Those days had been so carefree in comparison to the present. She watched as he went to his chair and lowered himself into it. Now that she was with him, it was even harder to imagine him doing the things she remembered.

"Have you seen Mallory lately?"

"I saw her earlier today. I stopped by for a visit before I went to my counseling session." She watched carefully to see how he took the information.

His face darkened with a frown. "Counseling? I thought you had given that up."

"I didn't know you were aware of it at all."

"Your mother told me."

"I had stopped going for a while. Now I've started again."

"Marriage counseling is a pack of nonsense. All it takes for a marriage to succeed is for everyone to know who is in charge. When everyone's role is clear, everything else falls into place."

"Who would you say is in charge in my marriage?" she asked smoothly.

"Your husband, of course. I don't like Russell. I've never made any bones about it, as you well know. But he's the husband and the head of the house. That's the way it's supposed to be."

"Not in my marriage. We make the rules together." She was surprised how calm she sounded. "Besides, I'm not going in for counseling about my marriage."

"Oh?" His dark brows drew together across the bridge of his nose.

"I've been having nightmares. For a long time, actually."

"Everybody has nightmares." He made a dismissing motion with his hand.

"I keep having the same one over and over."

His frown deepened. Although he didn't ask, she knew he was wondering what the nightmare was about. She wasn't about to tell him. The memory was still too new and too fragile. One burst of his lawyer's logic and it might be lost again.

"My counselor thinks I'm dealing with repressed memory syndrome."

"Bullshit!" Addison jumped to his feet and leaned toward her across his desk. Even though she knew he wouldn't hurt her in his office, she quivered inside. "Repressed memory syndrome! Crap! That's all it is! Pure crap!"

"Not really. Up until very recently, I had a huge hole in my memories. Did you know that, Dad? I couldn't remember a single thing that happened between the ages of eight and sixteen. I don't think that's normal. Do you?" In her anger she was almost baiting him. She took care not to flinch away from his piercing glare.

"That's crazy! You just forgot. Big deal! Nobody remembers their entire lives. The boredom would be overwhelming." He paced to his window and back to the desk.

"I'm beginning to remember, and believe me, it's not exactly boring."

For an instant something akin to fear flashed through his eyes. Then it was hidden. "You're falling for the latest medical scam. That's all it is. For a while everyone was hypoglycemic. Then all kids had attention deficit disorder. Now it's repressed memory syndrome! It's just something the medical community has dreamed up to fleece money from suckers like you! I thought you were brighter than this!"

She watched him in silence. She had learned in court many revelations could come from simple silence.

"These psychiatrists get together and decide what to bilk the public with from time to time. I'm sure they do. What sells on the newsstand? Incest! But their clients don't remember incest having happened to them. So they dreamed up this repressed memory syndrome. They say you just don't *remember* it having happened. But it did! Oh, yes, it did! Then they can skim the cream off your bank account regularly for years." He leaned toward her again. "Bullshit! You take my advice and stop going to this quack! She's making a fool of you!"

Kirby sat there quietly until she could control her voice. "I never mentioned incest, Dad. You did. I only told you I have repressed memories."

He stared at her as though he'd had a stroke and was paralyzed.

She stood and went to the door. "This has been a very interesting visit. If we were in court, I'd have a good case going right now. Wouldn't you say that's true, counselor?" She turned and walked out the door.

She was visibly shaking by the time she reached her car. It was difficult not to run or to look fearfully behind her. She was as afraid of Addison as she had been as a child. When she was safely locked inside her car, she looked back at the building. He hadn't followed her. Addison wouldn't have placed himself in so weak a position as to run after her with explanations or protestations.

She hugged the steering wheel and leaned her forehead on her hands. Did the syndrome hide things other than incest? She hadn't thought to ask Lauren. If it only pertained to incest, it wasn't surprising that Addison would say what he had. Naturally he would stay up with changes in the law and changes in society affected by those laws in order to write his appeal opinions. But either way, he had introduced the word "incest" into the conversation. Not her. She didn't like what that told her.

Instead of going to Mallory's house, Kirby went home. She was too shaken to tell her sister all that had happened. Once she was home, she went up to her bedroom and dialed Mallory's phone number. When Mallory answered, Kirby said, "Lauren says it would be a good idea not to let Tara see Dad alone."

There was a long silence. "I understand."

Kirby knew Tara must be standing within hearing distance. "I had a memory while I was in the office. I can't talk about it. It's too upsetting. Then later I had words with Dad. That's why I didn't come by. I just want to take some aspirin for my pounding headache and rest for a while."

"Sure. I understand. And I'll do what Lauren suggested."

When she hung up, Kirby went into the bathroom and took two aspirin. Her head was hurting terribly and she felt as if she was coming down with a cold. She wondered if it was only stress. Only stress. That was an understatement.

She clicked on the TV. The evening news anchorman's expression was shifting from casual-informative to grave.

"Yesterday Houstonian Gary Chandler was arrested and charged with molesting a child. This morning he was arraigned and his bond was set at twenty-five thousand dollars. You may remember he was convicted last year for indecency with a child but his conviction was overturned on appeal. He insists that he's innocent and that he never hurt a child in his life. Only a few minutes ago, he was released on bond and had this to say."

The film footage of Gary Chandler began to roll. He looked earnestly at the interviewer. "I'm being framed. It's my ex-wife. She'll stop at nothing to discredit me." He looked like a choir boy all grown up. He was even wearing a gold cross as a lapel pin.

The anchorman returned. "The incident allegedly occurred at Hermann Park near the train ride when the girl, whose name is being withheld—"

Kirby clicked the TV off. She couldn't bear to hear another word. Chandler had struck again. Another little girl had been sexually molested. If the appeals court hadn't overturned his conviction, which Kirby had fought so hard to obtain, Chandler would be in jail where he belonged and the little girl would still have her innocence.

And now that innocence was gone forever. Taken away the same way her father had taken away her innocence all those years ago.

Chapter Twenty-two

"I need to be getting home," Kirby said to Mallory as she pulled the new T-shirt over Tara's head. "I picked this up at a sale yesterday and wanted to see if it fit while I can still return it."

Tara struggled into the shirt, dodging when the sharp point of the sales tag poked her. She hadn't said a word since Kirby arrived.

"What do you think?" Mallory asked her. "Does it fit?"

"It's too tight," Tara mumbled.

"It looks okay to me," Mallory said. "You have your other shirt on under it."

"I think she's right," Kirby said. "Look how it pulls across her shoulders. I should have gotten a larger size. You're growing so fast, Tara! I'll bet you're going to be tall."

Tara looked away.

Kirby was watching her niece more than just checking the fit of the shirt. Something was very wrong. "Have you seen Grandma and Grandad lately?" she asked as if they had just crossed her mind.

"She was over there yesterday," Mallory admitted, not making direct eye contact with Kirby. "I had a dentist appointment and I wasn't sure how long it would take so I dropped Tara off there."

Tara pulled the shirt off and dropped it on the floor. She was sullen and moody.

Kirby picked up the shirt and started to fold it. "I'll take this back and exchange it. Was Grandad there yesterday?"

Tara glared at her. "Will everybody just leave me alone?" She ran from the room.

"She's been like that ever since I picked her up. Mom said Dad would be at the office all afternoon, but he came home early. She was on the phone with Freddie Rae Powers and you know how long-winded that woman is. I gather the conversation was about plans for some Republican fund-raising party and had gone on for at least an hour."

"I thought we agreed that Tara wasn't to be left over there!"

"I couldn't help it! It takes forever to get an appointment with my dentist and what could I have given Mom as a reason for not leaving Tara? How was I to know Freddie Rae would call or that Dad would come home when he did? I can hardly restrict my own mother from talking on the phone in her own house, can I? It was just by accident that Tara was there when Dad came home early!"

"I'm sorry. I shouldn't have snapped at you. Of course you couldn't." Kirby hated the thoughts that were forming in her mind. "Do you think Dad did anything to her?"

"I don't know." Mallory wrapped her arms around her body. "I just don't know. Tara won't talk about the visit. You saw what she's like. Something had to have happened." Her eyes were moist as she met Kirby's gaze. "What am I going to do? What reason can I give Mom for not letting Tara go over there? What if we're wrong!"

"Mallory, if Dad is molesting Tara, it doesn't matter what Mom thinks!"

"But what if he isn't?" Mallory insisted.

Kirby silently shook her head. After a moment she said, "If only we had some proof. Some way of knowing positively. I agree that we can't accuse him if there's a chance we could be wrong." She looked at her sister. "Mal, you've never actually said. Did he do anything to you? When we were children? If it only happened to me . . ."

Mallory opened her mouth to answer but was interrupted by

Derrick coming in the door. "Hi. I didn't expect you to be home this early."

He dropped a bag of wrapped Christmas gifts on the coffee table. "These go under the tree." Kirby could smell Scotch on his breath from across the room.

"I assumed they would." Mallory picked up one with her name on it. "I wonder what Miss Allerman picked for you to give me this year."

Derrick ignored the dig. He went to the liquor cabinet and took out the bottle of Scotch. "Drink, Kirby? I know you do, Mallory."

"No, thanks," Kirby answered. "I have to return something to a store and can't stay."

"Don't let me keep you."

Mallory frowned at him. "Don't be rude, Derrick."

He looked at them as if he hadn't thought they would take it as rudeness. "I just meant she doesn't have to stay on my account."

"How are things going at the office?" Kirby asked in an effort to be friendly.

Derrick tossed down a gulp of Scotch. "About the same as usual. Haufman and Jeffers are working out well." He poured Mallory a glass of bourbon and handed it to her. "I hear Gary Chandler has been arrested again."

"I'm surprised you didn't get a call to represent him."

"I think he's going with another firm. I didn't have time to take him and he didn't want Haufman or Jeffers."

"I've already told Leon Zimmerman that I want to handle his prosecution if the Grand Jury indicts him."

"I don't know why. It will only be overturned again." Derrick dropped into a chair and propped his feet on the coffee table. "It's a waste of time, really."

"I couldn't agree less. The man is fondling and raping little girls. It can't be allowed to continue."

"Look, if he's convicted, it will go to the appellate court and your father will overturn it again. Chandler knows this. He's not worried."

Kirby stared at him. "What did you say? *Dad* will overturn it *again*? He couldn't have. I was the prosecutor. It would have been a conflict of interest for him to hear the appeal. He was bound by law to recuse himself and not discuss anything about the case with anyone. Zimmerman said he did recuse himself.''

''Wake up and smell the coffee, Kirby. Even you aren't that naive. Naturally Addison's name won't appear on any of the documents, but that doesn't mean anything. He's told me the judges talk among themselves. He asked his chief justice to see to it that the Fourteenth reversed the district court's decision, as a personal favor. It's done all the time, I imagine.''

''You knew about this? That implicates you in a conspiracy to obstruct justice!''

Derrick laughed into his glass. ''There's no proof. The world isn't black and white. It's often a matter of who knows who and who owes who a favor.''

''Why would Dad do such a thing? He has no reason to care if Gary Chandler is sent to prison or not. They can't possibly know each other. Can they?''

''How should I know? All I can say is, your dad didn't think he was guilty and wanted him to go free. And he did.''

Kirby looked at Mallory, then back at Derrick. ''Has Dad done this before? In child molestation cases, I mean?''

''I have no idea. I don't question him about things like that. He volunteered the information or I wouldn't know about the Chandler appeal. I assume he did it because he knew Jim Haufman handled the appeal for Chandler and he wanted me to know. It was like a favor to me and the firm. You know how he likes the firm to win.''

Kirby felt nauseous. Derrick was a talkative drunk, and in his own home, he apparently felt no need to curb his tongue. ''I have to go.''

Mallory followed her to the door. ''I don't know what to say. Maybe Derrick's wrong.''

''I doubt it. He sounded too positive. Why would Dad care about Gary Chandler? Surely he doesn't regularly overturn all molestation cases! That wouldn't make any sense at all and would be noticed in time. Why Chandler?''

''I don't know. Maybe he honestly felt Chandler was innocent.''

''No way. The little girl testified as to what happened to her.

Even his own daughter testified! He was convicted fair and square. No one railroaded him."

"I don't know what to tell you." Mallory looked miserable and helpless.

"Don't worry. I'll handle it." Kirby glanced at her watch. "I have to run before the store closes. Do you think one size larger will do it?"

Mallory nodded. "Tara appreciates you buying it for her. She was just upset."

"See if you can get her to tell you what happened, but don't force her. She has to say the words on her own." Kirby didn't add that Tara's direct testimony would be necessary if they had to take Addison to court.

Mallory understood. She nodded mutely.

Kirby got to the store only minutes before closing time, but there were still many cars in the parking lot. The sale was a good one.

She parked and hurried through the cold, damp air into the store. Jordan's wasn't as convenient a place to shop as Brennahan's but Kirby hadn't gone back to Brennahan's since Josh's bout with shoplifting because of the embarrassment she still felt.

She selected a larger size shirt for Tara, and while she waited for a clerk to wait on her, she looked at the display nearest the cash register. The mannequins were set up as if they were a family sitting around a Christmas tree. There were bright lights and red balls as well as gold ribbons on the tree and a mountain of packages beneath. The little girl mannequin wore red footed pajamas not unlike some Kirby had owned as a girl. She smiled at the thought that styles had come full circle again.

The father mannequin was bending over the girl and was reaching out his hand. On his face was a sappy smile that best suited store mannequins. The mother mannequin was turned away as if she were looking down the aisle toward the coat racks and jeans.

Suddenly Kirby felt fear drive through her. The father mannequin's smile was suddenly sinister. The child seemed not to be playing, but drawing away from him in horror. The mother was oblivious to her daugther's danger.

Kirby backed away, her eyes wide and frightened. She bumped into the woman behind her, who glared at Kirby before leaving with her purchases.

"May I help you?" the sales clerk said.

Kirby pushed the bag containing the smaller T-shirt toward her. "Too small. I need to exchange it for this one." She couldn't take her eyes away from the mannequins.

"Are you all right, ma'am?" the clerk asked.

Kirby nodded. It was as if everyone was watching her, knowing what her father had done to her. "Hurry!" she whispered to the woman. She felt as if she was going to vomit.

The clerk continued glancing at her suspiciously as she made the exchange.

As soon as it was done, Kirby grabbed the T-shirt and bag, not giving the clerk time to package it for her. She gripped it in her fists as she hurried away. She was too aware of the group of mannequins behind her and of the stares of customers as she almost ran toward the door.

"Kirby?" a familiar voice called.

She looked over to see Maria Zimmerman smiling at her. Behind her was another display of mannequins, this one of male models glaring defiantly at the shoppers.

Kirby turned and broke into a run. She didn't stop until she was outside. The cold air burned her lungs and she was shaking so hard she had trouble putting the key into the car door lock. She jumped into her car and locked the door.

For a long time she sat there, shaking and trying to tell herself it had only been a flashback. That it had lasted longer than usual didn't a mean a thing. She was terribly embarrassed. Maria Zimmerman, her boss's wife, would think she was rude if not downright crazy. Everyone in the store between the children's department and the exit would have seen her running away like a frightened child.

Kirby put her head down on the steering wheel and let herself cry.

Would these feelings ever pass? She couldn't bear the idea of flashbacks like this one recurring all the rest of her life.

She fumbled getting her car phone out and dialed Lauren

Jacobs' number. It seemed forever before Lauren answered. "This is Kirby Garrett. I've had a flashback. In Jordan's!"

Lauren's voice was calming. "Okay. Where are you now?"

Kirby glanced around to be certain she wasn't still hallucinating. "In my car. In the parking lot."

"Are your doors locked?"

Kirby nodded, then realized Lauren couldn't hear that. "Yes. They're locked."

"Okay. You're safe. Look around you. Are there people around?"

"Yes." She was gripping the phone so tightly her hand hurt.

"You can get help if you need it. You have a car phone, obviously. You aren't helpless and alone. Now. Tell me what happened."

"I feel like an idiot!" She wiped at her eyes and reached for a tissue. "I ran out of the store! I actually turned and ran!"

"What happened?" Lauren repeated calmly.

"It was so dumb! I saw a display of mannequins around a Christmas tree and panicked. I feel stupid even calling you!"

"No, it's fine. I'm through for the day. You caught me on my way out the door, but I'm in no rush."

"I remembered a Christmas when I was little. We had been decorating the tree. Mallory fell and skinned her knee so Mom took her into the bathroom to get a bandage. While they were out of the room, Dad trapped me in the corner so that the tree hid me from the door. He . . ." Kirby closed her eyes and tried not to sob audibly.

"It's okay, Kirby. It happened a long time ago. It's over now. This is just a memory."

She nodded, hardly moving her head because all the muscles in her body were taut, and forced herself to say, "He touched me. He opened my pajamas and put his hand inside."

Lauren's voice was soothing and calm. "I understand. This is a new memory, isn't it?"

"Yes. I hate remembering!"

"I know it's rough on you, but it's an important breakthrough. Do you realize that?"

Kirby managed a shaky laugh. "I thought you'd say something like that. Should I be glad?"

"Probably, but I know it's painful. We would both rather have discovered that nothing happened to you at all. But since it did, it's good to get it out into the open."

"Is it? It doesn't feel good at all."

"No, it hurts. I understand that. But once you deal with it and take control over it, it can't continue to hurt you."

"The flashbacks. Will they go on forever?"

"I don't know. But you'll learn ways to deal with them when they do happen. That's something we can work on. Every time you have a flashback and see some other part of your history, it will belong to you. You're giving yourself power, even if it doesn't feel that way."

"It doesn't."

"Think of the flashbacks as if they were dragons. If you're with a dragon, it's safer to know where it's hiding, isn't it? And how big it is and if there's more than one?"

"I hadn't thought of it that way."

"We'll work on it."

"Lauren, thanks for taking my call."

"No problem. I want you to call me when a crisis occurs." Kirby drew in a ragged breath. "I'm feeling better. Still like a fool, but better."

"Don't let it worry you. Everyone does odd things from time to time, even in public. I doubt anyone noticed anything all that strange."

"Maybe." She was still remembering the odd look on Maria's face as she turned and ran away.

"I'll see you in a few days."

"Right. And thanks again."

Kirby was still shaken when she arrived at home. Russell met her at the door. As soon as he looked at her, he knew something was wrong.

"I had a flashback," she said. "In Jordan's."

"I thought you were going to Mallory's."

"I went there, the T-shirt didn't fit Tara, so I went back to Jordan's." She dropped her purse onto the table and collapsed onto the nearest chair. "I feel terrible."

"Do you want to tell me about it?"

She shook her head. "I can't. I can't say these things to you."

"Don't shut me out, Kirby. I want to help you."

She studied him thoughtfully. "I guess I'm having trouble talking to men right now. It's not you. It's what you represent."

"That's not fair. I never hurt you. I never would."

She reached across the table and took his hand. "I know. But you don't like Dad as it is. I don't want to tell you something that will make it impossible for you to be in the same house with him. We see them every Sunday at dinner! How could you sit at his table knowing what he did?"

"How can you?" he countered.

"I don't know. That's been on my mind a lot lately. I guess the stress of Christmas is making it worse."

"Kirby, I know what happens in incest. I have an active imagination. If you need to talk to me, I can handle it. If you don't want me to say anything to your father, I won't. I'll play this exactly the way you want me to."

"I guess that's just it. I don't know what I want from this. I can't imagine not seeing him again, but I dread being around him these days. Ever since I confronted him in his office the other day, I've been looking over my shoulder, fearing reprisals."

"He can't hurt you anymore."

She glanced around to be sure neither of her sons was in the dining room. "I'm worried about Tara. She's changed. Mallory left her with Mom in spite of me telling her not to. Dad wasn't supposed to be there, but he came home before Mallory returned. Mallory shouldn't have taken a chance like that. Something apparently happened, but Tara won't say what."

"What do you think happened?"

Kirby shook her head miserably. "I think Dad hurt her. Mom was on the phone, according to Mallory, and had been tied up with Freddie Rae Powers for an hour or so. Dad was there and that left him more or less alone with Tara. Mallory said Tara hasn't been the same since she picked her up."

"Damn!"

"How could Mallory do that! She knows how this could damage Tara! How could she be so shortsighted as to take a chance like that!" Kirby buried her face in her hands. "Mom was there when we were children, too."

"Are you getting some clear memories?"

"Yes." Her voice came out in a whisper. "I've started recovering memories. That's what happened in Jordan's."

He stood and came to her side of the table and put his arms around her. For once Kirby was glad that he did. She needed so badly to be held.

"Do you want me to talk to her? Mallory and I have always been close."

Kirby nodded, her face pressed against him. "Maybe that will get through to her. She'll just have to hire a baby-sitter like everyone else when she doesn't want to take Tara with her. I'm encouraging her to make an appointment with Lauren and stop putting it off. Mallory isn't thinking clearly about this."

"I'll talk to her tomorrow."

"There's something else." She straightened and studied her clasped hands. "Dad was behind Gary Chandler's conviction being overturned. Derrick told me so."

"Your dad did that? Why?"

"I don't know. He shouldn't have any reason to know Chandler. There's no reason why he would care one way or another what happens to him."

"Maybe Derrick was wrong."

Kirby shook her head. "I doubt it. He said it as if it were a matter of fact. I can't figure out why Dad would interfere like that. Do you think they could know each other?"

"I have no idea. Like you said, there's no reason they should."

"Do you think Dad regularly overturns convictions of molestation?" She searched his face. "Would he do that?"

"I don't like Addison. You know that. But that makes no sense. He couldn't keep his job if it became known that he was so biased in favor of criminals."

"Not just any criminals, but child molesters. Don't you see what this could mean?"

"Of course I do. I don't have the answer."

Kirby was silent for a long time. "I've been trying to get

used to the idea that Dad molested me. It's turned my world upside down. That's one reason I'm so personally upset over the Chandler case. Naturally I'd be upset—I don't mean that, but this issue strikes too close to home."

"I understand."

She let him cover her hands with his. Instead of feeling trapped or restrained, this time it felt good. Secure. "I want to take him to court."

"Who? Addison?"

"Yes. I want him to pay for what he did to me, and probably to Mallory. He may be doing it now to Tara!"

"What about the statute of limitations? Hasn't it passed by now?"

"Not necessarily. In some states, the survivor has three years from the time she becomes aware of the molestation to bring charges. It's a relatively new law. I know a similar bill was introduced in our legislature last session, but I'm not sure whether it was put into law." She drew in a shaken breath. "That sounds so scary. I don't know if I can confront Dad in a courtroom over this."

"You don't have to. No one will ever know, if that's the way you want it."

"No. If he's also molesting Tara, I won't stand by and let it happen. Removing her from danger isn't enough. I want him punished."

"It won't be easy. He's well thought of in Houston. If you thought Gary Chandler was difficult to prove guilty, your dad will be three times as hard."

"He did it. I'll find a way to prove it."

Russell lifted her hand and kissed it. "I'll be with you all the way, honey. You know that."

"I know. I'll need you. This isn't something I can face alone. My memories are still too shaky." She thought for a minute. "I'm not going to rush into this. I have three years, assuming that law applies in Texas. I can firm up my confidence in my memories, get more to work on. There's no rush. Except for Tara's sake, that is."

"I'll talk to Mallory. If nothing else, she can leave Tara over here. Josh is a pain in the neck sometimes, but he would watch to be sure Tara didn't get hurt. Cody would love to have her around."

"That would be a good suggestion. Russell?" She hesitated. "Am I crazy? Is all this really happening? At times it seems so unreal!"

"It does to me, too. But you're not one to make up things, especially not something like this. If you're having memories, they're valid."

"Thank you," she whispered. "I needed to hear that."

"I love you. I'll always stick by you. Now that I know what's going on with you, you couldn't chase me away."

"I love you, too," she whispered, wrapping her arms around him and feeling closer to him than she had in many years.

"Russell?" Mallory said as she opened her front door. "I thought you'd still be teaching a class at this time of day."

"Thursdays are light for me." He stepped past her into the house. "I wanted to talk to you before Tara comes in from school."

"Sure. What's going on?"

"It's this business about your father." Now that he was here, he felt awkward discussing this with Mallory.

She turned and went back to her chair. Russell followed her and sat in the chair opposite her. Her miserable eyes met his. "I know Kirby is really upset with me. I'm upset with myself! But I had to have a tooth filled, and I had been trying to get in to see the dentist for weeks and that was the only day he could take me. Mom was expecting Tara and I couldn't think of an acceptable reason not to take her over there. And Mom couldn't come here because she was expecting a delivery that afternoon. I feel awful about it!" She curled her legs under her. With her brown eyes so filled with unhappiness, she didn't look much older than Tara.

"I'm not here to blame you. I know you love Tara and wouldn't deliberately put her in harm's way."

"Never! Dad was at work and I knew I'd be back to get Tara a good hour before he was expected home. God! I was so stupid!"

"Do you think anything happened to Tara?" Russell was finding it hard to accept because Addison didn't fit society's stereotypical child molester profile.

"I don't know." Mallory sighed, then corrected herself in a barely audible voice. "Yes, I do. Tara has been acting out ever since I picked her up. Something had to have happened."

"After this, why don't you bring Tara to our house. She's always been close to Cody, and Josh is usually home, too. I get home early on Tuesdays and Thursdays this semester. We can watch Tara."

Mallory's eyes became damp with gathering tears. "I appreciate it. You'll never know how much. I just don't know what to tell Mom. She's babysat Tara all her life. She's going to wonder why I don't leave her there anymore."

Russell nodded. "I know and I have no answer. I've asked myself what I would have done if it were Josh and Cody who were at risk. In many ways your mother is so frail. I can understand your wanting to protect her."

"I always have." Mallory was silent for a moment. "Russell, are you sure the boys weren't, you know, hurt?"

"I'm as sure as I can be. Cody still likes to go over there. Josh has changed lately, but the change coincided with the separation. No, I don't think Addison did anything to them."

Mallory glanced at him. "That's the first time I've heard you call Dad by his first name."

"He doesn't deserve my respect these days."

"Then you believe all this is happening?"

"Yes. I want to deny it, but I can't."

"Me, too." Mallory picked at a loose thread in the arm chair's fabric. "Do you think I ought to make an appointment with Kirby's therapist?"

"Yes, I think it would be a good idea. If not with Lauren, then with someone else. She's helped Kirby a great deal."

"Derrick would have a fit. Dad . . ." Mallory stopped. "Let's just say it's not a decision to make lightly."

"No, but a lot has happened. It wouldn't hurt for Tara to see her, too."

"Maybe. I know you're right, but . . . ." She sighed. "I'll make an appointment."

Russell stood and she walked him to the door. As she opened it, she said, "Thanks for coming by. I've been wanting to ask your opinion on all this but can never catch you without Derrick or Dad around."

"Any time." He smiled at Mallory and left, hoping she would call Lauren.

He turned back to the house and Mallory waved at him from the doorway, a tentative smile on her face. She looked less miserable than when he'd first arrived.

Yes, Russell thought, he had a feeling Mallory would definitely be calling Lauren.

Chapter Twenty-Three

"Leon, may I talk to you?" Kirby stood hesitantly in the doorway of his office. After lying awake all night, she had come to a decision.

"Sure. Come on in." Zimmerman pushed away the papers he had been studying and gave her his full attention.

Kirby closed the door and sat in the chair opposite him. "I don't want anyone else to know what I'm about to ask you. Not if the answer is no."

"No one will know. What's wrong? Is there some hitch with the Dobson case?"

"No, no. It's coming along fine. I need to know how if the statute of limitations on child abuse cases is figured from the date of the actual event, or if it's three years from the time a person remembers that the abuse occurred."

"I assume you're talking repressed memories. The legislature has been debating that issue, but as of right now, it hasn't been signed into law. Why?"

"I'm considering taking my father to court if it becomes law."

For a long time the office was silent. Zimmerman didn't change expression, but Kirby knew she had stunned him.

Finally he said, "You know repressed memory syndrome is difficult to prove."

"I know."

"It could be opening you up for a lot of nasty publicity."

"Will I keep my job if I decide to do this?"

"Of course. I hired you because you're a damned good attorney, not because you had never been molested." He made a steeple of his fingertips and leaned so far back in his swivel chair he was on the brink of tipping over. "At least I gather you mean that you're the intended complainant."

"Yes. I am. I know how difficult it would be to prove, but I have a sister who may agree to testify as well." She swallowed. "And I have reason to think he's starting to . . . bother my niece."

"Addison? Into incest?"

"I know it's hard to believe. I fought against believing it for a long time myself. But the memories are coming more and more clearly and there's no doubt in my mind."

"What about your sister?"

"Mallory is still riding the fence. If she becomes convinced that something really is happening to Tara, she'll do anything to protect her. Mallory loves her daughter with all her heart. I have no doubt of that."

Zimmerman leaned forward slowly and rested his forearms on the clutter of papers on his desk. "Kirby, I hope you take this the right way, but I could tear holes in your story that a Mack truck could pass through. Any competent attorney could."

"I know it won't be easy."

"I'm saying it may be impossible. And what if you fail? You'll have stirred up a hornet's nest of bad publicity. Addison could sue you for defaming his name and causing him financial injury since he might not be reelected if incest is even whispered in connection with him. And then there's your niece. What will this do to her?"

Kirby nodded. "I know. I thought about this all night. But if it's true, I have to do everything I can to stop him."

"As far as you and your sister are concerned, I assume it has stopped already?"

"Certainly!"

"Is the girl—Tara—willing to bring charges against her grandfather? As I see it, that's your only real chance of proving anything. I hate to be so blunt, but you and your sister have let it pass by for too long."

"That's why I asked about the statute of limitations. I didn't remember what he'd done until recently! I couldn't have brought charges sooner!"

"A lot of people don't believe in repressed memory syndrome. Me? I don't know if I do or not. It sounds pretty implausible, frankly."

"I wouldn't lie about a thing like this!" Kirby said indignantly.

"I'm not saying that you would. I'm saying the judge and jury probably won't believe you." He gave her a smile. "If I were you, I wouldn't go jumping into anything. Once this becomes public knowledge, it's going to start flying off in all directions and you won't be able to retract it. Think about it. Talk to your sister and your husband. Above all, talk to your niece. If she'll testify that it's happening to her or has within the last ten years, then we might have a chance of nailing him."

Kirby stood and went to the door, filled with conflicting emotions. On one hand, she was almost relieved that she wouldn't be able to follow up immediately on the knowledge she had been molested. On the other, she was angry that once more injustice was prevailing.

"Kirby? One other thing. I do believe you. It's damned hard to picture Addison doing something like that. I've known him for years. But I want you to know I take your word for it. It also explains why you were so hot to trot over the Chandler case."

"Thanks, Leon."

"Just give it some thought before you go off half-cocked." She nodded and left his office.

The Harris County DA's Office closed early that day as it was Christmas Eve. Kirby maneuvered as quickly as she could through the heavy traffic and was pleased to be greeted by Cody in their driveway.

"Christmas gift, Mom!" he shouted.

She smiled at him. He wouldn't be a young boy much longer. He was already so tall. "Aren't you jumping the gun a bit?"

"I just wanted to be the first one to say that to you."

She put her arm across his shoulders as they went into the house. "Where is everybody?"

"Dad and Josh had to do some last-minute shopping. Tara was here a few minutes ago, but she went home with Aunt Mal."

"So are you ready for Santa tomorrow?"

"Mom," he said with a grin, "I'm not a little kid anymore."

"No, you're not. I miss it, though. Do you know that? Sometimes it's hard to believe you and Josh are so grown-up. In two years I'll have all teenagers."

"I won't be a horse's ass like Josh."

"Watch your language," she corrected automatically.

"Sorry. But he has been one. I can't wait to go to Grandad's house tonight and open presents."

Kirby smiled, but only on the outside and only for his benefit. She had been dreading this event for several days. She had bought Addison a gift as she did every year, but she felt like a hypocrite this time. "It won't be long," she said to her son.

"Then tomorrow we open gifts here! Christmas is so cool!"

"My little mercenary," she teased.

"Tara isn't looking forward to going tonight. She said she didn't feel good enough to go, but I don't believe her. She felt fine before I brought Christmas up. What's going on with her anyway?"

"I'm not sure. Has she talked to you about anything unusual?" Kirby was surprised how calmly she could say that.

"Nope. I'm going to watch a videotape until it's time to go. Unless you can use some help wrapping more packages for me," he said with a leering grin.

"Forget it, pal. I've finished my wrapping and they are all under the tree. It's too late to butter me up."

He laughed and trotted off in the direction of the den and the VCR. Kirby watched him go. What would it do to her sons if Addison's crime of incest were made public? With a sigh she went upstairs to change into more comfortable clothes.

Leon was right about opening a can of worms. Kirby knew

incest was difficult to prove, even under the best of circumstances. Jurors wanted to believe in apple-pie moms and dads like Ward Cleaver. Especially if the accused looked like everyone's ideal father and grandfather and had a respectable job.

Kirby was worried about the prospects of Christmases yet to come. Of family gatherings that would never be the same again. Maybe there wouldn't be any more get-togethers at all. On the one hand, she hoped there wouldn't be. She didn't want to be under the same roof with her father. But on the other hand, theirs had been a close family with a long history of visiting together at least once a week. And what about her relationship with her mother? Could she continue her relationship with her and not with her father?

What would this do to her mother?

She sat on the edge of her bed and kicked off her shoes. None of this was simple, none of it black and white. One part of her still loved Addison as the charming, generous father she had known in her oldest memories. Another part hated and was repelled by the man she now knew him to be. Neither image was exclusively true, and that was the thing that was tearing her apart. If she could simply hate him, everything would be so much easier.

Kirby lay back on the bed and stared up at the ceiling in hopes of finding an answer. There was none.

Tonight she would go to Addison's house and celebrate Christmas as they had for as long as she could remember. He would give her a gift and she would give him one. They would smile, even laugh. Kirby couldn't imagine smiling at him or how she would be able to pull this off.

But not to go there was unthinkable. Addison would demand an explanation and it would all explode. Kirby wasn't ready for a confrontation. She and Lauren had discussed the possibility, but Kirby wasn't ready for such an emotionally charged step. Not yet. And Christmas was no time to vent those feelings. The entire family might fall apart.

She noticed the familiarity of having to balance her needs against the family's and against her father's in particular. All her life Kirby had made decisions based on whichever outcome would cause the least waves. Keep Dad calm at all costs had been her motto.

She closed her eyes and wished it would all vanish and that she could again believe Addison was a perfect father. Quick-tempered, yes; even occasionally violent, yes. But perfect none-theless.

How, she wondered, had she ever convinced herself of that? No man who beat his wife and children was perfect or even near perfect, and she had always remembered the beatings. How had she built such a dream world? And what would be left after it crumbled?

Reluctantly, she got off the bed and began changing her clothes. Somehow she would get through tonight. Somehow.

Christmas dinner at the Walker house always happened on Christmas Eve now that Kirby and Mallory had homes and children of their own.

Jane had gone all out in her preparations and even had tiny favors with place cards at each plate. Kirby found her place and sat down. She had barely spoken to her father since their arrival, and although she knew he was watching her, she refused to make eye contact. To her relief, Russell was seated next to her and was pressing her knee reassuringly under the table. Sometimes Jane mixed up the usual seating just to be different and festive. With all the leaves in the table, it stretched all the way across the dining room.

Candlelight from the numerous candles along the table and around the room added to the elegant ambiance of gleaming silver and crystal and polished mahogany. The table was cov-ered with the heavy white damask cloth Kirby remembered from other special occasions. For this special occasion, they were using the sterling silver, not the plate, and the good china. "The table is beautiful, Mom," she said.

"Thank you. I have to admit, I've worked on this meal since early yesterday. No one will leave hungry. That's for sure!"

Mallory was seated opposite Kirby, and when their eyes met, they exchanged smiles as they had as children, smiles meant to show their allegiance. Kirby tried to relax. This was a Christmas dinner like many others. She had only to act the way she always had.

Tara was clad in a pretty dress—a significant departure from the jeans she usually lived in. Covertly, Kirby had been watching her all evening. She looked particularly ill at ease and her gaze was firmly locked onto her plate. Cody was sitting on one side of her, her mother on the other. Kirby could tell she was also avoiding Addison's glances.

Addison said grace, as always, and the meal began.

Kirby passed the candied sweet potatoes to Russell and received the English peas from Josh, who was trying not to put any vegetables on his plate. Kirby fixed him with a reprimanding stare until he grudgingly put a few peas on his plate.

Josh's behavior had improved of late, apparently in response to Russell's constant vigilance. Russell was still juggling his class schedule in order to take Josh to and from school, but he was considering backing off on that. Josh's obnoxious friends hadn't been back since Russell confronted them. Kirby was beginning to hope he would eventually become his old self again.

"I like your dress, Tara," Addison said from the end of the table.

Tara ducked her head lower.

Mallory poked her and whispered something to her.

"Thank you," Tara said in a low voice.

"You should wear dresses more often. I've always said they make a girl look so much more feminine. Don't you agree, Derrick?"

Derrick glanced at Addison, then Tara. "Sure. I guess so. She doesn't much like wearing dresses anymore."

Tara stared at her plate.

Kirby's food went tasteless in her mouth. This was the first time, she suddenly realized, they had all been together since her memories started to surface. On the last Sunday get-together, Tara had been sick—or had claimed to be. As discreetly as she could, Kirby started watching the conversation and glances more closely, trying to find evidence that Addison was paying attention of an unusual kind to Tara. It wasn't hard to spot.

"Pass Tara the carrots. You be sure and eat plenty, baby. They make your eyes pretty," he said. Later, "Tara, will you go into the kitchen and bring in the bottle of wine in the ice bucket? Put it here by me." Then, "It's almost time to open presents. Will you sit in my lap and help me open mine, Tara?"

It was all said either jokingly or in the kindest manner, but Kirby could see hidden meaning in Addison's request that had escaped her before. He was all but openly flirting with the child.

Kirby glanced at her mother. Jane seemed determined to keep her eyes and her mind on the meal. If she was noticing anything unusual in Addison's attitude toward their grand-daughter, she wasn't showing it in any way.

Kirby noticed that Mallory was becoming increasingly uncomfortable, but it could be because Derrick was drinking the wine as if it were water and he was dying of thirst. Kirby tried to imagine what it would be like to have Derrick as a husband rather than Russell and quickly concluded that she wouldn't put up with him for a week. No wonder Mallory sometimes drank more than she should. Derrick was enough to drive anyone to alcohol.

"You're not eating, Kirby," Addison observed with a slight edge to his voice which Kirby recognized from her childhood. The words might be spoken in a friendly manner, but there was an implied warning as well.

"I'm not hungry."

"You'd better eat or you'll get as skinny as Mallory." Addison grinned at his younger daughter. "You've lost too much weight, Mallory. Have some sweet potatoes."

Mallory obediently put some on her plate. Kirby watched the family dynamics as if she were a stranger among them. Mallory pretended to eat the potatoes, but Kirby noticed that none of them actually went into her mouth. She wondered if Mallory might be on the verge of becoming anorexic. In the last few months, she had indeed lost quite a bit of weight.

"You can't be too rich or too thin," Derrick said between bites. "That's what they say. I say that's half right. I don't like skinny women."

Mallory frowned at him and put down her fork.

Interesting, Kirby thought. Dad can order her to eat and she pretends to obey. When Derrick does the same, she rebels. Maybe there's hope for her after all.

After dinner they went into the living room and gathered around the tree. Kirby still found herself observing, rather than being part of the scene. They were a pretty family, she thought. Like the ones on Christmas cards. They looked perfectly normal if one discounted Derrick's slightly glazed eyes and the perpetual drink in his hand.

But under the surface it was so different.

She found herself staring at Addison and hurriedly looked away. This could very well be the last Christmas they were all together as a family. If she got the chance to take him to court on incest charges or if Tara came forward with accusations, they would never be a pretty family all together again.

If her memories were correct, that might not be a bad thing.

The packages were handed out. One to each adult, two to each child from Jane and Addison. The way it was always done at Addison's house. Addison and Jane had their gifts to each other, plus the ones from their children and grandchildren. Like Kirby and Russell, Mallory and Derrick would celebrate Christmas at their own home the next morning.

Kirby's gift was a necklace nestled on an expensive scarf. Her parents never cut corners on gifts. Despite her mixed feelings for Addison, she murmured in appreciation of the beauty of the necklace and scarf.

"I hope you like it," Jane said. "It's a Hermès. If the colors are wrong, it can be exchanged."

"I love it." Kirby fastened the necklace around her neck, a swirl of gold and diamonds suspended on a delicate gold chain. "It's beautiful, Mom." She couldn't bring herself to include Addison in her thanks. Not yet. She didn't want to show him appreciation for anything, given what he had done.

"Your dad picked out the necklace. I chose the scarf," Jane said.

Kirby swallowed her rebellion for the sake of the others. "Thank you, Dad."

"You're welcome." He smiled at her, but his eyes were

speculative. She realized he was watching her as closely as she was studying him.

Tara opened her first gift and smiled. "Tapes! Cool!"

"I hope you don't already have those," Jane said.

"I don't." She leaned toward Cody to share a peek at her bounty.

"Open your other gift," Addison encouraged. "I think you'll like it, too."

Tara tore into the shiny red paper and when she opened the box, her face grew still.

"A gown?" Mallory asked. "Are you sure Tara opened the right gift?"

Kirby saw layers of pink and white ruffles and laces and gossamer fabric. Mallory held it up and it was clear that it was sized for a little girl, even if it did look as if it belonged to a bride's trousseau. Mallory's eyes met hers. Kirby didn't smile.

If nothing else had aroused her suspicions, this gown would have raised questions. It was totally inappropriate as a gift to a child. Where had Addison bought it? The gown was clearly seductive and Tara recognized it as such. Kirby couldn't imagine it being sold in an ordinary store.

"I thought it would be pretty for you to wear when you come over to spend the night," Addison said to Tara. "You know the boys started spending the weekend here when they were about your age. You can sleep in your mom's old room or the guest room, whichever you choose."

Tara's face had paled and her dark eyes seemed too large and frightened. She bent silently over the tapes in her lap.

"Aren't you going to say thank you?" Derrick prompted as the silence grew long.

"Thank you," Tara mumbled.

"Now Addison," Jane ventured timidly, "if Tara doesn't want to spend the night away from home just yet, that's okay."

"She has to grow up," he said with a hearty laugh. "She can't be a baby forever. We'll have fun. Didn't you boys have fun when you used to stay here?"

Cody and Josh both nodded enthusiastically. "It's neat, Tara. You get to stay up late and watch videos."

Tara leaned against her mother's legs in a bid for reassurance and didn't answer.

Mallory reached down and stroked her hair gently. "That will be up to Tara. I'm not going to rush her into growing up."

As the others opened presents, Kirby found a thought forming that wouldn't be dismissed. What if there *was* some connection between her father and Gary Chandler? As irrational as a connection would seem, they did live in the same town, so it wasn't impossible that they were acquainted.

She made a mental note to call Bill Davies and assign him the job of finding a link if there was one.

Mallory had been trying harder to behave. She hadn't been to the Schooner for weeks. It had been two weeks since she had been with a man at all. Not sexually, anyway. School had resumed now that the holidays were over, Tara was gone and Mallory had a need inside her that could no longer be denied.

She dressed and went out, driving along the streets, trying to decide where she would be most likely to find a suitable target. On a whim, she turned toward The Village, the shopping center closest to her house. The Village, spread across several narrow streets and only a few blocks long, consisted of a number of specialty shops, among them one carrying only teas and coffees, another items from Ireland or Britain, another rare books.

She parked and began her search through the shops on that block, pretending to be casually shopping for nothing in particular. Unfortunately, with the rush of Christmas buying and exchanging over, the stores were populated almost exclusively by their employees. Disappointed, she started back for her car, then decided to try her favorite store there, The British Market. As she wandered through the aisles of British soaps and books and china, actually enjoying browsing, she thought she heard someone call her name.

"Mallory?" she heard the voice repeat. She turned to see a familiar face coming toward her. Bob. A former lover. "I never expected to see you here. Where have you been?"

She smiled. "Here and there. It's been too long."

"You're telling me. I was beginning to think you had fallen off the face of the earth."

"Not quite. I'm still hanging on."

He looked around to be sure no one was within earshot. "Would you like to go somewhere for a drink? Or to my place?" he added in a lower voice.

She thought for a minute. She really had missed him. He was one of the few men she had seen more than once. A dangerous thought made her smile. "I have a better idea. Let's go to my place. I'll drive."

She took him to her house and noticed his surprise when she turned into the drive of one of the nicest houses in a neighborhood everyone considered to be affluent.

"You live here?" he asked.

"I have for years." She glanced around. No neighbors were outside. That wasn't surprising since it was biting cold and damp. She took him inside.

From Bob's expression, he was impressed as he passed through the dining room with its massive, leaded crystal punch bowl sitting atop a heavily carved oak sideboard which was flanked by matching china cabinets. In the living room he paused, eyeing the elegant decor as if he'd never been in a home so opulently furnished. "I think there's a lot you haven't told me."

"Only that my husband makes a good living."

"I see now why you didn't want to leave him and move into my apartment. This is like Buckingham Palace!"

"Not quite." She went to him and put her arms around him. "The bedroom is upstairs."

"You know you're taking a chance in bringing me here."

"Derrick almost never comes home during the day. I'll hide you in a closet if we hear anything."

"That's your husband? Derrick?"

She nodded. The name had slipped out. At least he still didn't know her last name. She didn't want any of her lovers being able to call her to make contact with her husband. Having opted for the excitement of having her tryst with Bob in her own home, she had overlooked the obvious—that he now knew where she lived and might come back to see her at a time when

Derrick happened to be home, or worse, come to the house because Derrick was home.

"Is this a picture of him?" Bob went to the mantel and picked up a photo of Derrick. "He looks familiar. I think I've seen his picture in the newspaper. Isn't he a lawyer or something like that?"

"Do you want to talk about Derrick or make love with me?"

"No contest." Bob put the photo back on the mantel and followed Mallory up the stairs.

Once she was in the bedroom, all her nerves tingled with excitement. If Derrick caught them in the living room, any number of excuses could explain Bob's presence. In the bedroom it was another matter entirely. Her pulses raced and he hadn't even touched her yet.

Bob started undressing her and Mallory pressed her hips against him as she unfastened his shirt. Other than the boy named Jason, no lover of hers had ever been in this room. As with Jason, Mallory found the excitement almost overwhelming.

Today, she thought. Maybe today.

Naked, they tumbled into bed. Bob was eager for her and Mallory matched his hungry passion. It had been weeks since anyone had embraced her, kissed her!

She was so aroused by his lovemaking, she was unable to pay close attention to sounds in the house. She didn't even hear Derrick's footsteps on the stairs.

"Mallory?" he said as he came into the bedroom. "Where did you put my—" He stopped as if he had run into a wall and stared at the tangle of bare arms and legs in his bed.

Mallory gave a strangled gasp and grabbed for the sheet. Bob looked as if he was about to faint or be sick. He scrambled out of bed and clutched his clothes against him.

"What are you doing home?" Mallory asked anxiously as she fished for her own clothes without releasing the concealing sheet.

"Who the hell is this!" Derrick exploded. "What the fuck is going on here?"

Bob was dressing as hastily as he could. He didn't waste time on excuses that wouldn't have mattered anyway.

Mallory yanked her sweater over her head, not bothering with her underwear. "Derrick, I can explain."

"The hell you can! I don't need any explanations! I can tell when some guy is screwing my wife!"

"I didn't know . . ." Bob finally said. He was buttoning his shirt, mismatching buttons and holes. "I mean, she said she wasn't married!"

"You liar!" Mallory exclaimed. "You knew I was married!"

Bob grabbed his shoes as Derrick advanced on him. He scooped up his coat as he circled Derrick warily. "I didn't know! I swear I didn't know!"

Mallory was furious with Bob for his lies. She should never have trusted him enough to bring him here! What had she been thinking! She slipped on her jeans as she shoved her feet into her shoes. "Derrick, just calm down and let me explain." She had no idea what she could say. No one could lie his way out of a situation like this. Lie! That was her only hope. "He forced me!"

Derrick wheeled on her, and before she knew what he was about to do, he slapped her so hard she fell.

Mallory scooted away from him as he stalked menacingly in her direction. Behind him, Bob was racing down the stairs. She soon heard him bumping into walls in his haste to get out of the house. She struggled to her feet. "Didn't you hear what I said? He forced me!"

"Don't lie to me, Mallory! That was no rape I walked in on. You were on top! If anything, you were attacking him! God! How could I be so stupid!" He swung at her again and caught her on the shoulder.

Mallory cried out and stumbled but caught her balance on the bed.

"How often have you done this, you bitch? Do you have men here all the time? You turned my home into a whorehouse!"

"I haven't! I swear I haven't!"

"Get the fuck out of my house!" he roared. "Go on! Get the hell out of my sight!"

She didn't need further encouragement. Warily she circled him and backed out the bedroom door. Derrick followed her, screaming curses and insults at her until she flinched in terror.

She reached behind her for the stair rail, stumbled, and nearly fell.

Derrick shoved her and she grabbed at the rail, missed, and tumbled down to the landing. She scrambled to her feet and ran down the last steps. She was sobbing and starting to hurt all over. He ran after her. "My coat," she pleaded. "Let me at least get my coat!"

"Get out of my house, you stinking bitch! Freeze for all I care!" He struck at her again but this time she ducked.

She ran outside and down the sidewalk. Bob was already out of sight. She hoped she never saw him again. But where could she go?

Automatically she ran to Kirby's house. She hammered at the door until Russell opened it. "Mallory? What's wrong?"

She fell into the warmth of the house, sobbing so hard she couldn't speak.

Russell put his arm around her and helped her into the den. Both boys stared at her. "Out," he said abruptly. "You can watch TV in our bedroom."

Mallory collapsed onto the couch and curled into a ball of misery. Russell knelt beside her. "Mal, what happened? Did someone hurt you?" He gently turned her face toward him. "Damn! Did somebody hit you?"

She nodded speechlessly. On a sob she burst out, "Derrick!"

"Derrick hit you?" Russell stared at her. "Why? It doesn't matter. Is he at home? I'm going to go over there and beat the son of a bitch to a pulp!"

Mallory grabbed his sweater and pulled him back. "No! Don't go over there!"

He sat beside her on the couch and supported her. "Tell me what happened."

"I . . ." She felt sick having to admit this to Russell. "I had a man over there. Derrick caught us. In bed." Humiliation overwhelmed her and she turned away in sobs.

"You had a man in your own house? In bed?" Russell stared at her as if he didn't recognize her. "Mal, why would you do such a thing?"

"I don't know! Because I'm so lonely! Because Derrick

never comes near me anymore! I don't know. A thousand reasons!''

"Okay. Okay." He put his arms around her. "How badly are you hurt? Do you need to see a doctor?"

"No! God, no." She pushed away from him and touched her face. "Does it look bad?"

"There's a bruise on your cheek. Do you want to call the police and have him picked up?"

"I can't do that! He had a good reason to hit me! I was having sex with a man in our bed!" She almost shrieked it at him.

"Okay, okay. I hear you. What happened to the man?"

"He ran away, the spineless worm! He left when Derrick hit me. He didn't even try to defend me!"

"I don't know what to say. Maybe I had better go talk to Derrick."

"No! Not yet. Don't leave me until Kirby comes home. Please?"

"Okay. I'll wait. Derrick probably needs time to cool down anyway." He thought for a minute. "Where is Tara?"

"She went over to Melissa's house after school today. Oh, God! What am I going to tell Tara? What will Dad say? He's going to be furious."

"Then don't tell him. Derrick probably won't either. Why do you and Kirby think your father has to know every single thing you think or do? You made a mistake. I think you're fully aware of that. Bringing more people into it won't solve anything."

"But Tara . . ."

"Tara can spend the night here. I'll put the boys together and the two of you can have the extra room. I don't think you should go home tonight."

"No. I don't know if he will let me come home ever again."

Russell spoke to her gently, as if she were Tara's age. "Why did you take such a chance, Mal?"

"I don't know. I have no idea why I do half the things I do." She buried her face in her hands. "Maybe I'm going crazy."

"I think you should tell Kirby everything that happened.

And I also think you should start seeing a therapist. Kirby told me you were considering making an appointment with Lauren Jacobs."

"I made it, but canceled it." She drew in a ragged breath. "I'll call her tomorrow."

They heard Kirby coming into the house and Russell called her to come to the den. Kirby was as upset as Russell when she saw the huge purple bruise forming on Mallory's face.

"Stay with her," Russell said. "I'll go talk to Derrick and see if I can calm him down."

"By now he's probably drunk enough to listen to anything," Mallory said wryly. "I'm sure he headed straight for the Scotch."

Russell kissed Kirby's forehead. "I'll be back as soon as I can." He wondered what he could possibly say to Derrick to convince him to forgive Mallory. No better than their marriage had been in the past few years, Russell thought this could very well end it.

"Why would you bring a man to your house?" Kirby asked as she put a cold cloth on Mallory's cheek. "Didn't it occur to you that you could get caught?"

"I guess. Yes. I don't know, Kirby. It seemed like a good idea at the time." She cringed away from the cloth and eased it into a more comfortable position.

"Have you done this before? Who was the man? Are you considering leaving Derrick for him?"

"No, I'm not leaving Derrick for him. Why, he didn't even wait around to see what would happen to me, the sonofabitch!" She avoided Kirby's eyes. "His name is Bob."

"Bob? Bob what?"

"I don't know. He never told me and I didn't ask. It doesn't matter."

"Doesn't matter?"

"Would you stop with the questions?" Mallory sighed. "I'm sorry. It's just that I'm not feeling very proud of myself right now."

"I don't know what to say to you. I never expected you to do something like this."

"I'm not the person you think I am. This isn't my first affair.

It's not even the first man I've taken to my house. I guess it was the danger that we might be caught that was so exciting about taking him there. But I never dreamed Derrick actually would walk in on us!"

"How could you take a chance like that!" Kirby looked at her in concern. "You aren't taking any other chances, are you? With AIDS, I mean."

"No, I'm sexually frustrated, not suicidal."

Kirby hoped she was telling the truth. "How many affairs have you had?"

"I don't know." As soon as the words were out of Mallory's mouth, she looked surprised. "I guess I never thought about it."

"You never . . ." Kirby lifted the cloth to check the swelling. "He hit you hard. Has this ever happened before?"

"No. I didn't think Derrick had it in him."

"It's not funny, Mal."

"I know that! I'm not laughing!" Her voice broke and she tried to blink back the tears. "I'm not making light of this." She gazed at Kirby earnestly. "I don't know what's wrong with me. I need more sex than Derrick does. It's always been that way." She hesitated. "But I rarely get satisfied. Do you know what I mean?"

"I think so."

"It's so damned frustrating! It's like I have this need inside that constantly gnaws at me, never letting me rest. Derrick won't touch me most of the time. When he does, he just satisfies himself!"

Kirby drew back. "You shouldn't be telling me these things! It's none of my business what happens between you and your husband. Or you and your . . . lovers!" She had trouble even saying the last word.

"If I can't tell you, who can I tell?" Mallory pleaded. "I sure can't talk to Derrick about this!"

"You're right. I guess you can't. I'm sorry, Mal. It's just that I have trouble talking about sex."

Their eyes met for a long moment. "We're really messed up, aren't we?" Mallory said.

"Get into counseling. I promise you it will help." Kirby

hugged Mallory, much the same way she had when they were children and had to comfort each other because no one else was available. "Please, Mal?"

"I will. I've already promised Russell."

"Good," Kirby whispered. "Good."

Chapter Twenty-Four

"Hello, Raymond. How good to hear from you." Addison let the newspaper drop to his lap.

Jane looked up from her knitting.

The voice of the newest President of the United States, Raymond Stansfield, came to Addison over the line. "I've got good news for you. There's a letter on my desk informing me of a resignation in the Supreme Court."

Although he had been expecting this call, Addison felt his heart skip a beat. "Is that right?"

"Yes. Wrobleski is finally retiring. It's a matter of health. Your name will be given to the Senate soon as the man I've chosen to take his place."

For a few seconds Addison couldn't reply. This was the moment he had planned for all his adult life. "Thank you, Raymond. You'll never regret it."

"Of course, I have to give my staff committee a couple of other names, too. Political game we play. They'll leak those other names to the press so the Democrats will have a chance to shoot them down. Once they've pretty well unloaded on them, I'll announce I've selected you as my nominee."

"Who are the others?"

"Alf Newport and a man from North Dakota named Harry serman."

"I never heard of Iserman. Alf couldn't be trusted to be a school crossing guard."

"I know. That's my plan exactly. Newport isn't congenial and he never takes a firm stand on anything. Democratic research will also show he's an unreformed alcoholic and is probably dabbling in recreational drugs, too. I'll be properly surprised to find this out, naturally."

"Naturally. And Iserman?"

"He's fairly clean, but like you said, nobody has ever heard of him. He's a judge in a town barely large enough to be considered a city. He's as nondescript as they come. He'll be shot down because no one will be sure what he really stands for. I've been giving this strategy a lot of consideration and I think you're as good as confirmed."

"I appreciate this, Raymond. You'll see what I mean when the chips are down." In order to ensure this appointment, Addison had privately told Raymond that he would fully support Raymond's position on every issue before the court. It was a moral compromise, but in Addison's opinion, it was worth it. There was nothing he wanted more than to be a Supreme Court Justice.

"I'll tell the media about the resignation tomorrow and my selection committee will leak the two names under consideration as soon as the press gets to them. I imagine the news will break by the noon news briefs."

"I'll be watching."

"Remember, Addison, as far as the public is concerned, I'm not nominating you because you're my friend and helped me get elected but because you're the best man for the job. And you are," he added.

"I understand. Thank you again."

He hung up and sat for a moment staring at the phone. It was actually happening!

"Who was that?" Jane asked carefully.

He hated it when she spoke in that small, retiring voice. Nothing was more irritating than a woman sneaking quietly through life. "That was the President of the United States."

"Raymond? Why was he calling?"

Addison looked at her at last. She was no longer pretty and

her manner was apologetic even when there was nothing to apologize about. She would probably look good to the media. Certainly there were no skeletons in her closet that could be brought to light and cost him the position. "Call the family together. I have an announcement to make."

Mallory sat in Lauren's office, twisting the strap of her purse, crossing and uncrossing her legs.

"Are you nervous?" Lauren asked with a placid, nonthreatening smile.

"No, not at all," Mallory said too quickly. She added, "Maybe a little."

"I'm glad to finally meet you. Kirby talks about you often. She says you two are quite close."

"Yes, we are. She's my best friend." Mallory glanced around the office. "I didn't know what to expect."

"I try to make my clients as comfortable as possible. We wrestle with difficult topics in here and I want everyone to feel that this is a safe place for them."

Mallory drew in a shaky breath. "I'm not sure where to start."

"How about telling me something about yourself?"

"Well, I'm here because my husband caught me with another man—in our bed." She watched carefully to see how Lauren reacted.

"I see. Is that where you got the bruise?"

She nodded in embarrassment. "I wanted to wait until it was gone before coming here, but Kirby wouldn't hear of it. Also, this was one of Derrick's stipulations—he's my husband—for taking me back. He's never hit me before," she added.

"I'm glad to hear that. It's good that you came in now. I've seen bruises before."

Mallory laughed mirthlessly. "This is nothing compared to some I got from Dad." She caught herself too late; the words were already out. As before, Lauren took this revelation in stride.

"I assume your father has a rather bad temper."

"I pushed him too far," Mallory said automatically. "I mis-behaved a lot."

"That's no excuse for a child to be given bruises. Beatings are abusive, not instructive."

"Dad isn't all bad," Mallory protested. "He's really not!"

"No one is," Lauren replied quietly. "What else do you remember about him?"

Mallory was silent for a long time. "You're asking if he ever . . . touched me."

"If that's what you'd like to discuss."

Mallory crossed her legs again and curled her purse strap into a corkscrew. "Kirby didn't remember, but I do. Everything she remembers really happened. It also happened to me. But he did it in order to teach me what I needed to know in order to be a good wife! He didn't do it to hurt me!"

"So you really believe that?" Lauren sounded as if either answer was acceptable.

"I don't know what to think anymore." Her voice was scarcely more than a whisper. "No. It wasn't right for him to do those things to me." Her voice took on an edge of determination. "And he's not going to do them to my Tara!"

"I assume Tara is your daughter, is that right?"

Mallory's head bobbed.

Lauren nodded. "We're in complete agreement. The most important thing is not to give him the opportunity. He should never be allowed to get Tara alone."

"How can I be sure he won't?" Mallory cried out in exaspera-tion. "We live a block away. We eat Sunday dinner there every week. What can I tell Mom?"

"Eventually, she may have to be told the truth."

Mallory frowned. "I think that would destroy her."

"It doesn't have to be done today or in a harsh way. If you'd like—when you're ready—you can bring your mother here and I'll help you tell her."

"You'd do that?"

"When you feel it's time. Meanwhile, we'll find ways to help keep Tara safe."

Mallory relaxed a bit. "Kirby was right. I needed to talk to you."

"I have no magic solutions, but together we'll work things out."

"What if you get tired of seeing me? I seem to have an awful lot of things that need fixing in my life." Mallory was only half kidding.

Lauren smiled. "I'll be here as long as you need me. I'm not planning on going anywhere."

Mallory started to relax all over. She hadn't realized how much she had dreaded hearing the answer to that question. She hadn't talked much with Kirby about the counseling process, and for all she had known, Lauren might have had a limit on the number of visits each client was allowed. Mallory knew she needed a lot of help and had a great deal to work through. The thought of being abandoned partway through this was more frightening than taking the first step in coming here. "Where do we start? With Dad, what's happening with Tara, my crumbling marriage, or my affairs?"

"I think all those things are related. Let's start with what you remember about your father."

Mallory drew in a deep breath and began to talk about the things she had never told anyone, even Kirby. It wasn't pleasant, but at last she had hope of getting her life on an even keel. Lauren listened closely and asked questions only when she wasn't sure what Mallory meant. More quickly than Mallory would have guessed, she felt her trust in Lauren start to build.

"Why did Dad want us over here tonight?" Mallory whispered to Kirby. "Do you think he's mad at us? Could he have heard that we've been talking about what happened to us as kids?"

"How could he possibly have heard that?" Kirby hated the way her own mind was filled with dread. She felt as if she were a child again and about to be reprimanded.

"He always told us that nothing about the family should leave this house. Maybe—"

"Mal, he's not omnipotent! I haven't talked to anyone about it but you, Russell, and Lauren. I don't know what he wants to tell us, but it can't have anything to do with that." She saw her mother approaching and gave an almost imperceptible nod toward Mallory. It was a signal from their childhood to warn that silence was needed. A signal devised by children who feared the angry rages of a parent who was frequently out of control.

"Come into the living room, girls. Everyone else is already in there."

They went into the living room as their mother had asked and sat side by side on the sofa. Kirby was aware of the significance of news being delivered in this room. If it were an ordinary visit, they would be in the den.

"I received a call today," Addison said, glancing from one to another.

Mallory's eyes widened and she looked at Kirby. Kirby remembered how Mallory's demeanor had always given them away when they had been into mischief as girls. She met her sister's eyes and tried to mentally tell her to calm down.

"The call was from the President of the United States."

"Raymond Stansfield," Jane put in as if they might not know who Addison meant. He frowned at her and she became silent.

"He's bestowed a great honor on me. It wasn't entirely a surprise, but I had never expected it to happen." He paused for effect. "He will be nominating me to fill a vacancy as a Justice of the United States Supreme Court. Technically, I'm one of three men he's put on a list for consideration by his staff appointments committee. But he feels strongly that the committee will select me."

"There's a vacancy?" Russell asked. "I haven't heard anything about it."

"You will by noon tomorrow. Justice Wrobleski is retiring for health reasons."

Jane looked as surprised as the rest. Kirby suddenly realized that her mother also hadn't known the news until this moment. Addison had kept it from her until he told them all. It was as if his wife was of no more importance to him than his sons-in-law.

"Wrobleski hasn't been healthy," Russell admitted. "I read in the paper that he's scheduled for a triple bypass surgery."

Derrick looked thoughtful. "This will mean big things for

the firm. Even more prestige. No one in Houston but us will
be able to boast that their firm's founder has become a Supreme
Court Justice.''

''I'll admit that's occurred to me,'' Addison said with a smile.

''Will we have to move?'' Jane asked. ''Washington, D.C.,
is even farther away than Austin!''

Addison frowned at her. ''Certainly it is. What difference
does that make?''

''I had thought you were planning a move to Austin. I never
dreamed you'd go to Washington!''

''That's because you aren't capable of great dreams.'' He
looked at her with a raised eyebrow. ''Austin? Where did you
get such an idea?'' Then he looked away, clearly annoyed by
Jane's inability to keep up with the conversation. ''Never mind
that. It isn't important.'' Addison's broad smile returned and
he said to Derrick, ''Think what this will mean! It's a lawyer's
highest goal!''

Kirby remembered to murmur congratulations with the rest.
Her mind was spinning. Addison had overturned at least one
indecency with a child conviction, and as a Supreme Court
Justice he could influence the country's laws involving incest,
molestation, and pornography. As a justice, he could only be
removed from office by impeachment and a conviction of serious misconduct. Addison was too careful to let himself get
caught doing anything illegal, so for the rest of his natural life,
he could hold a position on the highest court in the land and
soften the laws against child molestation.

Once he was a justice it also would be far more difficult to
take him to court for molesting Mallory and herself. Kirby
glanced across at Tara and wished with all her heart that she
knew for a fact whether Addison was molesting her or not.
Kirby still wanted to believe that she was wrong about all of
it. Lauren had called it classic denial.

Tara was squirming in her chair and kicking at Josh. He
shoved at her leg but she kept on trying to put her shoes on
his pants leg. Josh glared at her and said, ''Quit that, Tara!''

''Josh,'' Kirby said as Addison turned on him with a frown.
''Don't do that.''

''She's kicking me, Mom. What do you want me to do? Just

sit here and get kicked?" He shoved at Tara's leg even though she had stopped pestering him now.

"Tara," Mallory said, "behave! I told you before we came over here that I expect you to mind your manners."

Tara's lower lip thrust out and she crossed her arms over her chest. "I wasn't doing anything. Josh's just trying to get me in trouble."

"I was not!" Josh exploded. "Dad, she's lying!"

"I am not!" Tara shouted.

Kirby watched the drama in shock. She couldn't imagine Mallory or herself doing such a thing. Tara was deliberately provoking a scene in front of Addison.

Derrick jumped out of his chair and caught Tara's wrist. "Come with me, young lady. We're going to have a talk."

Tara tried to twist free, and when she let out a wail, she was practically dragged from the room.

Kirby found her mouth had dropped open. She would have said Tara would never have done such a thing in her life under any conditions.

"I'm sorry, Dad. She's been on a tear all week," Mallory said nervously.

"She needs a spanking. You're too soft on her, Mallory. A child needs discipline or she'll grow up to be a delinquent." He fastened his eyes on Josh.

"I didn't do anything!" the boy protested. "She was picking on me!"

"I was thinking of your career in crime."

That drew Russell's attention. "My son is no thief."

"Not anymore he isn't." Addison leaned toward Josh. "For the next few weeks or couple of months, the press will be watching every move this family makes. If anything, and I mean *anything,* causes me to lose this position, I'm going to be furious. Do you follow me, Josh?"

Rebellion was angrily scrawled across Josh's face. He leaped to his feet. "I haven't done anything wrong since Dad came home! Why does everybody pick on me?" He stormed out of the room.

Kirby looked back at her father. Her heart was racing. If she had said half that to her father at Josh's age, she would have been severely beaten. Addison grunted his displeasure and with an angry scowl rose halfway out of his chair, then noticed that Russell, too, was on his way to his feet, and reconsidered and sat back down. Russell's unspoken warning had been effective in protecting Josh.

Russell, however, continued to glare at Addison until he leaned back in his chair. The confrontation was averted. Russell stood and said in a quiet voice, "I'll go talk to him."

Kirby was amazed at the scene she had just witnessed. Not only had no one ever dared talk back to her father or to act up in his presence, but Russell's stance had indicated that he wouldn't allow Addison to do as he pleased where Josh was concerned. Kirby felt fresh admiration for her husband. Russell was usually quiet and gentle, but not when it came to protecting his sons.

When Russell was gone, Addison scowled at Kirby and Mallory. "You two are doing a hell of a poor job raising those kids! Delinquents, every one of them!"

Cody looked up. "What did I do?"

Kirby reached out and touched his knee as a warning. "Maybe it would be a good idea for you to go watch TV."

Cody frowned at his grandfather, but he left the room.

"That was unfair, Dad," Kirby said. "Cody hasn't done anything at all and Josh has been on good behavior for months. Tara was only acting like an ordinary child."

"Are you calling me to task?" Addison demanded.

Kirby's mouth turned to dust. He still triggered the old responses in her. "I'm only saying that we have good children. It's natural for them to act out from time to time."

"Is that something your shrink told you?" he sneered. "That's one thing you'll stop right away. I'm not having anyone say that there's insanity in my family."

"No, I won't. Lauren is helping me and I'm going to continue therapy." Kirby was surprised how calm she sounded.

"Then I'll have to tell the press that it's a matter of marital counseling. I can't have them making something up."

"It's not marriage counseling. Russell and I are doing fine."

"Then what do you suggest I say when I'm asked why you're

seeing a psychiatrist?" he asked sarcastically. "I'd love to hear how you would answer the question."

"Would you really?" The room became too quiet. Kirby could scarcely believe she had said such a thing to him. She had every expectation that he would cross the room and hit her.

Addison looked as if he wanted to do exactly that. A muscle clenched in his jaw and his lips drew into thin lines from his effort not to strike her. Kirby faced him as if she were fearless. To her amazement, he backed down.

Mallory stared in disbelief.

Jane hurriedly said, "I think we could all use some coffee. My goodness, you children are on edge tonight." She gave Kirby the warning signal she had perfected when they were children.

Kirby leaned back and crossed one leg over the other. When her posture changed, Addison relaxed slightly. Kirby was hard-pressed to keep her face expressionless. It was happening just as Lauren had told her it might! She had refused to back down and he had retreated. True, it was over a small matter, but it was the first time it had ever happened. And she had diffused the tension by her body language! Kirby understood at last what Lauren had meant when she discussed becoming empowered.

Later that night when Kirby and Russell were in bed, she told him what had happened while he was talking to Josh in the other room. "I can't believe I actually said that to him!"

He took her hand. "I'm proud of you. There's no need for you and Mallory to walk on eggshells every time you're around him. You're adults. He can't hurt you anymore."

She rolled to her side to face him. "Until tonight I never really felt like an adult when Dad was angry. I've been paying closer attention to things you've mentioned about Dad over the years and I'm beginning to realize you're right. Dad really is tyrannical over us. When you said that before, I just thought it was because you didn't like him."

"He's losing his hold." Russell stroked his thumb over her hand. "Maybe he'll finally start to mellow."

"I don't know. It's not like Dad to back down. I'm afraid there will still be repercussions." She caught herself. "I say it so automatically, don't I? It's easy to forget that I'm not under his power anymore and that he can't come over here and punish me."

"You've come a long way." His voice was filled with pride for her progress.

"I have a long way still to go, though." She eased her bare foot closer to him until it touched his leg. "Russell, I can't let him become a Supreme Court Justice. You can see that, can't you?"

"Yes, I can. When you told me he was responsible for overthrowing the Chandler case, I knew he had to be stopped. I'm just not sure how."

"I'll have to tell what I know."

He drew her closer until her head was resting on his shoulder. "Are you sure that's what you want to do? It will mean embarrassing questions for Mallory and you. And for Tara, too."

"I have to do it."

"I know. I'll be with you all the way."

She smiled in the darkness. "I know. I love you, Russell."

He kissed her lightly on the lips, and instead of Kirby automatically pulling away, she kissed him back.

"Remind me to thank Lauren," he whispered as he took her into his arms.

Kirby smiled and kissed him again.

Within two weeks the Democratic senators had raised an uproar over the possible consideration of Alf Newport for the justice vacancy. As he'd said he would, President Stansfield expressed great surprise at discovering Newport's drinking and drug problems, and Newport passed into obscurity.

However, to Addison's consternation, both sides of the Senate seemed to be seriously considering Harry Iserman's credits. Stansfield's office had decided to leak Addison's name as another being considered so support would swing toward the man Stansfield was going to nominate. A week later the senators' opinions on the two men was almost evenly divided. The man no one ever heard of was running Addison a close race.

Kirby had decided not to make any public statements until

she heard whether Newport would be Stansfield's nominee. After all, Stansfield had his own interests to protect, according to Russell, who taught political science and knew more about these things than she did. He had convinced her that despite what Stansfield may have told Addison, it was possible that he might feel it was in his best interests to nominate Newport. On TV Addison was tall, handsome, and fatherly. Iserman answered questions brilliantly, but his demeanor was retiring and shy, almost subservient. Addison's charisma was pushing him far ahead in public opinion. And the opinion of politicians' constituents often swayed their views.

"I have to do it," Kirby said to Lauren.

"I can't advise you on that."

"Can you tell me what you'd do in my place? Am I wrong or overreacting?"

"If I were in your place, I'd be making phone calls," Lauren said. "If you'd like, you can use this one."

Kirby hesitated. Once this was done, it could never be reversed. Then she reached into her purse and took out the phone numbers she had already copied down and her telephone charge card. Without hesitation for reconsideration, she punched in the number of the first man on her list.

When someone answered, she said, "May I speak to Senator Frederickson?" Her eyes met Lauren's while she waited to be connected. Her old shyness threatened to return and she was glad she was calling from Lauren's office. "Senator Frederickson? I'm Addison Walker's daughter, Kirby Garrett. Fine, thank you. I wasn't sure you'd remember me." She drew in a steadying breath. "I'm calling about my father's possible nomination to the vacancy on the Supreme Court. No, just the opposite. I want you to reconsider backing him."

Kirby closed her eyes and concentrated on keeping her voice calm as the senator asked why she would say such a thing. "Dad is soft on the punishment of child molesters and I don't think he should have the power of a Supreme Court Justice for that reason. No, nothing is on his record, but I know for a fact he was responsible for overturning the conviction of a man named Gary Chandler who raped his daughter and molested at least one other girl. Chandler has been arrested again and charged with the same offense. And my father was supposed to have recused himself from the appeal in that case because I was the prosecutor. No, there were no charges of official misconduct brought against my father. Yes, as I just said, I was the prosecutor in that case. No, it's not a matter of professional jealousy. Senator Frederickson, this isn't an easy call for me to make."

Lauren leaned forward and nodded encouragingly.

Kirby plunged in. "I have reason to believe Dad may be involved in child molestation himself . . . Senator Frederickson, I . . . But you don't . . . Hello?" She took the receiver from her ear. "He hung up on me!"

"He didn't!" Lauren looked as surprised as Kirby felt.

She went to the next name on her list, that of a female senator, and punched in the numbers. "Senator Mays," she said when the woman was on the line, "I want to talk to you about Addison Walker's nomination to the Supreme Court . . ."

After several other calls, Kirby was baffled and disappointed. "I can't understand this. No one believes me." She was close to tears.

"It's okay to cry," Lauren reminded her gently. "I'm glad you called from here."

"This is the first time I've told anyone outside the family, and they all think I'm lying."

"I doubt they meant it personally. Maybe they didn't believe you're really Addison's daughter."

"I suppose that's possible. Anyone could use the phone and claim to be me. But I couldn't be more convincing in a letter. Anyone can write letters, too."

"I have to admit I didn't expect it to go like this. True, repressed memory syndrome is a new concept to some people, but it's as if none of them ever heard of it!"

"Some had, but I got the impression they didn't believe in it." Kirby pushed at the tear that escaped her eye. "How could they think I'd lie about something like this?"

Lauren handed her the box of tissues. "Don't get discouraged."

"I'm not. If anything, this has made me more determined than ever. If the senators I called are this uninformed, there might not be anyone in Washington who would stop Dad. He could even get some of the current child molestation laws declared unconstitutional!"

"I know. That's already occurred to me." Lauren looked at her with empathetic concern. "What will you do now?"

"I don't know. I don't think I should wait around for return calls from the senators who were out of their offices. I can't let any more time lapse. According to the news last night, Dad is pulling ahead of Iserman." She glanced at her watch. "My hour is up."

"I don't have anyone coming in this hour. We can run over our usual time today."

Kirby thought for a minute, then reached into her purse for the pocket-sized phone book she frequently used during the course of her work. She dialed Bill Davies' number. "Mr. Davies? This is Kirby Garrett. Fine, thank you. Anything yet on Addison Walker and Gary Chandler?" She listened to Davies' report. "I see. Well, don't give up yet. All right. I'll talk to you in a few days." She hung up.

"Who is Bill Davies?"

"He's a private investigator I've hired to see if there's a connection between Dad and Chandler. So far he hasn't found anything. I wasn't going to tell you until something turned up." She leaned back in the chair. "I keep coming back to Dad's risking his entire career by violating the law which prohibited him from influencing the appellate judges who were hearing Chandler's appeal. He knew it was wrong, but did it anyway. There has to be some reason."

"I can think of one," Lauren said.

"Other than the obvious, I mean. If I were a child molester, I wouldn't do anything to link my name to a similar case. It was unnecessary and Dad doesn't do foolhardy things. It's out of character for him."

"When is the Senate confirmation hearing?"

"Next month. I'm running out of time."

"I don't know how to advise you."

Kirby put the number back into her purse and closed it

decisively. "Repressed memory syndrome may be too far out, but there's one other avenue. I was hoping not to have to use it."

"Tara?"

Kirby nodded. "I'll call you if I get anything out of her."

"Be careful," Lauren advised. "If you put the idea into her head . . ."

"I know. I'm a lawyer. Remember?"

After leaving Lauren's office, Kirby drove to Mallory's house and saw Tara playing alone in the front yard. Instead of waving and running to the car as she would have done months before, Tara stood and simply watched as Kirby got out. "Tara, may I talk to you?"

They went into the house. Mallory met them in the den. "I thought I heard her talking to you."

"I made the phone calls we discussed and I got nowhere."

"No one believed you?" Mallory exclaimed. "What are you going to do now?"

"I have some questions I'd like to ask Tara."

Tara looked from one to the other. "Am I in trouble?"

"No, honey." Kirby put her arm on her niece's shoulder and they sat on the couch. "I just want to know some things and you're the only one who can help me with this."

Mallory edged toward the door. "I have something baking. Do you need me?"

Kirby shook her head. "Tara and I can work this out alone."

As soon as Mallory was gone, Tara said, "I'm in trouble! I can tell!"

"No, no." Kirby took one of her hands and held it reassuringly. "Tara, I've been paying attention to you lately and I think you had something really important that you wanted to tell me a couple of months ago. We were at my house, remember? I was busy and wasn't paying attention to what you were saying, but I want to hear. Will you tell me now?"

It was clear that Tara knew what she was referring to. She shook her head and slumped lower on the couch.

"I'm not going to force you to tell."

Tara cut her eyes up at Kirby. "How do you know what I was going to say? Maybe you won't believe me anyway."

Kirby took a deep breath and chose her words carefully. "What if I tell you the same thing once happened to me?"

Tara's mouth opened in surprise. "It did? Are you kidding me?"

"No. I'd never lie about something this important. Will you tell me what happened?"

"I don't know. Grandma told me it should be a secret between the two of us."

"Grandma knows?" Kirby couldn't keep the shock out of her voice.

Tara nodded. "I told her the day I got that real bad scrape on my leg. Remember?"

"I sure do. It was a terrible scrape. It almost got infected."

"It's okay now."

Kirby gently said, "What did you tell Grandma that day?"

In a voice that was so soft Kirby had to strain to hear her, Tara said, "Grandad kissed me. On the mouth like grown-ups do in movies." She watched Kirby warily.

"He did?" Now that she was hearing it, Kirby found it more difficult to hear than she had expected. "Has anything else happened since that day?"

For a minute she thought Tara would refuse to tell. Then the girl's dark eyes filled with tears and she nodded. Kirby waited. "There's this game Grandad likes to play," Tara whispered. "It's sort of like hide-and-seek, but I know where he's hiding."

Nausea cramped Kirby's stomach. "In the guest bedroom?"

Tara's eyes widened and she nodded. "Did he play the game with you, too? He said he did, but I didn't believe him."

"He told you about me?"

"Yeah. He said that it's what grandads do to teach their grandchildren how to be grown-ups."

Kirby thought she was going to be sick but she hid it. "What else happened, Tara?"

"He makes me take my panties off and touch him. Then he touches me." Her voice broke. "I didn't want to! I really didn't! I knew it was bad!"

Kirby pulled the girl close. "It's okay, honey. It's okay. You're not the one who did something bad. It was Grandad."

"I'm the one who touched him! I hate doing it! I don't want to be grown up!"

Kirby fought to control herself. "He wasn't telling you the truth, Tara. When you're grown up, it's not the same. You'll feel differently about everything and you'll only touch a man if you love each other."

"I love Grandad, too," Tara said quickly. "I didn't say that!"

For a moment Kirby could only hold her in silence. What Tara had said could have come from Kirby's own lips. "I know. But it's a different kind of love. When you're little, you don't love the same way a grown-up does. And Grandad doesn't love you the same way, either. It doesn't work that way."

Tara was quiet as if she was trying to understand. "Grandad doesn't love me?"

"Yes, he does. I'm sure Grandad loves you very much. But not the way two grown-ups love each other. It's not the way you're supposed to feel about a person in your own family." She didn't know if this was the way Lauren would have said it or not, but Tara deserved an answer.

"Do I have to keep playing that game?"

"No. You never have to play that game again. I'll see to that."

Tara sat up and smiled. "Are we through talking? I want to go outside."

"Sure. Run along." Kirby watched the girl trot out of the room.

Within moments Mallory came in. Her eyes were wide and dark. "I heard."

"He's molesting her." Kirby found it difficult to say those words, even though she already had known the truth. "We weren't mistaken."

"He's never going to see her again!" Mallory rarely got angry, but when she did, sparks seemed to fly from her eyes. "I'll have him arrested!"

"If you do, Tara will have to testify in court." Kirby rubbed the dull ache that was throbbing in her temples. "But you have to keep her away from him. Mal, Mom knows what's happening."

"No," Mallory whispered. "Not Mom. She can't know."

''Tara told her the day she hurt her leg on the tree.''

Mallory put her hand over her mouth as if she were feeling as ill as Kirby had moments before. ''Mom wouldn't let that happen!''

''She may have known it was happening to us.''

''That's not possible!''

Kirby lost her temper. ''Mallory, where do you think she was all day? She never left the house except to run errands or go to one of her meetings. Don't you think it ever happened when she was home? I remember her talking on the phone for hours and baking God knows what in her kitchen for half a day at a time. She was there!''

Mallory leaned forward, wrapping her arms around her middle. ''You're right,'' she said in a small voice. ''I just couldn't let myself believe that.''

''She may not have known the extent of what was happening. It's no excuse, but you know how she can justify almost anything. I have to believe she didn't know he was hurting us.'' Kirby looked at Mallory for confirmation.

''How could she not have known?''

Kirby noticed they had switched sides in the argument. ''I don't have any answers.''

''Tara told her and not me?''

''She told Mom that Grandad kissed her on the mouth. Unless Mom was paying attention, she might not have fully understood or asked the right questions. When I think back, Tara tried to tell me, too, but I had no idea what she was talking about. She's too young to know the right words. A 'kiss' can cover a lot of territory.''

Mallory thought for a minute. ''You know, I think she did try to tell me. Several times. I was busy and didn't really listen.''

''Well, we know now. You know you can never let Dad get his hands on her again.''

''As if I would!'' Mallory frowned at her sister. ''I love Tara! He'll never hurt her again.'' She paused. ''How far do you think he went?''

''I think it stopped at mutual touching. I don't think she's been raped.''

''Thank God!'' Mallory whispered.

"Lauren will want to talk to you about this."

Mallory nodded. "I know. I have an appointment with her tomorrow."

"Good."

"Kirby? Do you think Tara has been hurt . . . you know, in her mind?"

"Not irrevocably. She has some healing to do, as Lauren would say."

"I want to kill that sonofabitch!"

"So do I. But we can't, so we'll do whatever we can to keep him from this court appointment. If he's placed on the Supreme Court, it will be even more difficult to prove what he's doing." She reached out and patted Mallory's hand. "Don't worry. He's not going to get away with this."

Mallory nodded. "No. He won't. Not even if it means me testifying in court. I'm ready to do that now."

"Good," Kirby said in relief. While her own memories were vague and difficult to recall, Mallory apparently remembered everything. "Good," she repeated.

Chapter Twenty-Five

Addison Walker puffed out his chest as he looked around his office, feeling inordinately proud of himself. When he had been seated on the appellate court, he had looked on this office as the pinnacle of his career. Now he was on the verge of gaining stature that far exceeded this menial position. He did, however, regret leaving behind this office.

It was beautifully decorated. Jane might not be good for much else, but she had a flair for interior decorating. The deep-tone blue on the walls had been her idea, as had the Aubusson carpet in shades of blue, red, and gold. Kirby had picked the furniture: the mahogany desk and the oxblood leather uphol-stered chairs. With his gold-embossed law books lining two walls, it looked rich and wise. It had made a perfect setting for him.

He wondered how long it would be before Raymond pre-sented his name as nominee and how soon after that the Senate Judiciary Committee would call him to testify. If the judiciary committee approved him unanimously, his confirmation by the Senate would come swiftly and surely. The only thing which could possibly stand between him and his destiny was Harry Iserman, who was proving to be a sturdier candidate than any-one had thought possible. To keep anyone from saying Addison was being especially groomed by the President, Raymond hadn't phoned since his official call to tell Addison that he was being considered. Addison knew this was best, but it galled him that he was being talked about behind his back and that he didn't know what was being done by Raymond's staff to swing the balance in his favor.

When the phone rang, his first thought was that it was Raymond, calling to inform him the choice had been made. "Hello?"

"Judge Walker? This is Senator Mays," a woman's voice said.

"Good afternoon, Senator." Was this the call?

"I received a rather unusual phone call last week and I was wondering if you might help me understand it."

Addison hesitated. "Well, I'll do my best." He had met Senator Mays only briefly. Why would she be phoning him?

"I understand you have a daughter named Kirby Garrett?"

"Yes. Do you know Kirby?"

"No, I don't. However, she called me several days ago and suggested that I withdraw my support of you for the Supreme Court nomination."

Addison thought he must have heard wrong. "Kirby did what?"

"She seemed to think there is some dark secret in your background that would be of interest to the Senate Judiciary Committee."

Addison's anger started to build. He felt hot and uncomfortable. "There must be some mistake. Kirby wouldn't do that."

"Kirby Garrett was the name the woman gave me. She also called several of the other senators. I've talked to some of them and it seems that she told them essentially the same thing."

"No, no. There's some mistake. My daughter is behind me all the way. Someone must have called claiming to be her." Though the words fell from his lips smoothly and effortlessly, inside he was raging. He wanted to kill Kirby.

"I'm a little surprised that you haven't asked upon what grounds she feels you should be disqualified."

Addison fought to keep his voice calm and congenial. "I don't see what difference it makes. The call was obviously made from a deranged person, not my daughter."

"Today I also received a letter from her and the postmark is from Houston. The letterhead is that of the Harris County District Attorney's Office. I've checked and your daughter works there."

"Yes, of course she does. I've made that public. Kirby is an attorney." He mentally flailed about for some excuse that he could make for Kirby's actions.

"I've already checked."

"Well, what allegations have been made?"

"She's accusing you of child molestation."

Addison couldn't speak. His rage was building to gigantic proportions. If Kirby had been in his office at that moment, he would have beaten her half to death. "That's ridiculous!"

"All the same, it has raised questions among several of us. If there's any truth in the statement, it will naturally color our decision."

The wild, predatory animal that was his rage demanded release, but instead, he forced himself to speak calmly, as if this were patently and absurdly ridiculous. "I believe I understand what may be happening. Frankly I had hoped nothing would come of it, but I'm becoming concerned about Kirby's mental state."

"Oh?" Senator Mays sounded cool. Did she believe him?

"Lately I've seen a change in her. She and her husband were separated for a while." He knew this had become public knowledge. "They're back together now, but since the separation her mental condition has deteriorated. She's seeing a psychiatrist, you know."

"No, I wasn't aware of that."

"Yes, a doctor here in Houston. Naturally we had all hoped she would be able to help Kirby, but if Kirby's gone this far overboard, well, it doesn't look good." He switched to his facade of fatigue and fatherly concern. "My daughter sometimes has hallucinations. I've heard her say things that I can make no sense of."

"I had no idea."

"Apparently she experimented with a mind-altering drug in college, despite the efforts of her mother and myself to warn her away from such things. You know how rebellious young

people can be. It must have had a negative effect on her brain."
Everyone had heard of LSD trips recurring years after the drug
had been taken. It was plausible that other drugs available
during Kirby's teenage years could have had lasting side effects
as well, though at the moment he couldn't think of one by
name. Regardless, he'd said it, and whatever the negative consequences to his confirmation, he was sure that it would be less
than having anyone believe her assertion that he was a child
molester.

"I see. This does change things quite a bit."

"I had hoped it wouldn't come to light, to tell you the truth.
The entire family is upset over Kirby's, well, lapses."

"She's done this before then?"

"Never outside the family. She's a brilliant attorney and is
capable of holding her own in the courtroom, until now. She's
never before done anything of this magnitude. Oh, there have
been incidents when she's forgotten to cook dinner or pick up
her sons at school, but in general she's competent—or was."

"She could have hurt your career irrevocably."

"I can see that. Perhaps I should write or call the senators
she contacted and give them the right story."

"No, that might not be a good idea. It might be read as private
campaigning on your part. I'll speak to them unofficially."

"Thank you, Senator Mays," he said gratefully. "And I
certainly appreciate your letting me know what Kirby has
done."

When he hung up, Addison felt his rage reaching dangerous
proportions. He had to stop the bitch, daughter or no daughter,
and he had to work quickly. He had to silence her forever. But
how, short of killing her?

Killing her? No, that was too extreme. His head felt as though
it might burst. How dare she defame him in this way? Child
molester? Where had she gotten such an idea? Then a new
thought came to him. Drawing a deep breath, he pulled a tight
rein on the ferocity within him and appeased the beast by
swearing to himself that a more moderate plan would accom-
plish his goal. If no one believed her, it wouldn't matter what
she said.

He dialed Derrick's private line at the firm. Derrick answered. "There's a problem."

"Are you okay, Addison? You sound odd."

"I just talked to Senator Mays. She says Kirby has contacted her and several other senators on the Senate Judiciary Committee and told them I'm a child molester!"

"What! Kirby did what?" Derrick sounded stunned. "Why the hell would she do a thing like that!"

"I've seen this coming for a while. She's losing her grip on reality. She's angry with me for making you head of the firm instead of her, and she's trying to destroy me. You have to help me, Derrick. Find evidence that Kirby is suffering a mental breakdown. I'll have the papers signed to have her institutionalized."

"I'm not sure you can. She's married and—"

"Damn it, Derrick! I've got friends! Influential friends! Just do what I told you!" Addison was almost screaming over the phone.

Derrick paused. "How would I go about doing that?"

"Talk to Mallory. They tell each other everything. Maybe she'll have something we can use."

"What if she doesn't?"

"Find a way. Do I have to think for you? Goddamn it, figure out a way!" He slammed the receiver down.

Derrick held the dead phone, stunned for a moment, then slowly replaced the phone in its cradle. If anyone had sounded mentally off balance, it had been Addison. Nevertheless, he had his instructions.

He glanced at his wristwatch. It was almost time to leave for the day anyway. He put the papers he had been working on into his briefcase and headed for home.

When he reached the house, Mallory was alone watching TV. He had allowed her to come back home after the incident when he caught her having sex with a man in their bedroom, but only because he felt he had to. He couldn't afford to make Addison angry by doing something that might rock Addison's Supreme Court boat, especially since Addison had promised to help him get started in politics and he knew Addison's help would be essential. It was necessary for him to present a happy, stable married life picture to the electorate.

On the inside of their home, however, things were not happy at all. They seldom spoke or ate meals together, and she not only no longer shared his bed but she wasn't even allowed in what had been *their* bedroom. She hadn't even argued that the new arrangement wasn't fair. "Hello," he said as he put his briefcase on the table.

"Hi." She glanced at him, then went back to watching TV.

"Where's Tara?"

"Upstairs." She looked at the clock. "Why are you home early?"

"I need to talk to you about something." He turned off the TV and sat in his favorite chair. "Has Kirby been acting strange lately?"

"No, why would you ask a thing like that?"

Derrick had already figured out a line of reasoning that would work with Mallory. "I heard Miss Allerman talking to one of the other secretaries from down the hall. It seems she had seen Kirby doing something very peculiar, but they stopped talking before I could hear what it was."

Mallory thought for a minute. "I can't think what it could have been. I know Kirby has been having problems with panic attacks from time to time, but I think they're not happening as often lately."

"What happens when she has these attacks?" Questioning Mallory was simple, he thought. She was so easily tricked into giving him the information he sought.

"I guess she just gets frightened. I remember she told me about one she had in Jordan's. She was exchanging that T-shirt she bought for Tara and had a panic attack while she was there. She said she ran out of the store with everyone staring at her."

"I see." Derrick looked thoughtful. "Anything else?"

"Before she started seeing Lauren again, she told me she was having some difficulty leaving the house. You know, like agoraphobia."

"That does sound bad."

"No, not really. She explained it to me. It's just that she was having trouble in actually leaving the house. Once she was in the car, she was fine. It wasn't really agoraphobia—it was only *like* it." She looked at him earnestly, a tiny frown line appearing between her brows. "There's nothing wrong with Kirby. Now that she's seeing Lauren regularly, she's gotten much better."

"I see."

"I wish you'd stop saying that. You sound as if you're in court." She reached for the remote control and clicked the TV back on.

Derrick scowled at her. He wondered if he had made a mistake in letting Russell convince him to give her another chance. He couldn't tell whether her weekly visits with a therapist were changing anything. She didn't see his frown because she was already engrossed again in the show she was watching.

As he was leaving the room, Mallory called out to him. "What?" he asked, not bothering to make his tone pleasant. Every time he saw her, that scene in their bedroom the day he came home early played again in his mind, always renewing his anger.

"There's something I want to talk to you about."

"Well?" He was impatient, ready to be on his way.

"I saw Lauren today. She thinks it might be a good idea for you to come in with me next week."

"What for? I'm not screwing around with anybody." He almost enjoyed the brief pain he saw on her face.

"It's not about that. It has to do with Tara."

"Tara? You leave her out of this. She's fine. Nothing is wrong with my daughter."

"Derrick, please say you'll go. It's very important! I want Lauren there when we talk about it."

"I'll tell you what's important! It's important not to let Addison know you're seeing a therapist! He would have my hide if he thought I was allowing you to go!"

She watched him for a moment with a puzzled expression. "Why are you?"

"Because as rotten as our marriage is, I don't want a divorce. I'm hoping she can get you straightened out so you'll behave and not screw around anymore."

"I see." Mallory gave him a cool, dispassionate look that reminded him of Addison.

"Now what's this crap about Tara?"

She turned back to the TV. "Never mind. I'll take care of it myself."

"Good!" he affirmed, but his bravado fell flat. What was going on? Was there a problem with Tara that he didn't know about? Derrick wasn't a man to show his emotions easily, but that didn't mean he didn't feel them inside. He had adored his daughter from the first moment he saw her. Surely if something was wrong, he would know it. In all his life, Derrick had only loved two people more than himself. He looked back at Mallory and wondered if he could ever love her again. "Shit!" he muttered as he pushed through the dining room door.

Derrick went into the kitchen and called Addison to give him what little information he had gleaned from Mallory.

"That's all you could come up with?" Addison growled.

"That's all there is! If Mallory doesn't know any more dirt, there isn't any. As you said, they talk all the time!"

Addison muttered a curse and hung up. Derrick slammed his own phone down. He hated being hung up on, especially twice in one day. If he wasn't so concerned that Addison would block his career, he wouldn't be trying to help him at all. He had no choice but to try to squeeze more information out of Mallory.

The next day Mallory met Kirby for lunch at Kirby's favorite Mexican café downtown. "I'm glad you could make it on such short notice," she said as they were seated. "Derrick is up to something."

"You mean like another woman?"

"Are you kidding? I doubt he remembers what to do with a woman," Mallory said acidly. "He's still not sleeping with me. He makes me so mad!"

"So what is he doing?" Kirby ordered a taco salad and iced tea.

Mallory ordered the same. "He keeps asking me questions about you."

"About me? What sort of questions?"

"Stupid ones. Like is anything bothering you and do you still have panic attacks. Things like that. As if he really cared!"

"What have you told him?"

Mallory shrugged. "Nothing really. There's nothing to tell. I just thought you should know he was asking."

Kirby tapped her water glass thoughtfully. "Remember me telling you that I called some senators and wrote letters about Dad being a child molester?" She kept her voice lowered. "Even though they all responded to me as if I were some kind of kook, it may have something to do with that. One of them may have decided to check into my story and called Derrick since he's my brother-in-law and the head of Dad's law firm."

"I knew you shouldn't have done that." Mallory shifted uneasily in her chair. "If that's what has happened and if Derrick tells Dad, which he's sure to do, Dad's going to be furious!"

"He's been mad before. I can't let him get this appointment, knowing what we know." She studied her sister warily. "Are you getting cold feet?"

"Of course I am! This is damned scary!" Mallory hissed the words, then glanced at the neighboring diners to see if she had been overheard. "I'm afraid of him! You should be, too!"

"I am, but I have to do this anyway."

"I don't know, Kirby. If he got this appointment, he would have to move to Washington and he wouldn't be so close to Tara. You don't know how difficult it is to keep him away from her! Mom is asking all sorts of questions. So is Derrick."

"Tell them what happened."

"I can't do that! Mom would go all to pieces and Derrick would call me a liar and make my life even more miserable. I've tried to get him to go with me to see Lauren, so I could tell him there, but he won't go. You know he won't believe me without Lauren to back me up."

Kirby sighed. "I suppose you're right. But they have to know eventually. It's the only way you can protect Tara when you're not around."

Mallory nodded unhappily. "I'm around a lot more often than I used to be." It was true. Since she began counseling with Lauren, Mallory had been able to quell most of her compulsion to pick up men. She had had only two slips in the past month. She hadn't left Tara with her parents either time and never would again. "I haven't been much of a mother these last few years. I can see that now."

"You can't blame yourself. It should be safe to leave a child with her grandparents. You didn't know."

Mallory nodded, even though that wasn't strictly true. Unlike Kirby, she remembered what had happened. Lauren was helping her see how she had compartmentalized that memory and had convinced herself that Addison would never do such a thing again. "God, this is all so confusing! Life used to be so simple!"

"I know. Maybe it will be again someday." She straightened as the waiter put the salad and drinks on the table. "Do you know what I think? I think the reason Derrick was asking you about me is because Dad wants to know."

"I don't see how you having panic attacks has anything to do with Dad." Mallory salted her salad and started to eat.

"If he knows what I've told some of the members of the judiciary committee, he may have decided to defend himself by trying to discredit me. If he can find something that would make me seem eccentric or unstable, he could use that as an excuse for my having made that accusation about him."

"That never occurred to me. Did I do wrong in telling Derrick about the panic attacks?"

"No. At least I don't think so."

Mallory ate slowly. "I'll be more careful in the future. I'm glad I came down to tell you."

"So am I. Let me know if Derrick or Dad ask you any more questions."

On the north side of Houston in an older, rundown neighborhood, Bill Davies was standing outside a weather-beaten house trying to appear casual as he looked up and down the street to be sure no one was watching him. Wearing faded jeans with torn knees and a T-shirt imprinted with a beer slogan that was barely legible due to its many washings, he felt certain that if anyone did see him, he wouldn't look out of place.

No one attempted to stop him as he sauntered around the house to the back. An elderly woman across the fence was hanging dingy wet clothes on a line to dry. If she noticed him, she ignored him. He banged on the back door as he had on the front. As before, there was no answer. He hadn't expected one.

According to his confidential source, no one lived in this house. It was used for a different purpose.

At one time it had been a crack house. Davies had been in on the bust that led to the arrest of the four drug dealers who were selling crack to kids in the neighborhood. The county deed records showed the house had been owned by a string of businesses over the past several years, all of which were no longer in existence, and he had thought that was strange. Usually the drug dealers didn't go to that much trouble to conceal their tracks. They typically rented a place or borrowed it from a relative. Making drugs and trafficking them was generally an activity that required anything but a permanent location.

Davies had been keeping an eye on the house for that reason. He had seen activity around it for several months, but nothing that led back to drugs. That had also seemed curious. There was enough traffic to and from the house for something to be going on. His informant suggested it might be prostitution.

Davies had filed the information away for later use until the day he saw Gary Chandler leaving it. He had been so surprised, he had almost blown his cover.

He waited until the old woman next door finished hanging out clothes and went into her house, then kicked the rotted screen loose on the door, unlatched it, and went in.

The house had no furniture to speak of. Rags, bottles, beer cans, and other trash were strewn throughout. As he moved quietly through the house, roaches scurried for cover, and in one room he saw a rat digging in a pile of rubble.

When he reached the room in the middle of the house, he knew he had found something of real interest. Unlike the other rooms, this one had a bed against one wall. The sheets were grimy and unmade, the pillow looked greasy. Across from the bed was a tripod and a cheap video camera. It took no mental giant to conclude that the setup was there for making porno movies.

He started searching more thoroughly. In the top of the closet, he found several unmarked videotapes. The boxes were opened as if they had been used. Davies put one in the camera, rewound it, and watched several seconds of the video. In disgust, he pulled it out and shoved it into his jeans under his shirt. Kiddie porn! The worst of all.

He searched carefully for any clue as to who was using this place but wasn't optimistic that he'd find anything. The people involved with this apparently were pros and had left few signs. He wasn't too surprised that Chandler was involved in child pornography, given his arrest record for child molesting. That went together. But Davies' instincts told him there was something here that he was overlooking.

He left the bedroom and went into the kitchen. It was as filthy as the rest of the house. As he was passing through, he saw a piece of paper stuck in the door jamb. A telephone number was scrawled on it.

Davies copied down the number and left the house before any of the neighbors got curious enough to come see what he was doing there. The phone number might lead him to whoever was behind the porno operation. It might even lead to Chandler and a conviction that would stick this time.

Gary Chandler parked his car in the weedy driveway of an apparently deserted house in a north Houston neighborhood for the second time in two weeks. He rarely came to the house this often, but he had been depressed lately over his pending trial. Getting caught with the McIntyre girl had been the stupidest move of his life.

But she had been so sweet.

As usual, Gary glanced around before leaving his car. He had parked as always at the far end of the drive which curved into the backyard, so his car wouldn't be visible from the street. Even so, he was taking a big chance coming here during the day. If he was seen here and the use of the house became known to the authorities, it would mean a certain conviction.

The back door was unlocked and the screen torn loose. His brow furrowed and his eyes narrowed speculatively. This house had been chosen because it looked like the last place a burglar would strike. Only a handful of people knew what went on here.

He pushed open the door and listened. The house was quiet. Carefully Gary moved inside, pausing now and then to listen for sounds. He went directly to the room used for making the movies.

Everything seemed to be there, nothing stolen. If someone had broken in with theft in mind, the video camera and tripod would be gone. Maybe Eddy had left the door open by accident, even though it was most unlikely. Eddy had been chosen because he made very few mistakes. This wasn't an undertaking where mistakes could be overlooked.

They had quite a ring set up. Gary had only been to one actual filming session but he hoped to come to others. Eddy Compton made the tapes, duplicated them himself, and handled sales. A swarthy man Chandler didn't want to know supplied the kids. Where he got them, Chandler also didn't know. Eddy once told him they were runaways, and Gary thought that was probably true of the teenagers, but he had a feeling the little ones were being kidnapped. It was the little ones that Chandler was interested in.

He opened the closet door. Eddy had said his tape was ready and he could pick it up whenever he could come by. It was the same arrangement they had used for months, though he always had come at night before. Chandler felt around on the top shelf for his tape, found two, but neither had the mark that identified them as the one meant for him. Names were never used, only a coded symbol. As far as Chandler knew, Eddy didn't even know Chandler's real name. Eddy couldn't be trusted that far.

Stretching up on tiptoe, Chandler reached farther onto the shelf. Aside from a couple of dead bugs, there was nothing there.

He closed the door and frowned. It wasn't like Eddy to say a tape was ready and then not produce it. Eddy had his faults, but he was dependable in that respect.

With his next thought, fear rippled through him. What if the tape had somehow fallen into the hands of the police? Maybe

Eddy was setting him up in order to get out of some drug charge. The tape would be incriminating. He was on it.

He cursed himself for being so stupid as to let Eddy talk him into being on the tape. At the time it had been erotic. He was high and not thinking clearly enough to realize how dangerous that could be.

Chandler hurried out of the house and drove away.

As soon as he was out of the unsavory neighborhood, he picked up his car phone and dialed the number of his primary contact. "Addison," he said. "I think we've got a problem."

"What the hell are you doing calling me? I told you not to call me at work."

"I know, but this can't wait." Chandler maneuvered his car onto the freeway. "I've been at the house. My tape is gone."

"What tape? I don't know what you're talking about." Addison sounded as if he was about to hang up.

"Eddy made a tape the other night. I was to pick up my copy today. It's missing. Someone has been in the house."

"That's crazy. Why would anybody break in there and steal your tape?"

"What if Eddy is trying to set me up? You know he's been in trouble lately with all the drugs he uses. Maybe he's made a deal with the police."

"So what if he did? All he would do is implicate himself. There's nothing to tie you into the tape."

Chandler swallowed nervously. "Yes, there is. Eddy talked me into being filmed, too."

"What!" Addison's bellow made Chandler's ears ring.

"I was high at the time. I wasn't thinking straight. How was I to know the tape would turn up missing? Say, you don't think he'll distribute it around here, do you? Somebody might recognize me."

"You dumb sonofabitch!" Addison bellowed. Then he became quiet for a minute. "You've got to get out of the country."

"I can't do that! I'm out on bail!"

"Would you rather forfeit your bail money collateral or lose your freedom? If Eddy is double-crossing you, you have no choice."

"Where would I go? I've got a job---"

"Shut up and listen. I'll make arrangements for you to be on a midnight flight." There was a pause as if Addison was consulting his watch. "Damn! I have to make a flight of my own in less than an hour." There was another brief silence. "Be at Intercontinental Airport at midnight. I don't know which flight I can get you on and I don't have time to call you back. I'll leave instructions at the airport. Call your office and tell them you're sick and won't be in for a couple of days. And whatever you do, don't tell anyone you're about to leave town! Got it?"

"Sure. I've got it." Chandler swerved angrily around a slow-moving car. "I'll be at the airport tonight at midnight."

Addison hung up and stared at his phone for several minutes. "Sonofabitch!" he muttered. Then he dialed a number he had committed to memory.

"Eddy? Chandler is breaking. That's right. You've got to take him out. No, go to the airport and wait. He plans to be on a flight at midnight. No, I don't care how you do it, just do it!" He slammed the receiver down and leaned back in his chair. "Goddamned sonofabitch!" he repeated angrily.

Seconds later, his phone rang again. Forcing himself to be calm, he said, "Walker here." When the party calling didn't respond, he hung up the phone. It had to have been someone dialing a wrong number. Only his family and a few select others had the number to his private line. He hoped it wasn't Chandler trying to back out.

He could hardly believe Chandler had been so stupid as to let Eddy put him in a porno film. Addison had never known anyone who was as obsessive about sex. If Chandler had free rein, that was all he would do, in Addison's estimation. Usually that didn't bother him---his own sexual appetites were strong--- but to let himself be filmed!

Addison punched in the phone number for a travel agency. If Eddy screwed up, Addison wanted Chandler out of the country. Whatever happened, Addison didn't want to be implicated in Chandler's murder. Police investigators were certain to check the airport to see if Chandler was leaving town or picking someone up. Before becoming a judge, Addison had been a good lawyer. He knew how to close loopholes.

He booked Chandler on a flight to Toronto. He hoped Chandler had an up-to-date passport. Otherwise he would be stopped by Customs and sent back. But Chandler couldn't blame him for that.

Addison thought carefully, trying to see this dilemma from every angle. Was there anything that tied him to Chandler? Every base seemed to be covered, and he would be in Washington, D.C., when the murder or flight occurred. He hoped Eddy would be successful. There was less chance for a screwup if Chandler was completely out of the picture.

He glanced impatiently at his watch. If he didn't hurry, he would miss his own flight. Addison wanted to be far from Houston by midnight.

Pasting on his most fatherly smile, Addison picked up the suitcase and garment bag he had brought from home. His secretary looked up as he passed, and he gave her a congenial wink.

"Have a nice flight, Judge," she called after him.

"Thank you," Addison replied. Everything was falling into place, just as he had planned. If Eddy killed Chandler, there should be no glitches in his appointment to the Supreme Court.

Addison wanted this appointment so badly he could taste it. He hurried out of the building and flagged down a cab. He was on his way to real power! Addison smiled as the cab threaded its way through the traffic.

Davies dialed Kirby's office number. "I've got news. You're not going to like it much."

"What did you find?"

"I went to a house near the Heights that's being used for making kiddie porn. There were videotapes. The one I brought home has Chandler in it."

"Damn!" she exclaimed. "I had no idea he was into it that far!"

"That's not all. I found a phone number in the kitchen. When I dialed it just now, your father answered. My guess is it was a private line into his office, since I didn't have to go through a secretary.''

Kirby was dead silent.

"Hello? Are you still there?"

"Yes. Yes, I'm here. Could you give me that number, please?''

Davies read it to her. "I'm afraid there's more. I was able to pull some strings and find out who owns the house. It was sold at auction several years ago after it was confiscated in a drug bust. The high bidder was Falco Industries out of San Antonio. A few months later Falco sold it to an Oklahoma-based company which then sold it to an outfit in Alabama. All of those companies no longer exist, but a friend of mine who works for the State of Alabama did some digging and has reason to believe that one certain Michael Rousher, the principal in the Alabama company, was an alias for none other than Addison Walker." He waited for her to recover her poise. He had to hand it to her, though. She didn't go to pieces as he had been afraid she might. "I'm sorry I had to tell you all this."

"That's all right. I had to know. Thank you." Her voice sounded stiff, as if she were fighting down emotions.

"That's okay. Let me know if I can do anything else for you.''

"Are you sure about the alias being my father's?''

"No proof yet, but my friend thinks he can get it."

"Get that tape to Gunderman as soon as you can. And don't say anything to him or anyone else about my father's possible connection with this until I've had a chance to talk to Zimmerman.''

"Sure thing.''

Kirby hung up and buried her face in her hands.

It was what she needed, but the impact was no less shattering. Her father was somehow linked to a child pornography ring! She had never suspected anything like this. No wonder he had overturned Chandler's molestation conviction. Chandler could have implicated Addison.

At last she had a way to stop her father from moving into a position of such enormous power that he could make it easier for sick people like himself to prey on innocent children. When she had better control of herself, she called Detective Gunderman and told him she had proof on its way to his office that Gary Chandler was involved in the making of child pornographic movies. Gunderman agreed to get right on it and thanked her for her help.

She hung up without telling him her father might also be implicated. Although Addison's private line phone number had been found there, she had no idea how deeply he might be involved. He would argue that his number could have been written down by anyone and left there for a perfectly legitimate reason. He was, after all, a judge. It could have been placed there by someone who had a reason to call him in his official capacity, or even by a person who intended to make threatening calls to his office. He could argue that he had no knowledge of why his phone number was there and that he had nothing to do with these people. Even finding out that he owned the house where the illegal tapes were being made didn't mean he knew what was happening there. The connection was still tenuous.

As she rose from her desk to go see Zimmerman, there was a knock on her door and Zimmerman pushed it open.

"Leon, I was just coming to see you. I just got off the phone with Gunderman. Gary Chandler is going to be picked up by the police sometime today. It seems he had a business venture on the side. He was making child pornographic videos."

"What?" he exclaimed.

She nodded. "I just talked to Bill Davies. He has physical evidence to back it up."

"So we nailed the bastard!" Zimmerman grinned broadly. "Why don't you seem happy about this?"

"Dad's phone number was also found at the house. And through a circuitous route, it appears that Dad may be the owner of the house through use of an alias. Now that I have what I needed, I almost wish I didn't."

Zimmerman's grin faded as the implication sank in. After a moment he said, "You're not suggesting that we use what you have to try to stop your father's nomination, are you? Granted, if he's involved in something like this, his career is over! But we don't dare breathe a word about this until we have enough evidence for an indictment, assuming we can get enough hard evidence. His phone number being at the house is just circumstantial and his—"

"Wait, Leon. I know this isn't enough. I don't yet know for sure that he *is* involved, but I think we have enough to leak our investigation to the press. And I'm sure the President will have someone talk to us to find out what we have. It only makes sense. Stansfield wouldn't want the embarrassment of nominating someone who was under investigation in connection to a child pornography ring."

"Kirby! Wait just a minute. Do you realize you're suggesting that I stick my neck out like this, with only another two years until I can retire from this job? All this is too preliminary. What if we're wrong? Both our careers will be over."

"I know that, Leon. But what if Chandler confesses and names Addison as an accomplice? And we don't have to leak it until we have better proof. You know as well as I do that if my father is confirmed as an Associate Justice of the United States Supreme Court, we will be fighting against the whole Washington machine. We'd have to wait for him to be impeached before we could try him, wouldn't we?"

With Leon's face growing red with anger, he said, "I don't know. I've never been involved in trying to put a Supreme Court Justice in jail before."

"I'm sorry, Leon. I shouldn't have been pushing so hard. I know this has hit you cold. It's just that I *must* stop my father and this could be the way to do it."

"Please try to understand—" A knock on her office door stopped Leon in midsentence.

"Come in," Kirby called out.

It was Mrs. Parsons, beaming from ear to ear. "There's something on the radio I think you ought to hear."

Kirby nodded and Mrs. Parsons rushed in with a portable radio in hand. A news reporter was announcing that President Stansfield had placed the name of Judge Addison Walker before the Senate Judiciary Committee as his nominee to fill the vacant position of Supreme Court Justice and that there appeared to be no reason for opposition from any of the committee's members. The hearing before the committee was expected to be routine and swift, the vote likely to be unanimous approval of Walker, with confirmation by the Senate to follow soon after.

Mrs. Parsons clicked off the radio. "Isn't this just wonderful news! Mrs. Garrett, I know you must be so proud of your father. A Supreme Court Justice. Just think."

Kirby tried to force a smile for Mrs. Parsons' sake but couldn't. "Thank you, Mrs. Parsons. If you'll excuse us."

The DA's secretary took the hint and quietly left.

Kirby looked across at Zimmerman. "I have to have tomorrow off. Call it sick leave or vacation, I don't care which."

"What are you going to do?"

"I'm flying to Washington to take care of this personally. I'm out of time now."

"But how are you going to do it?"

"I don't know. But I will! I have to! Whatever I do, I won't involve this office without your permission. I promise."

"But maybe I'm wrong. It has all come so quickly, I haven't had time to sort all this out."

"No, Leon. You were right. You've worked too hard for too many years to jeopardize your retirement now. Maybe I can delay things until we have the proof we need. I'll be staying at the Mayflower in D.C. Call me if you get anything from Chandler that will help."

Zimmerman nodded. "Do take care of yourself, and take whatever time you need."

"If, God forbid, something happens to me, you're the only one other than Davies who knows Dad is somehow involved with Chandler. I didn't tell that part to Gunderman."

"If need be, I'll take care of it. You be extra careful. It's possible this porno ring may have connections as far away as Washington. There's no telling how big this thing is. The Mafia may even be involved. Keep yourself safe and don't take any chances."

She smiled. "I'm always careful." She hoped she looked more confident than she felt. She didn't want Leon to worry.

She asked one of the other assistant DAs to take the Abernathy case for her. She had an interview scheduled with the man and his attorney that afternoon and knew the case wouldn't take much background work. Abernathy had been caught in the act of robbing a convenience store and was expected to plead guilty. Her conscience wouldn't bother her since it was such an open-and-shut case.

As she drove home to pack, her thoughts bombarded her. Was it possible that her father was really involved in this? Despite what she now remembered of the incest, it was a big leap for her to accept that he might be part of a child pornography ring. If she thought confronting him over what he did to her at home was difficult, accusing him of this was infinitely worse.

She had to have proof.

As soon as she had packed and called Russell to tell him where she was going, she drove to her parents' house. She couldn't search his judge's chambers for evidence without a search warrant, but as his daughter, she had access to his house. Kirby hated doing this; it left an acrid taste in her mouth.

She recalled all too clearly the image of the man she was trying to topple. As if to urge herself to back away from this, she found herself thinking of Addison as he had been only months before. He was handsome, kindly, fair—the sort of father any girl would want. A father who bestowed generous gifts on his daughters and spoke of them to others with pride.

But she knew too much now. In reality the icon of Addison Walker that she had revered was severely flawed. The generous gifts he'd given always had had a high price connected with them, and his pride in her had been that of an owner, not a father. Kirby had once viewed some child pornography material during the course of a trial, and it had made her physically ill. Now she knew there was good reason for her reaction. If Addison was involved in this, even if he had never touched a child sexually, he had to be stopped.

Kirby was determined to do just that.

Chapter Twenty-Six

Jane looked at Kirby in confusion. "Your father isn't here, honey. You know that. He's flying up to Washington for the Senate confirmation hearings. He won't be home for at least two or three days."

"I know, Mom. I didn't come to see Dad. I only need to look in his safe."

"I understand, but that's not possible without him being here."

"Are you saying you don't have the combination? If he has nothing to hide, why wouldn't he give you the combination to a safe in your own house?"

Jane shook her head. "It's not that he's hiding anything. You know how your father is. He hates for anyone to mess about in his things. Especially me. He's told me hundreds of times not to clean his desk or to go into his office here when he's not at home."

"Mom, I have to look in there. If you don't have the combination, I'll have to call a locksmith or someone who can get it open." Kirby hated to pressure her mother like this, but she felt she had no choice.

"What is it that you think you'll find? What could possibly be so important it can't wait until he's home again?"

Kirby drew in a deep breath. "Mom, you're not going to

like this, but you're going to have to know sooner or later. Dad molested me as a child. He hurt Mallory, too."

Jane shook her head, and as her face crumpled, the color left her cheeks. "No, that's not possible. I would have known."

"Tara says she told you about Dad kissing her and you said it should be a secret between the two of you."

"That's because there was nothing to it. All grandfathers kiss their grandchildren and no one thinks a thing about it. It's all this junk on TV. It's putting ideas into Tara's head."

"No, Mom. You're wrong about this. I've talked to her, and from what she told me, Dad has been molesting her."

"But on TV—"

"Unless she's been watching X-rated movies, she couldn't have seen this on TV."

Jane began batting her watery eyes to hold back the tears. "I don't know what to say! Your father just wouldn't do something like this."

"Then prove I'm wrong. Let me look in Dad's safe." Kirby knew this was a long shot. Addison might not have anything in his possession that would tie him to Chandler and pornography. On the other hand, he might, and his safe seemed the most logical place to look. Before she left to go to Washington to try to stop him, she had do this one last thing.

For a moment Jane wavered, then nodded. "All right. I will. But you're not going to find anything and don't you ever tell your father that I know the combination."

Addison's home office, like his judge's chambers, was perfectly neat with everything in its place, just the way Addison liked his belongings. Kirby knew Jane would never have come in the room without permission. It was Addison's lair.

While Jane turned the dial on the wall safe hidden behind a painting, Kirby thumbed through the Rolodex on Addison's desk. There was no listing for Gary Chandler, but she hadn't expected to find one. He was too careful to write down anything that could be incriminating and leave it in plain sight.

"There," Jane said as the safe swung silently open. "Why, what are these? Why on earth would Addison put videotapes in the safe?" She took out three tapes and stared at them in amazement. "What an odd thing for him to do."

Kirby took them from her. They were a common brand that could be purchased anywhere and were unmarked, but the boxes had been opened. She looked in the safe, and in addition to the usual papers that might be found there, she also discovered several eight-millimeter films. Unlike the videos, they were the sort that could be bought only in stores that sold pornography. One was titled *Children of the Dark;* another was *Little Suzy.* Kirby didn't read further.

"I don't understand. What are these?"

Kirby stared down at the evidence. Until now part of her hadn't wanted to believe Bill Davies' report. "I think they're kiddie porn."

"No. That's not possible. They must be something else. Your father would never . . ." Jane let her words trail off.

"There's one way to find out." Kirby took the unmarked videotapes into the den and put one in the VCR. She stepped back and looked at the screen.

She heard her mother's muffled gasp from the doorway behind her. What they were seeing couldn't be misconstrued.

Kirby hastily shut off the tape. She couldn't look at her mother.

"I don't see how it's possible," Jane murmured, stunned. "I thought I knew him as well as I know myself!"

"Until this afternoon it never occurred to me that he could be into something like this either," Kirby said as she returned the video to its box. "I thought there must be some mistake."

"What does this mean?" Jane seemed confused. "The Senate will never make him a justice if they ever hear about this."

"I know. Mom, he hasn't been implicated yet, but something big is about to break. I'm going to take these tapes home. I can't leave them here and risk having him destroy them."

"Can't we just throw them away? I can put them in the trash and get rid of them." Tears brimmed in Jane's eyes.

"No, Mom. You can't throw them away. That would be tampering with evidence and you could be arrested. Do you understand?"

Jane nodded, her eyes large and miserable. A single tear rolled down her cheek and she made no move to wipe it away.

''But if we get rid of them, maybe no one will be upset with Addison.''

''No, Mom. It's not just a matter of him owning illegal tapes. What about the things he did to Mallory and me? To Tara?''

Jane sank slowly into the nearest chair and stared at the tapes in Kirby's hands. ''He could be arrested, couldn't he? Those videos—where would he get such things?''

''I'm reasonably certain these were made in a house in north Houston. We know the address. The police are rounding up the suspects now. I'm not sure how deeply Dad is involved.''

''What are you going to do?''

''I'm going to Washington.'' She checked her watch. ''I have to go now or miss my flight.''

''Are you going to confront him about these tapes?''

''No, I'm going to confront him about what he did to Mallory, Tara, and me. I won't allow him to get away with it or for him to be placed in a position where he could affect laws on pornography and molestation. I'm not sure what his connection is with the men who made these tapes but I can't wait around to find out.''

''But maybe—''

''Can't you see it would be even worse if he's arrested after he's appointed to the Supreme Court? Then it will reflect badly on our entire country.''

Jane caught Kirby's arm. ''Are you going to Washington just to get even with him? I've tried to raise you not to be spiteful. Why tell everyone what he did here at the house? Maybe he thought it was all right to act the way he did. You know what his side of the family is like. They don't know how to love. Not a single one of them!''

''No, any adult would know not to do what he did. There's no way to make excuses for him. He hurt all of us, including you. He has physically and emotionally abused us all my life. If I don't speak out, no one will ever know what he did, and I intend to be certain that doesn't happen.''

''But to act out of spite—''

''I'm not being spiteful. I'm protecting myself as I couldn't do when I was a child. I won't bring Tara's name into it if I can help it. The publicity would hurt her too badly. I've talked to Mallory and she agrees that this is the best thing to do. We're not going to sweep this under the rug and pretend it never happened!''

"Is Mallory going to Washington with you?"

"No, she can't bring herself to do it. I'm going alone. Please tell me you won't stop loving me for doing what I feel I have to do." Kirby had worried about this ever since she had decided to do all she could to keep Addison from being placed on the Court. She was determined to right the wrong done to her, but she was afraid it would destroy forever the love between her and her mother.

"All your life I've heard Addison tell you girls not to do anything that you wouldn't want printed in the newspaper. If it applied to you two, it must apply to him as well." Jane stood and hugged Kirby for a long moment. "Be careful, honey. You know what he can be like when he's angry."

"He's not going to hurt me or anyone else anymore."

Despite her brave words, Kirby was quaking inside. Addison would be furious, and she knew all too well how violent he could become. Jane was now in danger, too, because she had opened his safe and given Kirby the evidence she needed. Kirby could understand all too well why Mallory was starting to balk and make excuses for not getting more directly involved. Like Jane, Mallory was well trained to refrain from making waves.

Waves? This would be a hurricane!

Kirby was afraid, too. She knew Russell would protect her from physical harm, but her legal career could well be doomed. If she followed through on this—and she felt she had no choice but to do so—she had to stop Addison and put him in prison. If he wasn't locked away, she would be in great danger.

For a minute Kirby considered following Mallory's example. The Chandler investigation would reveal Addison's involvement and do the job for her. She could pretend to have known nothing about it and minimize the risk to herself. But the loss of self-esteem was too great a price to pay.

No! She was going to see this through, to be certain he was stopped and to show him she had done it. She owed it to herself for all those years of sexual, physical, and emotional abuse.

Kirby was determined never to waver again.

* * *

Kirby breezed into the Capitol Building, out of breath from the many steps out front, her mind so focused on her mission that she was hardly aware of the auspicious surroundings. Never having been there before and unsure in which direction to go, she stopped a young woman in the hall who identified herself as a Senate page. The woman volunteered to lead her to the chambers where the Senate Judiciary Committee was conducting its hearings. She thanked the page and approached the massive doors to the committee room. A uniformed guard stopped her and asked her name.

As he skimmed through a list of names on his clipboard, Kirby said, ''I doubt that you'll find my name there, but I want to address the committee.''

He looked at her as if she had lost her mind. ''You can't do that. They're conducting Judge Addison Walker's confirmation hearing.''

''I know. That's why I have to speak to them.''

''That's impossible. You aren't on the agenda. You'll have to contact the office of the committee chairman, Senator Mieckle, to discuss that possibility.''

''You don't understand, I'm Judge Walker's daughter.''

''That may be, but Judge Walker didn't put you on his list of invited guests.''

''I'm not on the list because he didn't expect me to be able to come because of my work,'' she lied. ''Can't you make one small exception? I'll be quiet as a church mouse.'' She put on her most guileless face.

''I suppose so, since you are his daughter. But don't tell anyone I did this, okay? If you want to observe, you can go in and sit in the back, but you have to be quiet.''

Kirby thanked the guard and quietly entered the hearing chambers. The room was filled, mostly by press people from the looks of them. Her father was sitting behind a large table in the center of the room. Facing him were the members of the judiciary committee. She recognized Senators Mays and Frederickson and others to whom she had sent letters and made phone calls.

Standing against the walls of the large room at about twenty-foot intervals, all dressed alike in dark suits with conservative ties, were men she assumed to be either Secret Service, FBI, or plainclothes guards of some sort. She was aware that several of them were watching her every move. Kirby slipped into the nearest chair to listen to the proceedings.

Addison's voice was strong, and from the expressions on the committee members' faces, his answers were what they wanted to hear. He was, after all, intelligent and knowledgeable. He looked like the perfect father figure, a perfect judge. There was nothing on record that could hinder him from becoming an Associate Justice of the Supreme Court of the United States. She knew that. The image of his public and private life was exemplary. Knowing what she did of him now, she was amazed that he had managed to maintain it so perfectly.

Since leaving her father's house and throughout the long flight to Washington, she had gone over in her mind hundreds of scenarios, where she could confront her father, what she should say to him, how much of his possible connection to the pornography ring she should mention to convince him to voluntarily withdraw from the confirmation process. She had been unable to settle on one that she thought was best. And now the time was drawing near when she would have to confront him.

As she stared at him, almost mesmerized by his charisma, her thoughts drifted to a time when he was younger, before his hair had turned silver. He had been dark and handsome. She had often seen women flirt with him, sometimes quite openly. He had never followed up on any of their advances, as far as she knew. Now that the memories she had repressed were returning, this made sense. They had been too old for him. Revulsion struck her like a lightning bolt.

"No!" she shouted as she leaped to her feet. Her voice resounded in the room. Heads swiveled in several directions, looking for whoever had shouted. "No! You can't appoint him to the Supreme Court!"

Several of the dark-suited men were running toward her. Kirby moved farther into the row of seats to evade them. "I'm

Kirby Walker Garrett! You don't know what he's done! He molested me as well as my sister!"

One of the men reached for her and Kirby jerked away. To the astounded senators she shouted, "You have to listen to me! Addison Walker isn't the man you want! You can't appoint him to the court! He's a child molester!"

The nearest man grabbed her, and Kirby felt him hauling her backward over the seats. She struggled to free herself. She continued to shout at the senators but even in her near-hysteria she knew she was damaging her case irrevocably.

Another man came to assist the one who was half-carrying her to the door. Kirby fought against them but her struggles were futile and she knew it. They deposited her none too gently in the hallway outside the committee room. A uniformed policeman was coming her way.

"All right," Kirby said, fighting to regain her composure. "I'm okay. I'm sorry. I didn't mean to—" She bit off her words. There was no excuse for what she had done. Tears sprang to her eyes. "I'll leave quietly."

The policeman escorted her to the door and she felt him watching her as she went down the bank of steps. She couldn't remember being so embarrassed in her entire life. For a person who kept her emotions so in check that she couldn't even allow herself to cry, she had done the unthinkable. She touched her cheeks and found them wet with tears. Shakily she hailed a cab and curled tightly in a corner of the back seat as it carried her back to her hotel. Just thinking about confronting him had panicked her so badly that she had become irrational. She was going to have to think of another way.

When she was back in her hotel room, she collapsed on the bed, exhausted. She wanted so badly to prevent Addison from moving into a position of power where he could further dilute the laws against child molesters, laws which were already so difficult to enforce that innocent children continued to be victimized while the perpetrators of these horrible crimes went unpunished. Somehow she had to prevent Addison from being placed in the highest court in the land. Who knew what damage he could do to the laws that were already too lenient?

With anger supplanting her fear and feelings of frustration, she got to her feet and fumbled through her purse until she found the list of phone numbers of the Senate committee members. Somehow she would have to find a way to talk with them in private, to convince them that she was not crazy. Methodically she called every name on the list. One by one, the responses were the same: the senators were in meetings and would be told of her call and request for an appointment as soon as they returned.

Kirby had no choice but to sit in her room and pace while she waited for someone to return her call.

By seven that evening, none had done so. Not wanting to keep the phone tied up lest she get a late evening call, Kirby made a quick call to Russell to tell him what was going on, assure him she was all right—which wasn't entirely true—and gave him her love. Frustrated, Kirby ordered a sandwich from room service and spent the remainder of the evening picking at the sandwich and looking at the television but paying no attention whatsoever.

She fell asleep with the set on but awoke abruptly to find the late night news on and a reporter discussing the progress of Addison Walker's confirmation hearings. Instantly she was alert. The station showed a sound bite with Addison smiling broadly and answering a question in the committee chamber. He looked fatherly, powerful, wise. In his summation, the reporter said the hearings were going smoothly and should result in unanimous confirmation. No mention was made of her outburst. That was news. It was controversial. Had Addison managed to get control of the press, too?

Kirby grabbed the remote control and snapped off the TV. What little sleep she got the remainder of the night was disturbed by a nightmare in which she was stuck in quicksand and was slowly sinking with no chance for help.

The next morning at nine she started calling senators' offices again. This time the secretaries were noticeably cooler toward her, some saying that the senators' calendars were full for the next several weeks and they were sorry they would not be able to meet with her during this visit to Washington. Unwittingly, she had destroyed her own credibility. She felt sure that after her outburst, Addison had done an excellent job of convincing the senators that his daughter was unbalanced, angry with him, and trying to cause trouble.

Only seconds after hanging up from the last of her calls, the phone beside her bed rang. It was Zimmerman. "Leon? Do you have something on Chandler? Did he implicate my father?"

"Unfortunately, the police didn't get to him in time. Chandler was shot to death on the way to the airport. It looks as if he was trying to get out of the country; a ticket to Canada was being held for him. He was shot as he was turning off Jetero Boulevard."

"Damn!"

"The police have a suspect in custody. His name is Eddy Compton. He's coming off a drug high and has the DTs so bad he's confessed to being the serial killer who was executed two weeks ago, robbing a bank in Chicago, and a bunch of other crimes that never happened. He's either very screwed up or very smart. Either way he appears to be loony tunes. I'm not sure we'll get anything useful from him for days, even if then."

"What about Dad? Did Compton mention him at all?"

"No. Not yet, but it might still happen. When we told him we were questioning him in regard to the murder of Gary Chandler, I thought I could see a glimmer of recognition in his eye but he denied knowing anyone by that name. The police have gone to the house where the movies are made. If Davies left Addison's number where he found it, it's only a matter of time before they begin looking for some connection to him."

"Thanks for letting me know." She stepped into her shoes as she talked. "I have to run. One way or another, I'm going to see to it that Dad doesn't win this one."

She hung up and caught a cab to the White House.

By the time she got there, a line of tourists was forming for the first tour of the day. Kirby circled around them and went to one of the guards at the gate. "I'm Kirby Garrett. My father is Judge Addison Walker and I need to see the President."

"That's not possible, ma'am."

"You don't understand. He knows who I am. He and my father are close friends."

"Yes, ma'am. I recognize Judge Walker's name. But I have no authorization to let you in. I have to follow orders."

Kirby had known this was a long shot. "Could you just call President Stansfield? Maybe he'll see me even though I don't have an appointment."

After several minutes of discussion, the guard called his superior. He spoke so quietly into the phone, Kirby couldn't hear the words. After hanging up, he turned to her. "I'm sorry, ma'am. I can't let you in. The President is too busy today to see anyone."

"Is that true, or was word left that he won't see me specifically?"

The man looked uncomfortable. "I believe the message was that he won't be able to see you specifically."

"I see. Thank you." She turned and walked back down the line of tourists, who were frankly staring at her. She wasn't going to give up. Addison also had gotten to Raymond Stansfield, but there still had to be a way.

She went to a public phone and reached into her purse for coins. Maybe Raymond wouldn't see her, but his wife might.

After nearly an hour of talking to secretaries and arguing with officials, she got Virginia Stansfield on the line.

"Kirby Garrett! How nice to hear your voice." The First Lady obviously hadn't gotten the word that Kirby was to be avoided. "Are you in town on business?"

"Not exactly." Kirby glanced out at the traffic and a man who was waiting to use the phone. "I know it's an imposition, but could I possibly see you for a few minutes?"

"I have a little while before I'm scheduled to go to a meeting. Where are you?"

"In Washington. And I can be at the White House in five minutes."

Chapter Twenty-Seven

"I'm not sure where to start," Kirby said when she was seated in Virginia Stansfield's private office.

"I'm afraid I don't understand. You look as if something is bothering you."

Kirby glanced at the open door to the secretary's office. "What I have to say has to be private."

Virginia got up and closed the door. "There now. Is that better?"

"Yes, thank you." On the short ride to the White House Kirby had rehearsed in her mind what to say so she would sound rational, in the event that Addison had already been there, too. But now that she was here, she couldn't remember any of the prefacing remarks that had seemed essential. There was nothing left to do but get to the point and hope she wouldn't be asked to leave before she had time to explain. "I've come to ask you to speak to the President about his nomination of my father to an appointment on the Supreme Court."

"I don't think you have a thing to worry about. Raymond has as much as told me that Addison is certain to get the committee's nod and a swift confirmation vote by the full Senate."

"No, you don't understand. I'm here to ask that the President withdraw the nomination."

Virginia looked puzzled. "Not get the appointment? Why not?"

"I'm not sure how to tell you." Kirby clasped her hands in her lap so her trembling wouldn't be so obvious. "This is very difficult."

"I've known your family for many years, and even though you and I don't know each other well, you can tell me what's bothering you."

"Dad is . . . not the man sort of man he seems to be. He's involved in something no one knows about yet." She was all too aware that she sounded too emotional and not entirely believable. "Have you heard of repressed memory syndrome?"

"Yes. It's rather well known these days." Virginia looked confused as if she couldn't understand what Kirby was getting at.

"It happened to me. A little over a year ago, I started having bits of memory return to me at odd times. At first I thought I was just overworked or imagining things, but it continued happening. What I was seeing was nothing I remembered from my childhood, but these were obviously memories and very real. Then I had an actual flashback."

"Oh?" Virginia leaned forward with interest.

"My husband insisted that I get into counseling. I was resistant at first, but it has helped me understand and deal with the memories. You see . . ." Her voice threatened to break but Kirby refused to stop now. "Dad molested me when I was a child."

"No!" Virginia actually paled. "Addison did that! I've known him for years and I never would have suspected he was capable of such a thing!"

"Neither did I until the memories started surfacing. I swear to you this is all true, as fantastic as it must sound to someone who knows him well."

"Do you have any proof of this?"

"No. Only my memories. But my sister, Mallory, was also molested and her memories are intact. We just discovered Dad is starting to do the same to Mallory's daughter, Tara. He has to be stopped."

"I agree fully! As you probably know, one of the causes

I've chosen to get involved with as First Lady is the prevention of child abuse. I knew it was epidemic in proportion, but one never suspects that you know an abuser! Certainly not Addison!''

"I want to keep Tara's name out of it if at all possible. I don't want her name to have to be connected with this unless it's absolutely necessary."

"I agree. She's how old?"

"Nine."

"Yes, it would be too traumatic to involve her in this."

Kirby looked earnestly at Virginia. "Please don't think I'm just doing this to be vindictive. It's only that no one protected me when I was a child and I have to do this for myself as well as for Mallory and Tara. Especially for Tara."

"I understand perfectly." Her lips shut firmly.

Suddenly it occurred to Kirby that Virginia might have more than political reasons for wanting to stop child abuse. She was understanding Kirby's story too easily not to have had some experience in her own background. "You really do understand, don't you?" she said in amazement.

Virginia stood and went to her desk. "I do." She lifted her head. Once again she was the First Lady and not just a friend of the family. "Naturally, that's not to be spoken of outside this room."

"No. Certainly not." Kirby forced herself to continue. "There's more. Just before I came here, I learned Dad has some connection with a ring of child pornography."

Virginia stared at her. "Why wasn't this revealed in the Senate investigation?"

"This was only discovered the day before yesterday. I'm still not certain how Dad is involved. The man he's somehow connected with is Gary Chandler. Chandler was convicted for molesting a little girl and I was able to get him sentenced to prison. However, the conviction was reversed by the Fourteenth Court of Appeals, the court on which my father serves. Recently Chandler was arrested again on the same charge and was released on bail awaiting trial. By chance I learned that Dad was responsible for the reversal."

"How could Addison do that? If you were the prosecuting

attorney, wouldn't he have had to disqualify himself from hearing the appeal or discussing it with the other judges?"

"He did recuse himself, officially, but he admitted to my brother-in-law that he had influenced the other judges to release Chandler." Kirby hesitated. "Naturally I was upset and wondered why he would do such a thing. I asked a man I know to see if he could find any connection between Dad and Chandler. Two days ago, he found the link." She lowered her eyes. This was difficult. In spite of all he had done, Addison was still her father, and until a short time ago, she had thought he was capable of no misconduct at all.

"I can see this is hard for you. Would you like some coffee?"

"No, thank you." Kirby couldn't have swallowed anything past the lump in her throat.

"What was their connection?"

"Apparently Chandler was involved in making kiddie porn. He was working with at least two other men and it was done in a house in north Houston." She forced herself to say, "It appears that Dad owns the house under an alias."

Virginia was startled. "Do you have reason to believe he knew what was going on there?"

"He knew. His unlisted phone number was found in the house. Only someone he knows well could have gotten that number. This made me suspicious so I looked in his safe at home and found some tapes that indicate he was at least receiving the porn. I don't know if he's more involved than that."

"That's certainly enough! I can hardly believe I'm hearing this! The investigations are so thorough! Why didn't any of this turn up?"

"As I said, it's only now coming to light. Dad's name hasn't been linked with the pornography ring. Last night the district attorney called to tell me that Chandler has been murdered. They caught the man who allegedly did it. Although he hasn't confessed, they found enough evidence to charge him with the murder, and they are hoping he'll confess his involvement in making the child pornography and name the others he was working with. Of course, he didn't name Dad, and he may not. But when the police get to the house where the videos were being made, they will find his phone number and will begin investigating his connection, if any. And I have the tapes I took from his safe. Naturally I'll have to turn them over as evidence."

"This is incredible!" Virginia stared at Kirby. "I can see now why it was so urgent for you to talk to me. I can't make any promises, but I feel confident that I can convince Raymond to withdraw his nomination of Addison. How public do you intend to go with the incest allegation? A press conference is certain to be called."

"It need not be made public at all now. You have the information and I have the satisfaction of knowing I stopped him."

"Very wise. The public is a fickle animal," Virginia said. "Just when a person thinks he knows where the public stands on an issue, things can change. I don't want to see this backfire on you or to cause you undue public embarrassment."

"Thank you. I remember all too well what happened in the Anita Hill case not too many years ago. If it was necessary, I would go through that, but it would be sheer hell."

"I agree. It won't be necessary." Virginia came back to her and offered Kirby her hand. "Thank you for telling me all this. You've saved my husband a great deal of embarrassment. And you've taken a step to protect innocent children from horrible abuse."

"Thank you for listening." Kirby felt as if a huge weight had been lifted off her shoulders.

Kirby was so relieved at having Virginia's promise to stop Addison, she hardly noticed her surroundings as she left the White House. Was it over at last? She felt exhausted, as if she had run for miles. She wondered what Virginia would tell the President and what his reaction would be. Shock? Disbelief? Everyone knew people were molesting children all over the world, but as Virginia had said, everyone assumed they didn't know anyone who would do such a thing.

The taxi let her out at the Mayflower Hotel and Kirby was relieved to reach the sanctity of her room. She lay fully clothed on the bed and curled up on her side, comfortable and safe and far removed from the faint sounds of traffic on the street below. This was her favorite place to stay in Washington. Although it was an older hotel, the rooms had a certain charm, an at-home familiarity that one didn't find in the newer hotels. In fact, she always stayed at the Mayflower. And Addison was sure to remember that—and might come looking for her.

Suddenly, this was no longer a place of safety, nor was any place in Washington. Anxiety and apprehension seized her. Her heart began pounding in her throat, and as she reached for the telephone, she realized her hands were trembling. Within minutes she had herself booked on the next flight to Houston. It would be close, but if she hurried, she could make it to the airport in time.

As she tossed her belongings into her suitcase, it occurred to her that Addison, too, would be flying back home soon. She couldn't remember how long her mother had said he planned to stay in Washington. What if she got to the airport and discovered they were booked on the same flight? She knew that at this point Addison would not cause a scene in public—his image was too carefully groomed to toss it away. But she would know he was there and that he would be waiting to catch her alone. It would be unlike him to let her public outburst go unpunished.

When would Virginia talk to the President? Kirby wondered as she left the room and hurried down the hall to the elevators. Would Stansfield call Addison while he was still in town, or would the Senate confirmation hearings continue in their usual course?

Kirby had the peculiar sensation of being someone else—someone who made public outbursts and stood up to Addison, even to the extent of going to the White House. A year ago, Kirby wouldn't have considered ever doing these things. She stepped into the elevator and impatiently pushed the button for the lobby. She was ready to be home.

Addison was in his hotel room that evening when the call came. "Hello? Mr. President?" He held his breath. Could the appointment happen so suddenly?

"You haven't been straight with me!" Raymond was clearly angry. "What the hell did you hope to do? Snow me and the rest of country as well?"

"What . . . what are you talking about?"

"Something has come to my attention that the background investigation didn't turn up. Did you think you could hide this from me? You could have embarrassed me and the whole country if I had placed you on the Court! What the hell were you thinking of?"

"I don't know what you're talking about." Addison frowned. "Have you spoken with my daughter? She's been going off the deep end lately. I have good reason to think she's having a nervous breakdown. She actually called most of the senators and wrote them letters alleging that I've committed some sort of crime." He tried to laugh as if that were ridiculous.

"Cut the bull! I've known you too long to swallow that line!"

"If it's not Kirby, what is it? I have a right to know!"

"You'll know soon enough. I'm not going into anything over the phone."

"I could come to the White House—"

"No! You can't! I want you to get out of Washington and as far away from me as possible. I don't even want you to ever say my name out loud! Do you read me?"

"Of course! But what are you going to say to the press? They'll want to know why you're withdrawing me as your nominee."

"No, Addison. You're going to voluntarily withdraw your name from consideration. I've called a press conference for you an hour from now in the lobby of your hotel. And if you say one word about this call, you'll wish you had never been born. Do you understand?"

"But how can I explain withdrawing? Everyone knows I want this position!"

"Think up something. But don't implicate me!"

Addison sat on the edge of the bed. "You owe it to me to tell me what's caused this. Maybe it's a misunderstanding."

"Does the word 'incest' ring a bell?"

"It *was* Kirby. Look, Raymond, she's not sane. I'm looking into having her committed as soon as I go back to Houston. She's been spreading this lie about me all over the country. I don't know why she's doing it. We've always been so close. Maybe it's at her husband's instigation. He's a Democrat and as far to the left as anyone can get. She's as smart as they come, but you know how women can be influenced. I'm sure of it. Russell is behind this." He was grabbing at straws, not realizing he was contradicting himself.

"Bullshit!" Raymond seemed to recall he was using a line that could be taped and tempered his tone. "You heard what I want you to do. At the press conference you'll withdraw your name. If you don't, I'm going to pursue this issue until you'll wish you had!"

"All right!" Addison felt his rage start to build. "I understand." When he found Kirby, he was going to make her sorry she'd ever thought of coming to Washington.

An hour and ten minutes later, Addison went down to the hotel lobby. A throng of reporters were waiting for him, some looking bored, others predatory, none particularly friendly. Addison plastered on his best smile and greeted them as if each were his personal friend.

A female reporter in a tailored suit thrust a microphone at him. "Can you tell us why this press conference has been called, Judge Walker? Does this mean your nomination has already been approved?"

Addison chuckled as if he found the question endearing. "Let's gather over here away from the elevators." He managed to maneuver the crowd in the direction he had chosen. It was a ploy he had used before to gain control of a situation.

When he had them gathered around and they were starting to press him with a volley of questions, he held up his hands for silence. The flashes from the still cameras nearly blinded him. "I'm glad you could all get here on such short notice. I'm afraid I've come to the decision to remove my name from consideration for Associate Justice of the Supreme Court."

More camera flashes. More insistent questions. A few reporters in the back were shoving to get nearer.

"I can't go into the details of my reason at the present, as they are personal, but I can say it's a matter of my wife's health." He had hit upon this lie as being one that would place him in the best possible light and evoke sympathy for him.

"Does this have anything to do with the woman who disrupted the hearings this morning?"

Addison's smile almost wavered but he caught himself in time. "No," he said with an expression of mild surprise. "No, it has nothing to do with that at all."

"Was that woman your daughter?" another female reporter called to him. "Could you tell us what allegations she made?"

Addison pretended not to hear her. Was it possible no one had understood what Kirby was shouting as she was hauled out of the room?

"I heard her say that you're a child molester," a man shouted from the back. "Is that why you're withdrawing?"

Addison drew himself up and fixed the man with his cold gray eyes. "No. There is no truth at all to any of that. Do I look like a child molester?" He chuckled again to show how ridiculous the suggestion was. "As I've already said, I'm withdrawing for reasons of my wife's health. We've been married forty years this coming June and, well, she needs me by her side just now."

Most of the reporters seemed to believe him. The questions veered from Kirby's outburst to Jane's fictional illness.

"Sorry, I can't answer any more questions." He glanced at his watch. "I have to run if I'm going to make my plane."

The woman in the suit pressed closer. "Have you told the President of your decision?"

Addison ground his clenched teeth in an effort to keep his smile in place. "The President knows of my decision," he said smoothly.

Although the reporters weren't ready to release him, Addison moved away, keeping his charm intact. He signaled the bellboy, and by the time he reached the elevators, one was waiting for him. He continued to smile and reiterate that Jane's sudden and serious illness was the only reason for his withdrawal. He made certain that the last the reporters saw of him, he was smiling.

The elevator doors slid shut and Addison's smile vanished. Ignoring the presence of the bellboy beside him, he jabbed at the number of his floor and was whisked silently away.

His face was drawn in a mask of silent rage as he stepped into the corridor that led to his room. Without a word, he handed his room key to the bellboy and nodded in the direction of his room. The young man hurried ahead to unlock the door. Kirby was going to pay for this! She had cost him the nomination he had sought all his life, and she had done it just when he was all but victorious. She had no proof that he had ever touched her or anyone else. She couldn't have! That meant it was his word against hers. Addison knew he would have no trouble discrediting her. He would never have Stansfield's backing again, but he could cause Kirby to lose her job and maybe her social standing as well.

Addison knew he was a dangerous enemy.

For a moment, he thought about Gary Chandler. Had Eddy been successful? Addison had no way of knowing until he returned to Houston. Either way, Chandler was gone and no longer a threat.

That left only Kirby.

Addison forced a smile back on his face as he entered his room and directed the bellboy to help him finish packing.

Kirby's flight back to Houston arrived on time, and Russell met her at the airport despite the late hour. When she saw him, she hugged him as if she had thought she would never see him again.

"He's been on TV," Russell said as they walked hand in hand to the car. "He withdrew his name from consideration."

"What reason did he give?"

"He said he wouldn't go into detail but claimed that your mother is in ill health and needed him to be with her. He put on a rather credible performance."

"God, he's going to be mad!"

Russell grinned. "Probably. I've always liked fireworks."

She laughed nervously. "I haven't."

"Don't worry, honey. He can't hurt you anymore."

She wished she felt that confident.

Jane called the next morning as Kirby was preparing breakfast. "Your father is home. I think you and Russell had better get over here right away!"

Kirby felt her mouth go dry. "He's angry, isn't he?"

Jane hesitated. "I believe that's true," she said carefully. In the background Kirby heard her father roar out a string of curses.

"Are you okay?"

"Yes. Just come over. Do as he says."

Kirby hung up. She was numb with fear. How often had her mother said those words to her? They had usually been before a beating.

"Was that your dad?" Russell asked from the doorway.

Kirby jumped. "It was Mom. We have to go over there."

"No, we don't. If you don't want to go, we'll go to work and ignore whatever he has to say."

Kirby shook her head. "I started this and I have to see it through. I'd better let Leon know I'll be late to work."

"I'll be right beside you. If I ask Mason to fill in for me today, I'm sure he will."

"What's going on?" Cody asked as he came into the room. "You guys look like someone died."

Kirby put the biscuits into the oven. "Your dad and I have to run over to Grandad's for a while. You and Josh stay here. These will be ready in ten minutes. Can you remember to turn off the oven and get to school on time?"

"Sure. I'm not a baby." Cody glanced from one parent to the other. "Something is wrong, isn't it?"

"I think so." Kirby hugged him and kissed his forehead. "Don't worry about it, though. We'll talk about it when we come back. Okay?"

"Okay." He turned and left the room.

Kirby wished she could be as calm. She went up to her room and felt on the shelf in her closet where she had hidden the tapes she took from Addison's safe. Trembling visibly, she put them in her purse. Going back downstairs, she said to Russell, "Let's go and get it over with."

By the time they arrived, Mallory and Derrick were already there. Kirby could hear Addison's ranting even before she went into the house.

Jane took her into the den. She was trembling and wringing her hands. Her eyes were large and fearful. "He's really mad! I don't know exactly what happened, but he's blaming you."

"Why is Mallory here?"

"He blames her, too, I guess."

"It's going to be okay, Mom."

Jane shook her head. "I don't think so. I don't think so at all."

Addison saw her approaching the den and shouted, "Get your ass in here, Kirby! You're in one hell of a lot of trouble!"

Kirby hid her fear and walked calmly into the room. Instead of sitting as Mallory was, she remained standing, facing him on his level. A quick glance told her Mallory was crying and Derrick was glaring at her with hatred in his eyes. Trust Derrick, she thought, to side with her father.

"What the hell did you tell Raymond Stansfield?" Addison shouted.

"Nothing. I didn't see the President. I talked to Mrs. Stansfield. I told her what you did and that I think this should disqualify you from holding the position of Supreme Court Justice." She met his fury without flinching.

"I ought to beat you half to death!"

Russell stepped closer to her. "You'll have to go through me," he said in a level voice. "No one is going to hurt Kirby."

In that instant Kirby loved her husband more than ever before.

"What exactly do you think Addison has done?" Derrick demanded. "You have really taken a lot on yourself, doing what you did! You've ruined his career!"

"No, he did that on his own." She looked at Addison as she said, "I told Mrs. Stansfield that you molested Mallory and me when we were children."

"You did what!" Addison's voice dropped to a harsh hiss. "You told the First Lady a lie like that?"

"It's no lie, Dad. I remember."

"You're crazy! I'm going to have you committed and locked up so tight you'll never see daylight again!"

"No, you're not," Russell said. "Kirby doesn't lie. Not about anything."

"I remember what you did in the guest room," Kirby said. "I remember enough details to be positive I'm recalling it accurately. Mallory does, too."

Addison wheeled on his younger daughter. Mallory pressed back into her chair as if she were afraid he would strike her.

"You! You put this into Kirby's head, didn't you! You and that goddamned psychiatrist! I'll have her license revoked!"

Mallory looked as if she was about to cry, but instead she lifted her head and straightened her shoulders. "Never again, Dad." Her voice wavered, then became stronger. "I couldn't stop what happened when I was a child, but I can stop it now. Tara will never have to go through the hell I did."

Addison growled like a wild animal and shouted, "I'll have you put away for spreading lies like this! You've ruined my career, you and Kirby! You're both crazy! I'll get you for this!"

"No, you won't!" Kirby stepped between them. "Your threats don't work anymore. Even if I hadn't remembered the incest, don't you think I remember the beatings? You can't treat people that way! Mallory is right. We couldn't do anything about it when we were children, but now that's not the case! You're finished, Dad. It's over."

"I'll sue you for slander! Who do you think the court will believe?" He was so furious a line of spital had formed at the corners of his lips. "I'll get you for this, too, Kirby. No one will believe you!"

She went past him and opened her purse. Without speaking, she put one of the tapes in the VCR and turned it on.

Eddy Compton's voice came over the speakers. The picture was self-explanatory. Before she could turn it off, something happened that Kirby hadn't expected. In the background of the film, she clearly saw Addison come into the room, glance at what was happening on the bed, and grin before the camera angled away to cut him out of the picture. Silently, Kirby pressed the off button.

It was the proof she needed and she felt sick for having discovered it.

Mallory's face had paled to alabaster and Derrick's mouth had dropped open. Jane was curled in her chair, sobbing quietly. Addison seemed about to go into apoplectic shock.

He spun toward Jane. "What have you done! You've been in my safe! My private safe! Have all of you turned against me?" he demanded.

"Addison," Derrick said hesitantly, "do you have some

explanation for this? I mean, that was a little girl on that video! And I could have sworn that was you I saw in the background!''

"I'm being set up!" Addison whipped his head from one to another. "You're all against me!"

Kirby answered Derrick. "It appears that Dad owns the house where this film and others like it are made. I don't know where the children come from, but I suspect they've been kidnapped. The police are looking into it. Also, there's been a murder. Gary Chandler was shot and killed as he was trying to leave the country." She looked at her father. "I assume you already know about this. Right, Dad?"

Addison opened his mouth as if he were trying to speak, but no sound came out.

"Derrick," Kirby continued, "I'm sorry to have to tell you this, but Dad has also been molesting Tara."

Derrick leaped to his feet and lunged at Addison. Russell caught his arm and pulled him away. "You hurt my daughter?" Derrick shouted. "You hurt Tara? I'll kill you, you sonofab-itch!"

Jane stood and looked at them, tears streaming down her face. Slowly she shook her head as if she were trying one last time to defend him. "Addison, aren't you even going to deny it?"

He tried to gain command again. "Of course I deny it, you damned fool! Kirby is making it all up! She's a liar!"

"No, Dad. I'm not." She went to the phone and dialed a number. "I need to speak to Detective Gunderman. Yes, I'll hold." She looked across the room at her family. They were frozen in a tableau of emotions.

She turned away. She couldn't bear to look at the havoc her actions had caused. "Detective Gunderman, this is Kirby Garrett. Yes, I'm back in town. I think you should send a squad car to my father's house. Yes, he still lives on Rice Boulevard." She listened for a moment. "It's about the Chandler murder and the pornography ring. My father is involved. Yes, I'm here at the house and I'll be here when you arrive."

She hung up and turned around to face her father. "Detective Gunderman is coming over."

"What have you done?" Addison whispered. His face had

gone gray and his cheeks showed age that hadn't been apparent moments before. "All I ever did was love you two." He stared at Mallory. "That's all I ever did."

"No, Dad," Mallory said in a choked voice. "You did a lot more than that." She stood and came toward him. Although tears still coursed down her cheeks, there was a new courage and determination in her movements. "No parent has the right to do to a child what you did to us. And that video! Were you doing that all along, too? Did you intend to take pictures of Tara like the pictures you took of that little girl on the tape?" She was quite near him now and trembling with anger. Shaking an accusing finger at him, she said, "I swear to God, if I ever find out you took pictures of my little girl, if you used her for anything like this, I'll kill you!"

"I never—" Addison began but Mallory cut him off.

"You've lied before." Mallory's voice was as steady now as hardened steel. "You'd better pray that I never find out you're not telling the truth about this."

"Tara is my grandaughter! I'd never . . . Ask her! Call her now and ask her!" The color had drained from his face, leaving it a dull gray, and he looked as if he had stepped into a nightmare. "Jane! Tell Mallory I wouldn't have made a video of Tara!"

Jane closed her eyes and buried her face in her hands. Her sobbing was the only sound in the room for several agonizing moments.

Addison backed from the room. At the doorway, he paused as if he were about to say something, then turned and walked away.

"Maybe one of us should go with him," Derrick said uncertainly.

"No." Jane was staring after her husband. "He won't leave the house. It's not like Addison to run away."

Kirby went to her mother and knelt beside her chair. "I'm so sorry, Mom. I wish it hadn't ended this way. I had no choice."

Jane looked at her for a long minute, then sighed. "I know. I should have taken better care of you. I didn't know. I swear I never knew he was . . . hurting you. And Tara . . . She tried to tell me. I didn't . . ." Her voice broke and a flood of tears coursed down her face. She buried her face in her hands. Kirby put her arms around her.

Suddenly there was a loud crack from somewhere in the house. Everyone jumped.

"What was that?" Mallory exclaimed. "Did you hear that?"

"It sounded like a gunshot," Russell said as he hurried from the room.

Kirby was close behind him as they searched for Addison and called his name. At the door to Addison's office, Russell stopped short. He turned to Kirby. "Don't come any farther! Derrick, take them back to the den."

Kirby was close enough to the door to see a wall spattered with red and gray matter. Suddenly she knew what she was seeing. A strangled cry burst from her and she tried to push past Russell.

He stopped her firmly. "No, Kirby! Go call an ambulance."

She searched his face. They both knew there was nothing an ambulance could do. "All right," she said. Her voice sounded as if it belonged to someone else.

In shock she moved down the hall. She took Jane's arm and led her back to the den.

"Is he dead?" Jane asked in a numb voice.

Mallory moved closer to Kirby.

"I don't know," Kirby lied. "Sit down, Mom. I have to call an ambulance."

The police arrived several minutes before the ambulance. When Kirby told them what had happened, they hurried down the hall to where Russell and Derrick still stood. Kirby listened to the hushed voices as if she were merely observing this, removed from it by a great distance. She could tell by the lack of frantic activity on the part of the officers that Addison was beyond their help.

Finally Detective Gunderman came into the den. He glanced at them all. "I'm sorry, Mrs. Walker. Your husband is dead."

Jane nodded as if she wasn't aware of the impact of the words. "He shot himself," she said vacantly. "I never thought he would do that. Addison shot himself." She looked up at the policeman. "He kept a gun in the office. It's been in there for years. I never dreamed he would . . ." Her words tapered off into silence.

Kirby put her arms around her mother and said to the others, "She'll be all right." She looked across at Mallory. "How about you? Are you okay?"

Mallory nodded almost imperceptibly, her face ashen as if she were on the verge of fainting.

"I have to ask you some questions," Gunderman said to Kirby. "For the record, I want to know what information you have about the Chandler murder and your father."

Mallory stood and took Jane's hand. "Come on, Mom. I'll take you to your room and stay with you."

Kirby waited until her mother and sister were out of the den, then she told the detective everything she knew about her father and the house in north Houston.

Epilogue

Kirby stood close by Russell, her hand securely in his. The preacher finished the graveside service with a prayer. Kirby didn't close her eyes, but continued to stare at the silvery coffin beneath the red spray of carnations. How fitting, she was thinking, that it should end with carnations. Even though she couldn't actually smell them, the scent seemed to engulf her.

She realized the prayer was over when everyone started moving about, and she brought her attention back into focus. She put her hand on Josh's shoulder and he didn't shrug it off. Addison's death had been difficult for Josh to understand. Cody looked away to hide the fact he was crying silently. Kirby wanted to hug him but knew he would rather have time to compose himself.

"Are you all right?" Russell whispered.

She nodded and squeezed his hand.

Slowly the mourners filed past, murmuring appropriate expressions of sympathy. Kirby maintained her poise. To the ones who said how sorely he would be missed, she nodded. To the ones who claimed to have been so close to him as to have seen this coming, she tried to look understanding.

Mallory was beside Jane several feet away. Derrick was standing with her and Tara was leaning against her mother as if she needed physical support as well as emotional. Kirby hoped Tara would come through this with as few scars as possible. Lauren seemed to think she would. Like Mallory, Tara was in counseling to get over the incest trauma as well as her feelings of somehow being responsible for Addison's death. They all had a long way to go, but they were on the mend. Even Derrick had been nicer in the past few days.

Slowly the crowd thinned. Kirby saw men in work clothes standing at a discreet distance. They seemed impatient for everyone to leave so they could finish the job of the burial.

"Come on," she said to her sons. "Let's go."

Cody fell into step beside her. "Are we going home now?" His voice was hoarse as if he were trying hard not to cry.

"No, we'll go to Grandad ... Grandma's house with the others."

Cody nodded and walked more quickly to the car where Josh was already standing.

"They're growing so fast," Russell said. "I miss them being little boys."

"I know. So do I." She glanced up at him. Even though he had never liked Addison, his face was tired and drawn. She was reminded again that Russell had been the one to find him. She squeezed his hand. "At least Josh is behaving more like himself again."

"He's basically a good boy. He was just getting off on the wrong foot."

As Kirby passed her mother, she stopped and gave her a long hug. Jane clung to her as if she would collapse if Kirby stepped away. Kirby patted her back. "It's going to be okay, Mom. Mallory and I will help you every way we can." It occurred to Kirby that Jane had never lived alone in her entire life. She had left her parents' house as Addison's bride. Widowhood would be a tremendous adjustment for her. "It's going to be okay."

Jane patted her and stepped back. She looked at Mallory, her face crumpling into tears. Mallory put her arm around Jane's shoulder.

"Are you ready to go, Mom?" she asked.

Jane nodded silently. For a long time she looked back at the silver coffin and scarlet carnations, then let Mallory lead her to the car.

Once they were out of the cemetery, Kirby leaned her head back and closed her eyes. "God, I'm exhausted! I don't know how Mom is holding up so well."

Russell reached over and took her hand. "It's not going to be easy for her."

"I could stay over there for a few weeks," Josh offered. It was the first time he had spoken since the service at the funeral home. "I don't mind."

"Maybe that would be a good idea. At least make the offer." Russell moved the car expertly through traffic. "Just be sure she understands it's only temporary."

After half an hour, they were in the familiar neighborhood of the Southampton subdivision. Kirby watched the houses as they drove by, each nestled in its established beds of spring flowers or greenery and sitting amid its manicured lawn. "Isn't it funny," she said, "how so much can change in your life, yet your world still looks the same way as always?"

"It's not the twilight zone, Mom," Josh said.

Cody punched him.

"Hey! I was only kidding! God!" Josh rubbed his arm and frowned at his brother.

"Don't argue," Kirby said automatically. Then, "Look at all the cars! Everyone at the funeral must have come here."

They found a place to park and went to the house. The door stood open to save the effort of answering the doorbell. Mallory had made arrangements for Jane's housekeeper, as well as for Ellen who worked for Kirby, to come directly here from the funeral home and start getting ready for the guests that were certain to come.

Now that the funeral was officially over, the crowd was more relaxed, less on its guard not to smile too freely, to laugh too easily. Except that it was still a bit subdued, the crowd could have been any of the numerous parties Addison and Jane had given over the years.

Kirby went directly to the kitchen. The housekeeper was bustling around, warming the dishes that needed it, placing spoons in the containers to go to the already laden table. Ellen was making certain names were on every container that had to return to its owner. Kirby spoke to them and offered to help, but the women waved her away. They had everything under control.

Josh was standing at the door and looking moodily down the hall. Kirby went to him.

"I haven't been in his office since . . . since it happened."

She put her arm around his shoulders and together they went down the hall. At the door to the office they stopped. It had long since been scrubbed clean of blood and looked as it had always appeared. As long as one didn't study the faint brownish stain on the carpet beneath the desk. No amount of scrubbing had been able to get that stain out.

"I have nightmares about him being gone," Josh said in a low voice. "I guess that's dumb."

"No, it isn't. I have nightmares, too."

He looked at her. In the past couple of months, he had grown taller than she was. It seemed odd to Kirby to look up to meet his eyes. "Mom, was it my fault?"

"What?" she exclaimed. "Of course not! Why would you think such a thing?" She touched his arm comfortingly.

"I was thinking about that day I was caught shoplifting. He was so mad at me and he said some things I can't forget. I thought maybe he . . . did this because he was so disappointed in me. I thought that was why he turned down the Supreme Court appointment."

"Oh, Josh," she sighed as she hugged him. "Honey, I never dreamed you thought that! It had nothing to do with that day. Grandad did something wrong—very wrong. It was about to be made public and he couldn't handle the idea."

"You wouldn't just say that?"

"I swear to you it's true."

After a while, Josh nodded and moved away from the door. "I'm going to go see about Grandma."

Kirby stood there alone, staring at the desk where she had seen Addison sit so often. How many lives had he ruined? If Josh hadn't asked her if it was his fault, he might have gone the rest of his life feeling guilty for Addison's suicide. Kirby felt an anger building in her that was inappropriate for the occasion. Today she had to play the dutiful daughter one last time. As she left the office, she paused and gazed for a long time at the closed door to the guest room. Then she went to join the others.

They didn't go home until late that night. Josh was staying at Jane's for a couple of days but Cody had been glad to return to his own home. He had been awfully quiet. As Russell unlocked the door, Kirby hugged Cody. "Are you okay?"

He nodded. Like Josh, he was growing taller. Eventually he might be taller than his brother. "It seems weird for Grandad to be gone."

"I know. I kept expecting him to walk into the room all the time we were there."

Cody looked at her in surprise. "Me, too."

"It will be awhile before we get used to the fact that he's gone," Russell said. "It was so unexpected."

Cody frowned. "Do you think Grandad loved me? I mean, he *had* to love me a little because I'm his grandson, but do you think he really loved me?"

"Yes. He really loved you." Kirby wondered what had prompted the question. Cody, unlike Josh, kept his hurts and thoughts private.

"I know he did," Russell said. "He thought the world of you boys."

Kirby managed a smile. "In a way, you were the sons he never had. He told me once that he regretted that your last name wasn't Walker so this branch of the family name wouldn't die out. That's why Josh's middle name is Walker."

Cody nodded. "Thanks. I'm going to bed now." He clattered noisily up the stairs.

Russell grinned after him. "Carpet an inch and a half thick and a pad under that, and he can sound like a stampeding herd of buffalo."

Kirby hugged him and let her cheek rest on his chest. She could hear the steady beat of Russell's heart and it was reassuring. "I love you," she said.

He put his arms around her. Even though she was more

accepting of his caresses, she noticed he never hugged her spontaneously. Her anger at Addison flared again. Would the past always haunt her?

For a long time they stood like that, silently embracing. At last Kirby said, "I wish I could stand like this forever. You make me feel safe."

"Do I?" She could hear surprise in his voice.

She nodded. "Is it too bad of me to be glad he's gone?"

"Not under the circumstances. I think everyone will understand when the investigation gets into full swing and his name comes up."

"It will be hard on Mom."

"It's going to be hard on you, too. And Mallory."

"At least Derrick wasn't drinking today. He was actually being supportive of her."

"Maybe he's not as bad as we've always thought. Addison could have been behind Derrick's actions as well. It's possible we'll never know how far his corruption reached."

"I don't want to know. It's difficult enough as it is." She straightened and took his hand. "Come to bed with me, Russell."

He put his head to one side. "Is that an invitation?"

She smiled. "Yes."

"Why tonight?"

"I don't know. For some reason I feel suddenly free. I don't know how long it will last, *if* it will last. But I want to make love with you."

A slow grin spread over his face. "I'll write Lauren a thank-you note."

"Don't you dare!" She laughed softly as she led Russell upstairs. She glanced at him over her shoulder. "I want to be the one to tell her." She was almost flirting with him, and for the first time it felt good, not frightening.

Inside their bedroom, Russell again took her into his arms. "I love you, Kirby. I think I've loved you ever since the first day I saw you."

"I fell in love with you at first sight, too. Did I ever tell you that?"